Praise for Detective Emilia Cruz

CLIFF DIVER

"From the moment I started the first one, I couldn't put it down. . . Her work touches on important issues affecting Mexico in a real, human way and is exciting, fast paced and utterly gripping." – *Mexico Retold*

HAT DANCE

[Emilia] is a force to be reckoned with." – *Mystery Sequels*

DIABLO NIGHTS

"Amato brings her characters to life with her vivid writing style and sets them on the streets of a Mexico steeped in Catholicism and corruption." – *OnlineBookClub.org*

KING PESO

"Danger and betrayal never more than a few pages away." – *Kirkus Reviews*

PACIFIC REAPER

"Carmen Amato . . . out does many of the best crime authors out there." – *Artisan Book Reviews*

43 MISSING

"A fast-paced procedural . . . a real page-turner . . . a very original plot." – *The BookLife Prize*

Also by Carmen Amato

DETECTIVE EMILIA CRUZ SERIES
CLIFF DIVER
HAT DANCE
DIABLO NIGHTS
KING PESO
PACIFIC REAPER
43 MISSING
RUSSIAN MOJITO
NARCO NOIR
BARRACUDA BAY
MADE IN ACAPULCO: The Emilia Cruz Stories
THE ARTIST/EL ARTISTA: A Bilingual Short Story
FELIZ NAVIDAD FROM ACAPULCO
THE LISTMAKER OF ACAPULCO

GALLIANO CLUB SERIES
ROAD TO THE GALLIANO CLUB: Prequel
MURDER AT THE GALLIANO CLUB: Book 1
BLACKMAIL AT THE GALLIANO CLUB: Book 2
REVENGE AT THE GALLIANO CLUB: Book 3

THRILLERS
AWAKENING MACBETH
THE HIDDEN LIGHT OF MEXICO CITY

43 MISSING

A Detective Emilia Cruz Novel

Carmen Amato

43 MISSING copyright © 2017, 2023 by Carmen Amato All rights reserved.

No parts of Carmen Amato's novels and stories may be reproduced in whole or in part without written permission from the author, with the exception of reviewers who may quote brief excerpts in connection with a review in a newspaper, magazine, or electronic publication; nor may any part of the books be reproduced, stored in a retrieval system, or transmitted in any form or by any means electronic, mechanical, photocopying, audio recording, or other means without the written approval of the author.

43 MISSING and the Detective Emilia Cruz novels are works of fiction. Names, characters, places, and incidents are the products of the author's imagination or are used fictitiously. Any resemblance to actual events, locales, or persons, living or dead, is entirely coincidental or used with permission.

Certain long-standing institutions, agencies, and public offices are mentioned, but the characters and situations involved are wholly imaginary.

Published 2023 by Laurel & Croton (second edition)
Trade Paperback Edition

Identifiers: ISBN: 979-8-9885363-6-9 (print)
ISBN 9978-0-9853256-9-5 (ebook)

Regarding names and monetary conversion

Regarding Mexican names: It is the custom in Mexico to use two surnames. The first is from the father's family and is always used. The second surname is the name of the mother's father. The second is sometimes dropped in conversation and/or to shorten the name in keeping with American and European naming conventions.

Conversion rate: For the purposes of this novel, $US1.00 = 10 Mexican pesos.

Spanish words: A glossary of Spanish words and terms commonly used in the Detective Emilia Cruz series is included.

**Keep far from the man who has power to kill,
and you will not be filled with the fear of death.**

Sirach 9:13

AUTHOR'S NOTE

43 MISSING is based on a true, unsolved crime.

A big, terrible, words-fail-me unsolved crime.

In September 2014, forty-three students from the Ayotzinapa Normal School disappeared while in the city of Iguala, Guerrero, attempting to commandeer buses to take them to a rally in Mexico City. Three years and dozens of arrests later, details around the crime are still sketchy and the families of the missing still do not have closure.

Neither truth nor bodies have been found.

I was just beginning the Detective Emilia Cruz series in 2014 when the 43 students disappeared. As time went on and the aftermath became spotted with half-truths and confusion, I wondered if I had the courage to address the crime. Fiction has been my way of bringing awareness to the scores of Mexicans missing amid the country's drug violence, but this crime and the possible secrets behind it, were almost unthinkable.

If Detective Emilia Cruz took on this investigation, I had to bring honesty and compassion to the project while creating both a believable motive and a firm resolution.

As I researched the idea that would become 43 MISSING, Francisco Goldman's reporting in The New Yorker magazine provided crucial details. I met him in October

2017 and thanked him for the superb reporting.

The motive for the assault on the students in the city of Iguala, not far from Acapulco, remains a mystery. One hypothesis reported by OpenDemocracy.net and other outlets which sparked my interest is that "the police were not after the students, but their bus . . . carrying shipment of drugs and/or money, which corrupt officers were trying to recover."

The novel 43 MISSING tackles many of the real anomalies related to the case, including a discredited motive, how the 43 bodies were disposed of, and multiple identical confessions.

The case quickly became a political hot potato and still is. Mexico's attorney general called the government effort "the most comprehensive criminal investigation in the history of law enforcement in Mexico" but has been unable to offer real proof about the students' fate. In 2016, the Organization of American States was called in as a neutral party but its investigation withered. The task force in 43 MISSING follows all of these failed attempts.

As I write this at the end of 2017, most pundits say the families will never know what happened. While the mystery of the missing is solved in fiction, I pray that it will some day be solved for real.

Carmen Amato
Fairfax County, Virginia

CHAPTER 1

Ready, Emilia Cruz Encinos told herself. Absolutely ready.

Her fingers beat a nervous tattoo on the steering wheel as she waited for the heavy steel gate to roll aside. With a final groan of metal-on-metal, it locked into the open position. Emilia took her foot off the brake and the heavy Suburban lumbered past the high concrete wall surrounding the police station in central Acapulco.

The uniform assigned to the guard shack trotted to the driver's window, forcing Emilia to stop and roll down her window. "Hey, Detective Cruz," he said. "Haven't seen you around lately. Been on vacation?"

"Sure," Emilia lied. "What's new?"

"Lieutenant Silvio's kicking ass and taking names," the uniform said, eyeing her with interest.

"Like nobody expected that," Emilia heard herself say. His face was familiar but she didn't know him well.

The uniformed officer gave an awkward laugh, slapped the Suburban's white paint, and went back to his post.

It was very early and the parking lot behind the squat stucco building was mostly empty. Emilia tucked the Suburban into a space, killed the engine, and gulped air. Her heart was racing, which was ridiculous. She was a detective who knew how to do hard things, going back to work.

In more than 12 years, she'd only taken two breaks, both

after being injured in the line of duty.

The first time she'd been shot.

This time was . . . worse.

Her eyes flicked to the rearview mirror. The uniform was watching her from the guard shack. With exaggerated gestures for his benefit, Emilia remade her ponytail, as if her hair was responsible for the delay in getting out of the car. Giving her hands something to do helped focus her breathing.

Emilia finally grabbed her shoulder bag from the passenger seat, and got out of the vehicle. In black jeans, loafers, denim jacket buttoned over her empty shoulder holster, and her detective badge on its lanyard around her neck, she could pretend it was just another day.

Because she was ready.

Emilia forced a tough strut into her walk as she crossed the parking lot and yanked open the rear door into the station.

Puentes, a young uniformed officer, was behind the holding cell desk. He gave a start when he saw her.

She shot him with her thumb and forefinger, the same as always.

"Detective Cruz," Puentes said haltingly.

I'm not going to shoot you. Emilia smiled, although her face felt brittle and her heart still thumped uncomfortably fast. "How are you doing?" she asked.

"Good, good." Puentes took a step away from the counter, putting more distance between them. "You?"

"Glad to be back." Emilia felt his eyes follow her down

the hall to the detectives squadroom. Puentes had seen her pull a gun on another cop. Emilia had been a fool to react to the garbage coming out of Detective Gomez's mouth, but the fear on that pendejo's face had been worth the mess that followed.

She pushed open the door and relaxed a fraction when she saw that the squadroom was empty.

The big space had been updated by the previous chief of detectives, Lieutenant Baez, but it looked even better than Emilia remembered. More organized. The walls were plastered with pictures and evidence cards from current investigations, but everything was aligned instead of the usual jumble of tacks and scribbles. The dozen metal desks each boasted two monitors. In the far corner, chairs upholstered in gray tweed ringed a sleek conference table. On the other side of the room, near the copier, a matching dark wood hutch held the coffee maker, a tray of clean mugs, and a built-in mini refrigerator.

Madre de Dios. New computers? A refrigerator?

"Cruz." Her former partner, Franco Silvio, filled the doorway to the lieutenant's office. "Grab a cup of coffee. We can talk before the rest of the crew reports in."

"Morning meeting still at 9:00 am?" Emilia asked breezily, like it was an ordinary Monday.

"Same as before," Silvio said.

Emilia dropped her shoulder bag on her desk and got herself a cup of fresh coffee. Silvio must have just made it, knowing she was coming in early.

A good sign.

She followed him into the office, past the placard on the door reading Lieutenant Franco Silvio. He closed the door and pointed to the pair of tweed chairs for visitors. As Emilia sat, he went behind the wide desk, coffee cup in hand.

Silvio's new responsibilities fit him well; he'd traded in his white tee shirt for the same color button-down, but still wore jeans and a shoulder holster and gun. The wiry crew cut, surly expression, and heavyweight boxer's physique remained unchanged.

"How are you doing?" he asked.

"Great, just great," Emilia caroled. "How's it feel to finally be the grand jefe?"

Everyone had known Silvio was long overdue for promotion even before she become his partner. His storied past, as well as a campaign to derail his career by the head of the police union, had kept him on the street until his talents won out.

"Finally getting some respect around here," Silvio joked but his expression wasn't light. "Been a little worried about you, Cruz."

"I'm ready to hit the ground running," Emilia said. She unbuttoned her jacket so he could see the empty shoulder holster. "Do you have my weapon?"

"Later." Silvio slid a folder towards her. "Here's your next assignment."

The desk was that of a busy man, with stacks of case files and random pads and printouts. The walls of the small office were newly painted and a framed poster announcing a championship match hung on the wall over a filing cabinet. Emilia recognized it from the room in Silvio's house where he kept his boxing memorabilia. That fight had been his last on the professional circuit in Mexico.

There were no other decorations. No picture of Isabel, his late wife.

Emilia put down her mug on the desk, next to a brass lamp casting a soft glow over the piles of papers. "The El Acólito case, right?"

"Nope," Silvio said smugly. "The national task force."

"Task force?" Emilia exclaimed. "Is the El Acólito investigation a national task force and nobody told me?"

Silvio shoved the file folder closer to her. "No, it's the Amistad 43 case in Michoacán." he said. "The one and only national task force."

Emilia blinked at him. "Seriously?"

"Any detective would give their right arm to get this kind of career shot," Silvio went on. "Not to mention an all expenses paid trip to Mexico City."

"I can't go to Mexico City," Emilia said, still not quite taking in his words. The Amistad 43 task force was a big deal. The media in Mexico had been talking about it for weeks.

"You have a week to get yourself together," Silvio said.

Emilia flapped a hand at the door to the squadroom. "No, I'm working the El Acólito case right here."

"You're not fit for duty," Silvio said bluntly. "No armed

assignment."

"Six weeks administrative leave," Emilia countered. "I did everything I was supposed to do."

"You never talked to the police counselor about what happened," Silvio said.

"I've done nothing but talk my head off about it," Emilia said, but her voice sounded uncertain in her own ears.

"I got nothing official, Cruz," Silvio said. "No doctor sign-off. Nothing."

"Nobody made you go to counseling after Isabel died." Emilia went into attack mode. Taking orders from her former partner was going to be bad enough, but at least Silvio should understand what she had to do. After, all, when his wife was murdered, he'd gone after the killer.

"Lieutenant Baez didn't make it mandatory," Silvio said.

"I covered for you," Emilia pointed out. "When Baez asked if you had anger issues, I said no, Franco's just being his normal pendejo self, he'll be fine."

"I didn't ask you to."

"But I did," Emilia said. "You owe me, Franco."

Silvio calmly folded his arms, heavy muscles straining the rolled sleeves of his shirt. "You have to be cleared by the police counselor before you can come back to the squadroom."

Emilia pressed a hand to her head. A vein throbbed with anger under her finger. He didn't use it much, but she knew Silvio had a heart buried under the stone face and mountain of muscle.

"Franco," she said, forcing herself to sound calm. "I'm here to find El Acólito. He's been running around free for six weeks. Who knows how many more people he's killed, raped, or sold. All I want to do is find him. There's no need to play games."

"I busted my ass to get you on the national task force," Silvio said, unmoved by her reassuring tone. "You need something that gets you away from Acapulco and time to get past what happened. The federales are on the El Acólito case. They're handling it."

"If I go, and I'm not saying I will," Emilia said. "Will I have access to the El Acólito files? Can I be working with the federales? If not, you know they'll fuck it up somehow. They always do. Giving up our jurisdiction—."

"Stop right there, Cruz," Silvio interrupted. "The bottom line is that the El Acólito investigation isn't your turf. Never going to be. I won't have you involved again."

So much for wheedling. Emilia's temper exploded. "Who are you to tell me—."

"I'm the fucking chief of detectives for the city of Acapulco." Silvio slammed his hand down on the desk, making the two mugs rattle. "It's my responsibility to make the assignments around here. Take it in, Cruz, that's the way things are now."

Emilia clenched her fists. "That's not fair, Franco, and you know it. I deserve—."

"How's Hollywood handling things?" Silvio interrupted. "This task force is as much of a favor to him as it is to you.

You're probably turning his hair gray."

Silvio's nickname for hotel manager Kurt Rucker often irritated Emilia but this time it stopped her in her tracks. "I . . . I haven't seen him in a couple of weeks," she admitted.

"Hollywood's been travelling?"

"I moved out."

"You moved out of the Palacio Réal?"

"Yes." Emilia had traded the penthouse apartment she shared with Kurt on the top floor of the Palacio Réal on Punta Diamante for a monk's cell in the rectory of San Pedro de los Pinos. It was much easier to hide from her life in a church than in Acapulco's most luxurious hotel.

Silvio spun his chair, tapped his keyboard, and swiveled the screen to show Emilia a spreadsheet. "You didn't register a change of address."

"I'm . . . it's a temporary place," Emilia mumbled. She couldn't stay in the rectory forever. "I'll do it when I'm settled."

"What about your car?" Silvio demanded.

"My car?" After everything that had happened, the clunky old Suburban's fate was the last thing Emilia was worried about.

"You're responsible for an official vehicle." He thrust a thick finger at the screen. "We're supposed to know where it is at all times."

Emilia snorted. "Aren't you the petty bureaucrat all of a sudden."

"Okay, Cruz," Silvio said, tamping down his obvious

annoyance. "We'll sort it out later. The important thing is this task force assignment. You could be the cop that solves the riddle."

"You're sure that's what this is?" Emilia narrowed her eyes at him in suspicion. "The Amistad 43?"

"Yes."

Emilia opened the folder, curious in spite of herself. Like everyone else in Mexico, she'd seen the news reports about the task force. It was a last-ditch effort to investigate the disappearance of 43 students from a rural teaching college from the village of Amistad in the state of Michoacán. The students had gone to Lindavista, a nearby city of about 80,000, to commandeer buses for a trip to a protest rally in Mexico City. But they'd been intercepted by local police, rounded up, and turned over to a drug gang.

The students were never seen again.

The Mexican Attorney General's office was under fire for fumbling multiple efforts to find out what happened. The task force would be the fourth investigation into the case in a year and a half.

The first investigation had taken place under the auspices of local law enforcement in Lindavista, assisted by the federale police and dogged by charges of collusion with the drug gang. When that petered out without finding either the students or their bodies, the Attorney General's office asked the Mexican Army to step in. The federales and the Army battled over jurisdiction, made three arrests in six months, and uncovered dozens of bodies in mass graves scattered across the state of Michoacán, none of which proved to be those of the 43 missing.

The third effort was a high-profile investigation sponsored by the Organization of American States. Eight senior law enforcement and justice department officials from as many Spanish-speaking countries descended on Mexico City to review the documentation and conduct a neutral investigation. After two weeks, they held a press conference, accused the Mexican government of stonewalling the effort, and closed up shop.

The international press sided with the Organization of American States and excoriated the Attorney General, providing an opening for the families of the 43 missing to renew their calls for transparency and accountability. As all of Mexico watched in anger, the narrative shifted from finding the 43 missing students, to protecting the current administration's shaky reputation.

The latest effort would create a task force of experienced law enforcement officials from across Mexico with no previous ties to the case. The hopes, not only of the families, but of a nation were riding on it. Being chosen as a member of the task force would have enormous career implications.

"No cop in their right mind is going to pass up a chance like this," Silvio went on. "This is the investigation of the century. Chief Salazar already sent your bio to the Attorney General's office in Mexico City. Plan for at least 90 days there."

"Three months?" The compressed timeline, coupled with

a rush of self-doubt that this was more responsibility than she could handle, set Emilia off again. "I'm not going to Mexico City for three months," she said. "I want to be here, hunting for El Acólito. Listen, I don't need a new partner. I'll work alone. Liaise with the federales if you want. But it's my case. I have to find him."

Emilia slapped the folder closed and tossed it onto the desk, knocking into Silvio's coffee cup.

"You're not listening!" Silvio caught the mug as it skittered off the desk. "You're assigned to the Attorney General's task force to investigate the missing 43 students from Amistad. Effective immediately."

"Tell Chief Salazar to send somebody else."

"How many different ways do I have to tell you, Cruz?" Silvio thundered. "You're not cleared to work on the street. You didn't talk to the doctor. I can't have you in the squadroom. Not yet."

"What are you saying?" Emilia demanded. "I'm too fucked up to stay in Acapulco?"

Silvio scowled. "I'm saying use the time in Mexico City to get your head together."

"Now that you're the big jefe," Emilia spat. "You've forgotten what it's like to work a case, is that it? Or is this your chance to finally get a woman out of the detectives squadroom?"

Silvio scooped up a pen and a spiral notepad and whipped them across the desk top. Emilia barely had time to react, just managing to snatch the pen out of the air before it hit her in the head. The blur of paper landed in her lap.

"What the fuck, Franco?" Emilia exclaimed.

"It's either the task force," Silvio said with iron in his voice. "Or write out your resignation."

Emilia gaped at him. It slowly dawned on her that he was serious.

"Now," Silvio said.

"Impressive leadership style," Emilia said shakily.

Silvio put his hands flat on the desk and waited, just like she'd seen him wait out suspects in an interrogation room.

Emilia shoved the notepad and pen to the floor, picked up the folder, and stood. "Thanks for the exile, Lieutenant." She loaded the last word with as much topspin as she could.

Silvio got to his feet. "Look, this is not how I wanted the conversation to go."

"Poor you," Emilia mocked.

"If you run into problems, call Lieutenant Baez. He's in Mexico City now."

"I know."

Silvio held out his hand to her.

Emilia shook her head, her whole body tight with anger. Silvio didn't move.

She finally slid a hand into his, expecting an impatient clench. To her surprise, Silvio pulled her into an awkward hug. Emilia broke away first.

"When I'm in Mexico City," she said, one hand on the doorknob. "Will you call if anything happens with El Acólito? Like, an arrest?"

"If I can." Silvio ran a hand through his bristly crew cut. "Call the police counselor before you go."

"Sure."

"Emilia," Silvio said. "Until you do, they're not going to give you a medical clearance. Or your gun."

"Good to know." Emilia wrenched open the door, grabbed her shoulder bag and left the squadroom.

She shot Puentes with her thumb and forefinger as she charged past him at the holding cell desk.

Once in the Suburban, Emilia cranked the air conditioning until it rattled the folder she'd dumped on the passenger seat. As her anger cooled, she realized that Silvio had unwittingly handed her a gift.

El Acólito used to live in Mexico City.

CHAPTER 2

"It's been six weeks," said Emilia. "Nothing's changed because of this new assignment. I'll find my brother and when I do, I'm going to kill him."

"Will that make you happy?" the counselor asked.

"It will even the score," Emilia replied.

The counselor didn't respond.

Emilia waited defiantly, shoulders tight, jaw tight.

Perched in the opposite corner of the room, the counselor sat in shadow, so that Emilia couldn't see her face. Didn't know if the woman was young or old, or if her expression ever changed.

"He's a rapist and a murderer and a human trafficker," Emilia said finally, unable to take the silence any more.

"Who raped you," the counselor said. Her tone was matter-of-fact.

"Among others," Emilia snapped. "He doesn't deserve to live."

"Why won't you say his real name?" the counselor asked. "El Acólito is the name of a Santa Muerte priest, a persona. A role he plays to lure women into his trafficking net."

Emilia wanted to haul the counselor into the light. Shout in the woman's face that the fear had nearly crushed her. Show the scar on her arm where she'd tried to break the chain. Tell about the gun in her face. How she knew he was going to pull the trigger. About the image she'd held in her mind for courage.

"He doesn't deserve the respect of a name," Emilia said. "He was called after an honorable man. Raphael Gamboa Escobar sounds too good for him."

"When he was an actor he called himself Rafa Gamboa," the counselor said. "Does Sophia know that?"

"My mother?" Emilia gave a harsh laugh. "She gave him away when he was three and spent the next 30 years pretending he never existed."

"Do you hate her for it?"

"I don't know," Emilia admitted.

"If she hadn't," the counselor offered. "Little Ernesto would never have grown up as Rafa Gamboa Escobar or turned himself into El Acólito."

"Probably not."

"So is she indirectly responsible for what happened to you?" On the other side of the room, the counselor shifted in her chair. Her face remained in shadow.

"I don't know," Emilia said again. It was a good expression to hide behind.

Blocks of white from the single window formed a pattern on the floor; a no-man's-land separating the two women in the dim room. The light was harsh and opaque, as if they were far from Acapulco and the Pacific coast's perpetual gleam of cobalt sky reflecting off turquoise ocean.

Everything else in the room was gray. Gray walls. Gray shadows.

"Sooner or later you're going to have to come to terms

with what Sophia did," the counselor said.

A clock ticked. The sound was muffled and far away.

"I could forgive my mother for giving away her child," Emilia admitted. "Her husband had just died in a horrible accident. She couldn't deal with two toddlers. Karina Escobar de la Vega was alone and grieving, too. With no children. When Sophia offered, Karina took my brother. Because he was crying and I wasn't."

"You were two years old. He was three. Do you wish Karina had taken you instead?"

"Yes."

The word hung in the air, twisting in the cruel squares of light between opposing corners.

"How does that make you feel?" the counselor asked.

Emilia straightened in her chair, knowing she was a mess and not just emotionally. She should have worn armor to this session, not just a white tank top, jeans, and sandals.

"And?" the counselor repeated, as if Emilia's answer was the most important thing she'd hear all day.

"I would have grown up in Karina's wonderful house in Las Brisas," Emilia said. "I would have had a father. Travelled. Competed at sports. Gone to college."

"Had a *quinceañera* party when you turned 15." The counselor took up the list. "Got married instead of working to support your mother."

"That's right," Emilia said. "If Karina had chosen me, I wouldn't have grown up with a demented mother in my uncle's apartment. Sold candy at the entrance to the

Maxitunel to pay my school fees because she wouldn't work. I could have been more than a beat cop, peeling dead bodies off sidewalks and wrestling drunks."

"A beat cop who literally fought her way into the detectives squadroom," the counselor said. "Although sometimes I think you've enjoyed that."

"I can hold my own," Emilia said.

"Tell me about Kurt Rucker," the counselor said.

"What?" Emilia wasn't ready for the abrupt shift.

"You left him," the counselor went on. "Certainly rich *gringos* are hard to come by for Mexican girls from the street like you."

"That's not the kind of relationship we have," Emilia said.

"You told Kurt you needed time to figure things out." The counselor was mocking her now. "But after six weeks all you can say is nothing has changed."

Emilia pressed her hands between her knees and stared at the dust motes swirling gently through the air. Her eyes followed them down. They'd come from somewhere in the shadows. Eventually they were all consumed by the light stamped across the floor.

"I can understand why you'd punish Sophia," the counselor said. "She tricked you. Used you, even as a child."

Emilia shrugged, eyes still on the doomed fragments of dust.

"But what are you punishing Kurt Rucker for?"

Emilia looked up. "I hate you," she said.

"Is he too blonde?" the counselor asked remorselessly.

"Too smart? Too strong? Too rich and accomplished? Are you punishing him for loving you?"

"Stop it," Emilia said.

From her dim corner, the counselor gave a little laugh of triumph. "No," she said, drawing out the word. "You're punishing yourself for loving him."

"This was supposed to be a conversation about me going back to work," Emilia said angrily.

"It is," the counselor said. "You've already traded your family and your lover for a shot at revenge. Will you also trade your job for a chance to find and kill Rafa Gamboa?"

"I know what you're trying to do," Emilia said.

"If you did, we wouldn't be here," the counselor replied.

CHAPTER 3

Emilia waited impatiently on the jetway, squeezed between groups of noisy tourists. At any moment, she expected to see Silvio race down the corridor, flash his badge, and yank her out of line.

The key to Rafa Gamboa Escobar's apartment in Mexico City was in her shoulder bag, courtesy of his foster mother, Karina Escobar de la Vega. It was where he'd lived as a moderately successful actor in Mexico City, starring in a *telenovela*, before he embarked on a lucrative criminal career as the Santa Muerte priest and human trafficker named El Acólito.

Emilia knew the *federales* were too busy chasing down his current crimes to probe into his past. But men like Rafa always left a trail of secrets.

Karina had also promised to find the name of a film director who'd known Rafa well. If Emilia got lucky, that person would be in Mexico City.

The line shuffled forward, the air suddenly hot and sticky as the passengers left the air conditioned terminal. Emilia found her seat and fastened the safety belt. People moved past, heading for the seats at the rear of the plane. None were Silvio.

The plane finally lifted off. Emilia caught sight of the Pacific glinting in the sunshine beneath them. A moment later it was gone, replaced in the window of the aircraft by the deceptively soft greens and browns of the mountains surrounding Acapulco Bay.

Kurt Rucker was down there, probably in his office in the Palacio Réal. Emilia formed a picture of him in her mind's eye. Blonde hair cut short with the merest suggestion of curl, wearing one of his trademark button-down shirts with the initials embroidered on the cuff. Knife-creased khakis.

He'd be busy planning deluxe events, approving five-star menus, and confidently assuring the corporate offices in London that everything at Acapulco's most luxurious hotel was running like clockwork. He was from New York and had served in *El Norte's* military before going to college. Kurt brought an ingrained sense of precision and responsibility to everything he touched, traits that seemed to rub off on everyone around him.

Each day it got harder and harder to pick up the phone. But it was also harder and harder to believe that he was out of her life for good.

The plane passed into the clouds and Emilia settled back in her seat. Passengers chatted in low tones. The man next to her opened a copy of *Reforma*, the main Mexico City newspaper. The flight attendant offered a beverage.

With a bottle of cola and a glass of ice on the tray table, Emilia opened the task force folder and skimmed the directions for meeting the driver at the airport and the check-in information for the Sheraton hotel in Mexico City's Colonia Cuauhtémoc district. All food and lodging expenses were paid for by the office of the Attorney General of

Mexico. There was also a daily stipend that would help fuel her hunt for Rafa Gamboa Escobar.

Five officers were assigned to the task force. Each biography was a brief rundown of career highlights. Hers sounded impressive, if short on recent specifics, and she wondered if Silvio wrote it.

Two captains, one lieutenant, and two detectives, including Emilia. The pecking order wasn't hard to anticipate. She was the only woman besides the coordinator from the Attorney General's office, a retired judge named Imelda Sarmiento de Suarez.

The most interesting item, however, was a signed letter from the Attorney General himself, Valenti Mendoza Lopez.

You have each been selected, not only for your record of investigative excellence, but to ensure neutrality and impartiality. No officer assigned to the task force has any connection to previous inquiries, persons involved, or even the state of Michoacán.

We rely on your skills to discard unsupported theories and make a final determination, based on concrete facts.

Emilia swallowed laughter. In a year and a half, the government had churned out plenty of theories and very few facts. She kept reading.

You will have access to all evidence accumulated since the incident in question. Given the sensitivity of the investigation, you are ordered to refrain from speaking to members of the press, or to families of the missing students, so as not to prejudice your conclusion.

Congratulations on this noble and important assignment.

The driver from the Attorney General's office met her flight. He steered Emilia to a big black SUV with a government license plate parked in a No Loading zone. She glimpsed a handgun in a belt holster when he opened the rear door for her.

"You must be Detective Cruz from Acapulco." A thin man in the back seat smiled warmly at her. He was old enough to be her father and spoke in a cultured and reassuring voice.

"Hello," Emilia said. She climbed into the car and the driver closed the door behind her.

He offered his hand and gave hers a firm shake. "I'm Juan José Miranda Robles," he said. "My flight arrived 30 minutes before yours."

"Nice to meet you," Emilia said. In a black collared shirt and matching pants, he reminded Emilia of the parish priest at San Pedro de los Pinos. From the task force biographies, however, she knew he held the rank of captain and headed up the Missing Persons Unit for the state of Oaxaca, one of the handful of states in Mexico to have such an effort.

The driver directed them to a cooler packed with bottles of water. Emilia grabbed one and offered another to Miranda; both drank deeply to lessen the dehydrating effects of Mexico City's high elevation.

The big SUV cruised out of the airport and onto a smooth highway. They passed a billboard as long as a city block advertising Telcel phone service. Banners bearing a man's jowly face and the name Oscar Suarez were affixed to light poles along the right side of the road and flapped in the rush of air from passing cars.

"I recall a phone call from a detective named Cruz some months ago," Miranda said. "Asking about crimes with a Santa Muerte signature. Was that you?"

"Yes," Emilia said, remembering the conversation herself. "You were one of the few I spoke to that didn't dismiss the call as a joke."

Miranda nodded; his hands clasped around the water bottle. Deep lines on either side of his mouth carved a perpetual strain into his thin face. Emilia guessed that he was close to retirement age.

"Later, I saw the Missing Persons alert for the El Acólito human trafficking ring," Miranda said. "A Santa Muerte priest luring women to so-called interventions to pray and then selling them over the border was almost unbelievable," he said. "But the full report was compelling. You are to be commended."

"Thank you."

"It was incredibly comprehensive with stunning details," Miranda continued. "Right down to his tattoos. I remember thinking that only someone who'd been inside his organization and very close to him could have written it."

He paused, evidently expecting a reply.

"We had great sources," Emilia said. The words scraped her throat raw.

The six-lane highway had a narrow median. A tall brown iron fence enclosed the road on both sides. In a half hearted gesture to camouflage the metal, trees were sandwiched in a narrow channel between the curb and the barrier. They looked brittle and thirsty against the dull blue sky.

"I'm glad the task force will have someone with your expertise," Miranda said.

"Thank you," Emilia said.

They began passing nicer buildings that Emilia supposed were apartments and offices and stores. Mexico City was huge, much bigger than Acapulco. Billboards for the Palacio de Hierro department store flashed by. More banners for Oscar Suarez urged drivers to vote for him for mayor of Mexico City.

"I expect our task here will be a difficult one," Miranda said after a small black pickup truck passed them, with POLICIA FEDERAL plastered across the rear bumper in big white letters. "Missing persons cases can be emotionally draining. Have you worked many?"

"No," Emilia admitted. "I've mostly worked homicide. But I'm always collecting information on women who have gone missing in and around Acapulco. Most are cold cases but I do what I can. I call them *Las Perdidas*."

"The Lost Ones," Miranda said. The lines around his mouth curved into a sad smile. "Have you had much success?"

"Not really." Emilia looked out the window as the SUV flew past another car. "I've found two. The first was in the morgue. The other thought she was in love with El Acólito. I couldn't stop her running off with him. She's still missing."

The SUV changed lanes and the road widened to four lanes in each direction. They drove under a huge suspension bridge; traffic circulated through a complicated road network in the air high above. More colorful billboards urged them to use purple mouthwash, buy gas at Pemex, and vote for Oscar Suarez.

"Do you blame yourself for her choice?" Miranda asked.

"No, but I want to do something about it," Emilia said. It was so easy to talk to this man, with his sympathetic manner and kind eyes.

"What about the women who were El Acólito's victims?" Miranda said. "The ones who were freed. Hopefully, they're beginning to heal."

"It's not easy coming back from something like that," Emilia heard herself say. "The fear in the middle of the night. Imaginary conversations where everything gets picked apart. The anger."

Miranda nodded but looked out his window as if to give Emilia some privacy. "What do you think helps the most?"

"Work," Emilia said, before the word *revenge* slipped out.

"Yes, the task force," Miranda said, managing to load the phrase with understanding. "Heart and hope will be our best weapons."

Emilia didn't answer. She'd been in Mexico City less than an hour and was already in trouble.

CHAPTER 4

At 8:00 pm, dressed in the skinny black dress, turquoise necklace, and strappy sandals she used to reserve for nights out with Kurt, Emilia presented herself for the first task force event. The concierge, wearing a Sheraton uniform, took her name before opening the door to a private suite on the executive floor.

Emilia passed through a lounge dotted with heavy upholstered furniture. A bartender presided over a long mahogany server stretched across the far corner. Four men formed a small knot in front of an array of liquor bottles. Miranda stepped away from the conversation as Emilia approached.

"Detective Cruz," he said. "How nice to see you again."

"Thank you," Emilia said but he was the last person she wanted at her elbow that night.

The other three turned to look. Two wore suits and were suddenly deeply interested in the newcomer. The third, out of place in a plaid shirt, jeans, and cowboy boots, merely nodded at her in lieu of a greeting and refocused his attention on his beer.

Miranda introduced Emilia to Captain Efrain Elizondo, chief of the Homicide unit in Guadalajara. Elizondo struck Emilia as the very definition of a successful Mexican civil servant. Handsome mid-forties, fit as a runner, wavy hair, and a suit that was tailored but not quite as subtly expensive as Kurt Rucker's Italian numbers. As he shook her hand, Elizondo exuded authority and confidence. Emilia couldn't help noticing that his grip was strong and his nails were manicured.

"Lieutenant Leonel Cardenas Diaz." The other well-dressed man muscled his way to Emilia's side and introduced himself. "All the way from Quintana Roo and the lovely paradise of Cancún. Glad to have you on the team, Detective Cruz. Can I get you a drink?"

Cardenas was a few years older than Emilia, maybe 35 or 36, with the type of aggressive charm usually accompanied by a chiseled jaw and abdominal muscles like corrugated steel. She could see the former and would stake money on the latter.

He didn't offer his hand but his eyes raked her from high heels to ponytail. The black dress wasn't cut low but it did cling to her curves. Emilia knew he'd try to get her into bed before the first week was over. Maybe even the first night.

"I'll have what he's having," she said and gestured to the man in plaid shirt and jeans.

The bartender popped the top on a Modelo Especial beer and tipped it into a glass so that the froth just skimmed the rim.

Emilia took the glass and held it out, offering a toast. "You must be Detective Anaya," she said. "From Reynosa."

"Miguel Anaya Vargas," he said and gulped down half his glass in one swallow.

A small commotion at the door to the door caught all their

attention. A slender woman walked in, accompanied by two bulky men in suits who were obviously bodyguards.

"Judge Sarmiento," Elizondo said smoothly. "A pleasure to finally meet you."

"Captain Elizondo," the woman acknowledged.

This time Elizondo made the introductions. Judge Imelda Sarmiento de Suarez was the task force's coordinator on behalf of the office of the Attorney General. Emilia had been impressed by the biography detailing her Oxford education, numerous professional awards, and enviable judicial career highlights. If Emilia had gone to college, she could have done all that, too.

Judge Sarmiento wore a black slubbed silk pant suit and a white lace blouse. A jangly collection of silver bangles decorated her right wrist, which was so thin the bracelets kept sliding onto the heel of her hand. Her hair was a blunt bob that came to her chin and hid any earrings she might have worn.

Without being prompted, the bartender poured her a glass of white wine.

"As this is a working dinner, let's all take our seats," Judge Sarmiento said.

They moved through the lounge and into an adjoining dining room where a table was set for six, with place cards by each plate. The judge and Miranda sat at the ends. Emilia found herself next to Elizondo and looking across at Anaya's plaid shirt, so out of place. Cardenas winked at her as he pulled out his chair. Elizondo's lips tensed in disapproval of the younger man's musclebound swagger.

Three goblets in graduated sizes topped each place setting. Conversation halted as two waiters circled the table, offering a choice of sparkling or still water for the largest glass, pouring white wine into the smallest, and serving elaborate goblets of shrimp and avocado in red *salsa cruda*.

"I'd like first to thank you all for taking time out from your careers to join the task force," Judge Sarmiento said. "You've left your families and homes to review material that can be quite disturbing. Hopefully there will be a conclusion that will allow our country to move beyond this terrible tragedy."

The woman had probably said the same words a thousand times, yet the expression on her face was sincere.

At the opposite end of the table, Miranda's expression was similarly genuine as he raised his wine glass. "A toast," he said softly. "May God guide our hearts and minds."

"Amen," Emilia replied without thinking.

Miranda smiled; everyone else had responded with the traditional "*Salud.*"

The setting had been a clever decision. It was intimate enough for the members of the newly-minted task force to relax, yet formal enough for the judge to make clear that she was in charge.

Despite the tantalizing scent of the food in front of her, Emilia's stomach was tight as tension settled over the table like dark clouds before a storm. Out of the corner of her eye, she saw Miranda, Elizondo, and Cardenas begin to eat. They each complimented the food. But she knew that just like her, they were silently sizing up the faces around the table, wondering who could be trusted.

The odds said that at least one cop in a group of five was dirty.

Only Anaya, the cowboy from Reynosa, seemed oblivious to the hum of nerves. He propped elbows on the table, hunched his shoulders, and slurped up the tangy seafood and sauce.

Next to Anaya, Cardenas deliberately hitched his chair an inch away. He caught Emilia's eye. The corner of his mouth quirked up.

Emilia pretended not to see and forced herself to eat. She wasn't going to judge Anaya on the basis of his table manners or give Cardenas the impression that she was easy prey.

Judge Sarmiento pronged a tiny piece of avocado. "I'm sure you all have different reasons for participating," she said. "But the main one should be that you want to see justice done. I speak on behalf of the Attorney General when I say that if we as a nation want to find out the truth, you are our last hope."

Elizondo cleared his throat. "I'm sure I speak for all of us when I say that we all agreed to serve on this commission for that very reason."

"We'll spend at least 45 days here in Mexico City reviewing all the evidence collected so far," the judge said. "My office has made arrangements for secretarial support, transportation, and the like. After your review, the task force will relocate to Michoacán and view the crime scenes. Once we return to Mexico City, you'll be tasked with writing a final report."

The waiters took away the appetizer dishes. The judge had barely eaten a third of her shrimp but nodded for the dish to be removed. A beautifully composed plate of breaded veal and potatoes topped with olives and capers appeared in front of Emilia. The waiter filled the middle glass with red wine.

Anaya looked around the table and Emilia realized he was searching for the obligatory plate of tortillas. Given that they were in a luxury hotel in a cosmopolitan city, there was only a napkin-topped basket full of the same French rolls the pastry chef made at the Palacio Réal. Emilia slid the basket to Anaya, getting a gruff murmur from him and a silent snort from Cardenas.

"Of course, the press is going to be very curious about the progress of your investigation," the judge went on. "My office will send out weekly releases as to the direction and progress of your work. As for anything personal, please remember that statements have to be approved for release by my office."

"Does that include speaking off the record to the victim's families?" Miranda asked quietly.

"I'm referring to all discussion about the investigation beyond the people in this room," Judge Sarmiento said sharply. "You've been provided with guidelines which preclude any contact with families of the missing."

The tension in the room pressed down, heavy and uncertain.

"We're all aware of our roles as impartial investigators," Elizondo said. "It's why no one from the state of Michoacán or who had any involvement in previous investigations was eligible for the task force."

"Exactly." Judge Sarmiento nodded. "It is critical that you all remain impartial. I don't have to remind you the issues this case has brought forward in terms of government accountability and charges of collusion. None of you has any links to the case. That cannot change."

Anaya wiped his plate clean with half a roll, shoved it in his mouth, and pushed the plate away from him, nearly knocking over his empty wine glass.

"I'm sure you have questions before the official start tomorrow." Judge Sarmiento looked away from Anaya's wobbling glass.

The judge's smile was forced. Emilia wondered how she had the strength to stay upright, given the amount of food she hadn't eaten.

"Will you be working with us day-to-day?" Cardenas asked, after a long pause during which everyone fiddled with their food.

"I'm the Attorney General's representative," Judge Sarmiento said. "My role is to provide oversight. Captain Elizondo is the senior police officer and will make the day-to-day decisions."

"Does the hotel know why we're here?" Cardenas asked.

The judge rearranged the potatoes on her plate. "The hotel is aware but has agreed to discretion. We don't anticipate issues with the media."

"What about transportation?" Anaya asked, the first time he'd spoken since sitting down. "And weekends."

Emilia was surprised at such inane questions. They could deal with logistics later.

"We have a car and driver at your disposal," the judge said. "Other than that, Mexico City has an excellent public transportation system. There is a *sitio* taxi stand right in front of the hotel. Of course, you'll be reimbursed for any business travel within the city."

"But are we working weekends?" Anaya found the bottle of red wine the waiter had left on the sideboard and refilled his glass.

"I hope not." Judge Sarmiento looked at Elizondo. "The task force should proceed in an orderly and civilized manner."

The senior captain cleared his throat. "We've yet to be acquainted with our workload."

"Is there a budget for the task force?" Miranda asked.

"Yes, but it's not optimal," the judge admitted. Her bracelets jangled as she cut a potato into miniscule bites. "If you need additional funding, it will have to be justified to the Attorney General. I shouldn't have to tell you what a year of intense investigation has already cost our government."

Elizondo nodded sagely, conveying to all that he was well acquainted with budgets and bureaucracies. "What about secretarial help?" he asked.

Emilia felt anger rise from the well. Why were they all nattering on about logistics and housekeeping rather than the actual issues at stake?

"Of course," the judge said. She pronged a morsel of potato. "We have a secretary, two librarians, and my own personal assistant will take on additional duties as needed. I'm sure you'll find that to be quite enough support."

Emilia tossed down her fork. Silver clanged against fine china plate.

Everyone flinched.

"Judge," Emilia said. "I understand why impartiality is important, but none of us has jurisdiction in either Michoacán or Mexico City. How are we going to make an arrest if we find the perpetrators?"

Next to her, Elizondo tensed, his mouth drawn in irritation.

"An arrest is not our top priority," Judge Sarmiento said slowly. "The key purpose of this task force is to identify the resting place of the bodies of the students and answer the question of what happened to them. I would have thought the letter from the Attorney General made that clear."

"We don't care who was responsible?" Emilia pressed.

From across the table, Anaya stared at her raptly, even as he scraped at his teeth with the nail of a pinky finger.

The others watched the judge.

"If you identify culprits and have solid evidence," Judge Sarmiento said. "The arrest will be made by the Policía

Federal Preventiva."

"The *federales* have been involved before and botched it," Emilia said. "Doesn't that conflict with our need for impartiality?"

Next to her, Elizondo gave a discreet cough to signal his disapproval at her persistence. "I'm sure what you meant to say, Detective Cruz—."

"I meant to say." Emilia raised her voice over his. "The *federales* have already had their shot at finding out what happened to the missing 43 students and there are more questions about their complicity than we can count."

"What do you suggest, Detective?" This from Miranda.

"I'd assumed we'd be given special arrest authority," Emilia said. "We're not just here to shuffle paper and worry about getting reimbursed for taxi rides, are we?"

"You make a valid point, Detective," Judge Sarmiento patted her lips with her napkin. "We can't lose sight of the optics."

"Optics?" Emilia echoed.

"Detective," Elizondo snapped.

His tone cut through her anger like a knife.

"My apologies, Captain," Emilia murmured.

He gave her a curt nod; apology accepted.

The conversation subsided into idle comments about the hotel and their respective travels to Mexico City. Elizondo studiously ignored Emilia. Anaya was mostly silent, as if he'd returned to his own world.

The meal wrapped up with orange sorbet and chocolate

candies. Coffee was served. The judge finished quickly and stood. Everyone followed suit.

"Please." Judge Sarmiento spread her hands, setting her bangles jangling. The only course she'd finished was dessert. "I apologize for having to rush off, but I have an appointment with the Attorney General this evening. This suite is available to you for the rest of the evening. Please make yourselves comfortable and take this opportunity to get to know each other before the workday starts tomorrow."

She left. Waiters cleared away the detritus and the group of five police officers drifted into the adjoining lounge. The bartender had been dismissed, but the rows of bottles and glasses beckoned. Someone turned on the television.

Glass doors opened onto a patio. Emilia walked out, lured by the dramatic night view of the El Ángel monument bisecting the famous Paseo de la Reforma boulevard. Atop its soaring column, the golden angel was lit from below by a lavender glow. Emilia picked out a dozen statues and the four obelisks that guarded its base. Traffic was thick, even at this late hour. Red and white lights circled the monument.

"Quite a sight, isn't it?" Cardenas came to stand next to her as the light illuminating the column shimmered to green. He had a glass of whiskey in his hand. "Hidalgo's remains are supposedly in there."

"Maybe it's supposed to remind us," Emilia said.

"How's that?"

"The angel is a monument to the heroes of our revolution," Emilia said. "Those men wanted something better for Mexico than a dictatorship. I don't think they intended to create a country where people disappear and others cover it up."

Cardenas came closer. "Are you a romantic, Detective Cruz?"

"Sure," she said. "Isn't everyone?"

"Interesting question you asked at the table," Cardenas said.

Emilia took his glass, sniffed at it, and handed it back as if she didn't care for cheap liquor. "Somebody had to."

Cardenas rolled the whiskey around the bowl of the glass. "Nice to know that the Attorney General's office is more worried about image than anything else. Nobody imagines that we'll turn up anything new or have to make an arrest. They just want to find the bodies, give them a decent burial, and shut up the families."

"We could do both," Emilia said. "Find the dead and get a murder conviction."

"Not likely," Cardenas said. "This was never going to be any more than a paperwork exercise."

"I'm not here to be the Attorney General's sacrificial lamb," Emilia warned.

Cardenas laughed. In another place and time, Emilia would have fallen hard for his mix of leading man looks and brash confidence.

"Can I give you some advice, Detective?" he asked.

"No."

He laughed again, then grew serious. "You and Captain

Elizondo."

Emilia raised her eyebrows at him. "What are you, a matchmaker?"

"Elizondo is the kind of senior officer who can help you get ahead," Cardenas said, watching Emilia closely. "I'm sure you know the type. After all, that's how you got here, isn't it? I'm sure you've noticed that everyone is senior to you. And you're a woman . . ." He let the implication drift into the night.

Emilia gave him a brittle smile as she considered her options. If she punched Cardenas in the gut or body-slammed him with the small iron table over by the door, there would be a major dust-up that would reverberate all the way back to Silvio in Acapulco.

"Do you know what a black widow is?" she asked.

"Like the spider?"

Emilia made a show of looking around to make sure they were alone on the patio. "The first was a lieutenant named Fausto Inocente. He died smiling. You know what I mean? I led the investigation, too."

"Black widow. Okay, I get it." Cardenas nodded, but there was a note of uncertainty in his eyes. He'd clearly intended to put her on the defense. Expected her to get angry. Deny his unspoken allegation.

Emilia shrugged. "Look it up."

It was the best kind of lie, one that would niggle at the other cop until he succumbed to curiosity and checked. When he did, Cardenas would find out that Lieutenant

Inocente had died under questionable circumstances and that Emilia had led the investigation. The verdict of death by misadventure would leave him wondering.

Cardenas lifted his chin and flashed a sudden grin. "I like your dress," he said.

Emilia smiled wickedly at him, suddenly enjoying herself. "Of course you do."

She turned and went into the lounge. She and Cardenas knew where each stood. He thought she was hot and she knew he was a *pendejo*.

The two captains, Elizondo and Miranda, were ensconced in overstuffed chairs in front of the television, each with a brandy snifter in hand. Anaya was draped over the bar with a shot glass and a half-empty bottle of top-shelf tequila.

Emilia poured herself a brandy. It was the same brand that Kurt liked. The taste reminded her of warm nights talking with him on the balcony outside the penthouse.

She took the glass to an armchair facing the television. "Thank you for joining us, Detective," Miranda said and raised his glass in a salute. Elizondo did the same, although the gesture was more perfunctory than his colleague's. Emilia hoped she hadn't shot herself in the foot already.

A nightly news program was on.

"So far the only member of the task force the media has identified is Judge Sarmiento de Suarez," Miranda said.

"I'm not sure that's a good thing," Elizondo said. "Her being singled out."

"And not you?" Cardenas had followed Emilia into the

room. He topped up his whiskey, dropped onto the small sofa, and put his shoes on the coffee table.

"I was thinking of her safety, Lieutenant," Elizondo said icily.

A breaking news logo twirled onto the screen and dissolved to reveal an unsmiling female newscaster. "The warden of the Multifoco maximum security prison in Michoacán state has been found dead in his office," the woman announced. A photograph of a man with cropped gray hair and a drooping moustache was projected to her right to create a screen-within-a-screen effect. "General Manuel Cordes Villalobos held the position for eight months, during which time he imposed controversial restrictions on several high profile prisoners, including Diego Barrielos Luna, head of the now-defunct Hermanos100 cartel."

As the newscaster spoke, the inset switched to a video of Barrielos Luna in custody. Mexico's most notorious and violent drug lord, his arrest two years ago had been a major coup for the government. It broke the back of the Hermanos100 cartel, which had operated throughout central and western Mexico and was thought to be responsible for thousands of drug-related murders. Famous for his preference for young women, Barrielos Luna was known as the Barrel Bomber for his method of dispensing with rivals in vats of acid.

In the video, Barrielos Luna was escorted by a squad of men in unmarked black military uniforms with their faces covered by black balaclava masks. Wearing a short sleeved orange prison jumpsuit, the drug kingpin had bedroom eyes and an insidious smile revealing straight white teeth. His hands were cuffed in front of him.

Emilia was drawn to the television. She'd never seen a picture of Barrielos in short sleeves before and was transfixed by the sight of a Santa Muerte tattoo wrapped around a meaty forearm. The Death Saint, forbidden by the Catholic Church in Mexico, was depicted as a black-robed Grim Reaper holding a globe in one hand and a scythe in the other. A white skull face leered from under a hood.

The image was absolutely identical to the tattoo inked onto the chest of Rafa Gamboa Escobar, aka El Acólito.

Human trafficker.

Murderer.

Rapist.

Brother.

"Detective Cruz?" Miranda's voice was like a tap on her shoulder. "Is something the matter?"

"No, no." Emilia backpedaled and sat again, her heart hammering. "No, I just wanted a closer look."

The newscaster continued with footage of the late General Cordes talking to reporters from inside the Multifoco prison. "A spokesman for the Michoacán state Office of Public Security said that an autopsy would be conducted to determine the cause of death."

Anaya crashed his empty tequila glass down on the bar top, the impact like a gunshot. Everyone gave a start.

"The investigation will be weak and easily forgotten," Anaya snarled. The stocky man in the incongruous plaid shirt had washed down nearly half a bottle of tequila, plus beer and wine with dinner, yet his eyes were clear and his movements precise.

"We have to pray that justice will be done," said Miranda.

"This is Mexico," Anaya retorted. "Prayers are worthless."

Emilia recalled the regional details provided in the task force folder. "The Multifoco prison is a few miles outside Lindavista," she said. "The town where the 43 students went missing."

"Are you always so full of interesting tidbits, Detective?" Cardenas drawled from the sofa.

"Nothing to do with us," Elizondo said.

CHAPTER 5

The building where the task force was to investigate the disappearance of the 43 students was only two blocks away. Emilia dressed in her gray pants suit, and walked past the United States embassy, where cement and metal barriers narrowed the sidewalk along Paseo de la Reforma. In the daylight, surrounded by dense traffic, the El Ángel column looked less ethereal, and more like a smog-stained city monument. Clumps of tourists milled on street corners, waiting for a break in the stream of cars so they could dart across to visit the mausoleum below the column.

She arrived at the same time as Judge Sarmiento, who introduced her personal assistant, a young man named Guillermo Ramirez. Cardenas, Elizondo, and Miranda were again in business suits, while Anaya stood out in plaid shirt, jeans, lizard boots, and straw cowboy hat. They were issued identification cards, which required fingerprinting and photos, plus an electronic card to open the door to an office suite on the third floor of the building.

In the suite, Ramirez made a short speech welcoming the task force members to legal librarians Ignacio and Daniel who would help catalogue the case file data. Tina, a terrified twenty-something, would be the task force's secretary.

Emilia took an instant dislike to Ramirez, who made a point of referring to himself as Licenciado Ramirez to draw attention to his college education. He wasn't much older than the secretary, wearing pointed black shoes and a form-fitting black suit with a chalk stripe. His hair was slicked into a pompadour, complete with sideburns that ended below his earlobes. The effect was that of a smug and overdressed elf.

He was to be both timekeeper and snitch, Emilia decided. Ramirez's thin fingers played with a clipboard, and he checked an oversized chrome watch every few minutes.

"It's time to go downstairs," he announced as soon as introductions were over. "If you'll follow me, please." Ramirez didn't wait for anyone but led the way out of the office suite.

Emilia saw Elizondo exchange glances with Miranda. The two men fell into step. Anaya trotted behind them, his boots ringing on the marble floors.

Cardenas maneuvered himself next to Emilia. She noted wryly that his gray suit was the same shade as hers. At least her blouse was pink while Cardenas wore a dark blue shirt and a floral tie. She guessed that he liked to stand out.

Doors opened as Ramirez led the little parade down the corridor to the elevators. Men and women stared silently as the task force members passed by.

"Good morning," Miranda said and smiled at the onlookers.

No one smiled back.

Ramirez stopped in front of the elevators.

A dozen doors slammed shut, one after another, all the way down the corridor. *Thump thump thump.*

"I'm sensing a lot of warmth," Cardenas said to Emilia

out of the corner of his mouth.

The elevator doors swooshed open, Ramirez shepherded them inside, using his clipboard like a paddle. Elizondo's face was expressionless. Miranda wore a tight smile. Anaya seemed amused.

"I'm sure you realize," Judge Sarmiento said to Elizondo but loud enough for everyone in the confined space of the elevator to hear. "Many in the Attorney General's office feels they have done everything humanly possible to expose the truth and find the missing students."

"Understandable." Elizondo's tone betrayed no emotion.

Emilia admired his coolness; she would have been bitingly sarcastic.

Clutching his clipboard as if it held the 11th commandment, Ramirez ushered them off the elevator, through a small lobby, and into an auditorium.

The upholstered seats were red and fanned out from an elevated stage framed by dramatic floor-to-celing red draperies. The walls were paneled in thin strips of dark mahogany. Enormous circular seals flanked the stage and floated out from the walls like planets from a lost galaxy; the Great Seal of Mexico on the left and the logo of the Procuraduría General de la República—the full title of the Attorney General's office—on the right.

Emilia stayed with Cardenas as the task force members followed Ramirez down the side aisle. The auditorium had seating for about 300, she guessed, and it was half full. Several police and military uniforms were in the crowd. Not surprisingly, she didn't recognize anyone. The rest of the audience wore suits and dresses. Emilia had the dismaying thought that Mexico City was much more formal than Acapulco. She'd need more clothes.

Their front row seats were adorned with name cards. Emilia found herself between Judge Sarmiento and Cardenas. The judge smiled wanly but didn't make eye contact. Anaya was on the other side of Cardenas. Miranda and Elizondo took their seats at the end of the row.

The stage was empty except for three modern leather armchairs set in a row behind a podium adorned with yet another national seal. Above the podium, the word *Welcome* was projected onto a huge screen.

The lights dimmed, cymbals crashed, everyone got to their feet, and the Mexican national anthem played. As a choir sang about the resounding roar of the cannon, three people entered the auditorium through a door set in the paneled wall. As if choreographed to the music, they climbed the steps to the stage level and stood in front of the chairs.

The music ended with a flourish, the lights came up again, and the audience applauded the sight of the Attorney General, Valenti Mendoza Lopez, coming to the podium. Blocky and pugnacious, Mendoza Lopez looked like a well-dressed bulldog. He took a pair of reading glasses from the breast pocket of his dark suit jacket, settled them on his nose, and motioned for the audience to sit.

"Thank you," he said. Emilia marveled at his gravelly

voice. He sounded in person exactly the way he did on television. "I'm pleased to extend a personal welcome to the members of the Amistad 43 national task force. Captain Efrain Elizondo of Guadalajara, Captain Juan José Miranda Robles of Oaxaca, Lieutenant Leonel Cardenas Diaz of Cancún, Detective Miguel Anaya Vargas of Reynosa, and Detective Emilia Cruz Encinos of Acapulco. You have each been chosen, not only for your record of investigative excellence, but to ensure neutrality and impartiality. No officer assigned to the task force has any connection to previous inquiries, persons involved, or even the state of Michoacán. We rely on your skills to discard unsupported theories and make a final determination, based on concrete facts."

On her right, Cardenas butted her arm with his elbow. When Emilia turned to look, he raised his eyebrows and she realized that Mendoza Lopez was reading the same welcome letter that had been in the advance packet.

Emilia gave a tiny shrug as Mendoza Lopez continued the recycled words. Anaya caught her eye, too, and hitched up the corner of his mouth in what probably passed for him as a grin. Beyond Anaya, both Miranda and Elizondo sat like grim statues.

"Let me sum up." Mendoza took off his glasses and draped an arm over the podium. Perhaps his posture was meant to be sincere but it came off as threatening and Emilia resisted the urge to shrink back. "When this is over, no doubt we will all owe the members of this task force a debt of gratitude for taking on such a difficult job. Please be assured that the office of the Attorney General will lend every assistance so that collectively, as a nation, we can put this sad moment in Mexico's history behind us."

There was polite applause as he backed away from the podium, lumbered down the stage steps, and left through the door in the paneled wall.

Another man sprang to the podium and introduced himself as Francisco Navarro, chief of staff to the Attorney General. He actually introduced himself twice, once behind the podium and again after clipping a small microphone to his lapel and moving to the left side of the stage. Next, he aimed a tiny remote at the screen. The welcoming slide dissolved into a satellite photograph of a city. Emilia could clearly make out the grid pattern of streets and an east-west highway running across the top of the view before it curved away to the south. Three red circles outlined locations on the photo; two on the west side and one on the bottom right that intersected with the southern turn of the highway.

"On the afternoon of 24 September of last year," Navarro began. "Students from the all-male Amistad Normal School teaching college entered the city of Lindavista to find transportation to Mexico City. Their intention was to participate in a demonstration marking the anniversary of the October 1968 student shootings in Tlatelolco Plaza. In keeping with student tradition for this event, they planned to commandeer the municipal buses that serve the citizens of Lindavista."

Cardenas shifted restlessly in his seat and Emilia resisted the urge to do the same. Navarro was simply reciting basics anyone with a newspaper or a smartphone had known for months. The students, or *normalistas*, probably seized buses every year to go to the annual demonstration in Mexico City. Thankfully, students in Acapulco could afford the economy class bus fare.

On Emilia's left, Judge Sarmiento tapped furiously at her cell phone.

"The students came into Lindavista from the west at approximately 7:30 pm," Navarro plowed on. He aimed the remote at the huge screen again and a red dot danced on the screen. "The group fractured. Some students entered a store, purchasing snacks and drinks, and behaving in an unruly manner."

The red dot jerked upward to the largest circle. The highway was a horizontal ribbon above it. Emilia decided that the unlabeled block north of the highway was the Multifoco prison, now in need of a new warden.

"A second student group went to the municipal bus station." Navarro said. "They commandeered two buses and drove through the city toward the highway toll booths."

The red dot hopped across the screen to the circle on the bottom right. "Their intention regarding the toll booths was to blockade highway lanes and by doing so, extort funds from drivers to pay their expenses while in Mexico City."

The auditorium was completely silent except for Navarro's voice. No whispers, shuffling of feet, coughs or sighs. Not even gum chewing.

Navarro's voice was flat and emotionless. "The group at the store flagged down a bus on the street and ordered the driver to the highway. The driver first returned to the bus station, departed the bus, and locked the students inside. One of the students was able to use a cell phone to call friends in the other buses now blocking the toll booths at the entrance to the highway. Those buses returned to the station and rescued their comrades."

The red dot returned to hover over the bus station below the strip of horizontal highway and the Multifoco prison.

"The reunited group commandeered two more buses and the four rode convoy-fashion through the streets in the direction of the toll booths."

Navarro stepped closer to the screen and the red dot flew in sweeping circles across the entire satellite image. "As you can see," he said. "The buses repeatedly journeyed past the *zócalo*, disrupting a charity event headlined by the wife of the mayor, Pilar Garay de Avila."

A bright image of a town square filled the projector screen. A huge pink banner strung between buildings advertised Caritas Señoras while pink and white *papel picado* streamers crisscrossed the blue sky between buildings. On the cobbled square, tables were dressed in pink checkered cloths and baskets of pink roses. The photo looked like a publicity shot from a magazine, an outdoor wedding reception or a teen's birthday party.

Judge Sarmiento made a tiny sound of disapproval.

Emilia glanced at the woman but the judge's lips were puckered and her entire attention was on her smartphone screen.

As Navarro rocked on his heels by the screen, the outdoor party was replaced by a shot of a white building surrounded by a tall wall topped with coils of razor wire. POLICIA was emblazoned on an arch over an opening in the wall wide enough to drive through.

"The Lindavista municipal police were alerted to the disruption," Navarro said. "The buses were tracked to the toll booths at the entrance to the highway. The students were ordered to stop the disruption to toll booth operations. When they failed to obey orders, the police fired upon them, forcing the buses off the road. The police then took the students into custody."

A toll plaza replaced the police building on the screen with cars lined up to pay. "According to members of the municipal police department," Navarro continued. "Acting on orders from Lindavista mayor Pedro Avila, the students were turned over to members of the El Choque drug gang to be taught a lesson. Gang members, however, misinterpreted their instructions. The students were shot and their bodies burned in a rural area used as a regional dump. The burned remains were bagged up and disposed of. The bags have not been recovered and the burn site has not been found."

The screen now filled with staggering statistics. Millions of pesos spent on investigations so far. Over 20,000 documents. Countless arrests of both police and gang members, as well as Lindavista mayor Pedro Avila and his wife. More than 200 people from the Attorney General's office involved, with as many *federales*, state officials, and local law enforcement.

Emilia was shaken by the numbers. All this churn had now boiled down to five cops who were expected to find all the answers.

The screen returned to the original welcome display and Navarro went back to the podium. "I join Attorney General Mendoza Lopez in wishing the task force good luck in bringing closure to this heinous episode, using the fresh perspective of . . . outsiders."

The last word hung in the air.

As if sensing the sudden hostility, Judge Sarmiento jabbed at her phone and switched it off.

The members of the task force were escorted back to the third floor suite set up for their use. With Ramirez at her elbow, Judge Sarmiento urged them to take the rest of the day to settle in and acquaint themselves with the librarians and secretary after their lunch break. Later in the week, she'd meet with them to discuss plans for their fact-finding trip to Lindavista. After perfunctory handshakes and a round of *good luck*, the judge swept off, Ramirez tagging behind like a well-trained poodle.

The door sighed shut on hydraulic hinges, like a vacuum

seal. An awkward silence settled over the group of five police officers.

Emilia studied the space where she'd be closeted with four strangers. On the perimeter, low partitions created a semblance of privacy for five workstations. The computers looked powerful, with bigger monitors than those in the detectives squadroom in Acapulco. The desk chairs were a mishmash of colors and heights.

A conference table surrounded by eight upholstered chairs anchored the center of the room. A hodgepodge of filing cabinets clustered together near the doorway to an inner office set aside for the secretary and librarians. Whiteboards on wheels, discolored by the faded erasures of a thousand previous uses, waited in a corner like discarded racecars in a garage.

Everywhere Emilia looked, cardboard file boxes promised a herculean task. There were boxes on the table, under the table, stacked between desks, crowded against the kitchen alcove. They formed a channel between a storage cabinet and the door. The labels suggested a galaxy of different contents and sources: *Misc DVDs, Lindavista 2 of 46, Federal Police Property*.

"Well." Elizondo cleared his throat and motioned them all to take a seat at the conference table. He pulled out a chair and paused.

Everyone did the same. The chairs were stained and filthy. Anaya sniffed audibly, like a bloodhound. The stink of urine was unmistakable.

"No doubt there was a rush to get the space ready and some things were overlooked," Miranda said. He dragged his chair to the door. Everyone followed suit. The stacked chairs were left outside in the hall and desk chairs brought to the table.

"Probably like the rest of you," Elizondo said. "I'd assumed that for an issue of national importance of this magnitude, there would be more support. The fact that this situation may not meet our initial expectations changes nothing. But if anyone feels they cannot deal with things as they are, please speak up now."

Emilia looked around the table. Everyone was silent.

"To do that," Elizondo continued. "We can't travel the same road as before. The broad conclusions of previous investigations can't prejudice us. To combat this, I would like to divide the work by category of information."

"An entirely different approach," Miranda added. "That will keep us from falling back on preconceived notions."

"Exactly," Elizondo said. "And maximize the talents of everyone here."

As if the two senior officers had already decided, Miranda volunteered to take on the documentation provided by the Amistad Normal School and the families of the missing students, to include reports from private detectives hired by the parents. He'd also help Elizondo review the witness statements and arrest records.

Elizondo asked Anaya to tackle the issue of terrain and weather, both of were relevant to claims of what happened to the bodies. Cardenas would review the forensic reports and build the master timeline with input from the rest of the task force.

"Detective Cruz," Elizondo turned to Emilia. "You probably have the greatest attention to detail among the five of us. I'd like you to review the video interrogations, documenting any relevant portions or anomalies, and construct a network analysis, graphing out the relationships between those involved."

The greatest attention to detail. Elizondo's expression was unreadable. Was this a patronizing way to remind Emilia that she was the sole female because she'd irritated him last night? Or had Miranda praised the details in the El Acólito alert report?

"I can do that," Emilia said.

"We'll meet every day at 4:00 pm to review and adjust as needed," Elizondo continued. "Are we agreed?"

Everybody murmured assent.

"Let me add something before we get started," Miranda said as Elizondo sat back, giving the other senior officer the floor. "We have a relatively short time in which to achieve what hundreds of investigators before us have not, which is to find out what happened to 43 young men on the cusp of adulthood. Forty-three men who wanted to become teachers and help their communities out of poverty."

Miranda's soft voice commanded attention. Emilia found herself nearly transfixed by his intensity.

"We can only do that by working together as tightly as

possible. This is not the time to hoard information or go it alone. Given the size of the team—."

"And the warmth with which we were greeted," Cardenas added.

Miranda nodded. "Ninety days does not seem like long enough time to review, collect new information and reach a conclusion. But we will achieve our objective and bring solace to the families of these missing young men."

Everyone claimed a desk and the task of organizing began. The librarians returned from lunch and looked shell-shocked as Elizondo explained how the task force would proceed. Boxes were opened, papers organized, file drawers rearranged, white boards repositioned.

As they sorted the boxes, Elizondo made an unwelcome discovery, which a call to Ramirez confirmed. While their computers were connected to the internet and had been given storage space on the Attorney General's server, nothing online awaited the task force. No databases, no electronic case records. Only the boxes and boxes of paper.

Emilia found cardboard crates of DVDs. Most disks were unlabeled. The cases were cracked.

The afternoon wore on. Miranda asked the secretary to order dinner. Everyone ate empanadas and salad at the conference table before tackling the boxes once again.

The five task force members stayed until midnight, when they walked back to the Sheraton in a group. Emilia envied Anaya his jeans and plaid shirt. Her gray pants and pink blouse were streaked with grime from wrestling dusty boxes.

The column supporting El Ángel strobed from lavender to green to frosty blue as they walked along Reforma.

Cardenas fell into step next to Emilia. "How about a drink in the bar?" he asked. "Celebrate our first day working together. You can tell me more about being a black widow."

"But then I'd have to kill you," Emilia replied.

It was nearly 2:00 am by the time Emilia crawled into bed. She left the bathroom light on so that a bright wedge of light cut through the hotel room. It wasn't that she was afraid of the dark, she just didn't like being in darkness.

Her thoughts circled tiredly. A task force of five people drowning in paper was laughable. Without more help from the Attorney General's office, they had no chance of finding out what had happened to the 43 missing students.

She'd have no time to hunt for Rafa Gamboa Escobar, either.

CHAPTER 6

Emilia added Pedro Avila, the mayor of Lindavista, to the list of people she hated. The list was still headed by Rafa Gamboa Escobar, but Avila—and Judge Sarmiento's assistant Ramirez—were neck and neck for the number two slot.

Silvio was a distant third.

In only two days the task force had developed a sense of rhythm and Emilia knew it was due to Elizondo and Miranda. They were already acting as a leadership team; Elizondo organized and authoritative, Miranda creating a climate of caring urgency. Neither senior officer was afraid to get their hands dirty and wrestled boxes and sorted paper like everyone else.

The first transcript of Avila's three interviews was 40 pages long, which Emilia realized with a sinking heart meant at least 2 hours of video. Avila denied everything. He didn't know the students from the Amistad Normal School were coming to Lindavista on 24 September, the same day his wife was scheduled to speak at a charity rally. He didn't know the students planned to commandeer buses. He denied giving an order to harm or hide the students, only for the police to clear the disruption at the toll booths.

Avila claimed to have spent the day in his mayoral office in the *alcaldia*, except for a late lunch at a restaurant. Along with a few prominent business leaders, the local military commander and the Lindavista chief of police joined Avila for lunch with two owners of businesses they hoped to attract to the city. The event was intended to demonstrate that security was a priority and commercial facilities were protected.

Emilia suppressed a gulp of ironic laughter.

Avila was a *pendejo*, but his file made for interesting reading. He was born and raised in Lindavista but attended college in Mexico City. His family owned furniture stores and Avila inherited the business ten years ago. He'd been mayor for three. His wife Pilar had an office in the *alcaldia*, and was noted for her charity work and commitment to education.

Avila and his wife had been arrested on 29 September, five days after the students were rounded up by the Lindavista police. Eighteen months later, he was under house arrest for misuse of public assets—namely the Lindavista police department—but still mayor.

The transcript of Avila's first interrogation showed that he'd been questioned by S. Camacho. Whoever S. Camacho was, they weren't a particularly gifted interrogator, sticking to a recitation of events on 24 September and repeatedly saying "Were you aware" in a way that let Avila respond with a simple "No." Silvio would have crucified S. Camacho for not asking open-ended questions.

After 29 pages of back-and-forth dialogue, Avila finally said something interesting.

S. Camacho: How were you notified as to the traffic disruption at the toll booths?

P. Avila: I don't remember.

S. Camacho: Were you still at the restaurant?

P. Avila: No, no.

S. Camacho: Did you return to your office after the lunch?

P. Avila: Yes. I think I was at home. I instructed the police to get the buses moved and get traffic back to normal. Arrest those responsible.

S. Camacho: How did you convey this order?

P. Avila: It wasn't anything special, you know. I picked up the phone. Told them what to do.

S. Camacho: Did you instruct the police to turn those responsible over to the El Choque gang?

P. Avila: Well, that's not the right word.

S. Camacho: Arrest?

P. Avila: No. Gang. They're not a gang.

S. Camacho: I don't understand.

P. Avila: El Choque is a club. A security club. Yeah, a club. From time to time the club functions as an auxiliary arm of the police.

S. Camacho: What did you expect this security club to do?

P. Avila: Teach those kids a lesson and send them home to Amistad. Nothing more.

"What garbage," Emilia exclaimed out loud.

"Problems?" Cardenas scooted his desk chair around the

partition separating their desks.

"The mayor of Lindavista referred to the El Choque gang as a security club," she said.

"Points for inventiveness," Cardenas observed.

"How's the timeline going?" Emilia asked.

"How about I tell you over drinks and dinner tonight?"

"How about you tell everybody at the 4:00 pm meeting?"

"Two can play hard to get, Detective." Cardenas wheeled his chair back to his own desk.

The DVD of Avila's first interrogation was one of the few disks with a label. Emilia skirted a pile of boxes, got a cup of coffee from the kitchen alcove, plugged in the headset, and started the video.

In person, Avila was a handsome man in his fifties with graying temples and a prominent jaw. His eyes were bloodshot, there was stubble on his chin, and his collared shirt was wrinkled. The video had been recorded on 30 September, a full day after his arrest.

The static camera captured Avila's face and torso as he sat at a table. No one else in the interview room was in the frame. The mayor stared unblinkingly at his unseen interrogator. His hands were not cuffed but merely clasped, although he occasionally rubbed his eyes. He didn't hesitate as the voice of S. Camacho asked question after question.

Emilia thought again that Camacho displayed little skill. Silvio would have led Avila in circles and made him double back upon himself until he tripped and fell on his face.

It wasn't until S. Camacho asked the question about El

Choque that the pace of the interview slowed. Avila didn't immediately answer but blinked rapidly. Emilia heard footsteps and the rustling of paper. Avila's eyes followed off camera movement. He gave a tiny nod.

Chair legs scraped against concrete. More rustling.

Emilia watched the time counter in the lower right corner of the video frame.

"El Choque is a club. A security club. Yeah, a club," Avila finally said a full two minutes later. His voice grew more assured as he explained El Choque's relationship with the Lindavista police force.

Emilia stopped the video and flipped through the transcript again. It gave no indication of pauses or activity in the room. She scribbled a note to herself and kept going.

S. Camacho was also listed as the interrogating official on the transcript of the first interview with the mayor's wife, Pilar Garay de Avila. If the transcript was correct, Pilar had not been questioned until two days after her arrest.

Two days of mounting pressure.

Two days to formulate her story.

Emilia stuck the DVD into the machine and decided Pilar had spent two days crying.

Pilar Garay de Avila was at least ten years younger than her husband, with long highlighted hair, a wide, thin-lipped mouth, and bold black eyebrows. Her eyes were smudged with old mascara and red from weeping. Her lips trembled throughout the interview during which Pilar either squeezed her hands together until her knuckles turned white or plucked nervously at the cuffs of her cashmere sweater.

That is, when she wasn't crying.

At the beginning of the video the voice of the again unseen S. Camacho asked the woman for her full name.

"Pilar Garay Villahermosa de Avila," Pilar said, her voice quavering.

"Please state your whereabouts on 24 September."

"I was at home. In the morning." Pilar faltered, her eyes tearing up again. "I can't do this. I need to speak to Lola. Please tell me where she is."

Lola. Their daughter, Emilia thought, although there was no mention of children in either file.

"Please answer the question."

Pilar gulped several times. "I was at home at first. Lola was there. Later in the morning we went to the *alcaldia*. To my office there." She paused. "May I have a tissue?"

As the camera remained fixed on Pilar, Emilia heard the thump of a chair hitting a wall, followed by footsteps. The squeal of door hinges and the low murmur of male voices.

A minute later a box of tissues was placed on the table along with a glass of water. Pilar took two tissues and pressed them to the inside corner of her eyes.

The sound of a chair being dragged across the floor drowned out her sniffles. "After going to your office," the unseen Camacho prompted. "What did you do next?"

Pilar balled up the tissues in her left hand and yanked at her sweater sleeve with the right. "I practiced my speech for the Caritas Señoras event."

"Tell me about the Caritas event," Camacho said.

Pilar stumbled through an account of the Caritas Señoras charity, which raised funds to keep girls in school. The charity paid school fees, bought books and uniforms, and even provided daycare for babies so teen mothers could continue their education. Emilia was impressed by the work Pilar described and the way she brightened a bit by talking about it.

"Were the streets around the *zocalo* blocked off for the event?" Camacho asked.

"I don't know." Pilar slumped against the back of the chair, the damp tissue still balled in her hand.

"How did you get to the event?"

"The driver for the *alcaldia*," she said. "I always travel in the official car."

"Did you notice any buses between the *alcaldia* and the *zocalo*?"

"The car has tinted windows," Pilar said helplessly. She looked around. "Where's Lola? No one will tell me where she is."

Emilia punched the button to stop the video. The woman's distress was real. Lola had to be her daughter. She pulled Pilar's file off the stack on her desk and was just about to open it when Elizondo loomed over the partition. He pointed to his ear and Emilia slid the earphones down to her neck to hear him.

"Detective Cruz, I wonder if you could lend me some assistance," the captain said.

"Of course."

Emilia followed Elizondo to his cubicle where he handed her two transcripts. "Can you please read these and tell me if you notice anything of interest."

Elizondo pulled out his desk chair and motioned for her to sit. Emilia lowered herself into the chair, while Elizondo rested against the desk and folded his arms.

The first transcript was dated 3 October, nine days after the students had been rounded up in Lindavista. Questioned by a *federale* unit in the village of Henrico, 25 miles north of Lindavista, Alfredo Nuñez admitted that he was a member of El Choque. About halfway through the six-page transcript, Nuñez admitted to killing the students.

Emilia knew her mouth was open as she read the blunt statement.

We put them on trucks and drove to the Colima dump. We shot them one at a time. All 43. They were like sheep. They just waited to die. Afterwards, we made a pyramid out of the bodies. We used gas to make a bonfire. Everything burned in about 12 hours. The newest members of El Choque shoveled the bones into bags and threw them around the dump.

Emilia looked up at Elizondo, her stomach churning. "This is what the last investigation concluded."

"Can you please look at this file as well," Elizondo said.

He exchanged the Nuñez transcript for a new one.

The interrogation of Pablo Guzman Hoya was also conducted by the *federales* on 3 October. A minute into the document, Emilia gasped.

We shot them one at a time. All 43. They were like sheep. They just waited to die. Afterwards, we made a pyramid out of the bodies. We used gas to make a bonfire. Everything burned in about 12 hours. The newest members of El Choque shoveled the bones into bags and threw them around the dump.

"Their statements are exactly the same," Emilia exclaimed. "Exactly."

Elizondo's usually stern expression twisted into grim acknowledgment. "Guzman Hoya was arrested the same day," he said. "But in Lomas Altas. Fifty miles away."

"Wait." Emilia laid the two transcripts side-by-side on the desk. Elizondo was right. The two arrests were made the same day, but miles apart.

"There is a slim possibility the interviews were transcribed by the same person and a mistake was made." Elizondo looked at her meaningfully. "But we need the interview footage to verify what these young men actually said."

"It could take awhile," Emilia warned. "Most of the videos aren't labelled."

"Get the librarians to help you."

Emilia nodded. "I'll do my best."

"Thank you, Detective," Elizondo said. "You can keep

the files."

Emilia went back to the video booth and ejected the DVD of Pilar Garay de Avila's interview.

The mayor's wife could wait.

CHAPTER 7

As Emilia took a chair at the conference table for the 4:00 pm meeting, she wondered how long the task force members could keep up the pace of 16-hour days. It was only Wednesday and she felt punch-drunk. Manually searching the uncatalogued video archive for the two duplicate confessions was hugely time consuming.

All she'd discovered so far was that each DVD held multiple video files. Some had as many as five recordings.

Judge Sarmiento popped in, Ramirez and his clipboard in tow. The judge had a quick word with Elizondo and Miranda before disappearing again.

Cardenas slid into the chair next to Emilia. "Drinks later, Detective?" he murmured.

"Sorry," Emilia said. "I'm working late."

"What a coincidence," Cardenas said and took out a little notebook. "So am I."

Elizondo called the meeting to order. As they went around the table, the group discussed the Avilas, the Lindavista police, and the charity rally held the day the students came to Lindavista. Cardenas scribbled in his notebook. The timeline was slowly coming together.

Emilia felt the weight of Elizondo's disapproval when she said she'd spent the day watching videos but had yet to find footage of either man who'd confessed to killing the students.

By Thursday afternoon, Emilia knew that unless something changed, she'd be chained to the DVDs forever, yet still never impress Elizondo with answers. She took a handful of disks and went into the adjacent office where Tina, the secretary, and the two librarians were at their desks.

"I need some help," she said to the librarians. "We need to find a way to digitize the video files and make them searchable."

Daniel handled the DVDs as if they were new and unusual. Ignacio looked tense. Tina stopped typing to watch the exchange.

Finally Ignacio shook his head. "We don't have the technical support to do that," he said. "We'd have to have a commercial contract."

Daniel handed the DVDs back to Emilia. "I asked about an online video archive," he said. "I was told it would take six months and cost at least 10 million pesos. Special software, you know. A video server. And we'd have to get permission to host the server on the official network."

"There's a privacy law," Ignacio hastened to add. "We'd need special permission from everybody in the videos to have their personal information made available to anyone who could access the server."

"This is a criminal investigation," Emilia exclaimed. "Collating information is what we do."

Daniel shrugged. "I'm sorry, Detective," he said. "That's what we were told.

Emilia narrowed her eyes. "Who told you?"

"Licenciado Ramirez," Daniel said nervously.

"Thank you."

Emilia stalked back to her desk and threw herself into her chair.

"Trouble in paradise, Detective?" Cardenas peered at her over the top of the partition.

"We need a video database," Emilia said. "Apparently Ramirez vetoed the project as too hard and too costly which is why we still have a pile of disks. Also, apparently we need permission from anyone who's on film."

Cardenas smiled, too handsome for his own good. "Want to talk to him?"

"If you get him to give us a video server," Emilia said. "I'll buy the drinks."

"Stand back, Detective." Cardenas stood and adjusted his tie. "Watch and learn."

As they approached the bank of elevators, two men waiting for the doors to open turned away and walked rapidly down the corridor.

"People here are so friendly," Cardenas gushed, looking after them.

Emilia nearly laughed.

Ramirez greeted the two cops with great sincerity, listened to Emilia's justification for a video server with sympathy, and rebuffed every argument Cardenas presented.

"We'll have to discuss this with Judge Sarmiento," Cardenas said finally. "Without a video server, a large portion of the evidence is useless."

"She's out of the office today," Ramirez said, his mouth pinched in smug superiority.

Emilia found herself clutching the arms of the chair as she and Cardenas sat in front of the assistant's desk like the accused before a judge. This odious little man, with his little bit of power, was going to prevent her from hunting for Rafa Gamboa Escobar. The apartment key was in Emilia's room at the hotel, but she was going to spend every *maldita* waking moment looking at video footage until the task force ended because of Ramirez.

Anger flooded Emilia's veins. Bile rose in the back of her throat.

Emilia got to her feet, unable to stay another minute. She said something and blundered towards the door. Cardenas pulled it open and they left.

"Tonight," Cardenas said as they got into the elevator. "We should discuss our approach over drinks and dinner. Later on, when we're horizontal, we'll come up with a better strategy."

Emilia jammed her hand against the red button and the elevator juddered to a stop. "Has it occurred to you," she shouted. "That we've been set up? Five strangers, 90 days, and a fucking mountain of crap?"

"You're just noticing it now?" Cardenas stuck his hands in his pockets, as relaxed as she was distraught.

Emilia stared at him, searching for a biting retort, but laugher tinged with hysteria bubbled up instead. Silvio would have yelled at her, spiraling them into a heated argument that threw off sparks. Cardenas was only interested in getting her into bed.

She sagged against the elevator wall and covered her face with her hands. Misery and mirth spilled out in equal measure.

"I don't mind crazy women," Cardenas observed. "But I do like to know ahead of time."

The fit of laughter ebbed and Emilia dashed the back of her hand against her eyes. "I've had too much coffee," she said lamely.

Cardenas stepped forward and punched the button. The elevator lurched and continued its descent.

At the 4:00 pm meeting, Elizondo instructed Emilia to keep searching for the duplicate confessions. Anaya wanted her to look for video footage of the Colima dump, especially if it showed land formation he could compare to maps. Miranda asked to be told if Emilia found video of a particular rally held by the families of the missing students and gave her the date.

"Sure," Emilia said unhappily.

Cardenas didn't put in a request but spent the meeting writing in his little notebook.

"Um, Detective?" Tina asked hesitantly. "Are you in here?"

Emilia came out of the toilet stall. "Hello, Tina."

The secretary had big retro tortoiseshell glasses and hair clipped into an equally trendy updo. "I was going home for the day," she said. "But I saw you come in here."

Emilia turned on the faucet and hit the dispenser for a blob of liquid soap. "Something on your mind?" she asked.

"I heard you talking about the videos earlier," Tina said.

Emilia nodded.

"I think maybe my boyfriend could help."

"How so?"

"He works for a company that imports cars from Germany," Tina said. "He's really good at his job."

Excellent. Please waste my time telling me about your hot mechanic. Emilia got a paper towel and rapidly dried her hands. "I don't think we need any car expertise. But I'll let you know—."

"No, what I meant to say." Tina stopped Emilia from opening the door. "They have all these videos. How to fix the cars. How to sell the cars. Cars on race tracks. That sort of thing."

"Okay," Emilia said slowly.

"That's what my boyfriend does," Tina said excitedly. "He manages all the videos. He runs the company's YouTube channel and even changes the videos from German to Spanish."

"What's he doing tonight?" Emilia asked.

CHAPTER 8

Tina's boyfriend Paco had a skimpy goatee, sprayed-on ripped jeans, and a head full of video technology. Emilia bought them all tacos at a place on Rio Lerma called El Caminero. The place was crowded and Tina led the way through the crush out to a table on the tiled patio. They sat on sun-warmed metal chairs under a big market umbrella.

Emilia watched as the thin young man wolfed down six chicken and *chorizo* sausage tacos for 92 pesos and washed them down with a beer. Between bites, Tina explained the situation to him.

"How long are the videos?" he asked.

"We don't know," Emilia said.

Paco nodded and picked up his last taco, squeezed a wedge of lime over it and added hot sauce from the bottle on the table. "Say you have a hundred. All on DVD. Not uploaded."

"Yes." Tina smiled at Emilia as if to say *Isn't he smart!*

Paco shrugged. "Well, that's your first problem. All the videos need to be uploaded before you can do anything else."

"That's the issue." Emilia put down her own untasted taco. "There's no video server."

Paco shook his head. "Nobody needs a video server any more. You create a protocol, upload to the cloud, and add a search program. Simple."

"You mean upload to YouTube?" Emilia asked.

"Nah," Paco said. "You don't want sensitive stuff all over the net, right?"

"Right."

"So you have to create your own holding zone in the cloud," Paco said. "Get all your video uploaded into an indexed library, then overlay a text-from-audio capability. Makes the audio fully searchable."

Tina bounced in her seat. "That's what you want, isn't it, Detective?"

"I think so," Emilia said. She had no idea how to make any of that happen. She'd used YouTube as a research tool plenty of times, of course; drug gangs in and around Acapulco loved filming themselves committing gruesome murders, but she'd never had to build a technical solution herself.

Paco wiped his hands on a paper napkin, dove into the knapsack on the tiled floor near his feet and came up with a tablet. "Let me show you how I have it set up for my company."

Emilia finished her tacos while Paco tapped and swiped and Tina beamed with pride.

"Look." Paco stood the tablet against the umbrella pole. "Here's a video. Now, say I want to search it for a word. Um, say, brakes." He typed the word into a small search box under the video frame. A tiny icon of interlocking gears popped up for a moment, then dissolved into a bar running the width of the image, spliced with thin blue lines in three places.

"Three hits," he said. "Every place you see a blue line, the word 'brakes' is in the audio." Paco slid his finger to the first line and tapped. The video image jazzed through several seconds and coalesced into a sleek sports car circling around a track. The camera zoomed in on the tires. A mechanical voice intoned " . . . brakes capable of stopping—."

Paco tapped to kill the sound. "Now if you want to search a whole library, I can set it up to do a global search. You'd get a list, like from a search engine, and every video on the list would have the word you want. It's not the most powerful program." Paco took a swig of beer. "It can only search one phrase at a time. But it's pretty useful."

"I think that's what we want," Emilia said slowly. This was going to cost a fortune. "How much does something like this cost?"

Paco took another big swallow of beer. "I can partition off space on my company's cloud if you want. Totally secure. Give you storage space so you can create a video library with the same search capability."

"What about your company?" Emilia frowned. "I don't want you to get into trouble."

"The storage space is there and been paid for already," Paco said. "I'll set up a database shell for you tonight, if you want. I'll send Tina the link. When you're done we'll migrate the whole thing someplace else. Nobody needs to know."

"That'll work, won't it?" Tina asked Emilia.

"You'll have to do the hard part," Paco warned. "Upload

each individual video file."

"I don't want to get you in trouble," Emilia repeated. She stared at the tablet and the blue indicator lines under the tiny video picture.

With this capability, what could the task force discover?

Emilia watched as Tina and Paco walked away. Their heads were bent toward each other and Paco had one arm flung possessively around Tina's shoulders. Something green and envious lingered at the edge of Emilia's thoughts for a moment before she headed east along Reforma and allowed herself to be swept up by the evening swirl.

Shops and restaurants beckoned. She felt anonymous and untethered. Lonely in a crowd of strangers. No one to go home to, no one who needed to know where she was.

A column of white and glass lattice towered over the south side of Reforma. A glass awning under the number 222 beckoned to pedestrians and Emilia followed the crowd into a sleek and spacious shopping mall. White mezzanine railings snaked around three floors overlooking a vast central atrium, connected by white tubular escalators and soaring V-shaped supports.

"A seat, señorita?"

Emilia had inadvertently stopped in front of a restaurant carved out of one side of the atrium. Big white umbrellas created an oasis of casual dining. "I'd like a glass of wine,"

Emilia heard herself say.

He guided her to a seat where Emilia splurged on pinot grigio and a small tapas plate of peppery olives. As she watched shoppers come and go, excitement about the video project crept in. If they pulled it off, maybe she'd find a crucial piece of previously overlooked evidence pointing to the fate of the 43 missing students. Prove that she was just as good an investigator as anyone on the task force.

With a major win like that under her belt, Silvio would have to let her back in the squadroom. No matter what the police counselor said.

She finished her wine, paid the bill, and decided to take the rare opportunity to extend her wardrobe. In Acapulco, work attire meant jeans, tees, and a light jacket to cover her shoulder holster. But here in Mexico City she was working in the Attorney General's office. Her reliable gray pantsuit wasn't enough.

Emilia headed for the escalator that would carry her up to Bershka on the next floor. The escalator going down was loaded with people, including a *gringo* who averted his eyes and focused on his phone as he passed Emilia going in the opposite directions. The *gringo* was a few years older than her, maybe in his mid-thirties. Curly light brown hair. Gray polo shirt. Navy pants. He had a carrier bag from the Aldo shoe store.

It wasn't anything she could put her finger on, but the man's subtle move bothered her. Emilia wondered if he was a reporter looking for members of the task force.

She ended her spree in the huge two-level Zara clothing store. Emilia liked the way she looked in the European store's trademark cardigans, sleekly cut pants, and funky jackets. She felt reckless as she staggered to the cashier with an armful of clothing.

As Emilia left the store on the second level laden with shopping bags, the *gringo* was idling by the window of Cristal Joyas, the jewelry and watch store. The Aldo bag was at his feet, as if while waiting he'd grown tired of holding it.

She had to walk right by him to get to the escalator.

He didn't turn to look or give any other indication of interest as Emilia marched past, bags jammed together in her left hand to leave her right hand free.

Just in case.

If he stared at her receding figure as the escalator carried her down, she didn't feel it. If he was behind her on the street, she didn't spot him.

CHAPTER 9

The process to upload the first video took 30 minutes.

Emilia watched enough to figure out the particulars of who, what, where, and when. She switched to Paco's indexing program, created a new document, navigated through the fields, and filled them in from her scribbled notes. Once the document was done, she uploaded the video. The program automatically noted its length and language.

Tina took a handful of DVDs and uploaded them, too. By 3:45 pm on Friday, the fledgling video library boasted exactly 23 videos. With Tina hanging over her shoulder, Emilia entered the word "sheep" into the search window.

The little gears twirled and faded. No results bar appeared. No little blue lines.

"Maybe there's no video with that word in it," Tina offered.

"*Madre de Dios*," Emilia muttered. "I hope this works."

"If it doesn't," Tina said stoutly. "Paco will fix it."

Tina's faith in her man was absolute. Emilia turned to the secretary. "Have you been together long?"

"A year," Tina said. Her eyes gleamed behind her lenses. "This weekend is our anniversary."

"Congratulations." Unexpected emotion gripped Emilia's chest.

She and Kurt had almost made it to a year together in the penthouse. Almost.

Emilia grabbed another DVD and stuck it into the computer drive.

By the end of the day the library held 37 videos. Elizondo looked unimpressed as she described the project at the 4:00 pm meeting.

It was strange to be in the big task force space alone on Saturday morning. Emilia made a pot of coffee, stacked the DVDs on the conference table and began the laborious process of watching and taking notes, creating a new indexing document, and finally uploading the video.

The room was silent except for the click of her computer keys.

"Why, thank you ever so much, Lieutenant Silvio," Emilia said out loud, watching the little gears spin as the video uploaded to the library. "This is a wonderful career experience. I'm so fucking grateful."

Ramirez had organized a tour of the pyramids at Teotihuacán for the task force and Emilia supposed that the others had gone. Elizondo had flown back to Guadalajara for a family matter and would be back Sunday evening.

On a Saturday morning like this, Kurt would be swimming or surfing. If there was a local race today, he and Jacques, the head chef at the Palacio Réal and a fellow triathlete, would be competing.

Silvio would be in the squadroom, setting up an

investigation into Acapulco's latest murder.

Emilia's best friend Mercedes Sandoval would be teaching a class of young dancers.

Sophia would go to the market as if she'd never told lies to her daughter, while her husband sharpened knives at the grinding wheel set up in the courtyard.

Rafa Gamboa Escobar would be . . .

As if to halt Emilia's train of thought, the gears stopped twirling. Another upload success that had only taken 30 minutes from start to finish.

At noon, Anaya walked in carrying a plastic bag. "How's it going?" he asked.

Emilia swiveled her chair around. "Hey, there," she said. "About 300 videos to go."

"Good stuff?" He thumped the bag on the conference table.

"I don't know," Emilia admitted. "I'm only watching them long enough to find out what they are so I can upload them to the database. What are you doing here? Didn't you go on the tour?"

"Nah," he said. "We don't have time for that shit."

Anaya came over to her desk, plaid shirt, jeans, boots, and belt buckle as out of place as ever in the modern office setting. He smelled faintly of cigarette smoke and peppermint.

"Can you show me how to do that?" he asked.

"Thank you," Emilia said fervently.

Anaya caught on quickly, although Emilia suspected he

was much more comfortable on the streets than stuck in front of a computer. After ten minutes she was surprised to hear *ranchera* music blare from his desk, guitars and trumpets driving a heavy counterpoint to a man's voice.

Anaya held up an MP3 music player, a cord trailing through the air from his desktop. "You like Vicente Fernández?" he asked.

Cowboy music.

"Sure," Emilia lied.

Two hours later, Anaya opened the plastic bag he'd brought in and hauled out sandwiches, apples, four beers, and a small bottle of tequila. Emilia was touched that not only was he willing to spend his day helping but thought to bring enough food to share. He refused her offer of payment and downed a beer in one swallow.

Emilia and Anaya were finishing the sandwiches at the conference table when Cardenas walked in. The man obviously spent time in a gym and was even better looking in jeans and a tee shirt than in a suit, although Emilia would never admit it to his face.

"Here I was, Detective Cruz," he said. "Worried that you'd be working yourself to the bone today without anything healthy to eat. But I walk in and you're swilling beer in the middle of the day."

"Did you go on the pyramid tour?" Emilia asked.

"Yes, I did." Cardenas tossed her a bar of gourmet chocolate. "They were tall and dusty and a bit too reminiscent of human sacrifice for my taste."

Anaya laughed.

"I thought I might be able to help out with your video project," Cardenas said. "After which you'd fling yourself into my arms."

"And my clothes would fall off," Emilia said.

"That's the usual order of things," Cardenas said.

"I'll tell you what," Emilia said. "In return for this chocolate bar, I'll teach you how to upload videos."

With the three of them working, the video library grew steadily for the rest of the day. Emilia lost track of time as they traded jibes and listened to *ranchera*. Anaya handed around the bottle of tequila. Emilia took a swig, as did Cardenas, but the detective from Reynosa finished it without any sign of drunkenness.

As the night wore on, they all got quieter. It was long past midnight when Emilia put her head down on her desk and fell asleep.

She woke, stiff and sore to realize that the lights were off and the room lit only by the glow of their three computer monitors. Both Cardenas and Anaya were stretched out on the floor and snoring. Emilia crept past them, curled up on the sofa near Tina's vacant desk, and fell asleep.

Something brushed her shoulder and she tried to bat it away, only to hear Miranda's voice. "Detective? Are you awake?"

Emilia blinked at him groggily. "*Madre de Dios.* What time is it?"

"A bit after 8:00 am," Miranda said.

"On Sunday?"

"Yes," Miranda said. "How long have you been here?"

"Since yesterday morning," Emilia said. The all-night video party came back to her. The three of them had indexed and uploaded more than 180 videos. "Cardenas and Anaya came in, too."

"So I gather," Miranda said. "They've gone to find coffee and breakfast food."

"Great." Emilia pushed herself to a sitting position and smoothed her hair. Her spine felt crooked and she could feel lines in her face where she'd rested against the seams in the sofa upholstery. She looked up at Miranda. "What are you doing here?"

"Put me to work, Detective," he said.

Cardenas and Anaya came back with a tray of Starbucks lattes and a box of pastries. Full of caffeine and sugar, Emilia washed up in the restroom, then taught Miranda how to upload.

The four worked steadily for about three hours, until Emilia called a halt to test the search function again. The others gathered around her terminal. She typed in the word "sheep."

She held her breath as the gears twirled and faded. Just when she thought that once again, nothing would happen, the search returned two videos.

"We did it," Emilia gasped. The videos listed were the interrogations of Alfredo Nuñez and Pablo Guzman Hoya, whose transcripts were still on her desk.

"Click on it, click on it," Cardenas urged.

Emilia's fingers flew over the keyboard as she called up the Nuñez video. Just like the video Paco had showed her Thursday evening, the results bar stretched across the bottom of the video frame. A thin blue line showed the point in the video where the word appeared. She advanced the footage to the line and started the video.

. . . sheep. They just waited to die. Afterwards, we made a pyramid out of the bodies. We used gas to make a bonfire. Everything burned in about 12 hours. The newest members of El Choque shoveled the bones into bags and threw them around the dump.

"Why is he so happy?" Anaya scoffed.

Emilia stopped the video. Nuñez had obviously been beaten; his nose and one eye was swollen and his shirt was torn and streaked with blood. Yet he seemed highly pleased to be speaking into the camera.

"Let's see the other one," Miranda said.

The interrogation room was different, but overall the Guzman Hoya video was disturbingly similar. A badly-beaten young man, confessing to a hideous crime as if it was a joke.

Their statements were exactly the same as the transcripts.

"I think Captain Elizondo will want to see this tonight, rather than waiting for the morning," Miranda said.

The conference table was littered with fast food wrappers and empty soda cans as Emilia uploaded the very last video, for a total of 420. The gears were still turning on her screen as Elizondo walked in.

"We have quite a surprise," Miranda said to him. "Detective Cruz has achieved a real miracle."

"So you said." In jeans and a black blazer, Elizondo looked more approachable. He set a paper bag on the conference table and pulled out two six-packs of beer. "I took you at your word that we have something to celebrate."

"We can search all the videos," Emilia said. "All the statements and confessions that were taped, no matter who did it. There's stuff in here from Lindavista police, the *federales*, the Attorney General's office." She gestured to the men standing by her desk. "Everyone helped."

"Well, Detective," Elizondo said. "Show me how it works."

"I can type in the word we're interested in," Emilia said. "The program will show us all the videos that contain that word. You'll see the two duplicate transcripts."

Once again she typed the word "sheep" into the search box. The gears twirled, winked out, and a search list appeared with seven entries.

"What the fuck," she heard Cardenas exclaim in a strangled whisper.

Emilia clicked on the first, the Nuñez video. She explained the blue line to Elizondo and hit "play."

"Go on," Elizondo said after a minute.

Emilia opened the second video on the search return list. Guzman Hoya's battered face proudly confessed to mass murder.

Before she played the third video, Cardenas taped a map of Michoacán to one of the wheeled white boards. He marked the cities where the men had been arrested and the dates of their confessions.

The task force room was silent except for the clicking of Emilia's keyboard. Five more young men, all bruised and beaten, happily admitted to having killed the missing students, burning their bodies, and watching gang members bag up the remains.

Each confession was exactly the same. Word for word, as if seven different actors had performed the same play in seven different interrogation rooms.

Emilia closed the last video. All eyes swung to Cardenas and his map. Seven pushpins fanned out east from the city of Lindavista.

"I was not expecting this," Elizondo said.

CHAPTER 10

Emilia found herself wedged into a corner of a ramshackle restaurant featuring steak *a la plancha* and not much else. The whole team was there, Anaya with his own bottle of tequila and the rest drinking beer. Elizondo looked like he didn't go to hole-in-the-wall *parrilla* places any more and kept looking around. Miranda clearly saw it as Anaya's territory. Cardenas looked at home.

They all got served flatiron steaks with stripes of charring on the outside and the meat cooked rare and bloody inside. The waiter flung down a bushel of fries and another round of beers.

For the first time in a long time Emilia felt part of something good again. Remembered why she'd stuck with being a cop when she could have parlayed it into something easier like being a bodyguard or a security guard in a department store. She was the lone woman, as she was in the detectives squadroom in Acapulco, but like she'd told the counselor, she could hold her own.

The war stories started halfway through the steaks. Some funny, some violent, some recounted the loss of a fellow cop or a bystander who ended up in the wrong place at the wrong time.

Emilia joined in with comments and laughter but didn't share a story of her own. Worried that Miranda would say something about the El Acólito case, she was surprised when

Anaya waved his fork in her direction. "Cruz here found the San Marco killing field in the hills above Acapulco. You remember hearing about that one? Honduran drug smugglers. Bodies cut up into hams."

Suddenly all eyes were on her.

"How did you find it?" Elizondo asked. "More technical wizardry?"

"Hardly." Emilia put down her knife. "The coast around there is very rural. Little villages stuck on the mountains above the ocean. A simple-minded boy cut the fingers off the hands of the dead and sold them."

"Sold them?" Cardenas asked incredulously.

Emilia nodded. "We didn't realize it at the time, but it was a very linear investigation. The finger kept getting sold. Eventually we found all the buyers and sellers."

"A body parts ring," Miranda offered.

"Nothing so organized," Emilia said. "A woman who ran a food stall in Acapulco bought the finger. She sold it to a man who makes fake religious relics. He made it look like the finger of Padre Pro, the martyr and sold it to a high end antiques dealer. That man sold it to a Catholic store." She blinked, remembering shopping there with Kurt, worried that he was going to spend too much. "By chance, I saw it in the store and thought it was the real thing."

"What was the break that cracked the case?" Elizondo looked at her intently, steak and beer forgotten.

Emilia shrugged. "We found the forgers who made the so-called documents saying it was Padre Pro's finger. Two brothers who ran a little operation out of their mother's house. She was a scary *puta*."

Miranda gave Emilia an encouraging smile. "Detective Cruz was also the officer who identified the El Acólito human trafficking ring."

"No stories there." Emilia bent her head over her plate and concentrated on sawing off a piece of steak. "That case sounds more interesting than it was."

To her intense relief, Miranda didn't push it. The conversation moved on. When they were walking out, Emilia pulled Anaya aside. The tequila bottle was half empty, yet like the previous night, he didn't seem at all affected by the alcohol.

"How did you know about the San Marco killing field?" she asked.

He pulled his mouth to one side and made a sucking noise. "Years ago, I was a boxer. Welterweight. On the pro circuit for awhile. Knew a real big guy from Acapulco. Heavyweight."

"Franco Silvio," Emilia said.

If Anaya had boxed at the same time as Silvio, he couldn't be that much older. Silvio was in his early forties, but Anaya looked 20 years older than that. Tequila and border violence had sucked him dry.

"I hear he's doing all right," Anaya said. "Fucking bad about his wife, though."

"He was my partner," Emilia said. "Got promoted to lieutenant."

Anaya nodded. "Finally."

"He tell you anything else about me?" Emilia asked. Silvio had probably gossiped like a girl to his old pal from the boxing ring.

"You look for missing women." Anaya sucked the inside of his cheek again. "Your *Las Perdidas*. Do you ever find them?"

"Not often."

"Why do you keep looking?"

"Somebody has to."

Anaya grunted and turned away to light a cigarette, a signal he'd finished speaking to her.

Emilia kept walking. Of all the things Silvio must have said about her, she wondered why Anaya chose to focus on her hunt for missing women.

CHAPTER 11

She called Silvio in the morning.

"Hey, Cruz," he said by way of greeting.

"Anything new on the hunt for Rafa Gamboa?" Emilia asked. She pictured him in his starched white shirt and jeans, grimy coffee cup in hand, piles of files on the desk.

Silvio snorted. "Nice to know you don't give up," he said. "Nothing has happened."

"Okay," Emilia said. "Thanks."

"You call just to ask?"

"Among other stuff."

"How's the exile going?"

"It's all right," Emilia admitted. "Five of us and everybody's decent, even the seniors. Hard workers. Clean."

"Five clean cops." Silvio seemed to be in an uncharacteristically jovial mood. "You sure they're all Mexican?"

"I met a buddy of yours," Emilia said. "Miguel Anaya Vargas from Reynosa. Said he fought welterweight on the same circuit as you back in the day."

"Yeah, sure. He fought his way out of Reynosa only to go back as a cop. We keep in touch."

"You might have told me you knew him."

"So?"

"You told him about the killing field up by San Marco," Emilia said. "He blabbed about it to the whole team."

"He talks too much?"

"The point is," Emilia said impatiently. "What else did you tell him about me?"

"Don't get crazy, Cruz." Silvio's voice lost its humor. "We discussed cases. Not your personal issues. Working style, that kind of shit."

"My working style?" Emilia asked suspiciously.

"I told him—." Silvio paused. Slurping noises came through the connection before he spoke again. "You're a clean cop, a decent investigator, and you puked your guts out the last time you saw maggots chewing on a headless vic."

"You did, too."

"We weren't talking about me."

"Well, thanks," Emilia said acidly. "Sounds like you summed up my career for him pretty well."

"Credit my silver tongue and all that shit," Silvio said.

"You're such a *pendejo*, Franco," Emilia grumbled. "When was the last time you went drinking with him?"

"With Anaya? Why?"

"He can really knock back the tequila," she said. "Forget welterweight. I'm talking heavyweight."

"If he's knocking back the tequila, he's got good reason.

"Which is?"

"This is between you and me," Silvio said. He was no longer joking, nor was he his usual gruff and grumpy self.

"Okay," Emilia said.

"Six, seven years ago," Silvio recalled. "Anaya was working a case. I never found out the particulars and don't want to. He got warned off. Kept going anyways. His wife and two teenaged daughters got snatched. They made the wife watch as they tortured and killed the girls. The woman was found wandering a highway a couple of days later. She's been in a home for the insane ever since." Silvio paused. "She doesn't even know him any more."

"*Madre de Dios*," Emilia gasped.

"Cut him a break," Silvio said. "Anaya's got nothing left to lose."

CHAPTER 12

The task force had bonded into a team over the weekend and Emilia knew she'd been the locus of the shift. Everyone was less formal, yet at the same time, the sense of urgency had heightened.

Elizondo took responsibility for digging further into the duplicate confessions and kept Emilia busy Monday looking for confessions of other El Choque members. Cardenas and Anaya came up with more search terms. She didn't get back to the taped statements by the mayor of Lindavista and his wife Pilar until late Tuesday.

Emilia watched Pedro Avila give the same answers for the third time as he'd given before in an interrogation room, although he seemed much more relaxed. Each time, the voice behind the camera and the name on the transcript was the same: S. Camacho.

Pilar looked like a completely different woman in her second taped interview than in the first, so much so that Emilia checked the dates. The two videos were 5 days apart, during which time Pilar had presumably been in jail. In the second video, she wore a gray prison shift, but her hair was styled and her makeup expertly applied. She certainly hadn't been crying but carried herself with an air of subtle amusement.

It was a fishing expedition. S. Camacho never rephrased or pressed for details, allowing Pilar to direct the conversation. Even Gomez, the most incompetent detective in the Acapulco squadroom, could have done better.

Pilar went from amusement to boredom. Her shoulders relaxed. Her eyes were halfway closed.

Pale pink nails gleamed as she fingered a set of rosary beads, the cross hidden under the heel of her hand.

Emilia got herself another cup of coffee. The new video library was a potential source of pure gold but only if she knew which words unlocked the treasure chest.

She typed in "Camacho."

The twirling gears were replaced by a list of twelve hits.

Emilia scrolled through the list. By now she could tell which videos were interviews; the interrogating officer's name appeared as a blue line at both the beginning and the end when he introduced and closed out the session for the benefit of the recording.

The first five were the idiot cop's interviews with the Avilas. Camacho had also interviewed a woman named Lola Dominguez. Emilia wondered if that was the person both Avilas had mentioned in their recordings, rather than a daughter.

Emilia's jaw dropped when she saw that the last video on the list was the interrogation of Lieutenant Sergio Camacho of the Lindavista police on 13 October, by the Michoacán *federales*.

"*Madre de Dios*," Emilia mumbled under her breath. S. Camacho had been arrested, too.

She played the video.

Camacho was nothing special to look at. Early forties, short straight hair, heavy moustache, soft jaw. He'd be fat in a few years. When he straightened his shoulders, the buttons of his collared shirt strained, revealing a white undershirt in the gaps.

Beyond his doughy looks, Camacho's expression was blank, as if he wasn't the sharpest tool in the shed. Emilia knew it was an act before she even heard the audio.

Camacho denied aiding and abetting the El Choque gang in the murder of 43 students.

Yes, he'd interviewed the mayor of Lindavista and his wife.

Yes, the chief of police of Lindavista had assigned him to that duty.

No, he hadn't received special instructions before conducting any of those interviews.

No, he didn't know anything about police helping the mayor cover up what happened to the students.

As far as Sergio Camacho knew, the students had attempted to steal buses and had been stopped, then turned over to the El Choque security club. No one thought they'd be killed. He personally had not been involved in any of the scuffles at the bus station, toll booths, or anywhere else the buses had visited the night in question.

Emilia drank her coffee as the interview dragged on.

Camacho and his questioner were evenly matched; whatever was thrown at him Camacho easily batted away. Indeed, the thickset lieutenant was much craftier as a suspect than as an interviewer. But having watched all the previous videos, Emilia could see the extent to which he'd protected the Avilas.

Throughout the interrogation, Camacho looked straight ahead. Emilia couldn't help comparing his interview with Pilar Garay de Avila's last session. Both were surprisingly sure of themselves in the face of charges they'd colluded to dispose of 43 people.

The only flicker of uncertainty came when Camacho was asked about Erik Flores, the owner of the bus service in Lindavista.

Officer: Tell us about Erik Flores. What was his involvement in the events?

S. Camacho: I expect he lost a lot of money.

Officer: Why is that?

S. Camacho: The buses were damaged. His property was destroyed.

Officer: Have you spoken to him about it?

S. Camacho: No, I wasn't assigned to talk to him.

Officer: Only to the mayor and his wife?

S. Camacho: That's right.

Emilia played the brief exchange about Flores twice. Camacho's agitation was barely perceptible; only a simple flutter of his eyelids betrayed his nervousness. She watched the rest of the video but he never flinched again.

She went back to the search list and clicked on the video of Lola Dominguez. The date was the same day as Pilar Garay de Avila's first interview. A police officer named D. Martinez was listed as the interviewer along with the now-familiar name of S. Camacho.

Lola was a pretty girl in her early twenties who looked frightened out of her mind. She answered every question rapidly, the words fountaining out of her. She was the personal assistant to the mayor's wife and had been with Pilar all day on 24 September, first going to the Avila residence to brief Pilar on the day's responsibilities like she always did. At 9:00 am or so she rode with Pilar in the mayor's car to the *alcaldía*. Lola's day ended when Pilar dismissed her. If there was an official function in the evening for the Avilas, she attended too, usually to help Pilar make a speech or introductions. Emilia got the impression that whatever Pilar needed, Lola was always there for her.

"We went to the *alcaldía*," Lola gabbled, obviously eager to please her interrogator. Eight minutes into the video and Camacho had already made her sob twice. His voice and choice of words were much harsher than when speaking to the Avilas.

"What time did you go to the rally?" Camacho demanded.

"Maybe 12:00 or 12:30," the girl stammered. "I went to make sure everything was ready. Decorations, the microphone. Pilar hates when things aren't organized properly."

"But you said you were with Pilar the whole day." A new

voice asked this question and Emilia assumed it was Martinez.

"I was." Lola nodded vigorously. "I was only at the *zocalo* for about an hour. The driver took me back and I told Pilar everything was ready. We left for the rally in the mayor's car at 2:00 pm."

Emilia stopped the video, backed it up 5 seconds and replayed Lola's last statement. "How long was this stupid rally?" Emilia muttered. She made a note to check if the organizers had been interviewed and restarted the video.

"We stayed all afternoon," Lola said after prompting by a new voice, presumably that of Martinez. "It was so hot. They should have put up a tent. Pilar had to wear sunglasses and was worried people would think she was rude."

There was an indistinct murmur of male voices. Both cops were still off camera.

The voices stopped. Footsteps scuffed on the floor. Lola's eyes followed movement out of camera range. A door opened and closed.

"When did you leave?" Martinez asked.

"Um, about 5:30," Lola said, her attention back to the unseen questioner.

"Was the rally still going on in the *zocalo*?" Martinez spoke rapidly.

Lola blinked. "The food and drinks were done. People were milling around saying goodbye and thank you and things like that."

"Where did Señora de Avila go after you returned to the

alcaldia?” Martinez was rushing now.

Lola’s shoulders slumped. “The driver took her home. I went with her and picked up my car from their house. Then I went home, too.”

“When did you get to the Avila home?” Martinez again.

“I’m not sure. Maybe ten minutes after we left the *zocalo*?”

“Was there anyone at the house when you got there?”

Lola shrugged. “The maids. The cook. The gardener. They’re always there.”

A pencil scratched against paper. “Are you sure,” Martinez asked very clearly. “The mayor’s wife, Pilar Garay de Avila, was no longer at the rally by 6:00 pm?”

“Yes, I’m sure.” Lola looked bewildered. “She was home before me and I know when I got home. My mother was waiting for her television program to start.”

Emilia stopped the video. She looked around, surprised to see darkening twilight through the windows. Miranda and Elizondo were both at their desks. Anaya was marking up a map tacked to a bulletin board. At the conference table Cardenas chewed on a pencil eraser as he leafed through a file.

Emilia wheeled her chair across the space to the table. “Gentlemen? I have something you’ll want to see.”

Cardenas gave a start. “An eighth confession?”

“Not quite,” Emilia said. “A statement by the personal assistant to the wife of the mayor of Lindavista.”

Just like on Sunday evening, the four men clustered in

back of Emilia's cubicle. She unplugged the headphones and adjusted the volume on her computer before replaying the last three minutes of Lola Dominguez's interrogation.

As they heard Lola gave the times of Pilar's attendance at the rally, Cardenas cut his eyes to the huge timeline marching across a freestanding whiteboard. The timeline traced the students' movements during 24 September in detail; their trips to buy snacks, the efforts to commandeer buses, the movements of the four buses they'd commandeered. As one day slid into the next, the timeline captured police actions as well as those of El Choque. All the tiny details that were the result of painstaking research through the files.

As yet there was no time entry for the rally in Lindavista, the one detail upon which the Attorney General's previous investigations turned.

Cardenas loped to the whiteboard and grabbed a red marker. "The rally ended at 6:00 pm, more or less."

"Add it," Elizondo said.

The next event on the timeline was 7:30 pm, when the students were first seen in Lindavista.

"The rally was long over before the students got into town," Miranda said slowly. "The police didn't intercept them on the buses until after 10:00 pm. Four hours later."

"Bottom line," Cardenas said. "The students never disrupted the rally."

"Have we just discarded the assumed motive?" Miranda asked.

Elizondo's face tightened. "I think we'd better discuss this with Judge Sarmiento," he said to Miranda, then turned to Emilia. "Detective Cruz, can you isolate that particular piece of film and put it on a disk?"

"I can give you the original," Emilia said. They'd labelled the original DVDs as they were uploaded and Tina had created a filing system for them. Emilia plucked the correct disk out of a box at her feet and handed it to Elizondo.

He and Miranda left.

"This is gonna make us some new friends," Anaya said. He reached into his back pocket and pulled out a dented hip flask, took a deep swallow and walked out.

Emilia shut down her workstation and found her shoulder bag. She punched Cardenas lightly on the shoulder.

"Come on," she said. "I'll let you buy me that dinner."

CHAPTER 13

Cardenas was becoming a friend, if it was possible to be friends with such a relentless flirt. But there she was, in her skinny black dress in the hotel restaurant at 9:00 pm, eating overpriced chicken with *chile ancho* sauce for which neither cop had to pay.

"This is insane," Cardenas said. "The Attorney General's case hinges on a simple question of timing that no one had actually bothered to ask."

"No wonder the mayor and his wife never admitted to anything," Emilia added. "Do you think they were framed?"

"I have no idea." Cardenas licked his fingers. "I've never seen such glaring problems with basic evidence and documentation."

"Deliberate incompetence or just regular incompetence?" Emilia asked softly.

Cardenas grimaced, but the sour expression only heightened his good looks. Every woman in the restaurant had gaped when he walked into the place.

"Who knows," he said. "There have been too many fingers poking at this. We need a dozen librarians, not two who are half asleep most of the time."

"What do you think Judge Sarmiento said about the rally timing?" Emilia asked.

"Probably some embarrassing hogwash delivered in a mechanical voice from the phone glued to her hand,"

Cardenas said. He made a slashing motion across his throat. "Okay, enough about that. I want to hear about the real Emilia Cruz."

Emilia shook her head and reached for her wine glass. "Men prefer to talk about themselves," she said wryly. "Tell me about the real Leonel Cardenas."

"Ordinarily I love talking about myself," Cardenas said. "There's so much good stuff women always want to know."

"No doubt." Emilia made a face.

"But tonight," he said. "I need to know if my theory is correct."

"What theory?"

"You're hiding a secret."

Emilia nearly coughed up a lung. "Why would you say that?"

"You're excessively driven."

"Women can't be driven?" Emilia counterattacked before Cardenas probed in the right spot. "They can't want to get shit done?"

Cardenas held up both hands to stop the onslaught. "I said excessive. Excessively driven. You attacked those videos like the devil was on your tail. You uploaded twice as fast as me or Anaya. Do you know how many times we tried to have a conversation? You were like a robot."

"You just can't cope with a woman who can do something better than you." Emilia lathered the last of her *chile ancho* sauce onto a bite of chicken.

"What about your little breakdown in the elevator after

talking to Ramirez?"

"I told you. Too much coffee." She popped the spicy forkful into her mouth.

"No, you're a little too intense about this investigation."

"We're a national task force," Emilia said. "Or haven't you noticed?"

"Do you have some personal connection that nobody knows about?" Cardenas pressed. "Lost a brother?"

"No." Emilia drank some wine. Cardenas's jokes and flirting hid a quick and assessing intellect.

"Nephew? Cousin?" he persisted.

"I'm the junior person here. I want to show that I can contribute." Emilia pointed at the untouched spicy sauce on his plate. "Do you want that?"

Cardenas moved the cup to her plate. "I'm more than happy to help you prove your point."

"You get high marks for consistency." Emilia had to laugh. "But it's never going to happen."

"I can make you change your mind." His supreme confidence was more humorous than anything else. "Even if you are a black widow."

"Okay, I'll come right out with it." Emilia put both elbows on the table and looked at him over her clasped hands. "I'd never sleep with a man as ugly as you."

Cardenas pretended to be mortally wounded. "*Jesu Cristo*, Detective. That really hurt."

"Seriously, I won't put either myself or the task force at risk for a hit-and-run driver."

"Are you implying I have a past?"

Emilia threw up her hands. "It's written all over you. I bet you have a dozen kids littered across Cancún."

"Only one." Cardenas picked up his cell phone. A few swipes across the screen and he held it out to Emilia. "This is Nico. Nicolas Cardenas Serrano. He's six. Smarter than both of us put together."

The sturdy little boy had his father's wavy hair, square jaw, and impish smile. He wore blue shorts and white polo and held the strap of a Spiderman backpack.

"He looks just like you," Emilia said. "What about his mother?"

"Nico lives with her." Cardenas grinned at the picture before tapping the screen and replacing the phone on the table. "We're separated."

"You slept around," Emilia surmised.

The waiter came by, deftly whisked away the empty appetizer dishes and set down their entrees.

Cardenas squinted at her over his grilled sea bass. "Our relationship is never going to get off the ground if you jump to conclusions, Detective."

"Am I wrong?"

"No." Cardenas grinned ruefully. "Look. Nico and I draw pictures for each other."

He pulled a small notebook from his hip pocket and handed it to her.

Emilia recognized it from the 4:00 pm meetings. While she thought he was taking notes, Cardenas was drawing. The

El Ángel monument, the Starbucks next to the hotel, the *parrilla* restaurant, an imaginary dragon. "These are good," she exclaimed.

"I text Nico a new picture every couple of days." As Cardenas leaned over to replace the notebook in his hip pocket, his gaze carried beyond Emilia's left shoulder. "Miranda and Elizondo are here," he said.

"Let's go ask them what Judge Sarmiento said," Emilia said and rose.

"No." Cardenas reached over the table and yanked on her arm to make Emilia sit down again. "Mom and Dad are arguing."

Emilia discreetly twisted in her seat.

Sure enough, the two most senior members of the task force were at a table in the corner. Both were red-faced as they gestured aggressively over untouched plates of food.

"*Madre de Dios*," Emilia murmured and faced front again. "Something bad happened."

Ten minutes later, the two captains stalked by on their way out. Miranda stopped when he noticed Emilia and Cardenas. "Lieutenant, Detective," he said. "How was your dinner?"

"Great," Cardenas answered for both of them. "What did Judge Sarmiento say?"

"The judge was not available," Elizondo said.

"Enjoy the rest of your evening." Miranda trailed Elizondo out of the restaurant.

"*Rayos*," Cardenas swore softly. "They're seriously

pissed.”

He walked Emilia to her room and held out his hand for the keycard. “Allow me.”

“Not on your life,” Emilia said.

“What are you saying?” Cardenas lounged against the wall by the door, all big innocent eyes, tousled hair, and miles of well-muscled shoulder. “That you won’t be able to resist me after all?”

Emilia rolled her eyes. “Don’t make me have to hurt you, Lieutenant.”

Cardenas looked down at her. “Maybe if I knew who he was I’d feel better about being snubbed.”

“Kurt?” Emilia heard herself say. Kurt’s aqua eyes glinted in her mind’s eye and a sudden hunger to be with him gnawed at her. “He’s . . . he . . . I mean,” she stammered, caught unawares by the wave of emotion.

“He’s not waiting behind the door to punch me in the head, is he?” Cardenas asked.

“No.” The humor helped Emilia collect herself. “We’re on a break.”

Cardenas considered. “Well, then, all the more—.”

“No, thank you, Lieutenant.” Emilia stuck her keycard in the slot. The light turned green and the lock gave a muffled click. “Good night.”

“All right. See you tomorrow.” Cardenas gave her a nod and took a step down the hall before turning back to her. “Hey.”

Emilia paused with the door half open. “What?”

"Has he seen you in that dress?"

Emilia laughed. "Good night, Lieutenant."

Emilia lay in bed in her hotel room and stared at the comforting ray of light from the open bathroom door. The digital display on the clock read 3:20 am.

Deliberate incompetence or just regular incompetence?

She never thought she'd be so caught up in the task force. From assessing the personalities of her fellow cops, to solving the video problem, to grappling with the horrific confessions, the task force was a bigger job than she'd anticipated. It left her neither the time nor the emotional capacity to start the hunt for Rafa Gamboa Escobar. The key to his apartment was still in her shoulder bag.

Emilia rolled out of the bed and washed her face in the bathroom. Left the door open and paced the room barefoot in her oversized tee shirt.

Ten steps to the door, ten back to the window.

El Ángel was dark now, but cars still cruised Paseo de la Reforma.

She thought about dinner with Cardenas. She'd had fun. It had been a long time since she'd enjoyed a give-and-take conversation. Laughed for the right reasons.

If she knocked on Cardenas's door right now, he'd answer.

Ten steps to the door, ten back to the window.

Emilia sat on the bed. The phone was right there on the bedside table.

The clock read 3:57.

Emilia took a breath and dialed. Three rings and the machine clicked on, as she knew it would. His private line didn't go through the hotel switchboard.

You've reached the office of Kurt Rucker, general manager of the Palacio Réal, Acapulco. Please leave a message.

Kurt's voice spoke the line twice. First in English, then in impeccable Spanish.

Emilia pictured him behind his big desk. White shirt, khaki pants, blonde hair. Eyes the color of the water beyond the cliffs at La Quebrada.

Organized. Calm. Caring.

She hung up before the beep. Ten minutes later she was sound asleep.

CHAPTER 14

Once again, Emilia was in the dim room, facing the counselor. Two boxers in opposite corners before the bell. The barred window tumbled blocks of light across the floor.

"He's undeniably handsome," the counselor pointed out. "Smart. Hardworking. Relatively young to be a lieutenant. So why did you sleep alone last night?"

"For a start," Emilia said. "It would jeopardize the task force. Plus, he sleeps around. I don't want somebody like that."

"What do you want?" the counselor asked.

I want things to be the way they were before.

They sat in stony silence in the gray room with the never changing pattern of light marking the boundary between them. There was no ticking clock this time.

Emilia broke first. "I want someone who knows me. I don't want to have to tell my whole history and wait to be judged."

"Is that why you called Kurt?" the counselor asked. "What did you talk about?"

Emilia dropped her head into her hands. Her cheeks were warm against her palms. "We didn't talk," she mumbled. "I just listened to his voice on his office answering machine."

"That doesn't sound very satisfying, especially compared to what Lieutenant Cardenas is offering."

"I'm not interested in Cardenas," Emilia said. "I'd just be

one more conquest to him.”

“Like with Rafa Gamboa Escobar.”

Emilia gasped as anger tightened every muscle.

“Ah, Emilia,” the counselor said with an odd laugh. “You’re like an old bottle. Nothing in there except dust and anger.”

“What?”

“You’ve filled all the empty places in your life with anger,” the counselor said. “Every idea in your head, every decision you take comes from a place of anger.”

“I have every right to be angry,” Emilia fumed.

“You’re angry at your own memory,” the counselor went on. “You think you should be able to remember the rape, but he drugged you and you can’t.”

“I think about it,” Emilia said. Tears filled her eyes and she brusquely swiped at them with the back of her hand. “See him pushing into me and I do nothing. I wonder how long it took. If his men watched. Laughed at me.”

“Why?” the counselor demanded. “Are those useful thoughts? Do you ever expect to get answers?”

“I don’t know,” Emilia cried. “If I kill him, maybe it will stop.”

“Is that why you left Kurt Rucker?” the counselor asked swiftly. “To avoid experiencing with him what you see in your mind with Rafa?”

“No,” Emilia said, revolted. “Kurt’s not like Rafa at all.”

“Not a murderer.”

“Kurt’s an honorable man!”

"Do you think Kurt would approve of you committing murder?"

Emilia clamped her mouth closed. Kurt had been her oasis, her refuge from the dirt and crime on Acapulco's streets. She'd fled because she couldn't do what she had to do from that protected place. Didn't want to soil it.

But admitting to those reasons took more courage than she had.

The counselor stirred in her dim corner. A white tank top was all that Emilia could see of her clothing.

"So here you are," the woman said. "A lonely glass bottle of anger ready to be smashed into pieces like a coward. Rafa Gamboa Escobar controls you through that anger as much as when he chained you like a dog."

Emilia jumped up. "He doesn't control me!"

"He controls you every time you say you're going to kill him," the counselor said mildly, as if Emilia's agitation was invisible. "He controls your most important relationships. Your relationship with Kurt, for a start."

"No," Emilia protested, but it was true.

"What about the members of the task force?" the counselor pressed. "You're doing good work. Making breakthroughs no one expected. You might even have impressed Captain Elizondo, not that he hands out compliments. What will they say when you kill Rafa? Won't they feel as tricked and used as Rafa made you feel?"

"Go away," Emilia said.

"Not yet," the counselor said.

CHAPTER 15

The task force space hummed with tension the next morning. Judge Sarmiento would be coming in that afternoon for a formal briefing, Elizondo announced. He wanted to show both the timeline and the network analysis.

Emilia entered connections between the players collected by the task force into a computer program that diagrammed linkages. The result was a huge spider web that she could display on a rolling whiteboard.

In the center of the board, Emilia used a black marker to write the names of Pedro Avila and his wife. From this hub, she drew spokes leading to all the people who directly connected to the mayor and his wife. This created a first tier of 28 people, among them the Lindavista chief of police, Pilar's assistant Lola Dominguez, and a score of Lindavista cops and city officials. Erik Flores, owner of the buses commandeered by the 43 missing students, had the most tenuous connection to Avila; he'd been at the mayor's business lunch on 24 September.

Emilia added connections, creating a second and third tier, until the whiteboard was a series of concentric circles of color-coded names. She used blue for the names of police officers who'd been arrested for complicity. Red was for El Choque gang members, all of whom connected to either a Lindavista cop or another gang member.

Off to one side , she wrote the names of the seven who'd

given identical confessions. Despite claiming to be El Choque members, they didn't connect to anyone. Not even each other.

Miranda surveyed the huge diagram. "What does this tell us to do next?"

"I'd like to follow up on Erik Flores," she said.

"The Lindavista transport king," Miranda said. "Who lost his buses thanks to the police."

"One of the cops who was arrested had an odd reaction when asked about him," Emilia said.

"What kind of reaction?"

"A twitch. A flinch."

A smile creased Miranda's face. "Enough to matter?"

"I'd like to check."

"Go ahead, Detective," Miranda said. "After the video success, I'm inclined to give you free rein. That's been nothing short of spectacular."

"Thank you." Emilia wished it had come from Elizondo, but it was nice to hear nonetheless.

Tina brought Emilia a thin file. Flores had given two statements to the Michoacán *federales*, neither of which had been videotaped. In both, he came across as a successful businessman appalled that his company was caught up in such a terrible situation.

An online search took her to the website for the Flores Transito company. The site was loaded with pictures of buses, freight trucks, and happy mechanics. Erik Flores was in most of them, a fit forty-something usually wearing a white polo shirt embroidered with his company's logo of a red flower.

There was even a picture of the happy Flores family at their ranch in western Michoacán. Erik, his wife Adelita, and teenagers Maria Lourdes and Juan Miguel posed with horses and a fluffy dog.

The wife wore skinny jeans, riding boots, and a red sleeveless blouse that revealed toned arms. She looked vaguely familiar.

Emilia decided that Señora de Flores reminded her of a certain type that frequently passed through the Palacio Réal. Women who paraded themselves through the Pasodoble Bar in bikini tops, chunky jewelry, and sarongs artfully tied to show off one leg.

They reeked of entitlement.

"We still place the mayor, Pedro Avila, and his wife, at the center," Elizondo said, standing in front of the whiteboard covered with Emilia's spider web of names. "But new information calls into question the previously accepted motive."

Emilia watched Elizondo. She knew he was comfortable in the limelight like this, instructing and informing and radiating personal power. But he was tense, too.

So was Miranda.

They all were.

Sitting next to Judge Sarmiento at the conference table, her assistant Ramirez jotted something on his clipboard with a silver fountain pen. The judge clasped both hands around a huge Starbucks coffee cup. She was so thin the veins protruded, blue and vulnerable.

Cardenas wheeled the timeline whiteboard next to the network analysis. All eyes focused on what was now a giant billboard showing a continuous history of the case.

Elizondo used a laser pointer to focus a red dot on the set of timeline entries for the charity rally on 24 September. "The Caritas Señoras event took place in the afternoon of 24 September," he said. "Streets were blocked off leading to the *zocalo* town square. By 6:00 pm, the event was over and the roads were clear. We have one statement on video from a witness and this morning confirmed the timing with the event organizers."

As you could have done.

The nib of Ramirez's pen scratched across the paper. Judge Sarmiento let go of her coffee cup with one hand to smooth her hair. Her makeup was skillfully applied but nothing could disguise the rings of fatigue under her eyes and the downward slope of her mouth.

Cardenas returned to his seat at the conference table and cocked an eyebrow at Emilia. She lifted a shoulder in a tiny silent shrug in reply. Next to Emilia, Anaya folded his arms as if shielding himself from the discussion.

"The students were first seen in Lindavista 90 minutes after the end of the rally," Elizondo said. "At that time, they were several miles from the *zocalo*. The mayor claims he first learned that the students had seized buses more than two hours later. As a result, we can only conclude that the charity rally is not a justifiable motive for the police attacks on the students in the commandeered buses."

"But your diagram still puts Mayor Avila and his wife at the center of the case." Judge Sarmiento gave a fleeting smile of condescension. "So the timing of the charity event doesn't matter, does it?"

Elizondo remained standing by the whiteboard, his face impassive. "It's an anomaly we're not prepared to overlook," he said. "Especially in light of a potentially much more serious discovery."

The laser pointer created a circle of red light around the list of seven names.

"Seven different suspects confessed to the murders of the 43 students," Elizondo said. "Using the exact same wording. Identical word-for-word confessions. Each confession recorded at a different place and time."

"What?" Ramirez stopped writing and blinked at Elizondo, his pen wavering in mid-air.

Judge Sarmiento frowned. "I don't understand."

"Seven separate yet identical confessions," Elizondo said. He sat down next to Miranda. "We have both the video footage and the transcripts."

"You're mistaken," Judge Sarmiento said dismissively.

Elizondo nodded at Emilia. "Could you please run the videos for us, Detective Cruz?"

Emilia went to the computer where the demonstration was ready to run. A large television, bolted to the wall just an hour ago, came to life with the video library search screen. The curser blinked next to the word "sheep." Around the conference table, heads raised as one to watch.

"We are able to search all of the video testimony gathered over the course of all of the investigations," Emilia said. She heard Ramirez suck in his breath as she went on. "Using a text-to-speech conversion program. A simple keyword search returns a list of all the videos in which that word is spoken."

One by one, Emilia played all seven video confessions. Cardenas rolled out the map showing where and when each man had been arrested.

As Emilia watched the men say those chilling words over and over on the large screen, she was struck again by the rehearsed nature of the confessions. The men weren't affected by what they'd done but proud they'd remembered the exact thing they were supposed to say.

She glanced around the room. Did anyone else see it?

After viewing all seven confessions, Judge Sarmiento's face was pale. "Are you people trying to make the Attorney General's office look foolish?" she asked, her voice tight with anger.

It wasn't the reaction Emilia anticipated. Shock, certainly. Horror. Even confusion. But not suspicion and anger.

"Both the video recordings and the transcripts are from

files turned over to the task force," Miranda said. It was clear that neither he nor Elizondo expected the judge's reaction. "We thought it was important for you to see this because we'll need to alter the schedule for visiting Lindavista. There needs to be time for extended interviews with each of these men at the Multifoco prison. We also want to interview Mayor Avila, his wife, and several others."

Elizondo nodded. "We'll have a list to your office shortly so that the additional arrangements can be made."

A jeweled brooch on her chest rose and fell as Judge Sarmiento's breathing became nervous pants. "I don't know if such a request can be accommodated," she said.

"This isn't a request," Elizondo replied.

Judge Sarmiento's eyes bored into Elizondo, the others around the table forgotten. "This is a very dangerous game, Captain Elizondo," she said. "It is not in the task force's charter to create evidence."

"This falls under the category of deconfliction," Elizondo said, his voice even. "To ignore such a glaringly questionable set of statements would border on criminal behavior."

Judge Sarmiento slapped a hand on the table, making her Starbucks cup wobble. "I hardly need a lecture on legal process, Captain," she exclaimed. "What you are asking to do is a potential breach of a legal charter. We cannot exceed the task force mandate without authorization from the Attorney General himself. Perhaps even the President."

Elizondo said evenly. "I assure you—."

"I'd like a written explanation of those confessions," the judge interrupted him. "Details of who made those recordings. And the transcripts."

"We already have a written report for you," Miranda interjected. He passed a folder across the table.

"No," Judge Sarmiento said sharply. "I want any paper copies numbered and restricted to Licenciado Ramirez, myself, and this task force. No emails. Is that clear?"

"Yes," Elizondo said. His jaw didn't move as he spoke the single word.

"I have another appointment," Judge Sarmiento said. She stood up and nervously smoothed the lapels of the white boucle jacket she wore over a matching silk blouse and black pants, lingering on the brooch as if to calm herself. "I'll discuss your report with the Attorney General at a suitable time. I don't need to remind you that the task force is his top priority. In the meantime, perhaps you can revisit your conclusions as to motive."

Judge Sarmiento swept out of the room, Ramirez trotting ahead to open the door for her. It closed behind him, the air-cushioned hinges sighing with the effort to prevent the door from slamming.

The five task force members were left slack-jawed around the conference table.

Miranda pointed at Elizondo. "This changes things," he said.

The other man shook his head. "It still crosses the line, Juan José."

"There is such a thing as loyalty to a higher power," Miranda said softly.

"What are we talking about?" Cardenas inquired.

Neither Elizondo nor Miranda acknowledged the question.

"Excuse me." Miranda stood. "I believe I have exceeded my ability to contribute."

He turned off his workstation and left. Again, the door hissed as it slowly closed.

Elizondo pinched the bridge of his nose and looked around the table at the confused faces of Emilia, Cardenas, and Anaya. "Tomorrow will be a work holiday," he said. "I don't want to see any of you in here. We'll reconvene the day after tomorrow and go back to basics. Lieutenant Cardenas and Detective Cruz, please revisit the issue of motive. Who wanted the students out of Lindavista the night of 24 September and why. Find something we can work with."

Cardenas glanced at Emilia. They both nodded.

Elizondo turned to Anaya. "Detective, when do you think you'll have a final report on the Colima dump?"

"End of the week," Anaya said.

"Good, good." Elizondo looked at each of them in turn. "Any questions?"

"No, *jefe*," Emilia murmured and heard the others say the same.

Elizondo stood up. "Lieutenant Cardenas, please let the support staff know they will not be needed tomorrow."

He walked out.

"I hope Mom and Dad aren't getting a divorce," Cardenas said.

CHAPTER 16

Rafa Gamboa Escobar had lived in a modern apartment building in the trendy Polanco district.

As Emilia entered the building, the key in the pocket of her jeans, she wondered what she'd find. This is where he'd lived as his acting career took off. Rafa had been the handsome boyfriend in *Rosa Quintana,* a hugely popular soap opera.

When the *telenovela* finished its run and Rafa left for parts unknown, his foster parents had left the apartment alone in hopes that Rafa would return. Now that they knew he was a wanted criminal, they planned to sell it.

A security guard in a glass booth at the entrance studied Emilia's identification, returned it through the slot and buzzed her in. The lobby looked like a miniature of the Sheraton, with paneled walls, a marble floor, and a long concierge desk topped with a bowl of candy and a floral arrangement almost as tall as Emilia. The air conditioned space was freezing.

She showed her identification again to the man behind the desk, along with a letter Karina had provided. "I called earlier," she said. "To look at apartment 203. Señor Gamboa's place."

"Yes." The man looked mournful. "Are you the real estate agent?"

"No, I'm Señor Gamboa's sister." The words tasted vile

in her mouth.

"He moved away so suddenly," the concierge said. "But the apartment is just as he left it. The woman comes in to clean once a month but as I've told Señora Escobar, we've always taken good care of her son's home."

"He died," Emilia heard herself say.

"*Por Dios*!" The concierge crossed himself. "He was so young, such a charming man. Always so considerate of the staff here." He looked at her expectantly.

Emilia looked away uncomfortably, not sure why she'd lied and unwilling to dream up some tragic end to complete the fabrication. She saw a bank of mailboxes behind the man's shoulder. "Are there any tenants still here who knew him? Who were friendly with him?"

"He was quite a busy young man," the concierge said. "Perhaps Señor Menendez. An older man. He lives across the hall."

"Do you know if he's in now?"

"No, I don't believe so. He's a banker."

"Perhaps when he comes in you can ask him to call me." Emilia put her card on the counter, dug out a pen, and scribbled her name over the printed cell phone number.

The concierge picked it up. She knew he was nonplussed by the unconventional calling card but experienced enough not to show it.

"I suppose you want to go up now." He moved out from behind the counter.

"I'm fine alone," Emilia said. "I have the key."

"Yes, yes." He walked her to the elevators; glossy brass doors set into the paneling. Emilia saw a wavy golden image of herself before the doors parted. The concierge darted in ahead of her, holding the doors open with one hand while he punched the button for the second floor with the other. "Second door on the right as you come out of the elevator," he said.

"Thank you," Emilia said, wishing he wasn't so trying so hard to be helpful.

"My condolences to your family." He stepped away and the doors closed with a soft swish.

From the hall layout, Emilia decided there were six apartments on each floor. A window at either end showed different views of Polanco's high-rises, upscale stores, and busy traffic. A big green sign for Starbucks rose above the architectural clutter.

The second floor hallway was wide and Emilia's feet sank into plush gray carpeting punctuated with gold fleur-de-lis motifs. The walls were covered in subtle gray and white murals that repeated the street scenes outside. No doubt the perspective of the murals changed on each successive floor to match the view from the windows. Everything reminded Emilia of wealth and privilege and that she had neither.

The apartment still had the name Gamboa written in a stylized script above the doorbell. She walked up and down the hall before taking out the key. The name Menendez was written above the doorbell of apartment 206.

Emilia's hand shook slightly as she fitted the key into

Rafa's lock. Her heart pounded so loudly if anyone had walked up behind her she would not have heard them.

She stepped inside, closed the door very quietly, and halted in the dark entrance, suddenly unsure of herself. Waiting for laughter or his mocking voice. Telling her she'd never find him, that he would always be one step ahead. Toying with her, scaring her.

"No," Emilia said out loud. She found a light switch. A chrome and glass chandelier sparkled overhead.

The living room was long and narrow and divided into zones. Two brown leather sofas faced each other, the ends centered in front of a wide window covered in slatted blinds. To the left, the end of the room was outfitted as a study, with a stylish chrome desk and dark wood bookcases. At the opposite end of the room a marble-topped round dining table was ringed by four dark wood chairs. A larger version of the hall chandelier hung above.

A doorway by the dining table led to a small kitchen, the kind for people who ate out for most of their meals. A fancy cappuccino machine sat on the counter. Emilia opened cupboards, finding dishes and pans but no food. The refrigerator was still hooked to electricity but empty save for a jar of ammonia with a hole punched in the lid, no doubt courtesy of the cleaning service Karina Escobar had maintained for so long in the vain hope that her foster son would return.

Beyond the kitchen, a tiny hallway led to a laundry closet, maid's room, and a bathroom. All the cupboards were empty. Emilia's cross trainers squeaked against the tile floors.

She passed through the living room again, went down a short hallway and found two bedrooms, both with en suite bathrooms. The larger of the two rooms had a king-sized bed in it.

Rafa's bedroom. Emilia groped for the switch, her heart racing again. Soft light spread across a simple white bedspread. More slatted blinds shaded the windows.

She found herself opening drawers with rushed and jerky movements. The bedside tables were empty but a few items of clothing still hung in the closet. Emilia ripped hangers holding shirts and pants to the floor, adrenaline and anger mounting in equal measure.

"You *pendejo*!" she yelled. "You fucking *pendejo*!"

A shelf came crashing down as she pulled at another handful of hangers and she stumbled backwards to avoid being hit by the length of wood. Emilia banged her head against the opposite wall and gasped. Stars twinkled across her vision and she slid to the floor.

Tears came, hot and unwelcome, yet cathartic at the same time. Emilia cried until she was afraid she'd be sick. She forced herself to her feet. The impersonal kitchen offered cold water for her face and a chance to get herself under control.

"Rafa Gamboa Escobar," she said out loud. Her voice shook but breaking the eerie silence gave her courage. "You are wanted for crimes including murder, sexual assault, human trafficking, fraud, and impersonating a caring human being. Your home is subject to search and seizure."

As if in response, the air conditioning clicked on.

She went through the bedrooms, looking for papers, addresses, anything that would provide a clue to his present-day whereabouts. The living room bookcases held scripts and ornaments. A few books on acting. A biography of Sir Lawrence Olivier.

Rafa had aimed high.

She opened the blinds, felt along the window sills. Found placemats in a small teak buffet in the dining area. The coffee table was bare but for the television remote.

Emilia sank into one of the sofas and looked around. It was a beautiful place. She tried to imagine Rafa's life in the apartment. The handsome up-and-coming actor. Parties to further his career and celebrate every step forward. An endless string of women dazzled by his looks and family money.

Why hadn't it been enough?

Coming had been a waste of time. The only thing she knew about Rafa Gamboa Escobar that she hadn't two hours ago was that he'd taken everything of importance with him. Emilia dug her hands into the sofa cushions in frustration.

Her fingernail scraped metal.

Emilia spun off the sofa and pulled up the cushion. A heavy key was nearly buried in the seam of the canvas stretched over the springs.

She picked it up. A tiny cardboard label was tied to the

key with string.

Casa Odisea.

Odyssey House.

Emilia reeled out of the apartment building with keys in her pocket and the concierge's sympathies in her ears. A taxi took her back to the Sheraton.

Three hours of online searching led nowhere. The closest Emilia came to connecting the key to Rafa was a housing development in Veracruz. When she called the Casa Odisea sales office, no one by the name of Rafa Gamboa Escobar had purchased a plot.

There were no other leads worth following.

She called Karina Escobar de la Vega in Acapulco. Rafa's foster mother picked up on the second ring.

"Emilia, I was wondering when I'd hear from you again," she said warmly.

"How are you, Karina?" Each time Emilia spoke to the woman, regret dogged the conversation. But for one twist of fate, Emilia might have been the one to grow up in the big white house in Acapulco's wealthy Las Brisas neighborhood.

Instead, Rafa had been the chosen one and destroyed everything he'd been given.

"Everything is fine here," Karina said. "Are you still in Mexico City?"

"Yes." Emilia looked at the busy street below. It was always rush hour on Paseo de la Reforma. "I've just been in Rafa's apartment in Polanco."

"Was it hard?"

Emilia sighed, not really able to put into words the way she'd felt there. "At first," she said. "Do you know of a place called Casa Odisea?"

"What is that?"

"I found a key with a label that says Casa Odisea." Emilia took the key out of her pocket. "I think it's a door key."

"I've never heard of it." Karina sounded upset.

"Did Rafa ever mention a neighbor?" Emilia asked. "Señor Menendez. The building concierge says he's a banker."

"We never met him but Rafa mentioned him several times." Karina's tone grew lighter. "Antique collector of some note. But generous. He used to loan Rafa books. Old books. First editions, that sort of thing."

"I'll try to talk to him on the weekend," Emilia said.

"Are you sure this is a good idea?" Karina asked gently. "I know you need closure, Emilia, but maybe it would be better to let others find him. Maybe instead you should make your peace with Sophia."

"Karina, don't forget that this is my job," Emilia said stiffly. "I'm a cop and Rafa is a criminal."

"I'm never going to forget that," Karina said. "You asked me about people Rafa worked with in Mexico City. I've found the name of the director who fired him. That was

Rafa's last acting job before he disappeared."

As Emilia grabbed the hotel's complimentary pen and pad, she heard the click of Karina's heels on tile, then the fluttering of paper.

"Here it is," Karina said. "Paulina Reno." She read off a number.

Emilia copied it down. By the time they finished the conversation, Karina was crying. Emilia said something lame and promised to call again soon.

CHAPTER 17

Emilia was alone in the hotel gym the next morning before 6:00 am, burning up nervous energy on the elliptical. By 8:00 am she was showered and dressed, but the hotel concierge told her that stores in the area didn't open for another hour. Emilia dropped the Casa Odisea key in her shoulder bag and headed over to the Starbucks coffee shop connected to the hotel. A swank shopping gallery full of exquisite silver jewelry and Pineda Covalin silk scarves led to an atrium dotted with tables topped with green umbrellas bearing the Starbucks logo. Emilia followed the rich aroma of coffee down the steps and into the big shop, where a queue of thirsty patrons snaked past armchairs and assorted tables.

Starbucks catered to a mix of well-dressed Mexicans and *gringos*. No doubt the latter were on their way to work in the US Embassy next door. The front entrance of the coffee shop faced Paseo de la Reforma. Through the broad glass panes Emilia could see the morning pedestrian rush and lines of traffic jerking around the base of the El Ángel monument.

She bought a grande-sized latte, a piece of lemon cake, and a copy of the *Reforma* newspaper. Every chair was occupied so she made her way through the crush of people back to the atrium, managing to snag the last unoccupied table. She pried the lid off the coffee cup, popped a piece of cake into her mouth, and opened the newspaper, feeling smart in one of her new Zara outfits. Boxy navy jacket, simple navy shell, and skinny mustard ankle pants. Navy pumps with a kitten heel. Hair brushed into her usual ponytail to show off little silver hoop earrings.

The new clothes felt like armor.

Reforma's top story blared out in tall headlines. The United States had requested extradition for Diego Barrielos Luna, the Barrel Bomber, to face indictments in five different courts for multiple charges including drug trafficking, kidnapping, and murder. As with every high profile criminal extradition case between *El Norte* and Mexico, the death penalty was a major stumbling block. Mexico did not have a death penalty and would not extradite its citizens to countries that did. Either Mexico would have to make an exception or the United States would have to promise that the death penalty would not be sought if and when Barrielos Luna came to trial.

"Is this seat taken?"

Emilia looked up to see a *gringo* with wavy brown hair standing by the empty chair on the other side of the table. Instead of a gray polo and navy pants, he wore a pinstriped suit, starched shirt, and a muted paisley tie. His Aldo store bag from the 222 Reforma mall had been replaced by a battered brown leather briefcase in one hand and a tall paper Starbucks coffee cup in the other. A folded copy of *Reforma* was tucked under one arm.

Sure enough, all the other seats in the atrium were taken.

Emilia hoped her expression didn't give her away. "Go ahead," she said.

"Thank you." He set the briefcase down on the ground by his feet and slid into the seat.

They sat in silence, both sipping coffees, their respective newspapers spread before them. Emilia pretended to read the article about Barrielos Luna while watching the man out of the corner of her eye.

On the other side of the table, paper rustled as the man flipped a page. He cleared his throat. "Excuse me," he said in accented Spanish. "But do you shop at the big mall up the street? The 222 Reforma mall?"

Up close, he was a bit older than she'd first thought, with hazel eyes and deep smile lines on either side of his mouth. His clothes looked expensive. Gold cufflinks peeked out of the sleeves of his suit jacket.

"Occasionally," Emilia said.

"This probably sounds like the worst pick-up line in the world," he said. "But I'm quite sure I saw you a few days ago. You had a big bag from Zara."

"You have sharp eyes," Emilia said. Adrenaline surged into her system.

"I remember things that make a positive impression."

Emilia tipped her head in acknowledgment of the impressively subtle compliment, her skin tingling in anticipation of danger. He was suave and well-dressed but running into him a second time in a city of 30 million people couldn't be a coincidence. Cops in Mexico couldn't afford to believe in coincidences.

The man extended his hand. "Tom Lennox. I'm the Legal

Attaché at the embassy over there."

Emilia blinked. "You're a *norteamericano* diplomat?"

"Yes." He smiled, hand still in the air. "Legal Attaché means I'm a diplomat but also our top cop in a foreign country."

"Yes, I know." Emilia shook his hand. "I'm Detective Emilia Cruz Encinos."

Lennox had a firm grip but released her hand quickly "Fellow law enforcement?"

"I'm a police detective."

"You're probably someone I need to know." Lennox pulled a business card out of the inside pocket of his fine wool jacket. "Do you work here in Mexico City?"

"I'm from out of town," Emilia said.

"Where are you from, if you don't mind my asking?"

He was a diplomat. There was no harm in telling. "Acapulco," Emilia replied.

He handed her the card. An embossed golden eagle decorated the center above his name and title. The embassy address on Reforma was printed at the bottom, along with a telephone number.

Emilia offered her card in return, the same mix of printed phone number and handwritten name she'd given the concierge at the apartment building in Polanco.

"Emilia Cruz Encinos." Lenox read her name thoughtfully. A moment later he raised his eyebrows in recognition. "You're part of Judge Imelda Sarmiento's task force."

Emilia drew back.

Lennox stiffened, apparently realizing his error. "I'm so sorry," he said, eyes widening. "Of course you aren't broadcasting that to everybody wandering the local Starbucks."

Emilia gave a tight smile and made a show of folding her newspaper.

"Please." Lennox leaned forward conspiratorially, inviting Emilia to meet him over the table. "The embassy legal team was briefed on the task force. I thought the idea of bringing in an impartial investigative team was genius. Not even the American press could find fault with the approach."

"Glad to hear it," Emilia said.

"You're staying at the hotel?" Lennox indicated the Sheraton on the other end of the wide gallery.

"Yes, it's very nice."

Lennox pocketed her card and gathered up his newspaper. He'd been reading the same article on the Barrielos Luna extradition request. "Maybe we'll run into each other again," he said and stood. "Thank goodness Starbucks is right near the office. Sometimes only coffee keeps us going."

"That and stress," Emilia said lightly.

Lennox laughed as he picked up his briefcase and tucked the newspaper under his arm again. "It was nice meeting you, Detective Cruz," he said. "I'm sorry if I said anything to make you feel uncomfortable. I think the task force will do a tremendous service to Mexico and the families of the missing. Thank you for taking on such a challenge."

It was a kind and gracious thing to say, and certainly more heartfelt than anything from a member of the Attorney General's staff. "*Gracias*, Señor Lennox," Emilia said gratefully.

She watched him stride through Starbucks, nodding to several *gringos* standing in line; no doubt fellow diplomats from the embassy next door. He walked out the door giving out onto Paseo de la Reforma and turned left toward the embassy. A moment later, the pinstriped suit was swallowed up by throngs of busy pedestrians hurrying to their busy jobs in the busy commercial district.

CHAPTER 18

The encounter with the diplomat was forgotten by the time Emilia found the tiny shop. It was on Rio Lerma, near the restaurant where the task force had celebrated after completing the video library. Emilia remembered the blue sign with white letters proclaiming *Cerrajero*.

"*Buenos dias*!" The locksmith reminded Emilia of her Uncle Raul. The same kind smile and the same wiry build of someone who'd done hard labor all his life. The same greasy blue coveralls, too, the kind every tradesman in Mexico wore.

Emilia returned his smile and greeting and held out the Casa Odisea key from Rafa's apartment. "What can you tell me about this?"

The locksmith took the key in work-roughened hands and turned it over a few times. He stepped behind the tiny counter and produced a large magnifying glass. He raised both the key and the glass to catch the light from the open door, turning them both this way and that.

Emilia waited.

Gray metal shelves stretched from floor to ceiling along the wall, loaded with either gray metal drawers or gray metal bins. Bits of gray metal tools poked over the lip of most of the bins and the drawers tipped haphazardly, so old and rusted they couldn't slot into their runners any more. Every other wall was covered in pegboard nearly obscured with loops of wire and chain, rubber tubing, and dusty packages of household bits and bobs. A gray metal cabinet was topped with a length of plywood to serve as a counter. It was crammed with tins of lubricating oil, an untidy pile of receipts, and a cardboard box of loose keys. A dirty can jammed full of pens and pencils and metal files sat on top of an old-fashioned accounting ledger.

The locksmith held out the key. "It's from a Fanal Series 180 lock," he said.

Emilia took it. "Is that special?" she asked, willing him to say, *Yes, only three ever made and I sold each one personally.*

"Top of the line," the locksmith said instead. "Popular with quality builders."

"House builders?"

"Residential and commercial." He raised two fingers, canted his hand sideways to mimic the locking mechanism, and pretended to insert a key. "High security overlap, two safety rods, and a latch bolt. Houses, yes, but warehouses, stores, schools."

"An exterior door," Emilia clarified.

"*Alta seguridad*," the locksmith confirmed. High quality security.

Emilia regarded the key. It unlocked a door, behind which something important was kept, something that needed extra protection. She looked up. "Where are these sorts of locks sold?"

The locksmith brightened. "I can get one for you. Do you

need it today? Tomorrow?"

Emilia shook her head. "No, I don't need a lock. I need to know where these Fanal locks are sold."

"Any place," the locksmith said with a shrug. "Big home stores sell them. Building contractors can order them directly from the company."

"What about the number on the key?" Emilia pressed. She read off the string of tiny numbers stamped into the head of the key. *12441.* "Can you trace the serial number?"

"Only the Fanal company can do that."

"Do you have a customer service number for the company?" she asked.

He rubbed his chin. "Maybe I can find you a better lock."

The implication was clear. She wasn't buying anything and he was running out of patience.

Emilia pulled 100 pesos out of her wallet and dropped it into the old cardboard box full of loose keys. "I don't need a different lock," she said. "Just information about this key."

The locksmith gave her a wink, produced an old flip phone from the pocket of his coveralls, laboriously clicked through a contact list and placed a call. Emilia put the key on the counter. She stood in the shop doorway and watched well-dressed people hurry to work along Rio Lerma's wide sidewalks. She wondered what the day would hold.

Had Miranda and Elizondo resolved their difference?

Loyalty to a higher power.

Was Miranda referring to the Attorney General?

"Hola, Chavo, *que tal?"* After some chatter about

grandchildren and the lousy performance of the Cruz Azul *fútbol* team, the locksmith asked if Chavo still knew that Fanal distributor. "*Oye, bueno.*"

The locksmith waved at Emilia, holding the thumb and forefinger of his free hand close together but not touching, in the familiar gesture meaning *wait a minute*. He read the serial number of the key into the phone. More back and forth with the person on the other end. He finally broke the connection.

"So now we wait," the locksmith said. "My friend will call if he finds out anything. Come back later. He'll have called by then."

Later. Emilia almost laughed. Sometimes she regretted that being a cop meant she'd lost the wonderfully imprecise and unique Mexican sense of time.

He fished Emilia's money out of the box and held it out to her. "You didn't buy anything."

"I can't, really." Emilia shook her head. "You've been really helpful."

"No, no." The locksmith laughed and fluttered the bill at her. "Just tell your friends to come here."

"Let me buy you a coffee," Emilia said.

He grinned. "But we don't tell my wife, eh?"

Emilia laughed as she took the bill. He really did remind her of Tío Raul.

She stood in line at Starbucks again, bracketed by *gringos* speaking English too fast for her to eavesdrop. Then back to the *cerrajero* on Rio Lerma with two lattes.

As she squeezed into the little shop, the locksmith was speaking into his cell phone and scribbling on an old receipt. "*Sí, sí. Bueno.*"

He ended the call and pushed the receipt across the counter to Emilia. "This Series 180 was one of an order of more than 5000 shipped from Fanal to a builder."

She handed him a latte and scooped up the receipt.

In childish block printing he'd written *Coba Construcción, Monterrey.*

"Thank you," Emilia said fervently. She headed briskly towards the Attorney General's building, but stopped when she came upon a bench. She sat, fished out her cell phone, and tapped the company name into the search app.

Coba Construcción had gone out of business three years ago.

Emilia stowed her phone in her shoulder bag and kept walking, her legs like lead and Rafa Gamboa Escobar's mocking voice in her head.

CHAPTER 19

The next few days were an emotional roller coaster. Emilia was heartsick over the failure of the Casa Odisea key to provide a clue to Rafa's whereabouts, worried about the edgy dynamics within the task force, and emotionally bruised by the horrific stories she found in the files. Elizondo and Miranda were still at odds over something neither would share, making for terse conversations. Anaya's hip flask was omnipresent.

Emilia found herself gravitating towards Cardenas, who alone seemed impervious to the strained atmosphere and grueling 16-hour days. His innuendo-laden banter, which Emilia parried with witty jabs, devolved into a running joke.

His humor, combined with a ruthless work ethic, helped Emilia over the hurdles, especially when it came to missing or poorly developed information. It didn't matter if the evidence gathering and questioning had been conducted by the Lindavista police, the *federales* or the Attorney General's office. They'd all been sloppy. It made Emilia realize how much she'd learned from Silvio.

On Saturday, as they were sitting down to the daily 4:00 pm meeting, Anaya taped a sheaf of maps to the whiteboard over the network analysis diagram.

"The bodies weren't burned," he announced without preamble.

The room grew quiet, except for the tapping of a keyboard

in the adjacent office. Emilia could barely even hear her own breathing. It was as if they were all holding their breath.

Miranda swiveled his eyes to Cardenas, who was closest to the door.

Cardenas slipped out of his chair, noiselessly closed the inner door, and returned to the table.

"The Amistad Victims Rights Fund commissioned a study six months ago," Anaya began. "They started on the theory that the bodies had been burned at the Colima dump, like everybody thought, and hired a Spanish fire consultant to conduct the investigation."

He adjusted one of the maps. "This is a satellite picture of the dump taken 28 September, supposedly two or three days after the bodies were burned. Our seven suspects claimed the bodies were piled together. But there's no big scorch mark, no heat signature."

"But if the picture was taken days later," Elizondo said impatiently. "Wouldn't there have been enough time to clean it up?"

"The devil's in the details," Anaya said. "To burn 43 adult human bodies so fast, they'd have had to use gallons of accelerant. Gasoline brought in a tanker truck or in barrels prepositioned at the site. If they burned all the bodies at once, it would have made a bonfire you could see from space."

"*Por Dios*," Miranda murmured.

"The consultant checked with the *norteamericanos*," Anaya went on. "Records from the International Space Station don't indicate anything like that."

"What if they burned them individually?" Emilia asked.

"Forty-three fires in two days?" Anaya said. "There would have been 43 scorch marks. The garbage pickers at the dump would have noticed, too."

"Maybe they cut them up," Cardenas said. "Tried to burn them but it was taking too long, so they bagged them up so they'd blend with the rest of the garbage out there."

Emilia swallowed hard; he made it sound so clinical.

"Wouldn't there be a heat signature coming off the decomposing bodies?" Elizondo asked. "Even now?"

Anaya shook his head. "There's too much organic matter there," he said. "The *norteamericanos* did a satellite sensor pass. The Geological Survey people. They didn't get anything."

He unfurled a black and white map across the table and everyone stood to see better. It was a simple elevation map, with shading to show height. "This is the survey that the *federales* did of the dump last year," he said. "But the dump's landscape is constantly changing. More garbage gets tossed every day, kids pick through it to find shit to sell, and the whole thing is constantly settling. Had an earthquake a couple of months ago, too."

A wave of nausea made Emilia lift her chin and breathe deep.

Anaya stuck a thick finger on a jagged black mark on the right side of the map. "This is the ravine where one of the cops accused of collusion said the remains were dumped. The *federales* didn't find shit. For all we know, the ravine has disappeared by now."

Elizondo indicated the edge of the map. "How far did the *federales* go? What's beyond the dump?"

"Rugged hills," Anaya answered. "El Choque gang territory. Too far from Lindavista for police jurisdiction. To the extent that law enforcement is anybody's responsibility, it's up to the *federales*."

"Should we continue to focus on the Colima dump or not?" Miranda asked the group. "We don't have time for dead ends. So far we have no motive and no bodies."

"On the other hand," Cardenas said, irrepressible as always. "We're up seven confessions."

Elizondo gave the younger man a dark look, which Cardenas completely ignored.

"The *federales* still think the dump is the most likely place to find the bodies," Anaya went on. "One of the problems is size. The dump doesn't have defined borders. It's a couple of square miles of hills and gullies covered in garbage from Lindavista and half a dozen other towns in Michoacán."

"Every confession says the bodies were burned close to or in the dump," Elizondo said. "Even if that's wrong, which this research says is the case, the dump appears to be only logical place to hide such a large number of corpses."

"But the confessions," Emilia burst out. "Why would seven men falsely admit to burning the bodies and dumping the remains?"

"We'll have to ask that question, Detective," Miranda

said. "When we visit them in prison."

"Maybe they want us to keep looking there," Cardenas said. "Because it means we won't be looking elsewhere."

Anaya rolled up his maps and photographs. "I'll check tomorrow if the *norteamericanos* can give us satellite footage of the land east of the dump," he said.

"It'll wait," Miranda said tiredly. "Sunday is a day of rest."

CHAPTER 20

Emilia caught Esteban Menendez at home in his apartment in the building in Polanco. He was an elderly gentleman who graciously welcomed her into his home.

Menendez's apartment was full of cut crystal and Spanish antiques. Emilia perched gingerly on a silk striped settee while Menendez's maid brought out a vast silver tray bearing a sterling coffee service and delicate porcelain cups. In black trousers, white shirt, and narrow black tie, with a mane of white hair combed straight back, Menendez looked like a Spanish *don* unexpectedly thrown forward in time. If it hadn't been for the scene of skyscrapers and stores out the window, Emilia might have believed herself to be in a colonial hacienda.

The maid, wearing a black dress and white apron, set the tray on a tea table. She poured out coffee and retreated. Menendez picked up a small tongs. His hand hovered over a sugar bowl as he looked at Emilia.

"One, please," she said hastily.

He dropped a sugar cube into her cup and carefully put down the tongs. "Cream?"

"Yes, please."

Menendez carefully tipped a drop onto the rapidly dissolving sugar cube.

Once the coffee ritual had been completed, Menendez gave a long sigh. "My condolences to your family."

It took Emilia a moment to remember that she'd told the concierge that Rafa was dead. The news had no doubt been passed along.

"Thank you," she said, wriggling to get comfortable. The settee cushion was hard as a rock. "We weren't close. I'm trying to learn more about him and the concierge said you and he were friends."

"Rafa was charming," Menendez said. "A brilliant mind."

"Did he talk to you about places he liked to go?" Emilia asked. "When he needed to get away?"

"Places?" Menendez frowned, his white eyebrows dipping together in an expression that made him look like a querulous owl. "What sort of places?"

"Anyplace, really," Emilia said. "I'd just like to know the sort of places he liked to go."

"His movie friends might know that." Menendez sniffed and crossed his legs. He wore blue felt scuffs with gold crowns embroidered on the toes. "I was much more interested in Rafa's mind."

"How so?" Emilia took a sip of coffee.

"His education had been curtailed and he was very anxious to make up for that."

He dropped out of college. But Emilia was sure Menendez was not a person who would respond well to being corrected. "And you helped him?" she asked.

A clock chimed. Menendez checked a gold pocket watch. Emilia guessed he was comparing the two antique timepieces.

She couldn't get a bead on the older man. Arrogant and fussy, he hardly seemed like a natural friend for a rising television star loaded with testosterone.

Menendez closed the watch and returned it to his pocket. "Rafa turned to me for advice as he studied. His mind was like a sponge; he absorbed knowledge very quickly. Philosophy, ancient cultures. Languages. Rafa had an appetite for the classics."

"When he left," Emilia asked. "Did he tell you where he was going?"

Menendez was clearly annoyed by her change in conversation. "Rafa went out to seek his fortune on a bigger stage."

"Where was that?"

Menendez held onto his cup with one hand and waved the other at the view out the window. "Rafa could go anywhere. He understood he had a destiny."

Emilia nodded like she understood, but she was getting a strange vibe off the fussy old man. Silvio often scoffed at her so-called women's intuition but he always paid attention to it.

"Does Casa Odisea mean anything to you?" she asked. "Did Rafa ever talk about going there?"

"Casa Odisea." Menendez rolled the words around on his tongue.

"A place Rafa might have mentioned," Emilia suggested.

"*The Odyssey* was one of the books I lent Rafa," Menendez said.

"Could I see it?" Emilia asked eagerly.

"It's in the library." Menendez stood and placed his cup on the silver tray.

Emilia followed Menendez down a hall, twisting to avoid a startling number of antique tables, chairs, trunks, cabinets. Many were topped by stuffed birds and small animals. Glass eyes formed an obstacle course to navigate around. Emilia tensed when she saw a fox in mid-stride on a table; she wanted to touch it but didn't. Menendez was ahead, but she was sure he'd know.

He stopped, selected a key from a ring from his pocket, and unlocked a wide door.

"I let few people in," Menendez said, quickly shutting the door as if concerned with uninvited guests. "This is my private collection."

"Thank you for inviting me," Emilia said, overwhelmed.

The air was cooler here than in the sitting room where he'd served her coffee. A fan hummed quietly in the background. Shelves stretched 12 feet from floor to ceiling on all four walls. Almost every inch of self space was taken up with antique books. The only furniture was an exquisite black and gold desk, with slender legs culminating in carved cloven hoofs, and a sculptural clear acrylic chair. Emilia felt as if she'd stepped into one of the luxury lifestyle magazines that Kurt sometimes read.

"What an amazing room," Emilia exclaimed. "You are quite the collector, señor."

Menendez opened a desk drawer and took out a pair of

thin cotton gloves. He went to a shelf and carefully took out a book. "Rafa read this copy of *The Odyssey*," the old man said. "He respected all it had to offer."

Cradling it in his gloved hands, he showed Emilia the flyleaf. A name was scrawled across the paper, starting with a big H and displaying a prominent lower case loop midway through. She didn't recognize the signature or make out the name but no doubt it was that of a famous dead person whose previous ownership of the book made it special.

"Did he ever mention a place connected with the book?" Emilia asked. She'd get a copy of *The Odyssey* and scan it for clues. "A house, maybe? A place he went to?"

"Rafa and I spoke about the themes in the book," Menendez said stiffly, obviously irritated that she hadn't been impressed by the signature. "The great heroic quest."

"May I?" Emilia gestured at the immense shelves.

"You may look but not touch. Many are priceless relics of man's intellectual history." Menendez slid *The Odyssey* into its slot on the shelves.

Emilia slowly walked around the room, peering at the titles. Most of the books were leather-bound, with foxed pages and frayed binding. Most had no markings on the spines and without being able to pull them out and look, there was no way to tell what they were. Those spines with lettering revealed a wonderful diversity of languages. A few titles were written in Latin; still others in Cyrillic letters. Emilia recognized English, French, Italian, and a language she guessed was German.

"If Rafa was going to go on a quest," she asked, as she surveyed the shelves. "Where do you think he'd go?"

Menendez didn't reply.

Emilia looked over her shoulder.

Menendez pulled out the transparent chair and sat behind the desk. "I was your brother's tutor," he said. "Not his confidante."

"Of course," Emilia said, wondering why Rafa had needed a tutor. She studied the beautiful old volumes again.

One book was encased in mottled green leather with bold black letters handwritten in English. Emilia went up on her toes to read *The Spells of Lucifer*.

Two spines over, her eye spotted a Spanish title, *Inquisition and Exorcism*, on a crumbling tome.

On the next shelf she found a second English-language title: *Miracles of Darkness*.

And another. *Reaping the Five Stages of Death.*

Emilia felt cold and clammy. She glanced at Menendez sitting primly at the desk in the nearly invisible chair, his gloved hands folded, his slippered feet resting between the cloven hooves.

"Yes, Rafa read that one, too," Menendez said.

CHAPTER 21

Emilia shivered despite the warm sunshine and the happy burble of the Sunday crowds in the Zona Rosa near the El Ángel monument. She didn't know if Menendez was some sort of Satanic worshipper or just a strange man with a proclivity for collecting antique books about the occult. Either way, she'd seen enough to know where Rafa had gotten the inspiration for his El Acólito stage show.

She was about to reach for the door handle of the El Péndulo bookstore when a pale hand grasped it first. "Permit me."

Emilia stepped aside. "Señor Lennox?"

"Detective Cruz," he said, obviously surprised to see her. "What a pleasant coincidence. You're making the rounds of Mexico City's best spots just like a local."

"Yes," Emilia said. "Coffee shops and bookstores."

"El Péndulo is the best of both." Lennox pulled open the door and they walked in together. "Have you had lunch?" he asked. "May I treat you to something in the café? They call it the *cafebrería*."

"Café and *librería*," Emilia said. "That's clever."

She tried not to grin like a school girl at his invitation and was glad she was wearing something nicer than jeans. Lunch with a diplomat in the fabled El Péndulo bookstore would certainly be something to remember. It might even cancel out the encounter with Rafa's bizarre neighbor.

"Thank you," Emilia said. Lennox knew enough about the task force that she wouldn't have the stress of guarding her conversation. "I'd like that."

They sat in the café. Lennox was clearly pleased she'd accepted his invitation. He didn't wear a wedding ring and Emilia wondered if he was lonely, living the stressful life of a diplomat in a strange city.

"I love this place," Lennox said. "They have a nice selection of books in English and great coffee."

"You speak well enough to read in Spanish," Emilia said.

Lennox laughed. "You are too kind," he said. "My conversation is adequate and I can get through the newspaper. But that's all."

As if she'd heard their conversation, the waitress gave Lennox an English language menu and Emilia the Spanish one. They laughed and compared the listings, finally deciding on salads, plus *agua de jamaica* for Emilia and sparkling water for Lennox.

He was easy to be with. Reserved but not stiff. Friendly but not flirtatious. Just two professionals sharing a meal on a lazy Sunday afternoon.

"I was actually thinking of calling you on business this coming week," Lennox said as they dove into their salads. "To talk about the task force."

"I can't say much about it," Emilia said. "We're not allowed to make any public statements before we deliver our final report."

"Of course, of course," Lennox said. "Don't worry, I'm

not fishing for a status report I can run up the flagpole to Washington. As much as everyone wants to know what is happening, I don't think that would be appropriate. And of course, given the state of things in Washington, it would leak to the press in a matter of minutes."

Emilia held up both hands in protest. "I'm not going to be responsible for that."

"Absolutely not," Lennox said seriously. "No, I was hoping to talk to you about Diego Barrielos Luna. The Barrel Bomber."

"I only know what's been in the news," Emilia said and poured dressing on her romaine. "The task force doesn't have anything to do with him. Unless there's something Washington knows and isn't telling."

"No, no. Nothing like that," Lennox said. "I wanted to talk to you about the extradition proceedings."

Emilia mixed the greens to coat them with the vinaigrette. "I don't follow."

Lennox put down his fork. "Washington has formally requested that Mexico extradite him to the United States to stand trial for murder and drug dealing, among other charges. I'm actually dealing with your Attorney General's office to get the extradition order through and get the man over the border. But frankly, your government seems too distracted to deal effectively with our request."

"But it was in the news," Emilia said. "Just the other day, in fact. Negotiations are ongoing over the death penalty issue."

Lennox picked up his fork again. "The word 'negotiations' means I'm waiting for someone to return my phone call."

"Oh."

Lennox sighed and chased a tiny tomato around his salad plate. "The death penalty discussion is only one part of the problem," he said. "Barrielos Luna's lawyers have already filed six *amparo* appeals challenging the Interpol extradition warrant on behalf of the United States. The usual claptrap about extradition interfering with Mexico's right to exercise national sovereignty."

"It's the process," Emilia said. "If the extradition is legitimate, the appeals will delay the proceedings but doesn't mean the extradition will be denied. In the meantime, Barrielos Luna is stuck in the Multifoco prison."

"Mexico's record of approving extradition requests is spotty, at best," Lennox argued. "There's no pattern for which requests are approved and which are denied."

Emilia sipped her *agua de jamaica*. Working crime on the streets of Acapulco hadn't left much time to consider international judicial issues. But Lennox was right. Some cartel kingpins lost their appeals and were sent to face charges in *El Norte*. Others stayed in jail in Mexico, almost certainly still running drug operations from a designer prison cell. If there was a pattern, it was likely based on payoffs to judges.

"What does the Amistad 43 task force have to do with the extradition?" she asked. "Those missing students haven't anything to do with Diego Barrielos Luna."

Lennox put a dab of dressing on the tomato. "How can I say this without seeming to criticize your government?" he said slowly. "The task force is sucking all the oxygen out of the room, so to speak. No one in the Attorney General's office can focus on anything else until your final report is delivered."

Emilia nearly choked on a crouton. If anyone else in the Attorney General's building was concerned about the task force, they certainly hid it well. At some point in the last week, every member of the task force, including the feuding Elizondo and Miranda, had remarked on their isolation.

"Cutting 30 days off the task force's schedule would be a huge help," Lennox said.

This time Emilia did choke, coughing up crumbs until she was able to swallow more icy hibiscus tea. "Thirty days is a third of the time allotted," she managed. "I doubt that's even remotely possible."

"I don't want to sound overly dramatic," Lennox said. "But there's reason for urgency. He's escaped custody in Mexico twice already and everybody is holding their breath that he doesn't do it again. The man is a Houdini."

"Houdini?" The name scrawled across Menendez's cherished copy of *The Odyssey* came into focus in her mind's eye. "Who's that?"

"Harry Houdini," Lennox said. "The American escape artist who dabbled in spiritualism."

"Escape artist," Emilia repeated. Of course. That's just

what her brother was.

Lennox wiped his lips with his napkin. "The sooner your task force wraps up, the sooner we can get the extradition process over. I want Barrielos Luna over the border and into an ironclad American jail."

"I don't think I can help," she said. "The only person I know in the Attorney General's office is Judge Sarmiento."

"Who do you think owes me a phone call?" Lennox's eyebrows drew together in annoyance. "She's never in her office. No doubt she's spending all her time trying to keep her husband out of jail."

"What?"

"She's married to Oscar Suarez," Lennox said. "He's running for mayor of Mexico City while trying to disguise the fact he's going to be arrested for money laundering any day now."

"Her husband is Oscar Suarez?" Emilia remembered the face flapping from banners during the drive from the airport. "I didn't know."

"So you see the dilemma," Lennox said. "When we ran into each other, I thought, hey, here's someone who can help."

Emilia shook her head. "I'm just a single person on the task force. I don't control the schedule."

"You do want Barrielos Luna in jail, don't you?" Lennox pressed. "Punished properly for his crimes rather than living like a king in Multifoco."

"Yes, of course," Emilia said.

"He's wanted for as many crimes in the United States as in Mexico," Lennox went on. "Murder, extortion, money laundering, drug dealing. I have a list as long as my arm in the office."

"I'm sure," Emilia said. "His nickname isn't Barrel Bomber for nothing."

"If he stays here, we both know he'll escape again," Lennox's voice was lower now and more intense. It was clear he felt strongly about the issue. "You know as well as I do that extradition is the only way to keep him behind bars. Mexico can't even keep its own prison wardens safe."

"Do you think Barrielos Luna had something to do with the death of the Multifoco warden?" Emilia ventured.

Lennox pushed his empty plate away. "Don't you?"

Emilia swallowed hard.

"Look," Lennox said quietly. "Would it help you if I told you the US government was offering a $50,000 bounty to anyone who helps us complete the extradition within the next 30 days?"

Emilia sucked in her breath. Fifty thousand dollars was more than she earned in 18 months. With that much money in her pocket she could take a leave of absence. Travel the length and breadth of Mexico until she found Rafa.

She knew her mouth was hanging open and managed to clamp her lips together. As wonderful as it would be to have that money in her pocket, what Lennox was asking was laughable. Emilia thought of the mountain of files, the seven confessions, and the order to find the real motive. The task force needed more time, not less.

"It's not possible," Emilia said regretfully. "We've got a huge job and it gets more complicated by the day. I don't even know if the official 90 days is going to be enough."

"Will you think about it?" Lennox asked. "There must be a way to wrap it up."

"I can discuss it with the other members of the task force," Emilia said. "But I know they'll come to the same conclusion."

"I'd rather you didn't," Lennox said.

"Why not?"

"Someone associated with the task force is on the wrong side of the investigation," Lennox said. "Washington has been watching things. We're not sure exactly who it is, but we know it's not you."

CHAPTER 22

Emilia paced her hotel room that evening, distrust deepening with every step. Anaya's absences and nonstop drinking. Arguments between Miranda and Elizondo. Cardenas's jokes could hide almost anything.

Or was it rat-faced Ramirez?

She couldn't discount Judge Sarmiento, either. The woman was a mass of vulnerabilities. She was trying to preserve the reputation of the Attorney General's office while her husband's mayoral campaign went down in flames. No wonder she was as thin as a rake.

But it could also be someone else. One of the do-nothing librarians. Even Tina, the oh-so helpful secretary might have succumbed to a bribe.

She hadn't admitted it to Lennox, but what he said was easy to believe, especially if the culprit was Ramirez or Judge Sarmiento. Someone had made sure evidence was lost in boxes of messy paper files and unlabeled DVDs. Someone had limited their charter to keep the task force wandering in the dark.

And prevent them from making any arrests.

Emilia plunked herself on the bed with her cell phone and checked the time. It was only 8:00 pm, hardly late for most of the people she knew. Silvio picked up after the fourth ring.

"Cruz," he barked by way of greeting. "What's the matter?"

"Hey, Franco," Emilia said. "Nice to hear your voice."

"Yeah, sure." He gave a gruff laugh. "What's going on?"

"Kind of an odd thing happened and I want your take on it."

"Now?"

"Is now not a good time?"

"Uh, no." Silvio's voice faded, as if he'd pulled away from the phone.

"Do you want to call me back later?"

"Now is okay." He was suddenly at full volume again.

"You sure?"

"What's the problem, Cruz?"

"I met the Legal Attaché from the *El Norte* embassy," she said.

"Mixing it up with the high and mighty," Silvio observed. "I told you this would be good for your career."

"We met by accident," Emilia said. "Three times, which is sort of weird, given how many people—."

"What are you talking about, Cruz?" Silvio sputtered. "Some *norteamericano* is stalking you?"

"No, no, listen," Emilia exclaimed. *Madre de Dios,* but the man was as aggravating as ever. "He wants me to speed up the task force. Make it so we finish early."

"Are you in charge of the schedule?"

"No."

"So tell him to fuck off."

"He's a big deal diplomat, Franco," Emilia snapped. "You don't tell people like that to fuck off."

"Has this turned into a personal thing?" Silvio asked suspiciously.

"*Madre de Dios*, let me finish, you *pendejo*." Emilia felt her blood pressure rise. "He's negotiating the request for extradition for Diego Barrielos Luna. You know, the Barrel Bomber. He says as long as the task force is going on, the Attorney General's office isn't able to focus—."

Muffled sounds came from the other end of the connection. A feminine murmur. Silvio's gruff tone. Low laughter from both.

He was with a woman.

Emilia was so surprised that she dropped the phone. It bounced off her leg and onto the bedspread.

Silvio's wife had been dead for almost six months and if he wanted female company there was no reason why he shouldn't have it. Yet what woman would have the strength—and poor judgement—to take on Franco Silvio? Who would want a perpetually surly ex-boxer with control and commitment issues who lived in the house where his wife had been murdered?

"Cruz?" Silvio's voice boomed from the phone. "Are you there?"

Emilia scrabbled to pick up the phone. "Look, Franco."

"Cruz, what you're telling me is that you got a problem with some *norteamericano* diplomat sticking his nose in where he shouldn't. Does the head of the task force know?"

"No, that's just the problem—."

"If you need to go outside your chain of command,"

Silvio interrupted. "Call Lieutenant Baez. He'll know how things operate there. He'll help you out."

"Yeah, okay." It was a good suggestion and Emilia wished she'd done that instead of calling Silvio. Apart from his short stint as head of the detectives squadroom in Acapulco, Lieutenant Baez had spent his entire career in Mexico City. He had a bigger view of the world. "Um, while I've got you, has anything come in about El Acólito? Any sightings?"

"No, nothing."

The call ended with Emilia promising to call Lieutenant Baez and Silvio impatient to get back to the woman.

A shower helped Emilia switch gears. She climbed into bed with the remote control, a tiny bottle of wine from the mini bar, and her wet hair wrapped in a towel. Some *norteamericano* movie was on that she'd seen before. Action scenes zoomed across the screen, but Emilia barely saw them as she dried her hair and sipped cabernet.

Before the film was over, Emilia found the business card Lieutenant Baez gave her the day he resigned from the job in Acapulco. She'd been angry that he was running away from problems, but they'd parted on good terms and she knew he'd help her now.

He was a neutral party, too. No involvement with the task force or any of the previous investigations into the missing students.

Most importantly, he'd want her to have $50,000.

CHAPTER 23

It was clear that once the previous investigations had linked Pilar Garay de Avila's appearance at the charity rally, no other possible motive was investigated. Emilia and Cardenas decided to take a break from the files and consider possibilities rather than evidence.

"Maybe someone wanted to close the Amistad Normal School," Emilia suggested.

"There would be easier ways to do that besides massacring a quarter of the students," Cardenas said. "Set fire to it. Beat up the teachers. Raise their taxes until they're forced to close."

"Maybe someone tried and we just don't know," Emilia said.

She pointed to the whiteboard and Cardenas duly wrote *Close school*?

"Okay, what else?" Cardenas asked.

"Someone wanted to close the bus station."

"You're stuck on a 'closing' theme, Detective."

Emilia glared at him. "Erik Flores owns the transportation concession in Lindavista. From his website anyone would think he's rich. I mean, he owns a horse ranch. Maybe he has enemies."

"Blackmail?" Cardenas asked.

"Maybe," Emilia said. "We'd need to get his bank and business records."

Cardenas shook his head; they both knew that would be next to impossible given Judge Sarmiento's attitude. "If he was the target," Cardenas said. "Wouldn't he connect to more people on the network analysis?"

"What if Avila wanted to buy out the municipal bus concession?" Emilia waved a hand at the diagram and Pedro Avila's name circled in the middle. "Consolidate power."

"Was there anything in the files about how much the bus concession is worth?"

"I think so," Emilia said. She rifled through the files spread across the conference table, plucked out the thin dossier on Flores, and skimmed it. "No, there's no net worth." She raised her head. "But say he's coining money. Avila wants the concession. Maybe that was the real reason for their lunch on 24 September. Avila threatened Flores and Flores tells him to shove it.

"So Avila tells the police to make things tough for Flores," Cardenas continued her train of thought. "Run him out of town."

Emilia nodded. "Resulting in the police kidnapping 43 students and turning them over to El Choque for a lesson. Didn't hurt any of Avila's constituents."

"I can see it," Cardenas said. He hitched a hip against the edge of the table and tapped the marker against his knuckles. "Avila wanted an opportunity to embarrass Flores. Hurt him financially. Sees the kids from Amistad and thinks, hey, not anyone from Lindavista. Just those rabble-rousers from Amistad."

"Flores is scared," Emilia went on. "Never makes a statement to the police saying, hey, Avila wanted my business."

"Avila can't take the business now because everybody is watching." Cardenas started writing on the board. "Plus, he's still under house arrest."

Emilia pressed her hands to her temples. They'd been brainstorming all day, even as a clock ticked in the back of her mind. Lennox's $50,000 became more elusive with every hour.

"The problem is," she said tiredly. "Avila had easier ways to squeeze Flores than killing a bunch of students. Raise taxes. Arrest all the drivers on some goofy charge."

"But they didn't expect that El Choque would kill the students," Cardenas pointed out. "Just to beat them up and scare them."

"What if we have it backwards?" Emilia dropped her hands and straightened up. "Maybe Flores complained about his buses and drivers being hijacked by students one too many times."

"How often does it happen?"

"This was an annual event," Emilia reminded him. "Anniversary of the cops shooting students in Mexico City."

"So Flores knew something was probably coming."

"Yes. Emilia pointed at Cardenas. "Flores says, 'no more' and goes to the police to make sure they don't let it happen again. But the Lindavista cops are a bunch of *pendejos* and it all got out of hand."

"Avila knew about the relationship between the Lindavista cops and El Choque," Cardenas said, writing on the board. "But maybe Flores didn't."

"Even if he did, would it matter?" Emilia shrugged. "You said it yourself. No one expected the kids to be murdered."

"That's right." Cardenas stepped back to survey his list. "Just the way things are done in Lindavista. Cops and gangbangers working together."

"Not just in Lindavista," Emilia said.

"That's the bigger problem," Cardenas said. "Not ours to solve."

Emilia pushed herself out of her chair and walked over to the big whiteboard with the network analysis splayed across it. "What if we put Flores in the center instead of the Avilas?"

Cardenas grabbed his suit jacket and trotted out for food while Emilia sat at her computer and reworked the network analysis program. In 15 minutes, she had a lopsided scrum of names. Flores only connected to Avila and the cop named Camacho who'd reacted to the name when interviewed after his own arrest for collusion.

By the time Cardenas returned with takeout boxes of *arrachera* steaks and crisp fries, Emilia had finished the revised network analysis.

She sat at the table with her food, a can of cola, and bendy plastic utensils. The steak all but melted in her mouth.

Cardenas stayed standing, wolfing down fries with his fingers as he stared at the new diagram.

"It doesn't help," Emilia said, ankles crossed on another chair as she ate. "Waste of time."

Suddenly Cardenas tossed his half-eaten food on the table and dug through the takeout bag for a napkin. "What if Flores has been wildly successful?" he said as he wiped his hands.

"Really rich, you mean?" Emilia asked. "He probably is."

"No, successful in hiding his motive," Cardenas said. "Successful in staying under the radar."

"Where are you going with this?"

Cardenas darted to the timeline whiteboard and tapped a marker against the very first entry. "We started with the time the students were first sighted in Lindavista," he said. "But for all we know, this whole trajectory started the previous September when the usual contingent of Amistad students came into town, seized buses and went to Mexico City for the annual rally."

Emilia cut into her steak, sawing carefully so the plastic knife didn't bend. "You're saying the cops took action this time because Flores made a stink the last time."

"Exactly." Cardenas took a swallow of cola from the can he'd left on the table. "One complaint from a big-deal businessman was enough. Nobody wrote it down, there's no paper trail leading to him. When the big mess goes down, he sits tight and hopes it will blow over. So far it's been the right strategy."

"Simple and obvious. I like it." Emilia punctuated her words with her plastic fork. "Flores didn't want his buses hijacked. End of story. It had to have cost him thousands of pesos at least each time it happened. Lost cash flow. Wear and tear on the buses."

"Okay." Cardenas threw himself into a chair and attacked his steak with the plastic utensils. "I think this is our best theory so far."

"Nothing in the files to support it," Emilia reminded him.

"What's not there supports it." His knife snapped in two and the blade skittered across the diagram. Cardenas glared and pulled the steak apart with two hands. "Let's not take that as an omen."

Emilia grimaced around a French fry. "We'll have to interview Flores when we get to Lindavista," she said after swallowing. "Plus his employees. Business associates. The Lindavista cops."

"Make a list," Cardenas mumbled through a mouthful of steak.

Emilia got up, found a marker, and began writing. "How long do you think this will take?" she asked. "An extra three days? Four?"

"Zero if Judge Sarmiento rules it as creating evidence." Cardenas swallowed his last bite of steak.

"Can we call it fact checking?" Emilia paused. If Judge Sarmiento impeded their investigation into motive, she was almost certainly Lennox's culprit. But if she didn't allow extra time, it would help wrap up the task force that much earlier.

Fifty thousand dollars.

"Do you think anyone really expects us to find out the real motive?" she asked, shoving the takeout box with the remains of her lunch across the table to Cardenas.

He fished out the last piece of her steak and took a bite. "I don't really care who expects what," he said after wolfing it down. "We do it for the families of those kids."

"Right." Emilia nodded. "So we look at Flores."

"Let's write a report for Mom and Dad." Cardenas gathered up the empty takeout boxes and threw them away. "Let them take it to the judge if it looks like we're trying to bust the charter or whatever."

"Where are they?" Emilia asked. Anaya was at the army's geographic survey office but Elizondo and Miranda hadn't broadcast where they were going.

"Probably arguing in private," Cardenas said.

They spent the rest of the day putting together a report on motives they'd considered and discarded, as well as their contention that the team should focus on Flores and his interest in preventing his buses from being hijacked as the most likely motive for police action against the students.

At 7:00 pm, Emilia hit the Print button. As soon as the draft of the report came out of the machine she shut down her computer.

"Leaving so soon?" Cardenas yawned. "How about we go back to the hotel and have sex?"

"Can't," Emilia said. "I have a date."

"I thought you and he were on a break?"

Emilia dropped the report on his desk. "Dinner with my

ex-boss."

"You're standing me up for your ex-boss?" Cardenas picked up the sheaf of papers. "I'm wounded, Detective."

"Don't bleed on the carpet," Emilia said. "Ramirez will make you pay for it."

Cardenas chuckled.

"Good night, Lieutenant." Emilia slung the strap of her bag over her shoulder, headed for the door, and stopped. "What happened to the buses the students took?"

"They got shot up." Cardenas looked up from the report and frowned. "Nobody is disputing that."

Emilia rolled her eyes. "Where are they now?"

"You mean did they get junked? In a landfill? Back in service?"

"Yes."

"That's a new question," he admitted. "We should check if Flores got an insurance payout."

Emilia felt a tiny stab of guilt. Another time-eater. "Maybe it doesn't matter," she said, wishing she hadn't brought it up.

"Hard to know," Cardenas said.

CHAPTER 24

"Given that our circumstances have changed," Baez said. "I think that you could call me Alejandro."

"All right," Emilia said. "We'll make it Emilia and Alejandro."

The lieutenant hadn't changed much in the few months since he'd been her boss in Acapulco. Still stocky, still dressed in a dapper suit and tie, still the type of cop more comfortable at a computer than on the street.

The waiter hovered. Baez ordered for both of them. Emilia relaxed against the plush upholstery of the chair and enjoyed the sensation of being with a familiar face.

"I was so pleased to hear your voice when you called," Baez said. "Congratulations again on being selected for the Amistad 43 task force. You're a great detective, Emilia. I'm sure you'll make a big difference."

"It's my first assignment after, you know," Emilia said.

"How are you doing?" Baez's hand moved slightly toward hers.

The waiter appeared with their appetizers. Baez snatched up his napkin with both hands. "Excellent," he said, glancing at the plate of shredded hearts of palm salad arranged in a pyramid.

When the waiter left, Emilia reached across the table and tapped Baez's hand. "Thank you for asking," she said. "It means a lot."

"And?" He turned his hand up and gently grasped her fingers.

"I'm working through it," Emilia said. "I'll be fine. Really."

"I know you will." He gave a reassuring squeeze before releasing her hand.

Emilia dug into her hearts of palm. The pale slivers were dressed with strips of roasted red pepper and a tangy citrus marinade.

The restaurant in the trendy Condesa section of the city was upscale and modern. Water streamed over an entire wall of tiny blue tiles aglow from lights tucked under the soffit while huge blue and white *talavera* pots topped massive concrete pillars, greenery trailing down the sides. The blue theme extended to table linens embroidered with a logo meant to evoke the tile waterfall. Emilia wondered what Kurt would say about the décor.

Baez ate a few bites and put down his fork. "I feel that I should apologize," he said. "I'm sorry for leaving Acapulco when I did but I couldn't cope with what happened."

"It wasn't your fault," Emilia said. She pushed a pimento around the plate, wishing he hadn't brought up the subject. If she told him her plans for hunting down Rafa Gamboa he'd have a stroke. "You and I both thought the undercover operation was going to be a quick recon of El Acólito. We didn't know he was trafficking women on the side."

"Silvio knew we'd missed something," Baez sighed. "He and I have talked about it. He would never have approved the operation. But I did."

"Let's not spoil our dinner," Emilia said.

The host seated a couple at the next table. The woman nudged Baez's chair as she went to sit. She apologized for disrupting him while her escort made a joke about close quarters.

"That's what I get for make reservations at such a popular place," Baez said to Emilia.

"The food is very good," she replied. Baez clearly wanted to impress her.

In that vein, he talked about his new position as head of an administrative unit, overseeing payroll and human resources.

"The Oscar Suarez case is the biggest issue for us right now," he said after they were both served chicken *milanesa*. "I've had to approve overtime pay for at least a dozen financial crimes investigators."

"Suarez?" Emilia asked. The thinly sliced breaded chicken smelled delicious. "The man running for mayor?"

"He's under investigation for money laundering through his family's chain of grocery stores."

"He's the same Oscar Suarez married to the head of the task force I'm on," Emilia said. "Judge Imelda Sarmiento de Suarez."

"I know," Baez said. "She could be susceptible to pressure, if you take my meaning."

Emilia leaned forward; Baez had given her the perfect opening. "That's exactly what I need to talk to you about," she said. "I was approached by the Legal Attaché from the *El Norte* embassy. Thomas Lennox."

"I've heard that name," Baez said. "Not recently, but there was a money transfer case that Financial Crimes handled. I recall sending a memo forward that was going to be passed to him."

"He's very important, isn't he?" Emilia said. "A very senior diplomat."

"Well, yes." Baez let the sentence trail off as he sliced into his chicken.

"He's very concerned that Judge Sarmiento isn't acting on the extradition request to get Diego Barrielos Luna over the border and into a *norteamericano* jail." Emilia sipped the white wine Baez had ordered to go with the chicken. "He says that Washington wants our task force to wrap up sooner than planned so our Attorney General's office can focus on the extradition. As long as the task force is working, decision-making in Mexico City is frozen."

"I expect he's right," Baez said. "Between the task force and the Suarez case, nothing is happening. The Amistad 43 families are still protesting. The president's poll ratings are at record lows. Violent crime is on the rise in almost every state. Giving up Barrielos Luna would be yet another admission that national security is unravelling."

"And if he escapes again, things will get worse." Emilia was conscious that she was echoing Lennox's arguments. "He's escaped prison twice. The warden of the prison where he is now was found dead and he's mixed up in that somehow."

"Have you spoken to Judge Sarmiento about this, this--." He frowned.

"Thomas Lennox," Emilia supplied.

"Yes, Señor Lennox," Baez went on. "Have you spoken to the judge about it?"

"Not yet, because . . ." Emilia trailed off. Tables in the restaurant were close together. If she could hear their neighbors talking about a potential new car purchase, they could hear her, too.

"Someone on the team is a dirty cop," Baez said, mistaking her hesitancy to continue speaking.

"I think we should talk about this somewhere else," Emilia said.

"I can offer you red wine, white wine, vodka or whiskey," Emilia said, holding up a tiny bottle of liquor from the minibar in her hotel room. "There's a carton of orange juice, too, but it tastes like cardboard."

"I'll go with the whiskey," Baez said. He took off his suit jacket and loosened his tie.

Emilia got two glasses from the bathroom and poured whiskey for him and white wine for her. They toasted each other and Emilia took the chair at the desk.

Baez sat on the end of the bed and sniffed the whiskey. "This is very nice," he said.

"You might need it," Emilia said. "You see, what I didn't want to say in the restaurant is that you were right. Señor Lennox claims that somebody associated with the task force is on the wrong side, as he put it. He said Washington has been investigating and they know it isn't me."

Baez's eyes widened. "That's a serious allegation, Emilia."

"I know." She rolled the glass between her hands, the wine swirling. "I think it could be Judge Sarmiento. She didn't seem to think it was a problem that everything was paper. No digital files at all. We walked in and there were boxes and boxes of stuff."

"Don't jump to conclusions based on the amount of paper you inherited," Baez said. "That's the product of too many different agencies all handling a different part of the investigation. Every agency has its own system."

"They left us boxes and boxes of stuff. It took us a week just to figure out what was there," Emilia went on. "Plus, she insists that we can't legally develop new evidence."

"You can't fault Judge Sarmiento for setting parameters," Baez cautioned. "The task force's mission is to review, not necessarily be considered a new investigation."

"She's worried about the optics."

"Wouldn't you be in her shoes?"

"What about her husband and his dodgy finances?" Emilia pressed. "You said she could be pressured. Should she have recused herself from the task force?"

"Possibly," Baez said. "But her finances are completely

separate."

Emilia sipped her wine, irritated that Baez was steering himself into the same sea of indecision that had sunk him in Acapulco. "Lennox wants the task force to wrap up early," she said. "He doesn't think the Barrielos Luna extradition will go forward until it's over. Meanwhile, Washington thinks he might escape again."

"So you said." Baez said. "On the one hand *El Norte's* criminal justice system is so good that they can take thugs like Barrielos and lock them up tight. On the other hand, they're in love with any drug that makes them forget who they are. Mexico has to live with the paradox."

"I don't want to land in the middle of a political mess," Emilia fretted. "Lennox even offered—."

"I know you'll work it out, Emilia." Baez cut her off, rushing his words. "You're the most beautiful and interesting woman I've ever met."

"It's a good thing you're not my boss any more," Emilia said with a laugh. He sounded like Cardenas. "I'd have to tell you that was very inappropriate."

"Franco Silvio always knew how I felt about you," Baez said.

"Let's not talk about him." Emilia wrinkled her nose. "Lately when anyone says his name I smell brimstone."

Baez laughed awkwardly and sipped his whiskey, his eyes on Emilia over the rim of the glass.

The weight of his expectations shimmered between them.

Madre de Dios. This was the last thing she needed. Emilia

put her glass on the desk and stood up. "I guess things will work themselves out," she said. "It's late."

Baez put his glass on the desk next to hers. "I've got nowhere else to go tonight, Emilia."

She stood there, as if her bones had turned to jelly as Baez cupped her face between his hands. He kissed her gently. When she didn't resist, the pressure of his lips grew. Emilia finally kissed him back, experimenting with the feel of his mouth against hers.

Baez broke the kiss to taste her earlobe. His hands roamed down her body. "I've thought about this ever since you called," he murmured into her skin.

His lips found hers again. This time the kiss lasted longer. Emilia closed her eyes and relaxed into his arms. It was nice to feel a spark of something besides anger again.

"Do you need another drink first?" Baez murmured.

"Hmmm?"

"I want you to relax," Baez said. "I'll take good care of you, Emilia."

The breath caught in her throat and Emilia realized she was about to have sex with a nice man she didn't find particularly attractive. Nor did she want a romantic relationship with him. Maybe she'd sent the wrong signals by inviting him to her hotel room, but Baez was primed to think she'd called for something besides his professional advice.

Baez kissed her neck, his breath warm against her skin.

Emilia peeled herself away; confused, flustered, and

flattered all at once. "I need a minute," she said hastily. She grabbed her purse from the desk and fled into the bathroom.

She turned on the sink faucet full blast, flipped down the toilet lid, sat and buried her head in her hands. One night out with a familiar face and she'd been a fool. She didn't want Alejandro Baez.

He would never measure up. He would never be as good as what she'd lost.

On the other side of the bathroom door, Baez gave a discreet cough.

Emilia dug her phone out of her purse. It was late enough. One moment of guilty pleasure and then she'd apologize and send Baez home.

She dialed the office number, expecting the usual rings and canned message.

It rang once. Someone picked up. "Hello?"

"Kurt?" Emilia blurted.

"Em?" Kurt managed to inject shock and warmth into the word at the same time.

"Sure," Emilia heard herself say. "I said I would call, didn't I?"

"That was two months ago," Kurt said.

There was nothing she could say in response. The first thing that popped into her head came out of her mouth. "What are you doing in the office so late?"

"Some nights the apartment is just too empty," Kurt said. "Did you call there first?"

No, I wanted to listen to your answering machine.

"I need some advice," Emilia blurted.

"Okay." Kurt sounded wary.

"I'm in Mexico City," Emilia said. "On a task force to find out what happened to the Amistad 43 missing students."

"I know."

"How?"

"Franco Silvio told me."

"Why are you talking to him?"

"He asked me about a real estate investment," Kurt said. "Told me a little about the assignment. Nothing much."

"Oh." Silvio was buying real estate. He had a girlfriend. Things were happening in the lives of people who mattered and no one wanted to tell her.

On the other end of the connection, Kurt drank something. "So what do you need advice about?"

Baez tapped on the bathroom door. "Emilia? Are you all right in there?"

Emilia hastily pressed the phone against her shoulder, praying Kurt hadn't heard Baez's voice. "Five more minutes, please," she called softly.

"As long as you're all right."

Emilia blasted the faucet and waited until Baez moved away from the door.

Hopefully Kurt hadn't heard the exchange. Emilia cut the water to a slow drip and raised the phone to her ear again. "It's the task—," she began.

"Are you calling me," Kurt interrupted. "Before or after?"

Emilia stopped breathing. She'd never been able to lie to

him. "Instead of," she managed.

"Am I supposed to be pleased?" Kurt exclaimed. "Flattered? What's going on, Em?"

"I almost made a mistake," Emilia said, forgetting to keep her voice low. "But I didn't. And I'm calling because I need some help and you're the smartest person I know."

She heard the latch click, then the yawn of the corridor door opening. A moment later Baez's footsteps faded and the door slammed shut.

"Did he just leave?"

Emilia slumped in relief. "Yes. I'm in the bathroom in my hotel room."

"I think I just got an ulcer," Kurt said.

"Please don't hang up."

"Tell me what's going on, Em."

Emilia imagined him in his big desk chair. This late, he'd be in shorts and a polo shirt. He'd probably spent 12 hours in the hotel, worked out, and hit the office after dinner. If his door was open, faint music from the Pasodoble Bar would trickle in. He could eavesdrop on conversations between hotel guests and the night duty concierge. There might be a glass of brandy next to the computer keyboard.

She took a deep breath. "The task force Silvio told you about," she said. "Things have gotten a little complicated."

"I'm listening," Kurt said.

She told him about the diverse personalities on the team, Judge Sarmiento's personal distractions, and described how she'd met the diplomat from the US embassy.

"Lennox wants me to speed up the task force," Emilia summed up the situation. "He claims Mexico City can't focus on the Barrielos Luna extradition until the task force completes its work. Given the way Judge Sarmiento is acting, I think he's right." She paused. "What do you think?"

"You're sure he's the Legal Attaché?" Kurt asked.

"Yes, of course," Emilia said. "I'll read you his card. Hold on."

She opened her wallet and took out the embossed card. "Thomas J. Lennox," she read out, along with the phone number and embassy address. "There's a gold eagle on the card. The paper is very thick. Very official."

"And he wants you to get the task force to wrap up early?"

"In the next 30 days," Emilia said.

"Is that possible?"

"I don't think so," Emilia said. "We're sifting though a lot of confusing stuff. But if I could get things wrapped up early, Lennox says I'd get a $50,000 bounty for assisting the extradition."

"A bounty?" Kurt's voice radiated suspicion. "Are you sure?"

"Yes, that's exactly what he said.

"Em, the Legal Attaché is the FBI representative in a foreign country," Kurt said. "It's a very senior position. If the Legal Attaché wants to meet with the Attorney General's office, they aren't going to tell him no. There shouldn't be any reason for him to sneak around and dangle money in front of your nose."

"You think he lied about getting in to see Judge Sarmiento?"

"I don't know, Em." She could hear Kurt's discomfort in his voice. "It sounds off somehow."

Emilia left the bathroom and sat on the bed. Baez had left a note: *Maybe another time, Alejandro.*

"I've heard of rewards for information leading to a capture," Kurt went on. "But not for pushing along another country's internal criminal investigation."

"What you're saying," Emilia pressed. "Is that he basically offered me a bribe."

"You need to clear things up with him, Em," Kurt said seriously. "In his office, face to face. If the bounty is legit, he'll be able to talk about it there. If he waffles, you know he's blowing smoke."

"*Por Dios.*" Emilia sank into the pillows, hoping she hadn't walked into a trap.

"Do you know where the embassy is?"

"Right next to this hotel."

"If his big problem is not being able to see this judge who's working the task force, maybe you can offer to carry a message. You said she's there every few days, right?"

Emilia sat up. "That's perfect," she said. "It solves everything. She won't want me to be in the middle of it. Once she knows he's desperate enough to seek out an intermediary, she'll meet with him."

"That way, the task force isn't affected in any way."

"You're brilliant," Emilia said. "I knew you'd know what

to do.”

“Glad I could help.”

“Thank you.”

“So where does this leave us?” Kurt asked.

“I don’t know,” Emilia admitted. “I’ve been so angry. Like an old bottle full of anger, waiting to break.”

“Em—.”

“I miss you,” Emilia said.

She broke the connection.

CHAPTER 25

Emilia loitered at Starbucks on Monday morning, one eye on her latte and newspaper, the other on the people passing in and out of the coffee shop. Most were *gringos* but Lennox wasn't one of them.

The task force had a week to finish slogging through the files before departing for Lindavista. They still didn't have a motive or an alternate theory about what had happened to 43 bodies and didn't know if they would be allowed the extra time to conduct interviews. While Emilia hoped Lennox's offer of a bounty was legit, wrapping up the task force early was an impossible dream. They needed a team of 20 investigators, not five.

At 9:00 am she left her newspaper on the table, tossed her latte cup in the trash, and left Starbucks by the door leading onto Paseo de la Reforma. A few steps east and she was in front of the US embassy. Below a government seal with an arrogant-looking eagle, green curved awnings the size of a bus shaded the entrance. Concrete barriers, spouting greenery in an attempt to soften the look, stopped anyone who might have wanted to drive up the stairs and crash through the big glass doors.

A glass guard post, the tinted bulletproof walls thick enough to distort the view of the interior, bumped against the sidewalk. With her police badge and *cédula* identity card in hand, Emilia got in line to speak to the embassy representative inside.

To her surprise he looked Mexican, not *gringo*, and wore a uniform she couldn't identify.

"Can I help you?" Behind the glass, he spoke into a microphone on an adjustable arm, clicking it to speak and clicking it off when he'd finished.

A metal speaker was set into the glass at the level of Emilia's mouth. "I'd like an appointment with Señor Thomas Lennox, please." She bent to slide her badge and card through a tiny slot below the speaker.

The guard's microphone clicked, but his voice came through the speaker as if squeezed out of a lime. Emilia caught "appointment" and "Thomas Lennox?"

"Yes," she said. "Thomas Lennox. The Legal Attaché."

She watched as the man picked up a phone and murmured into it. A moment later a second man in uniform came into the booth and stood by his colleague. They conferred, both casting surreptitious glances at Emilia.

Badge and identity card were pushed out of the slot back to Emilia. The microphone clicked. "You must have made a mistake," the guard said, leaning closer to the microphone than before. "You're not on the visitor list and Thomas Lennox is not at post."

Emilia scooped up her items. "Can you tell me when he'll be in the office?"

"He's not at post," the guard repeated.

Emilia sensed the frustration of the two men with briefcases waiting behind her for their turn to present documents and gain admittance to the big square building. For $50,000 they could wait.

"Not at post," she repeated, drawing out the unfamiliar term. *Gringo*-speak, no doubt. "Does that mean he's out of town?"

The second guard in the booth came to the microphone. "Señor Lennox finished his assignment at the embassy two months ago. If you'd like to make an appointment with his replacement, you'll have to do that by contacting the Legal Affairs section. We can't help you here."

"That's not right," Emilia said, trying not to sound as irritated as she felt. "Lennox. Thomas Lennox. The Legal Attaché. Very tall. Brown hair."

"Yes," the guard said stonily. "He is no longer assigned to this embassy. He has departed Mexico."

"Then who—." Emilia caught herself just in time. She edged away, past the concrete barriers and the green awnings and the chatter of people with important diplomatic business to contract. Her hands were clammy as she held onto the strap of her shoulder bag. Her kitten heels carried her forward but Emilia had no idea in which direction. She had to think before she blundered into the task force team room and blurted out complete nonsense.

Kurt's words ran through her head. *I've heard of rewards for information leading to a capture. But not for pushing along another country's internal criminal investigation.*

A man having a heated cell phone conversation bumped into her and kept going, phone clamped to one ear. Emilia stumbled, cracked her elbow against a lamp post, and paused uncertainly. A woman with a briefcase maneuvered around her in order to step off the curb and cross the street.

Emilia found a café, plopped down at a table, and ordered a latte.

Her hands were so sweaty the paper sugar packet was soggy before she could tear it open and pour the granules into her cup.

Who exactly had offered her a $50,000 bribe for hurrying things along?

Emilia watched videos for the rest of the afternoon, glad that the screen and headphones gave her a measure of privacy from the rest of the task force. For hours, half her attention was on the inconsequential questioning and the monosyllabic replies. The other half circled around the question of Thomas Lennox.

Either the man she'd met was someone pretending to be Thomas Lennox, or the real Lennox was working for someone else besides his own government.

He must have known that she could check his identity. Either he didn't care or thought she was too stupid to bother.

If it hadn't been for Kurt, she would have been that stupid. No, starry-eyed at the thought of herself having lunch with a senior *norteamericano* diplomat and the prospect of money to fund the hunt for Rafa Gamboa Escobar.

The bottom line, however, was that Lennox—or whoever he was—had offered her an outright bribe. It was a little consolation that he'd couched it as an official payment; perhaps he thought she'd be more receptive.

Emilia tore off her headphones and headed for the kitchen alcove. As she made a fresh pot of coffee, Emilia had to give Lennox his due. The story about extraditing Diego Barrielos Luna to *El Norte* before he escaped from a Mexican prison again was a compelling argument; certainly one that would resonate with a clean cop. No, the extradition argument was nothing more than a fig leaf to cover his real intentions.

Of course, she'd fallen for it. *Madre de Dios*. Lennox was probably snickering up his sleeve right now, convinced that she was an *idiota*.

Could she get the team to wrap things up a month early? If it meant subverting the whole process and leaving the fate of the 43 missing students undiscovered, could she do it?

Could she close her eyes, pretend Lennox was who he claimed to be, and take the money?

Would she really trade her job—and her self respect—for a chance to fund a private hunt for her brother?

Emilia punched the button and the machine gurgled into life. As the coffee brewed, she washed her mug at the sink, her thoughts leaping from one thing to another.

If the Barrielos Luna extradition was simply an excuse, what was the real reason behind Lennox's attempt to wrap up the task force?

More than a hundred people had been arrested. Most were

still being held. Avila and his wife were under house arrest, and the police chief and the members of the El Choque gang were at the Multifoco prison along with Barrielos Luna.

The Avilas would be freed if the task force didn't find anything beyond the weak charge of collusion. The fate of the others was murkier.

"How is your day going, Detective Cruz?"

Emilia was so startled she dropped her mug. It clanged against the stainless steel sink but didn't break. She caught her breath, heart hammering.

Miranda appeared around the side of the partition, cup in hand. He raised it in a salute to the rich aroma of coffee. "I followed my nose."

Emilia gulped as her heart rate subsided. "It's almost done," she said.

"You seem a bit preoccupied today," Miranda said in that diffident way that invited confidences.

"You startled me." Emilia wondered if he'd ever been a priest.

"You and Lieutenant Cardenas seemed to be working well together," Miranda said.

"I'm just worried we're going too fast," Emilia heard herself say. "The files don't support our conclusions."

The coffee maker beeped.

Miranda took the carafe. He filled Emilia's cup and his own.

"This is a strange situation, Detective," he said as he tapped sugar into his brew. "We have so little to go on except our instincts." He paused and handed her the sugar. "Our morality. And integrity."

He held her eyes, his gaze direct but sympathetic, before taking his cup and heading to his desk.

Emilia sipped her coffee, holding the cup in two hands like Judge Sarmiento, shaken yet again that day. Had Lennox targeted Miranda as well? Told him of an unnamed traitor on the team?

Did Miranda suspect her?

She edged around the partition. Miranda was by Anaya's cubicle. The two men looked at a map. Elizondo was at his desk, upright as always, tapping diligently at his computer. Cardenas wore headphones and watched an interrogation video on his computer.

Had Lennox contacted each member of the team, not just Emilia? Did he deliberately sow mistrust in the mind of each member of the task force?

She dumped out the rest of the coffee and went back to her desk. Put on headphones and started a video just to make it appear that she was busy, but turned off the sound so she could think.

Who benefitted from closing down the task force, but also had the money and power to hire someone as good as Lennox to impersonate the Legal Attaché? Or pay the real Lennox to stay in Mexico, unbeknownst to the embassy people, and carry out this elaborate charade?

Who stood to benefit the most from the task force finishing as soon as possible?

Emilia stabbed the button to stop the video.

Pedro Avila and Pilar Garay de Avila, the mayor of Lindavista and his wife, fit both counts.

They had to be the key to Lennox, maybe to the whole investigation. Emilia switched to the network analysis program and called up the original version with the Avilas as the hub around which all the other connections linked. There was simply no other way to look at it.

Emilia printed off a copy. Along with two mugs of fresh coffee, she brought it to Cardenas's cubicle. He looked up from his computer screen and took off his headphones.

"Thought you might need this." Emilia held out a mug. "One sugar, spoonful of milk, right?"

"Are you leading me on, Detective?"

"Maybe," she said. "Got a minute to talk?"

Emilia wheeled over her desk chair and gave him the network analysis diagram.

"What's going on?" Cardenas split a chocolate bar from the stash in his desk drawer and handed her half.

"The Avilas," Emilia said. She had coffee in one hand and chocolate in the other. As if staying calm wasn't enough of a challenge. "I think we need to check them out again."

"But the rally motive doesn't fly."

"There has to be something else," Emilia said. "Too many threads connect to them."

"We weren't saying they're blameless." Cardenas frowned. "Avila still told the police chief to turn the students over to El Choque. But the more compelling motive lays the blame on Flores."

"I suggest we go down two tracks on the theory they'll converge," Emilia said. "Both Flores and Avila. If we dig deep enough, one of them will give away the motive."

"Is this women's intuition?" Cardenas asked.

Emilia jiggled her knee impatiently. "It's the analysis. There's no way to arrange all these links that doesn't put the Avilas in the middle."

To her relief, Cardenas nodded. "All right," he said.

"You take Flores," Emilia said. "I'll work on the Avilas."

Lennox was still waiting for her call. Waiting for her to say she could wrap up the task force in return for $50,000.

CHAPTER 26

If only one of the Avilas had said the word 'sheep' or said how much they hated Erik Flores, there would be something to go on. Emilia wondered if this wasn't why previous investigations simply grabbed onto the charity rally and hung on for dear life. It was the easy answer. But for the timing discrepancy, it would have worked.

Emilia went through all of the taped statements made by Pedro Avila again. She'd thought he was clever before. Now she decided he was smart and slippery. No doubt Avila had fingered Lieutenant Camacho to conduct their interviews.

She viewed all the interrogations of the chief of police and the cops who'd been arrested for collusion with El Choque, including Camacho. But no one spoke of a motive for the initial police move against the students, besides the fact that the students were unruly and disturbing the peace. Every one of them was a master of obfuscation.

She was finally down to a second pass at Pilar Garay de Avila's videos. As before when she'd watched the woman's two videotaped interrogations, Emilia was struck by the contrast. In the space of a week, Pilar went from tearful wreck to composed First Lady of Lindavista.

It wasn't so much that Pilar's hair was styled and her nails were done in the second video, but that she was so sure of herself. She reminded Emilia of an actress guest-starring on a talk show. Smiling, confident, even a little glib.

Why yes, José, I loved working on that film.

Yet she was still in jail.

In the first video she was frightened. She knew she was in trouble.

In the second video, the trouble had vanished. Pilar was amused. Her interviewer was Martinez, the cop who'd questioned Lola Dominguez.

Emilia crossed her arms and watched Pilar control the second interview. She knew something Martinez didn't.

The scene was identical to all the other videos Emilia had watched in the past few days. The seated figure. The plain table. A glass of water. Box of tissues. The disembodied voice asking questions that Pilar batted away.

As she talked, Pilar played with her rosary beads, her pink fingernails occasionally catching the overhead light to send a momentary glare into the camera lens.

"Who's this?"

Emilia paused the video. Anaya watched the screen over her shoulder. A coffee mug dangled from his hand.

"Pilar Garay de Avila," Emilia said. "Wife of the mayor."

"The one still under house arrest."

"Yes."

Anaya squatted down next to Emilia's chair to be eye level with the monitor. "What's she holding?"

"Rosary beads," Emilia said.

Anaya snorted. A heady mixture of tobacco, tequila, and cheap cologne wafted off his plaid shirt. "Can you zoom in?" he asked.

Three clicks later, the video was larger but also grainier. Anaya didn't move as Emilia restarted the video. Pilar smirked and spat out answers to questions and rolled beads between her fingers.

"Stop," Anaya said suddenly.

"What?" Emilia said as she clicked the icon.

Pilar's hands froze in mid-motion. What Emilia had previously taken for the cross dangling at the end of a rosary was a black and silver charm. A tiny figure stretched out its arms in a mocking imitation of Christ on the cross.

"*Madre de Dios*," Emilia whispered.

Pilar Garay de Avila held not a rosary but a set of worry beads celebrating Santa Muerte. Each silver bead bore a faint skull motif and the charm dangling from Pilar's fingers depicted the so-called Skeleton Saint as the reaper of death in a long black enamel robe. Its hood surrounded a silver skull with red jewels for eyes. One bony hand held a tiny globe to show dominance over all the earth. The other held a reaper's scythe. The charm was smaller than Pilar's thumb but it was unmistakable in the enlarged video.

"Black Santa Muerte," Anaya said. "Black means power over enemies."

"I know," Emilia said. Her chest felt tight.

It was the same exact Santa Muerte image she'd seen tattooed on Diego Barrielos Luna's arm and Rafa's chest as he whipped up an already frenzied crowd as El Acólito, Santa Muerte's chosen priest.

"That's a nice piece of shit," Anaya observed. "Probably

real silver and enamel. Where'd she get it?"

"I have no idea." Emilia rummaged through the files on her desk, looking for the written transcript.

Anaya plucked it out of her hands. "Doesn't say," he said after a minute. "Who visited her in jail?"

Emilia blinked. Five days elapsed between Pilar's first and second interrogations. No doubt she had a visitor in all that time. "You think somebody brought it to her?"

Anaya tossed the file on top of the pile. "Check the arrest record, but the *federales* should have confiscated anything she had with her at the time."

"You're right." Emilia gave herself a mental shake and found the right folder. Anaya was right; Pilar had surrendered almost nothing at the time of her arrest. No worry beads were listed on the form.

Anaya tapped the mouse to play the video again. "Look at how she's working those beads. Either she's a believer or she's got a lot of faith in whoever gave them to her."

Without the audio, Emilia could focus on Pilar's body language. The way her eyes flicked down to look at the beads, the way her shoulders relaxed when her thumb hit the Santa Muerte charm. Emilia could kick herself for assuming the woman was fingering a rosary, but she'd been too captivated by Pilar's poise and snide answers.

"Find out where the beads came from," Anaya said. "Whatever message those beads carry, she feels real good about it."

Emilia bit her lip. "If I call the Multifoco prison, does that qualify as creating evidence?"

"Tell them you're Judge Imelda Sarmiento de Suarez," Anaya said and snorted at his own wit.

Two hours and three calls later, Emilia had the answer.

Pilar had been visited in prison twice. Both times the visitor was her sister, Adelita Garay de Flores.

"We just won the *lotéria, mi amigo*," Emilia sang out. She shot around the partition and slapped a scribbled note on Cardenas's desk.

"Adelita Garay de Flores," he read out loud.

"Wife of Erik Flores," Emilia said.

"So?"

Emilia pumped her fist into the air. "Surprise," she said. "The wife of the mayor of Lindavista and the wife of the owner of the bus station are sisters."

CHAPTER 27

At the end of the day, Emilia snuck out of the task force suite and went up to Judge Sarmiento's office. A plan was beginning to take shape in the back of her mind, but she needed to know if the extradition of Barrielos Luna was going to happen or not.

Ramirez was sitting at his desk in front of the door to the judge's office, like an elf elevated to security guard. "Detective Cruz," he said, in a tone that suggested she was the unwashed peasantry. "What brings you up here?"

I've come to bring a chicken to the queen.

"Is Judge Sarmiento available?" Emilia asked.

"No, she's not in her office. Perhaps I can help you."

Emilia shuffled her feet a bit. "I was wondering about something.

"Oh, yes?"

"The Barrielos Luna extradition," Emilia said diffidently. She sat uninvited in the chair by his desk.

Ramirez stiffened. "The Barrielos Luna extradition is separate from the task force," he said.

Emilia scooted closer. "I know, I know. But is it on hold because the judge is coming with us to Lindavista?"

Ramirez edged his chair backwards. "The extradition is no business of yours."

"It actually is." Emilia let loose the lie. "My boyfriend is a cop, too, and is probably going to be one of the Barrel

Bomber's escorts when they take him to El Norte. We're planning the wedding so it would really help to know if it's going to be sooner. Or later."

Ramirez pursed his lips. "That's quite a presumptuous thing to ask, Detective. Congratulations on your upcoming wedding, of course, but I can't—."

"I just need to know when he'll be out of the country." Emilia burst into tears, with all the theatrical force she could muster. "You can't imagine how much money we've spent."

"Please, Detective." Panic spread over Ramirez's sharp features. "I'm sure it'll all work out."

"My parents, his parents—." Emilia sobbed, too overcome to finish her sentence.

Ramirez's body was nearly concave in an effort to pull away from her weeping yet not cede his territory. "Detective, listen to me. The extradition will go through as soon as Judge Sarmiento returns from Lindavista."

Emilia caught her breath. "Are you talking about the original timeline?"

"Yes, yes," Ramirez said, still flustered. "Nothing has changed. As soon as she returns they'll finalize the extradition."

Emilia stood up. "Thank you, Licenciado," she said, sniffing away the last of her crocodile tears. "You've been so helpful. I wish you were coming to Lindavista, too."

He preened like a peacock as Emilia left, having no idea what he'd just set in motion.

Emilia sat on the bed in her hotel room with a glass of wine from the minibar and her uneaten room service dinner. The discovery that Pilar and Erik Flores's wife were sisters would lead to something, but she might not be there to see it. The Santa Muerte dangling from Pilar Garay de Avila's worry beads had shown her a fork in the road. For awhile Emilia could go down both paths, but eventually she'd have to choose one or the other.

Rafa or the task force.

Just like the counselor said, she'd already traded her family and Kurt. The job was all she had left.

Lennox thought she'd swallowed the argument that the task force had to wrap up quickly in order to push Barrielos Luna's extradition. Well, Emilia now knew when the extradition was going to take place and it was within his desired timeline. If she took the bounty, Lennox couldn't accuse her of trickery, even if the task force kept going.

Success hinged on what she could make him believe.

The maid had replenished the supply of whiskey. Emilia rinsed her glass in the bathroom sink and opened one of the tiny bottles. The whiskey seared her throat, prompting a coughing fit that made her eyes water.

When it subsided, Emilia picked up her cell phone and slid her finger over the screen to wake it up. She slowly tapped in the number on Lennox's card. It went straight to voicemail, which didn't surprise her.

She waited for the tone. "Tom, this is Emilia Cruz. From Starbucks and El Péndulo. Let's connect when you have a chance." She reeled off her cell number and hung up.

He called her back within the hour, saying something about always checking messages from his machine in the office.

"What's your schedule for tomorrow?" Emilia asked. "I could come by your office at the embassy."

"I'll be out of town all day," Lennox said smoothly. He was a real pro, neither rushed nor nervous. "A conference that's been on my schedule for months. But I'll be here later in the day. How about drinks in the evening? The King Cole bar at the Saint Regis hotel is excellent. It's not far from the Sheraton and their signature Sangrita Maria should be on your list of things to do in Mexico City."

"Sounds intriguing," Emilia murmured.

"Excellent." Lennox's enthusiasm travelled through the connection. "How does 8:00 pm sound?"

"That's fine," Emilia said.

Starbucks, El Péndulo, the Saint Regis Hotel. Places where he was just another rich *gringo* blending in with other rich *gringos*.

But where she'd be noticed.

CHAPTER 28

The day dragged. Emilia watched videos, combed through files, and sifted through the city of Lindavista's website.

She went to the Saint Regis early, wearing the body hugging black dress. A quick survey of the elegant bar let her know she was there ahead of Lennox. Channeling every wealthy and arrogant woman who'd ever passed through the Pasodoble Bar in the Palacio Réal, she claimed a seating grouping with a clear view of the door.

Lennox did exactly what she hoped and paused in the entrance. Emilia took his picture with her cell phone. A moment later, Lennox was making his way toward her and Emilia's phone was stashed in her bag. Lennox greeted her with his fake diplomat smile. Emilia let him order her the fabled Sangrita Maria drink.

"How is it?" Lennox asked, gesturing to the tall frosted glass in Emilia's hand.

"Spicy," she said. *And wickedly strong.* Emilia knew she wouldn't finish the cocktail made with mezcal, red wine, brandy, and a pinch of *pasilla* chile puree. The alcohol, coupled with the adrenaline thrumming though her system, would make her too drunk to risk what she planned to do.

"Every Saint Regis hotel creates a unique version of a Bloody Mary." Lennox had a small glass of whiskey that had been served on a tiny silver tray with a crystal bowl of ice cubes and a pitcher of water. They served top shelf whiskey like that at the bar in the Palacio Réal, too. "The Sangrita Maria is unique to the hotel here."

"I can honestly say I've never had anything like it," Emilia said. She crossed her legs and nestled into the corner of the sofa.

The King Cole Bar was where the rich went to relax in low slung elegance. A long abstract mural anchored the bar along one short wall while long tufted sofas cut the room into soft parallel lines of privacy. Everything was muted and lush, from the caramel tweed sofas to the olive green occasional chairs, to the pale blue glow illuminating the surface of the bar and the cream curtains shrouding the spectacular view of the El Ángel monument. The Saint Regis was on Reforma, two blocks east of the Sheraton, but the view was just as remarkable.

"So how is the task force going?" Lennox was the picture of a handsome *gringo* out with an attractive local woman. Sure of himself and the outcome of the evening.

"We're scheduled to go to Lindavista at the end of the week," Emilia said.

"How long will you be there?"

"Well, that depends," Emilia replied.

"I see." Lennox smiled.

Emilia stirred her drink with the straw, feeling her heart starting to race. "The most important people we need to speak to are mayor Pedro Avila and his wife."

Lennox nodded without reacting in any special way to the

mention of the Avilas. "They shouldn't be hard to find. They're still under house arrest."

"In your position, from an official point of view, I mean," Emilia said slowly, as if she hadn't rehearsed her lines in front of a mirror. "Which is more important? Finding the bodies and knowing what happened to the students? Or getting Diego Barrielos Luna out of Mexico as fast as possible?"

Lennox tipped his glass and gently swirled the amber liquor, as if lost in thought. A jazz combo created an edgy mood around the black grand piano, but the music wasn't loud enough to disrupt conversation. Some trick of the room's acoustics, Emilia guessed. She didn't recognize any of the tunes.

"As the Legal Attaché, my government is on the side of justice for the victims of violent crime," Lennox said without a hint of irony or deceit. "So, yes, it's important that the bodies are found. But as a bystander who has watched events unfold over the past year, I know that's not going to happen."

"No justice, then?"

"I accept what I cannot change and work for what I can," he said. "Diego Barrielos Luna is probably running his drug empire from jail. It's only a matter of time before he escapes again. So from a strategic perspective, what's the best thing for Mexico's future?"

The man was an excellent actor, Emilia had to give him his due. He'd dismissed the reference to the mayor and his wife, and maneuvered the conversation to where he wanted it.

She wanted it there, too.

"I can meet your timeline," she said. "Get the task force to wrap up right after we go to Lindavista."

Lennox was still the picture of relaxation. His legs were crossed and one foot bobbed to the music. "How?"

Emilia shrugged. "You and I aren't the only ones who believe the task force is holding up the extradition. Plus, there's nothing to be seen this late in the game in Lindavista. As soon as we leave, the extradition will go forward."

"As soon as you finish in Lindavista . . ." Lennox let his words trail off. He raised his eyebrows at Emilia.

"Judge Sarmiento will be in Lindavista, too," Emilia said. "As soon as she's back in Mexico City, she's going to green light the extradition."

"Ah." He finished his drink and signaled for another.

Emilia tucked herself into the sofa cushions, playing with the straw in her glass so Lennox wouldn't see that her hands were trembling.

The jazz was light and racy; the piano's treble notes pranced through the syncopation. The waitress brought Lennox another whiskey. As before, he put in a single ice cube and let it clink around the glass before taking his first swallow.

"You'll get the bounty," he said. "As soon as the task force wraps."

Emilia poked at the ice in her drink with the straw. "I don't want the money," she said. "I want to meet Barrielos

Luna."

Lennox's body stiffened. "You mean visit him in prison? In Multifoco?"

"Multifoco isn't far from Lindavista," Emilia said. She'd surprised him.

The atmosphere between them was suddenly volatile.

"I don't control access to Barrielos." Lennox set his drink on the cocktail table.

"You're negotiating for his extradition," Emilia pointed out. "Certainly that gives you enough leverage to request a ten minute meeting."

"Why do you want to meet him?" Now that the first rush of surprise was over, Lennox was in attack mode.

"He's the biggest and most famous criminal of my generation." Emilia forced herself to sound starstruck.

"He's not going to sign autographs," Lennox scoffed.

Emilia edged toward Lennox, wiping away the power of his chagrin by the mere fact of her closeness. "Ten minutes in exchange for wrapping up the task force early," she said sweetly. "That's all I want."

They stared at each other. Emilia saw a deliberate blankness in his eyes that reminded her of Lieutenant Camacho's interrogation video. Lying men always gave themselves away in one way or another.

She didn't blink.

"I'll see what I can do," Lennox said and pulled away from her gaze. "But no guarantees. Multifoco isn't for the casual visitor."

"Arrange it before we head to Lindavista," Emilia said.

Lennox raised his glass. "I like your style, Detective Cruz." His voice was no longer friendly.

Emilia stood up. "I'll wait to hear from you."

This time she felt him watching as she walked away.

CHAPTER 29

"This is our last meeting before heading out to Lindavista," Elizondo said. "If you have any last minute tasks to complete, get them done tomorrow. But I hope you can take the day for yourself. Go to a museum. A movie. Be a tourist. We'll reconvene here at 9:00 am the day after tomorrow to pick up our files and convoy to Lindavista."

He passed out cards with car assignments to the task force members seated around the conference table. Three official vehicles with driver and bodyguard would transport them to Lindavista and be at their disposal while in the city. On the way there, the vehicles would stay together and maintain radio contact. Given the critical nature of the task force, every precaution was being taken to avoid notoriety and minimize the possibility of an attack on the convoy.

Emilia's heart sank as she read that she'd be in the first car with Elizondo. While the captain from Guadalajara had treated her as fairly as he'd treated the male members of the task force, she couldn't shake the feeling that they'd started off on the wrong foot and been stuck there ever since. Add to that her jitteriness over the situation with Lennox, and the four hour trip promised to be a nerve-wracking experience.

Cardenas tipped his card toward Emilia. He would ride with Miranda.

"Judge Sarmiento is unable to join us," Elizondo said. "You'll probably see it in the news tonight or tomorrow, but her husband has withdrawn his candidacy for mayor of Mexico City. Licenciado Ramirez will be coming with us instead of Judge Sarmiento." He passed a card down the table. "Detective Anaya, he'll ride with you."

Emilia suppressed a smile. Anaya would probably drink and fart away the drive while Ramirez cuddled up with his clipboard.

"The Attorney General's people have laid on a tour of sorts for us," Miranda said when Elizondo wrapped up the transportation and accommodation instructions. "Key locations including the bus station, the highway toll booths." He paused. "And the Colima dump."

Emilia raised her hand. "Do we have an appointment to speak to the Avilas?" she asked. "They're still under house arrest, remember."

"And the identical confessions," Cardenas said. "They're all at the Multifoco prison, so I presume we'll be spending quite some time there."

Multifoco. The word all but hung in the air in front of Emilia. She looked at her notes and tried to breathe through a minor panic attack.

"We have permission to speak to them but we have to make our own arrangements," Elizondo said. "Does anyone have any other outstanding issues?"

Me. Me. Emilia heard the word in her thundering heartbeat.

No one spoke up.

Cardenas pushed his chair away from the table, in

anticipation of the meeting's end. Elizondo held up a hand to halt him.

"Captain Miranda and I," Elizondo said. "Have a difficult issue to discuss with you all."

Cardenas shot Emilia a glance. She lifted a shoulder in half an *I-don't-know* shrug.

Miranda clasped his hands and rested them on the table. "A representative of the families of the missing 43 students contacted me," he said. "While we've been specifically instructed not to speak with the families, this representative claims to have key information which has never been provided to law enforcement."

"Captain Elizondo and I have discussed the approach at length," Miranda went on. "The impartiality of the task force has been universally accepted as the key to our success. Speaking to the families, even through a representative, and using any information given to us through this channel, would open us up to charges of having been wrongfully influenced. That would create difficulties."

Cardenas shifted in his seat and Emilia knew what he was thinking. This was the issue that had caused Miranda and Elizondo to quarrel.

Miranda was unable to deny the families an opportunity to help find their sons' killers. For him the task force was as much about restoring hope and bringing closure to the grieving families as it was about anything else. But Emilia was sure Elizondo saw the task force as a stepping stone to higher things. Repercussions to flouting the Attorney

General's rules would be serious. The task force members could be smeared by the Attorney General, lose their rank, transferred to a shit department like Traffic, or forced into retirement.

"Do you know what they have?" Slouched in his chair, Anaya folded his arms across his chest. "If it's so helpful, why didn't they make a statement? Put it out there."

"They waited because their previous statements were discredited as biased," Miranda said regretfully. "They were put down by the government and mocked in the media. Now they're afraid that any unilateral statement will be suppressed."

"Inconvenient information," Anaya said.

"Something like that," Miranda agreed.

Elizondo sat with his hands clasped and head bowed, looking intently at nothing.

"Nobody wants the families to show up 100 federal investigators," Cardenas said. "It's been 18 months. Everybody has already chosen sides."

"That's right," Miranda said quietly. "Is the Attorney General's reputation more important than justice for the dead and their families? Have we as a society forgotten about accountability? Have we forgotten our humanity?"

Emilia felt her chest tighten.

Ever since coming to Mexico City, she'd avoided putting herself in the shoes of the parents whose children had disappeared into a night of violence. Avoided thinking about the raw pain of losing a child and the agony of never knowing what had happened to him. Had those students died afraid? Calling out for help? Had they been tortured and mutilated, the fate of so many gang victims?

How could Emilia put on those shoes when she herself planned to commit murder? She'd locked the irony away but now Miranda's quiet words held the contradiction up to her like a shiny mirror.

"After much discussion," Miranda continued. "Captain Elizondo and I decided that the fair thing to do is take a vote whether or not we should talk to the representative. I've made up some ballots. Yes, means we'll find out what information we have and use it if necessary. No, and we'll refuse the meeting and stick to the mandate we've been given."

"The vote must be unanimous," Elizondo said firmly.

No one said a word as Miranda handed out little slips of paper, each printed with two words.

Elizondo set a clean coffee mug in the center of the table. "Please mark your ballot at your desk. When you're done, fold it and place it here."

Chairs scraped against the floor as all five members of the task force rose. Emilia kept her eyes down as she darted to her desk. She smoothed out the ballot.

New information would almost certainly mean an extra outlay of time. It upped the odds that Lennox would find out he'd been tricked into arranging the visit with Barrielos Luna.

Emilia's pen hovered over the ballot. What were the

chances that a bunch of Michoacán farmers had discovered anything that could change the outcome of the task force's final report? If it was so important, it would have been made public.

Had Miranda fallen into a trap meant to simply embarrass the task force and by extension, the Mexican government?

Was this any more of a long shot than her attempt to question Barrielos Luna?

She circled her answer in red ink, folded the ballot, and dropped it into the mug on the table.

Elizondo was the last to tuck his ballot into the mug. He didn't look at Miranda as he returned to his chair.

"Any others?" Miranda said.

After a few moments of silence, he drew the mug to himself, reached in and plucked out a ballot. Emilia found herself holding her breath.

"One vote for yes," Miranda said. He placed the paper in the middle of the table where everyone could see.

It wasn't Emilia's ballot.

Again he dipped into the mug, unfolded the slip of paper and read the circled word. "Yes."

The next ballot was the same.

And the next.

"Yes."

He unfolded the last slip of paper. Emilia watched his shoulders relax. Miranda glanced at Elizondo before speaking.

"The last vote is for yes," Miranda said, his voice

breaking. "It's unanimous. Thank you."
Emilia started breathing again.

CHAPTER 30

After ten minutes, Emilia decided that Café Cervantes on Prado Norte was where Mexico City's beautiful people went to see and be seen.

Paulina Reno was five or six years older than Emilia with an impressively sophisticated world-weary air. The movie director's hair was long and wavy with auburn streaks and her eyes were rimmed with black kohl to match her black ribbed top, skinny silk ankle pants, and strappy sandals. Silver rings with raw semi-precious stones adorned three fingers of each hand.

"So you're a cop come all the way from Acapulco to talk about Rafa Gamboa." Paulina sipped her cabernet wine. "What's he done?"

"He's wanted for human trafficking," Emilia said. No sense frightening the woman by listing out all Rafa's crimes or complicating the discussion by admitting he was her brother. "I'm talking to anyone who can shed some light on his habits. Interests. That sort of thing."

"It's been a long time since I've seen him." Paulina's slim fingers up slid nervously and down the stem of her wineglass. "Like I said on the phone, I doubt I can help."

"I wanted to talk to you about the movie," Emilia said. "You cast him in a movie but it didn't work out."

Little *tapas* plates waited to be sampled. Emilia took a garlic olive and looked at Paulina expectantly.

Paulina took a deep breath. "Five years ago, I was the assistant director on *Rosa Quintana*, the *telenovela*. Rafa was our leading man."

Emilia nodded.

"He was gorgeous." Paulina gave a rueful laugh. "Breathtaking. I'd never seen anyone the camera loved so much."

Emilia tasted her wine, remembering Rafa perform on stage as El Acólito. He wore only flimsy white cotton trousers and the Skeleton Saint inked across his bare chest. He'd been beyond handsome. She could only imagine his looks before the shocking tattoos and nomadic criminal lifestyle.

Paulina took an olive. "I left *Rosa Quintana* before the show ended to take a job in Miami. One of the *norteamericano* Spanish language networks made me an offer. A year there and I landed the director slot for a romance movie being filmed here in Mexico City. It wasn't a big budget film, but there aren't many opportunities for female directors in Mexico."

"You got to select the cast?"

"Yes. *Rosa* had just wrapped and I knew Rafa was free."

"As your leading man," Emilia offered.

"I thought I had more than that." Paulina nibbled at the olive and took a slow sip of wine. "Rafa's audition was amazing. His screen test was even better. Everybody watching it fell in love with him."

"Including you."

"Including me," Paulina repeated bitterly. "Once we started filming, it all fell apart. Rafa complained he didn't have as many lines as somebody else. He wanted endless script changes." Paulina looked up at the ceiling as if to remember. "The coffee on set wasn't the kind he liked. Costumes. His co-star. The time spent waiting for a shot to be set up. He complained about everything."

"Did that cause problems for you?" Emilia asked.

"Like you wouldn't believe." Paulina poured more wine for both of them. "He was a spoiled prima donna killing my first chance to direct a movie."

Emilia took a potato croquet and slid the dish closer to the other woman.

Movement across the restaurant caught Paulina's eye and she waved to someone beyond Emilia's range of vision. "Jorge Ramos," Paulina whispered. "You know, Che in *El Mundo Lago*. He put up his own money for the show to get the part."

"I've never seen it," Emilia said.

Paulina gave a tight smile. "You're not missing anything."

"So what happened with Rafa?" Emilia prompted. "And your movie?"

"He finally quarreled with the producers over making his part bigger." Paulina gulped wine; the conversation was making her agitated. "They gave me an ultimatum. Either fire Rafa or they'd fire both of us. We were only two weeks into the shooting schedule. If we replaced him, we'd still be able to finish on time. They suggested a replacement. Not as good as Rafa, but easier to work with and alike enough from the rear that we might be able to use some of the footage we'd already shot."

Paulina waved nervously to a hefty female who trailed the maître d' like a cruise ship behind a tugboat.

"So you told Rafa he was out," Emilia said to get Paulina's attention again.

"In the evening, at my place," Paulina said with a tiny shiver. "You know, a little booze, a little sex, a little bad news. I actually thought he'd get another job and we'd stay together."

"How did he react?" Emilia asked.

Paulina's hand shook as she selected a wafer-thin slice of Spanish chorizo sausage. "He beat the shit out of me," she said.

"*Madre de Dios*," Emilia murmured.

"Concussion. Broken ribs. Broken wrist." Paulina's voice shook. "Believe it or not, I was still in love with him. I told everyone I fell down the stairs at my apartment building."

"And Rafa?"

"Never saw him again." Paulina's upper lip quivered and she covered by biting into the slice of chorizo.

"I'm sorry," Emilia said.

Paulina finished the morsel of sausage. "I couldn't work. The producers started over with a new director and a new leading man. I spent months recovering at my parent's home. When I got back to Mexico City, Rafa had disappeared."

As if in silent agreement, the two women sat in silence with their wine until Paulina's trembling stopped.

"Did he ever mention a place called Casa Odisea?" Emilia asked at length.

"What's that?" Paulina asked. "A house? A hotel?"

"I was hoping you'd know."

Paulina shook her head. "No, I don't remember him ever mentioning a place with that name." A group of young women following the maître d' to a table caught her eye. "That's Betty de la Hoya."

"She was Rosa in *Rosa Quintana*, wasn't she?" Emilia asked.

"They had to cover her bruises with makeup," Paulina said and waved.

Betty detached herself from her friends and came over to Paulina.

Betty kissed Paulina on both cheeks, but despite the traditional greeting Emilia sensed a strain between the two women. Paulina introduced Emilia by name, omitting to add that she was a police detective.

"We've been talking about people in the business." Paulina made room for Betty in the booth and tugged at the woman's sleeve to make her sit. Betty was younger than Emilia, with honey-colored hair cut in a daring pixie and a loose cotton skirt and top that was bohemian high fashion.

Betty grinned. "I love gossip."

"Do you remember Rafa Gamboa?" Paulina asked.

"What a scoundrel," Betty said. She spoke lightly but her

shoulders hunched inward. Emilia was sure the motion was unconscious.

"When was the last time you saw him?" Emilia asked.

Betty blinked. "I don't know," she said. "Maybe a year after *Rosa Quintana* ended. I ran into him somewhere in Polanco. Outside a restaurant. I was with someone else. Rafa said he was going up to Baja for a film shoot."

"Did he tell you the name of the movie?" Emilia asked. "The names of anyone else involved?"

"No," Betty said. "Later, I decided he'd made it all up. If there had been a real movie Rafa would have boasted about the director. The producer. Something to impress us."

"You knew him fairly well before that?"

Betty glanced at Paulina. "Paulina and I both did," she said, her implication clear. "At different times, of course."

"When you were with Rafa," Emilia said casually. "Did he ever mention a place called Casa Odisea?"

"Casa Odisea." Betty blinked and the corners of her mouth turned down. "Yes, I remember that name."

Emilia's heart stuttered. "Do you know where it is?"

"I don't know," Betty said. "Maybe Acapulco."

"Does Rafa have a house there?" Emilia pressed. "A house called Casa Odisea?"

"No, no." Betty shook her head. "It was an adoption agency. Well, maybe more like an adoption investigation company. Rafa hired them to find his real family."

"What?" The word came out of Emilia's mouth in a squeak.

"He was adopted," Betty explained. "His mother never told him he was adopted, but he knew. He didn't look like her. There weren't any pictures of him until he was about four, either."

Emilia swallowed hard. "Do you know if the Casa Odisea people found out anything?"

"I doubt it," Betty said. "It's not like Rafa could give them very much to go on. Just stuff he remembered."

"Like what?"

"A different mother reading stories to him," Betty said. "A father who took him for rides in a big car. Playing with his baby sister."

Emilia felt her whole body tighten. "Rafa thought he had a sister?"

The young actress gave a sad smile. "He remembered her the best. Said that her hair was straight and his was curly. Finding her seemed even more important than finding his real parents."

Betty turned to Paulina. "I think that sister was the only woman he ever really loved."

Emilia felt her chest tighten.

Her phone vibrated with a text and she snatched it up, murmuring an apology to the other women. Lennox's number blinked on the screen. The meeting with Barrielos Luna was on.

CHAPTER 31

"You should resign from the task force," the counselor said.

"I'm not hurting anybody," Emilia insisted.

"Rooting around Rafa Gamboa's apartment is one thing," the counselor said. "Talking to the devil incarnate is another."

"Barrielos Luna isn't the devil," Emilia said. "He's a criminal. I've talked to plenty of those."

"Not like him."

"He knows Rafa," Emilia said doggedly.

"You're betting on a tattoo," the counselor said, her voice larded with disgust.

"It's not the only thing." Emilia clenched her fists. "Barrielos Luna likes young girls. El Acólito traffics them."

"You've traded away your life for a vendetta against your brother," the counselor said. "But is the truth about what happened to those 43 young men really yours to trade?"

The room was a boxing match, Emilia decided, and the light cutting across the floor from the barred window served as referee. Seated in chairs in the opposite corners of the room, she and the counselor circled around each other's words. In her white tank top and jeans, Emilia was ready to fight but somehow she never landed a blow.

"One question," Emilia said. "No one can begrudge me one question. He either knows Rafa or he doesn't."

"Rafa was looking for you," the counselor said. "For his real sister and mother. Perhaps there's some humanity left in him."

"I didn't see it," Emilia flung back.

She heard her own breath, angry snorts like a restless racehorse.

The counselor stood and adjusted her seat cushion. For the first time, Emilia realized that the woman was eerily similar; about the same size, with a long ponytail and white shirt.

"What about Kurt?" the counselor asked, after sitting again.

"He's got nothing to do with this," Emilia said quickly.

"He said you didn't hurt him," the counselor mused. "Even gave you the opportunity to slam the door closed once and for all. But you didn't."

Emilia looked at the dust motes floating in the shards of light between herself and her opponent.

"The door is still open," the counselor said.

"Maybe when this is all over." Emilia stood and rocked nervously from foot to foot.

"You mean after you've killed Rafa Gamboa."

"Yes."

The counselor's face was almost in the band of light. Almost.

"Let's talk more about the moment when you confront

Rafa," she said. "How do you see the scene playing out? What if he's unarmed? Will you kill an unarmed man?

Emilia stopped rocking and dismissed the ridiculous questions with an abrupt flick of her hand. "I'm going to track him down. If it takes making deals with a phony diplomat and talking to Diego Barrielos Luna, then that's what I have to do."

"How does killing him make you so different than whoever killed those 43 students?"

"How dare you compare me to those killers?" Emilia exclaimed.

"It's the same thing." The counselor's voice was harsh. "Taking a life. You as the judge, with an illegal gun, would be no better than that."

"Those kids did nothing to deserve what happened to them," Emilia threw herself into the chair again, hardly able to believe the direction of the conversation. "Rafa is a murderer and a rapist."

"Who deserves the punishment provided by a civil society."

Emilia laughed and the sound grated against the gray walls. "Civil society?" she repeated. "Sorry, this task force is about optics. Making sure the Attorney General and Judge Sarmiento aren't embarrassed."

"You could change that," the counselor said. "If you weren't so fixated on Rafa, maybe you'd actually make a difference. Choose to do good."

"I can do both," Emilia said stubbornly.

"I salute your singlemindedness," the counselor said. "I can even understand your anger. But Rafa controls you more each day. You let him lead the way. After all, that's what older brothers are for, aren't they?"

"I make my own decisions," Emilia retorted.

"Tell me how this ends well. Tell me the difference between you and whoever killed the 43 if you kill your brother."

Emilia stared at the increasingly familiar figure in the far corner. The light across the floor played tricks with her vision and the emptiness strained her ears. No comforting noise travelled from beyond the window; there was no sighing breeze, no patter of rain, no birds.

Thoughts of Kurt rose unbidden. Nights spent talking together on the balcony outside their bedroom. Watching the sun rise surrounded by the swell of the Pacific. Dancing in the Pasodoble Bar to the rhythm of a steel band.

"You still have choices, Emilia," the counselor said.

She raised her hand and shot Emilia with her thumb and forefinger.

CHAPTER 32

The ride to Lindavista was nearly silent, which was fine with Emilia. After being briefed on the security plan and issued temporary handguns, she and Elizondo climbed into the back of the first official SUV. The driver got behind the wheel. The bodyguard took the front passenger seat and clamped his assault rifle into a quick-release rack next to the console. Radio checks confirmed that the next two vehicles in the convoy were ready to roll. The driver admonished the others to stay alert and limit radio chatter before signing off.

Emilia wondered if Anaya had offered Ramirez a swig out of his hip flask yet.

As the convoy picked up speed on the highway heading south out of Mexico City, Elizondo fiddled with the rear air conditioning control. When the vents were angled to his satisfaction, he asked Emilia if she was comfortable. When she said yes, it was fine, he gave a curt nod and stared out of the tinted window. Emilia pressed herself into the upholstery and watched the city go by, only slightly distorted by the thick bulletproof glass.

For the next two hours, she thought of the conversation with Paulina Reno and Betty de la Hoya. Emilia wondered if Rafa was so twisted he'd think it was funny that he'd raped the sister he'd been trying to find. The real irony was that his sister was looking for him, too.

Emilia glanced at Elizondo, wondering what he'd say if

he could read her thoughts. His face was expressionless but his hand remained on the stock of the handgun he'd been issued.

As if he felt her glance, Elizondo turned away from the window. "Everything all right, Detective?" he asked.

"Yes, Captain," Emilia replied. "I'm fine."

She stared out the window as the heavy SUV left the city behind. The landscape turned to billboards and scrubby trees and the occasional cement hovel in a patch of cleared land, often with a few goats roaming amid thorny bushes. Occasionally they passed roadside villages, fields of blue agave plants, or the gates to an auto-hotel brothel where men literally drove in for a quick sexual encounter. The bodyguard in the front seat conducted radio checks every 15 minutes.

They stopped once at a highway comfort station. The kids selling candy and water and the adults hawking souvenirs and puppies didn't approach the heavy vehicles, which parked facing outward. With the bodyguards in position, they marched in a phalanx to the low concrete lavatories. Once there, however, it quickly became apparent that no one had thought of the security issues involved in getting Emilia safely in and out of the women's restroom. She had to wait until they cleared the toilet stalls and stationed a bodyguard at the entrance. Emilia sheepishly paid two pesos to the dumbfounded matron and collected her fold of toilet paper.

The trip resumed without incident. Emilia and Elizondo sat without speaking until the SUV passed under a double archway painted in the national colors of Mexico and proclaiming Lindavista to be the city with the view of the angels.

"Lindavista *de los angeles*," Emilia said out loud as the SUV rumbled under the red, white, and green arch.

"No doubt Captain Miranda would say 43 angels," Elizondo said.

The comment was so out of character Emilia had to stifle a gasp. Elizondo continued to look out of his window.

Lindavista was larger than Emilia expected, despite the number of times she'd studied the city map and pored over pictures. The roads were fairly well maintained and bordered by shepherd's crook iron streetlamps that spoke of the city's Spanish heritage. They passed a number of churches that all seemed in good repair as did most of the commercial buildings they passed. White, pink, and mango-colored stucco predominated.

The convoy stopped along the curb in front of a long two-storey white building. A sign with a stylishly minimal logo proclaimed they'd arrived at the Hotel Independencia. Thick columns supported a dozen arches running the length of the building, forming a shaded pergola. The column and arch motif fronted a long balcony on the second floor. On the roof, red clay tiles rose to meet a peaked ridgeline.

They were all assigned rooms on the second floor, with an extra room commandeered by the drivers and bodyguards as a command post. Prior arrangements had been made, Ramirez explained with a superior sniff, for the hotel to convert its smaller dining room into a meeting room for the task force. He and the two captains would have the keys, ensuring that the files, charts, or computer equipment left there would be safe.

Dinner was served in that room. Emilia found herself picking at the tasty *carnitas* in front of her, along with a clay dish of warm tortillas, as the next day's schedule was discussed. Both Miranda and Elizondo chose their words carefully, saying little about the interviews with the seven jailed suspects and nothing about the planned meeting with the family representative of the missing students. It was as if everyone was waiting for Ramirez to say he was tired and leave.

Anaya ended the meal when he got up and said he was going to find a bar and he didn't need a babysitter. Cardenas fairly rocketed out of his chair in his haste to say he'd come, too.

Emilia rose next, giving her apologies but she was very tired and planned to go to bed with a magazine; it had been a long drive.

By the time she'd unpacked her suitcase, the texts were flying with the schedule for keeping Ramirez occupied. In the midst of the exchanges, including some frankly funny bits from Cardenas, Emilia got the text she'd been waiting for.

You were supposed to text me when you got there.

And here it is, Emilia typed back to Lennox.

Lennox's reply popped onto her screen. *Thursday.*

He gave her cryptic instructions where to meet him and what time.

Emilia acknowledged and closed out of the message application.

She fell into bed with the bathroom light on, of course.

CHAPTER 33

"This place looks better than I thought it would," said Cardenas.

"I know," Emilia replied. "It's a pretty city. Not a place where massacres take place."

"I almost expected to see a dark cloud over everything." Cardenas glanced at the map, then tipped a finger to the right, letting Emilia know they had to turn at the intersection.

Yesterday, they had all driven the city, viewing the crime scenes in the downtown area from the safety of the SUVs. There had been no protests, no news stories about the national task force being in town so the next day they'd divided into squads of two or three to walk the students' routes and get up close and personal with the events of 24 September. Emilia and Cardenas, with the timeline and a small city map in hand, started at the convenience store on the west side of the city where the students had first been spotted.

While Emilia and Cardenas waited for the light to change and let them cross the street, Emilia uncapped her bottle and guzzled some water. Lindavista was built on a series of undulating hills and the elevation was high enough to be felt. The air was dry and dusty.

The light turned and they stepped off the curb. The street ahead sloped uphill and Emilia had to lengthen her stride to keep up with Cardenas. They passed a mix of gated residences and commercial enterprises sporting big signs. The buildings were a jumble of two and three story cement block structures.

"What's missing from this picture?" Cardenas asked as they passed by a small plumbing supply shop, the stucco walls wearing a fresh coat of pale green paint.

"No graffiti," Emilia said. This part of Lindavista was cleaner than Acapulco. Sidewalks were swept and free of animal droppings. A few walls wore handbills for theater events or hotline numbers for unwed mothers, but the lack of sprayed on insults, taunts, and slogans was conspicuous. Most doorways were adorned by pots of red geraniums, possibly the city's signature flower.

"And no beggars," Cardenas said.

It took them about 30 minutes to walk from the store to the Plaza Bolivar where the bus station was located. Emilia imagined that it had taken the big crowd of students a bit longer. They would have been excited, laughing and talking about their big adventure to the anniversary event in Mexico City. For many, it would be the first time they'd ever been so far from home. The group's leaders would be busy shepherding their friends and rehearsing how they would commandeer the buses.

From the top of a loaf-shaped hill, Plaza Bolivar commanded the northwest quadrant of the city. Set in the intersection of two main streets, and ringed by a cobblestone lane, the white limestone plaza was a charming spot. Flowering bushes and stone benches invited rest and conversation. The focal point was a larger-than-life statue of Simon Bolivar, liberator of the Americas, on a rearing horse. Mounted on a dark stone plinth, the statue was so tall Emilia had to shade her eyes and crane her neck to see Bolivar's stern face.

The city's colonial planners had saved their best architectural efforts for the neighborhood. A brilliant white cathedral dominated the street to the west. The massive church had an arched center entrance and twin white spires topped with domed caps and a cross in the traditional Spanish style. From the map, Emilia knew it was the Cathedral of San Miguel el Arcángel.

The city's museum of natural history anchored the street across from the plaza's southern side. Painted a soft melon shade, the long low building was built in a similar style to the hotel housing the task force, with a run of columns and arches suggesting a cool and dim interior.

Emilia and Cardenas passed the museum, crossed the cobblestone lane, and strolled past the enormous statue of horse and man. The two cops had been together all morning, getting a feel for the city and comparing notes, but Cardenas had been uncharacteristically subdued.

No one took any notice of them, but if anyone had, they would have passed for a married couple new to Lindavista. Both wore jeans and sunglasses and carried water bottles, cell phones, and a map.

A large outdoor café spilled across the northern side of the plaza, its perimeter marked by pots of red geraniums.

Waiters in black pants and long white aprons scurried from tables topped with red market umbrellas to a glass summerhouse decorated with green iron scrolls and filigree columns. A wide counter fronted the glass structure and behind it, Emilia could see the kitchen staff brewing coffee and slicing cheesecake.

"There's the bus station," Cardenas said.

"What?" Emilia looked up at him and he made a *jump over* motion with a forefinger.

The bus station was on the other side of the street from the café and the north side of the plaza.

"Care for an iced something?" Emilia asked.

Cardenas grinned. "Are you buying?"

They took the table on the end so that they could see both the bus station and the little shopping center around the corner, where a line of taxis waited for customers. They both got frozen coffee drinks that the waiter claimed were the specialty of the house, made with frothed espresso, agave syrup, and coconut milk.

Cardenas got out his pad and sketched the scene for his son. The city bus station might once have been a twin of the museum on the opposite side of the plaza but the colonial columns and arches were open to the sunny weather. Between the arches, Emilia saw a sales counter, two rows of chairs bolted to the floor, and two dozen or so customers milling about.

"Authorized mechanics only," Cardenas said.

Emilia cut her eyes to him. "What?"

"The sign by the gate on the left." Cardenas showed Emilia the opening in a tall wall to the left of the station. "They must have a maintenance area in back."

Emilia frowned. "Was that in the files? I remember pictures of the front, but not of a maintenance area."

"I think we're going to be saying that a lot," Cardenas said. "They gave us a hundred boxes of shit."

Along the other side of the building, a vast awning provided shade for half a dozen Flores Transito buses angled alongside. Other buses idled inside the terminal as people queued to board.

As Emilia sipped her cold drink and felt the jolt of caffeine hit her bloodstream, a bus rumbled out of the terminal and onto the street. The Flores Transito bus was gold and white, with a stylized logo of a red geranium.

The bus passed the cathedral and continued east away from the Plaza Bolivar. Through the arches, Emilia saw a woman roll a cleaning bucket into the vacant parking bay and swab the floor with a mop.

"Did you see that?" Emilia asked.

"It was a bus, Detective," Cardenas said. "Hard to miss."

"No, I mean the flowers," Emilia said. "There are red geraniums everywhere in this city. Even on the side of the buses."

"So?" Cardenas looked at her with his eyebrows raised.

"It's that . . ." Emilia trailed off. "I can't put it into words but Lindavista is so polished. Organized. Even the bus station. I know that sounds silly, but I have the oddest feeling."

"I know what you mean," Cardenas said, surprising her. "I expected to see a whole city in shades of gray and everyone bowed down with second hand guilt. At first, I thought it was just the contrast. Coming up for air after drowning in horrible confessions and discussions about how to dispose of 43 bodies, and finding out life is still going on in color. But there's something else."

"There's too much money here," Emilia said. What she was seeing was better than what she'd read. "For a city without any big industry or a tourist draw, it's awfully prosperous. No beach, no Copper Canyon, no silver mine. Just mountains and nice views but nobody comes for that."

"There's the Multifoco prison," Cardenas said. "In fact, if we stand by the statue, we should be able to see the fence."

They finished their coffees and backtracked to the statue. Emilia stood on the second tier of the plinth base and sure enough, there was the vast Multifoco prison complex stretching away to the northwest about two miles behind the bus station.

She was high enough to see the roofline of the sprawling gray flat-topped building and the top of the perimeter fence. A four-lane highway bordered the prison property for a short distance before curving south to cut through the eastern side of Lindavista. A vast chain-link fence topped with razor wire ran next to the highway, no doubt to deter escapees from getting close to a moving car. A deep man-made ravine made for a secondary barrier following the path of the highway, its steep sides lined with concrete blocks. Clean water burbled through the cut through the earth, as if the ravine was part of some water purification or retention effort.

"The prison is a pretty big place," Cardenas said. "Multifoco must provide a lot of jobs."

"Do you remember the news about the death of the warden?" Emilia asked. "Who's running it now?"

"I don't know," he said. "We should check it out before we go to interview those seven *pendejos*."

And Diego Barrielos Luna. Emilia gave an involuntary shiver at the thought.

"You okay?" Cardenas shook his head and held out a hand to help Emilia step off the plinth.

"Sure," Emilia said lightly. She wondered what Cardenas would think if he knew she hoped to find a clue to Rafa Gamboa Escobar's whereabouts inside the walls of the prison.

They wandered into the bus station where Emilia took a few pamphlets listing the bus routes. The help behind the counter wore gold polo shirts with *Flores Transito* and the logo embroidered on the chest pocket. The ceiling was high and slow-turning fans kept the air from smelling of diesel fuel.

They walked around but there was nothing to see beyond people buying tickets and buses coming and going. Nothing to suggest that one dark evening, a crowd of rowdy students had forced their way onto four buses, demanding in high spirits to be taken to Mexico City.

As Emilia and Cardenas headed for the street parallel to the cathedral, another bus rumbled out of the station and bounced across the strip of cobblestones in front of the Plaza Bolivar.

The woman with the mop and bucket quickly cleaned the floor where the bus had been parked.

CHAPTER 34

The Colima dump took its name from an eastern suburb beyond the highway that formed a curving ring road around the city. The dump was everything Lindavista was not, as if the rot and dregs of the city had been skimmed off and deposited on a lunar landscape of waste.

The land there was hard and chaotic; ridged by sharp masses thrown up by ancient earthquakes and riven by *barrancas,* narrow canyons that made for natural trash bins. Here and there a rocky outcropping poked up, but otherwise tons of garbage, much in plastic bags, formed a choppy white coating over the jagged earth.

A gravel track led to the official dump zone, where city garbage trucks offloaded their weekly haul. Workers spread out the refuse, using shovels and a backhoe. But beyond the officially sanctioned area, garbage strewn by all comers stretched out for miles.

The task force arrived in two vehicles. Emilia scooted out of the big SUV behind Anaya and Cardenas and the stench hit her like a blow to the chest. Drawing a deep breath was impossible. She hastily clamped on the surgical mask Miranda had handed out before they left the hotel. It helped but her eyes watered so badly she could barely see.

Their luck was holding. There was no one to notice that the national task force looking into the disappearance of the Amistad 43 had finally arrived at the supposed final scene of the crime. No protesters greeted them; no family members with signs and candles to demand answers they did not have.

In addition to the surgical masks, the task force members all wore rubber boots, latex gloves, and had long sticks for prodding the heap, as well as copies of the map Anaya had shown them in Mexico City. It was early, before the sun had a chance to fully warm the place, yet Emilia felt the heat of decomposition rise from the land.

"*Madre de Dios*," Miranda whispered. "We have come to hell."

"Watch your step," Anaya warned. "No telling what's underneath the top layer."

"Anybody who falls in is on their own," Cardenas said, but his usual bantering tone was flat.

The vastness of the place was almost inconceivable. Emilia and the others stayed with Anaya as he attempted to find the spot where the previous investigation claimed the bagged remains of the 43 students might be, but markers that had been left were gone. The mass of trash was constantly shifting.

"This is not accurate." Elizondo glanced from the map to the endless lunar vista.

"It was a guessing game to begin with," Anaya said. He took the lead, pointing out the ridges of land as a way to orient the group.

As Emilia skirted trash bags and rotting carcasses, sweat soaked through her tee shirt and the waist of her jeans. She had on a baseball cap and sunglasses above the surgical mask, yet her head pounded from the ripening reek of death and decay. Rats rooted through the ocean of trash, which rustled and heaved under the brightening sun.

"I'm not doing this," Ramirez announced.

The group stopped. Ramirez was behind the rest of them, scowling through his surgical mask. With the tall stick in one hand and the big rubber boots swamping his legs, he looked like a spoiled child refusing to go on a fishing trip.

"Licenciado Ramirez," Elizondo said. "Please stay with the group."

"No." Ramirez looked around wildly. "I did not agree to this!"

"It's a garbage dump, Ramirez," Cardenas called. "What did you expect?"

"I am not like the police," Ramirez screeched. "I don't play in rotting refuse."

"Get ahold of yourself, boy," Elizondo snapped.

Ramirez threw down the stick. "I won't do it!"

"You *pendejo*," Emilia exclaimed, anger flaring. She tramped over to Ramirez, grabbed the younger man's arm, and gave him a jerk. "You were the one who insisted on coming to see that we did things properly. If the rest of us can take it, you can take it, too."

"Don't touch me!" Ramirez's eyes bulged above the surgical mask. He tried to pull away but Emilia held on.

"Detective Cruz." Miranda was suddenly next to her. He put a gloved hand on Emilia's arm. "I think it would be better if Licenciado Ramirez waited in the car."

As if on cue, Ramirez yanked off his mask and vomited.

Emilia hopped back to avoid being splashed.

Miranda braced the younger man as Ramirez retched over and over. When he stopped, Miranda walked him to the vehicles.

"One down," Cardenas said.

Miranda came back. "We are all under a great strain, Detective," he said to Emilia. "But let us be considerate of those who are weak."

"Yes, Captain," Emilia murmured.

Beyond the stink and the rats, the problem was one of vastness and inaccessibility. Even if the bagged remains had been left near the edge of the dump, 18 months later there was no telling where that edge was now. Earth moving machines couldn't be used, either. They were too heavy to stay on top of the pile and the risk of plunging through the rubble into a bottomless, garbage-filled canyon was too great. The dump was like a living, breathing monstrosity; continually growing outwards and covering every cut and divot in the earth with a cruel blanket of scum.

A few trash pickers roamed the north side of the dump, not too far away from the official entrance, using sticks to poke at the bags, test the ground underneath, and scare away rats. Emilia knew the pickers would not stray far. If they fell into a ravine, the backhoe and city workers were the only hope of being rescued.

After six hours of rising heat, including two breaks for discussion and water, Anaya admitted defeat. The five task force members were never going to be able to do more than understand the difficulty of the task. If the students' bodies, or what was left of them, were somewhere in this vast sea of garbage, they were never going to be found. The *federale* map was useless, although it did give them an indication of how the perimeter of the dump had grown in the intervening time.

Everyone was silent as they piled into the vehicles. Emilia bounced against Anaya on one side and Cardenas on the other as the SUV lurched over the gravel track. She took off her mask and willed herself not to get sick now. Cardenas must have read her mind because he cranked up the rear seat air conditioning. Cold air buffeted her.

In Mexico City, when they'd talked about the El Choque gang members killing the students and burning the bodies, the discussion was dispassionate. Clinical. Theories, hypotheses, possibilities to investigate.

But confronted with the Colima dump, Emilia could no longer pretend this was an academic discussion. What sort of deranged person could dismember a fellow human and leave the body there to rot? Was the task force trying to find bodies or were they hunting a pack of sick murderers? Because no one could navigate that dump with the remains of 43 healthy young men. An army of madmen would have had to do it.

"*Rayos*," Cardenas swore, sniffing at his shirtsleeve. "We all stink. Bad."

Without warning, Emilia burst into tears. She covered her

face with her hands and sobbed, caught up in a private agony.

Could she be as bad as those killers? There was no way to escape the trash-filled hole she'd created out of her own life. Hate and anger at Rafa had carried her this far; if she didn't pursue him to the end, where did that leave her? And if she did, who would she be?

Cutting through everything was the sharp pain of missing Kurt and the precious moments of clarity that always came after confiding in him.

To her surprise, Anaya put his arm around her and pulled her close. Emilia rested her head against his plaid-covered shoulder and eventually her tears ran down. He released her when she wiped her eyes and sat upright again.

"That place fucks with your head," he said and offered his battered hip flask.

"Yeah," Emilia sniffed. She took a slug from the flask. It was decent tequila, not that she was a great judge of anything beyond a good mojito. The liquor burned its way down her gullet.

"Better give him some, too," Anaya said with a jerk of his chin at Cardenas pressed into the corner of the rear seat. "Hasn't made a pass at you all day."

Emilia managed a wobbly laugh as Cardenas took the flask. He made his eyes pop after swallowing and she knew he was clowning around for her benefit.

The three of them finished what was in the flask and fell silent for the rest of the ride back to the hotel in Lindavista.

CHAPTER 35

Emilia kept her appointment with Lennox on Thursday. Slipping away from the task force schedule gave her pause, but in the end she simply said she wasn't feeling very well and withdrew from the excursion to Amistad to see the school.

She met Lennox at a small restaurant a few blocks from the hotel. The *norteamericano* seemed at ease in his surroundings and in his role as the Legal Attaché, here to escort her to see the criminal his country wanted behind bars in its own sturdy jail.

"The clock is ticking," Lennox said as they sat in the restaurant. "But unless the task force wraps up in the next two weeks, I'm afraid your chance is gone."

Emilia closed her menu. "I'm not hungry," she said. "Why don't we just get it over with?"

Lennox slowly closed his menu as well. "This was your idea," he said. "Your price for considering my offer."

"That's right." Emilia stood up.

Lennox had a large SUV and a driver waiting outside. Emilia stared out the window, discouraging any attempts at small talk. Although she and Cardenas had seen the prison from the center of Plaza Bolivar near the bus station, there was no direct road there from Lindavista. They drove a route that took them on the highway south of the city before exiting on a purpose-built road winding north again to

Multifoco.

Emilia was familiar with the process of entering a prison. Identification checks, bag and body searches, waiting for the prisoner to be brought to an interrogation room.

Lennox, however, bypassed it all.

The SUV rolled up to a wide barrier of corrugated metal. A brace of uniformed guards with long guns popped out of the small cement shed next to the gate. Lennox rolled down his window and passed over a piece of identification in a leather wallet. Emilia supposed it was a false diplomatic *cédula*, because both guards came to attention before one of them stepped inside and hit a switch. A moment later, to the accompaniment of grinding metal and an electronic hum, the barrier slid to the side.

Once in the reception area, another uniformed guard ushered Lennox and Emilia through without checking identification. Five minutes later, Emilia found herself sitting in a large room next to Lennox, with two guards leaning casually against the wall on either side of the door.

Diego Barrielos Luna, the infamous Barrel Bomber himself, was across a metal table from her. No restraints, no glass to keep him from touching her. Nothing to suggest he was the most dangerous criminal Mexico currently had behind bars or that his drug empire had once been worth billions of pesos.

He was bulkier than in the television footage she'd seen the first night in Mexico City, with wavy black hair and eyebrows like two dark slashes over slightly hooded eyes.

He was often described in Mexico's more sensational media outlets as handsome and his penchant for teenaged girls was well documented.

Emilia wasn't so much struck by his muscled physique or sensuous eyes, but by the man's raw, restless energy. Neither the guards nor Lennox was in charge; Barrielos Luna dominated the room. His gray prison jumpsuit was a fashion choice. The top two buttons were undone and an expensive gold chain snaked around his neck.

The man's gaze raked over Emilia's head and torso. He turned approving eyes to Lennox.

"A gift, my friend?"

"This is Detective Emilia Cruz," Lennox replied. "We are here at her request."

"And what can I do for you, Detective Emilia Cruz?"

Emilia's carefully rehearsed questions flew out of her head as she realized her mistake. She knew that Lennox could not be trusted and she should have insisted that her true name not be shared with Barrielos Luna.

But there was no use leaving now.

Barrielos Luna smiled, showing a mouthful of straight white teeth. He reminded her of a shark.

"I'm interested in Santa Muerte," Emilia said.

"Santa Muerte?" Barrielos Luna rubbed his chin. "Have you come very far to ask me about the Boney Lady?"

"Detective Cruz is from Acapulco," Lennox said.

Barrielos Luna pushed his chair back and crossed his legs. He wore expensive loafers with little brass toggles across the instep.

Emilia felt the room close in. Barrielos Luna's freedom of movement was wrong. Multifoco was a maximum security prison but the guards were clearly not enforcing the rules for their most notorious prisoner. How many within the prison walls had been paid off?

"You have a tattoo," she said as her heart raced. "The black Santa Muerte. Power over your enemies."

"This is good." Barrielos Luna's smile widened. "She knows me well."

He rolled up his sleeve, extended his forearm, and made a fist. Santa Muerte bulged toward Emilia, the black hooded robe rippling over his muscle. The skeleton face had been inked by a master; the detail of the hands holding scythe and globe were superb. Not only was it the same image she'd seen on Rafa Gamboa Escobar's chest as he inflamed the crowd as the Santa Muerte priest El Acólito, but now she was sure the two tattoos had been created by the same artist.

"Where did you get that tattoo?" Emilia asked.

Barrielos Luna relaxed his hand and Santa Muerte's robe rippled again. "I don't remember," he said and pulled down his sleeve. "Why does my tattoo interest you?"

"It's very detailed," Emilia said. "Very good. Where should I go to get the same thing?"

He shook his head. "You are too pretty for a big tattoo like this."

"No," Emilia said. "I want one by the same artist."

"You came all the way from Acapulco to ask me where

to get a tattoo?" Barrielos Luna grinned, seeing right through her. "I don't believe you."

Emilia had read dozens of news articles about him over the years. Barrielos Luna was a killer who enjoyed tormenting his victims. Face-to-face with him, she knew it was all true. The hooded eyes were soulless. He made her feel naked and alone. No armor, no bravado.

She straightened her spine, keeping her hands in her lap. "Do you know El Acólito?" she asked. "The Santa Muerte priest."

Barrielos Luna looked at Lennox, who gave a tiny shake of the head.

"Maybe you met him three or four years ago," Emilia continued. "A tall man. Young. Handsome and strong. He conducts intercessions for women all over Mexico to pray to the black Santa Muerte."

"You want him to pray for you?"

"I'm looking for him," Emilia said. "He has a tattoo just like yours."

"Many people have Santa Muerte tattoos."

"No, his is exactly the same, just bigger," Emilia said. "Did you ever hear of a man who got a tattoo like yours across his chest?"

A design as large and detailed as Rafa's tattoo had taken days to complete. Whoever had done it wasn't some wanderer with a hypodermic and a bag of soot but an experienced artist with a shop. Rafa had stayed in the vicinity until the design was done; maybe he had a house or friends nearby. Emilia knew that if she could find the artist, she'd be a giant step closer to finding Rafa.

Barrielos Luna stretched, casting restless energy into all four corners of the small room. "You've seen this tattoo close up?"

"Yes," Emilia said uncomfortably. "It's exactly the same as yours."

"What is this El Acólito to you?" he asked. "Your lost lover?"

"The same artist did both tattoos," Emilia said, ignoring his question. "All I want to know is who did yours."

Barrielos Luna gave a bark of laughter. "A beautiful woman comes to me, yet she is searching for another man." He thrust his face towards Emilia's. His lips were naturally dark red. "No, I cannot recall ever having met this El Acólito. But if he is hiding from a beautiful woman like yourself, then he is a fool."

"I'm done," Emilia said abruptly to Lennox. She went to the door, snapping her fingers to make the guards jump to attention.

"It was a pleasure, Detective Emilia Cruz," Barrielos Luna said softly.

The image of Pilar Garay de Avila playing with the Santa Muerte worry beads pushed past Emilia's desperation to get away from the man and his silky voice. As the guard put a key into the lock, Emilia pivoted on her heel. "Do you know a woman named Adelita Garay de Flores?" she asked.

"Is she looking for El Acólito, too?" Barrielos Luna

countered.

"Maybe," Emilia said. "She prays to Santa Muerte."

Barrielos Luna spread his hands. "I am locked away in prison. I know no one any more."

Emilia slapped the wall by the door, the need to get away choking off her air. The guard unlocked the door.

Lennox followed her out.

CHAPTER 36

"You missed the big showdown yesterday," Cardenas said as he slid into the seat across from Emilia. He made a gesture to the hotel waitress as if he was pouring coffee

"A showdown?" Emilia lowered a forkful of eggs. "In Amistad?"

Cardenas's attention zeroed in on the waitress. The girl filled his cup, took his breakfast order, and sailed away, buoyed by his not-so-subtle flirting. Emilia rolled her eyes and kept eating as Cardenas dumped two packets of sugar into his cup and stirred, enjoying Emilia's reaction.

"Didn't know Captain Miranda had it in him," he said airily.

"Okay." Emilia sighed. "Every waitress in the world adores you and you are a fantastic storyteller. Now, what happened?"

"I seriously thought he was going to take a swing at Ramirez."

Emilia pointed at him with her fork. "You are the second most irritating man I've ever met."

"Okay." Cardenas pushed Emilia's flatware aside. "We went to Amistad as planned. The place isn't much. Unpainted concrete. Half the streets aren't paved, chickens running loose. The school is the only claim to fame but even that's not more than a basketball court and a jumble of concrete classrooms and dormitories. But the school turns out dedicated educators. Every teacher in this part of Michoacán is a graduate."

"So why did Miranda and Ramirez argue?" Emilia asked. Her cell phone, lying next to her plate, vibrated with a text message, making her spoon rattle. She grabbed the phone but didn't look at the screen.

"We toured the school and ended up in the office. Miranda started firing off questions, but in that nice way he has so the person doesn't even know they're being grilled." Cardenas was momentarily distracted by the plate of eggs and *chilaquiles* the giggly waitress set in front of him. The girl topped off their coffee cups and moved on, her cheeks pink after Cardenas gave her another special smile.

"It's in your DNA, isn't it?" Emilia asked.

"What's in my DNA?" Cardenas uncapped the table setting's obligatory bottle of picante sauce.

"Never mind." Emilia flapped a hand at him, even as her cell phone vibrated again. "So Captain Miranda asked questions."

"Ramirez interrupted," Cardenas sprinkled his food with hot sauce. "Went off about violating the charter by attempting to create new evidence. Destroying the trust placed in us. Even threatened to disband the task force if any of us is found to be in violation."

"For asking questions?" Emilia felt the blood drain from her face.

"Miranda asked the little *pendejo* to step outside." Cardenas wolfed down his breakfast as he spoke, oblivious to Emilia rigid with fear across from him. "Nicely, you know. Ramirez was full of himself, says 'gladly,' and the two of them walk out. Elizondo doesn't react but I can tell he's just developed an ulcer as big as Copper Canyon."

Cardenas washed down his eggs with coffee. Emilia waited, her scalp prickling with adrenaline.

"By the time the rest of us got out there," Cardenas went on. "They were nose-to-nose and Miranda was using some choice words to describe Ramirez's mental capacity. Ramirez's face was the color of shoe leather and if Elizondo hadn't intervened I think the *pendejo* would have actually burst. *Blam*. Bits of Licenciado Ramirez all over the Amistad Normal School."

"*Madre de Dios*." Emilia tried to make it sound like a joke. "What would we tell Judge Sarmiento? Spontaneous combustion?"

Cardenas grew thoughtful. "If Ramirez knew what we were doing today, he'd have a stroke."

"Do you think he'd shut down the task force?"

"Yes," Cardenas admitted. "But we all knew that when we voted."

Emilia's breakfast rose up and scorched her throat. If Ramirez found out she'd talked to Diego Barrielos Luna at the Multifoco prison yesterday, he'd crucify her. Even if she could argue that she was following up the Santa Muerte angle from Pilar Garay de Avila's worry beads, Emilia doubted he'd accept it as a logical next step. No, Ramirez would argue that Emilia had been attempting to collect new evidence and was in violation of the task force charter. The Attorney General's office would shut down the task force and she'd be responsible.

Trading her job for the chance to hunt down Rafa Gamboa was one thing. But as Cardenas kept talking, Emilia was finally honest with herself. Yes, she'd put the last chance to find out what happened to the missing 43 students on the chopping block.

All for nothing. Barrielos Luna had given her exactly zero to help her find Rafa Gamboa.

Cardenas waved his fingers in front of her face and Emilia flinched.

"What's the matter?" he asked.

"Nothing," Emilia said brusquely and shoved her empty plate away. "Just sorry to have missed all the fun. Captain Miranda is always so calm."

The waitress topped up Cardenas's coffee cup, giving Emilia a chance to check the two text messages. Of course it was Lennox again. He'd sent her a message last night, too, implying that she should make things happen now.

She deleted both texts as Cardenas scraped up the last of the *chilaquiles* on his plate. "Anaya volunteered to babysit Ramirez today," he said. "Reviewing maps at some regional geographic office."

"So that the rest of us can . . ." Emilia's voice trailed off.

"Exactly." Cardenas wiped his lips with his napkin and frowned at Emilia. "You're not thinking about trying to change your vote, are you?"

"No, of course not." Emilia stood up and grabbed her shoulder bag from the hook by the table, still fighting for control. "What's done, is done."

It didn't matter what the task force did now. She'd put them all into a trap that could spring closed at any moment.

Elizondo and Miranda left the hotel without a bodyguard, on the pretext of having breakfast at a swank restaurant near the museum. Emilia and Cardenas strolled out 30 minutes later, leaving a message that they were returning to the Plaza Bolivar and likewise did not need security services that day.

By 11:00 am, after two taxi rides and a walking tour to shake off anyone inclined to follow them, Emilia and Cardenas arrived at the address. It was a large house in a pleasant residential neighborhood south of the plaza. A guard was waited at the gate. Cardenas said they were there to see Señor Diaz and the gate opened swiftly. It closed just as quickly behind them.

There was no Señor Diaz, of course, but the mere fact that they were meeting in this anonymous place and having to use a code phrase spoke to the paranoia gripping the families of the missing students. A tight-lipped man in jeans and a red tee shirt escorted them into the house, his wary attitude making Emilia realize that the families were taking a greater risk than the members of the task force. The Attorney General's office, instead of seeing the families as a source of support and information, had succeeded in making them an enemy, one to be discredited and shunned. If the facts didn't fit the narrative, the facts had to be proven wrong.

By meeting, the families stood to lose both their credibility and their best chance to find out what really happened to their sons.

Emilia hoped that what they had to share was worth it.

She and Cardenas were ushered into a living room and parked on two folding chairs. In fact, the only furniture, apart from a large carved cabinet, appeared to be folding chairs to accommodate the throng of people.

Elizondo and Miranda were already seated, along with Jorge Sanz, a lawyer for the families. The director of the Santé Human Rights Center in Mexico City, Victoria Lizaso, was also there. She'd been one of the earliest advocates for the families, organizing multiple rallies in Michoacán and Mexico City to pressure information out of the *federales*, the Attorney General's office, and anyone else who might prove useful.

Emilia recognized both Sanz and Lizaso from dozens of photos and press statements. They made an odd couple. He was short and stout with a receding hairline. She towered over him, a mane of unkempt gray hair flowing over a *rebozo* shawl she clutched around ample shoulders.

More than two dozen others sat or stood around the perimeter of the room and Emilia knew without being told that they were all parents of the missing students. Both the men and women had the short heavy torso of Mexicans with mostly *indio* blood. Their faces were blunt-featured, their skin was dark and leathery, and their hands roughened by years of subsistence farming. Fear and defiance radiated out of them in equal measure.

Sanz made a short welcoming speech, Lizaso thanked the task force for agreeing to the meeting. Miranda answered for the task force members and introduced each of them to the group.

Once the preliminaries were over, the crush of bodies warmed the room with a yeasty tension. Emilia glanced at Cardenas as she took out her notebook. His eyes roamed the room, looking for trouble.

Sanz cleared his throat. "The previous investigations focused on four buses intercepted by the Lindavista police on the night of 24 September," he said. "The students in those four buses have not been seen since that night. But we would like you to know that there was a fifth bus. The students on that bus survived and returned to Amistad."

"A fifth bus?" Miranda echoed.

"Ten *normalistas* from Amistad commandeered bus number 402 in the rear of the bus station, where there is a gas pump," Sanz explained. "The other students got into buses parked in front of the station in the usual passenger loading area. Between 8:30 and 9:45 pm, four buses departed the main station exit and headed south along Avenida Victoria. The fifth bus departed around 9:30. Because it departed from the rear of the station, that bus took a different route and got a little lost before it turned east toward the highway."

Emilia bumped Cardenas with her elbow. When he turned to look at her, she tilted her notebook so he could see the list of bus numbers she'd copied down weeks ago from the files. Bus numbers 115, 702, 339 and 120 had departed from the front entrance of the station. There was no reference to bus 402 driving away from the rear.

Cardenas nodded to let Emilia know he understood.

Sanz continued, his forehead glistening with sweat in the overly warm room. "The students in the fifth bus heard the driver receive a call from another driver, saying there was a police action happening at the toll booths and he should detour. Before he could turn the bus around, police on foot approached the driver's side. He talked to them through the window but opened the emergency exit in the rear at the same time. The students ran out. When the police entered the bus, it was empty. The driver was roughed up, but in the end the police apparently believed his story that the bus was headed to the station for service."

One of the mothers let out a soft sob. Emilia didn't turn around to see but she heard the zip of a purse being opened and a soft sniffle into a tissue.

"Do you have the driver's statement?" Miranda asked.

Victoria Lizaso nodded. "He passed his statement to the Santé Center," she said. "With the proviso that we do not release his name."

"Tell us about the ten students who managed to get off the bus," Miranda gently pressed. "What did they see?"

"They saw their friends and brothers rounded up like cattle," one of the fathers burst out. "Like animals!"

Sanz raised his hand for quiet. "They scattered and hid," the lawyer said. "Most of them passed the night in the dark in the street, lost and confused and hearing gunshots. One by one, they all made it back to Amistad the next morning, only to find that their friends had disappeared."

"We need to obtain official statements from each of them," Elizondo said.

"No!" another father shouted, thrusting a finger into the air. "We have been betrayed enough times."

"You said they would listen," a woman accused Sanz. "Now they want more."

Elizondo's face tightened. "Without such statements, we may not be able to use this new information."

The room erupted.

"They are like all the others!" a man raged amid shouts of *Betrayal! Betrayal!*

A high voice pierced the chaos. "Our children die and they protect their own."

Emilia cringed as waves of anger and sorrow and scorn buffeted her. The pain she'd endured at the hands of Rafa Gamboa Escobar was nothing compared to what these families had been through. Their children had no doubt died violently yet the parents had endured a year and a half of lies and weak excuses and counteraccusations.

The only trust or compassion left in the process was what the task force could bring.

Miranda stood and raised his hands. "Please, please."

His voice was lost in the swelling anger.

Emilia watched Sanz motion to the task force members. They were escorted out of the house.

"Thank you for coming," Sanz said shortly. "I hope this information proves useful to you."

CHAPTER 37

Without consciously making the decision to go there, Emilia and Cardenas wound their way through Lindavista to the Plaza Bolivar. Neither said a word as Cardenas led them past the giant statue, across the street, and along the sidewalk running parallel to the side of the station. Emilia grabbed his hand so they'd look like a couple, lost perhaps but with no malicious intent, as they walked past the sign designating the space for mechanics and into the large maintenance area at the back of the station.

No one noticed as they kept going, past a gas pump and a service bay with a couple of guys in coveralls tinkering with the rear engine of a Flores Transito bus. Loud music played from a cheap radio somewhere inside the bay. Another bus sagged awkwardly with a flat tire. A carwash zone was empty.

The wide rear gate was open. They found themselves in an alley running parallel to the north side of the Plaza Bolivar. It emptied out on either side into larger streets that in turned connected to those radiating out from the plaza.

There was nothing significant about the alley, no indication that this was the gate of salvation. A field of weeds stretched ahead and beyond that a metal fence closed off further access. Emilia recalled the landscape on the other side, seen from her previous vantage point on the plinth of the statue in the center of the Plaza Bolivar. There was nothing but the man-made ravine, the highway, and eventually the Multifoco prison.

"I don't know what I expected to see," Cardenas said. "But this isn't it."

They strolled back to the plaza and took a table in the outdoor café under a striped umbrella, ordered frothy iced coffees, and watched buses come and go. Cardenas sketched the cathedral.

Providing public transportation to the citizens of Lindavista was a well organized process. The sales counter did a brisk business in tickets and brochures. Buses in service parked under the awning. When scheduled to start their route, the buses drove through the station and picked up passengers before pulling into the street and trundling past the cathedral along Avenida Victoria.

Every time a bus left its parking space or passed through the station, the woman with mop and bucket rushed to keep the floor sparkling clean.

Emilia's phone buzzed with a text message. She read it but didn't answer.

She had nothing to say to Lennox.

Emilia knew that Cardenas was more shaken by the meeting with the families than he let on. They stayed together the rest of the day, having dinner in some forgettable restaurant before returning to the hotel.

Miranda met them in the lobby. "Detective Cruz, could you come with me, please," he said. It wasn't a question. "Licenciado Ramirez would like to speak with you."

"What's going on?" Cardenas asked.

"This is a private issue, Lieutenant," Miranda said.

Cardenas threw Emilia a questioning look. She shrugged in return, as if she didn't have the faintest clue that she'd just destroyed everything.

She left Cardenas in the lobby and followed Miranda into the small dining room set aside for the task force. Elizondo was there, reading a file at one end of the table, a beer and glass by his elbow. Ramirez was positioned in the middle, like a judge in his courtroom, with files spread out in front of him.

"Finally," he said as Emilia and Miranda walked in.

Elizondo looked up. "Good evening, Detective," he said.

Emilia bobbed her head at the senior officer. "Captain."

"Licenciado Ramirez came to me with some troubling information regarding your activities with the task force," Elizondo said.

"Troubling information?" Ramirez sneered. "Serious allegation of misconduct, is more like it."

His elfin features were pinched in glee. Emilia immediately knew this was payback for confronting him at the dump.

"Misconduct is a strong word." Elizondo's voice carried a warning undertone.

"I represent Judge Sarmiento," Ramirez straightened his

shoulders. "We will not have the task force undermined by a lowly detective who exceeds her authority in the most arrogant and deceitful way imaginable."

The trap had sprung. Emilia felt sick.

Just like she'd feared, Ramirez had found out about her meeting with Barrielos Luna and would use it to close down the entire task force, all because she'd embarrassed him.

"I'm sorry," Emilia said, hoping that if she confessed and offered to quit, the rest of the task force could soldier on. "I thought there was a connection between—."

"You see!" Ramirez's voice upped an octave. "She admits that she co-opted a private company into assisting with the task force without official knowledge or permission."

"I did what?" Emilia asked, momentarily confused.

"Your clever video library," Ramirez retorted. "You knowingly revealed official government secrets to a private company in return for hosting video content on a virtual storage platform. A car importer, of all things."

"Nobody revealed official secrets," Miranda said, clearly exasperated.

"I'd like to hear Detective Cruz's explanation," Ramirez said primly.

Miranda and Elizondo waited. Ramirez picked up his pen.

Emilia took a deep breath. She'd been so fixated on Barrielos Luna that her brain was slow to switch gears to Paco, Tina, and the video library. "It was an offer of assistance," she began. "To share storage space and a text-to-speech interface the company already had."

Ramirez waved a finger at her. "Start with Tina, the secretary, who confused her loyalties. She has confessed to the whole scheme. She introduced you to Paco Ricardo Hernandez."

"He's a video expert." Emilia's heart sank, knowing Ramirez would vent his ire on the young couple.

"At this car importing company," Ramirez prompted.

"Yes." Emilia looked from Miranda to Elizondo. "If Tina hadn't been proactive and introduced us, we wouldn't have found the identical confessions or figured out the rally timing."

"Tina will not be penalized in any way for assisting the task force," Elizondo said to Ramirez.

"Tina's job is in serious trouble," Ramirez retorted. "As is the foolish hippie who attempted to sway the task force with his database project."

"There was no swaying," Emilia exclaimed. "Paco solved a huge technical problem for us. He was sure his company would want to help. Did you ask them?"

"You are not entitled to know the extent of the investigation into your misconduct, Detective," Ramirez said. "You revealed official secrets. Assume that your career is over."

"Attorney General's Office Refuses Private Sector Expertise to Solve Amistad 43 Mystery," Miranda said, as if quoting a news broadcast.

Ramirez frowned at him.

"If anything happens to Tina or Paco," Miranda said. "That's the headline in the *Reforma* newspaper. The subtitle will mention a certain Licenciado Ramirez who personally stood in the way."

"You presume to threaten the course of justice?" Ramirez looked incredulous.

"I'm willing to admit that Detective Cruz might have taken a different approach," Miranda said, with a glance at Emilia. "But given the lack of other options, her solution was ingenious. The private sector offered cutting-edge help and the task force accepted it. End of discussion. Unless, of course, you wish your office's lack of technical effort to be publicly known."

Ramirez stood and gathered his files with swift, jerky movements. "I will be calling Judge Sarmiento for further guidance," he said. "She'll be very disappointed in your response, Captain."

Miranda folded his arms. Elizondo poured beer into the glass on the table.

Ramirez left, slamming the door as he went.

"Well, thank you," Emilia said uncertainly.

"Sit down, Detective," Elizondo said loudly.

Emilia perched on the edge of the closest chair.

"You thought Licenciado Ramirez was going to raise a different issue," Elizondo said. "Please tell us what that is."

Emilia hesitated.

Both men looked at her expectantly.

"I saw Diego Barrielos Luna yesterday at Multifoco,"

Emilia said quietly.

"The Barrel Bomber?" Miranda queried.

"Yes."

"What business did you have with Diego Barrielos Luna, Detective Cruz?" Elizondo's voice was ice cold.

Emilia took a deep breath, hands clamped around the seat of her wooden chair. "He's a well known follower of Santa Muerte," she said and was rewarded by a sharp intake of breath from Miranda. She plowed on. "He's got a big tattoo of a black robed Santa Muerte. In the video of her second interview, the mayor's wife Pilar Garay de Avila was playing with black Santa Muerte worry beads. Supposedly her sister gave them to her. The sister who's married to Erik Flores, the owner of the buses."

"You decided there was a connection," Elizondo said. "Without mentioning it to anyone else."

Emilia nodded. "Yes."

"And is there?" Miranda asked. "Is there a connection?"

"He didn't give me anything," Emilia said.

Miranda sighed. "I assume you also asked about El Acólito."

"Yes," Emilia said. "Another dead end."

Elizondo drank some beer, playing with the tension in the room. "It didn't occur to you that we should know?"

"I'm sorry," Emilia hoped she sounded contrite and not guilty. "I thought if I handled it myself, no one else would get in trouble."

"You're not wrong there, Detective," Elizondo said

harshly. "Your little independent outing could land us all in a very difficult spot."

Miranda closed his eyes, as if calming himself, then sighed and reopened them. "After this morning, that's probably moot."

"Nonetheless, it limits her usefulness to the task force," Elizondo said. "If Ramirez finds out there will be hell to pay."

"I'm sorry," Emilia repeated.

Elizondo looked grim. "Ramirez is insisting on coming to Multifoco to observe the meetings with the seven who confessed. If you're there, too, we run the risk of a guard recognizing you or finding you in the security system as a previous visitor. You'll stay behind."

"I understand," Emilia said.

"You and Lieutenant Cardenas are meeting with the Avilas tomorrow," Elizondo said. "After that, go back to the bus station. Find out what's so unusual about the rear entrance."

"We walked through there today," Emilia said. "It's a big maintenance plaza with a gas pump. Nothing much to see."

"Try again," Elizondo said crisply. "I want you two there until you figure out what we're missing."

"What about Erik Flores," Emilia asked. "Can we have a chat? Ask him a few questions? Without mentioning a fifth bus, of course."

"Ordinarily, I'd say use your own judgement." Elizondo stood up and arched his torso in a movement that spoke of extreme weariness. "But in light of this conversation, the answer is no. The next time you have an independent thought, Detective, talk to me first."

The two captains left.

Emilia's legs felt like rubber as she found Cardenas sitting at a table in the bar off the lobby, apparently waiting for her.

"What was that all about?" he asked.

"Ramirez is going nuts over the video library," Emilia said.

She recounted the conversation with Ramirez and was rewarded with a low whistle from Cardenas. "That Paco kid took a hell of a risk," he said.

"You should have seen Captain Miranda," Emilia said. "He was calm but furious."

"I think our job is getting to him," Cardenas said.

"I, uh, told them about this other thing I did," Emilia said. "I met Diego Barrielos Luna."

She told Cardenas about arranging to see Barrielos Luna because of the link to Pilar Garay de Avila's Santa Muerte worry beads, again leaving out Lennox.

"I can't believe it." Cardenas shook his head. "You just waltzed into Multifoco and said you wanted to meet the Barrel Bomber? And they let you?" He started to laugh. "That took balls."

"It was a fool's errand," Emilia said bitterly.

It was late and the bar was nearly empty. A television mounted on the wall replayed last year's World Cup final.

The sound was low, diluting the cheering crowd into a background hum.

Emilia thought about ordering a drink but she was too wrung out. She stood up, swaying slightly with fatigue.

"Do you realize," she said to Cardenas. "This morning none of us even got to say, 'I'm sorry for your loss.'"

CHAPTER 38

Emilia felt curiously light the next morning as she and Cardenas were driven to the home of Lindavista mayor Pedro Avila and his wife Pilar. The meeting with Barrielos Luna was no longer a burden. It had been a useless effort, but couched in terms of the task force's investigation, it was no more than a forgotten detour.

"Hard times under house arrest," Cardenas muttered as a rolling gate clattered to the side. The SUV headed into a circular drive and stopped under a columned portico in front of a huge white stucco house. A maid in a navy dress and white apron waited on the steps that were flanked by glazed pots of red geraniums, as if that was the only flower that was allowed to grow in Lindavista.

They were led through a two-story foyer with a sweeping staircase trimmed with a brass scrolled rail, down a wide hallway decorated with oil landscapes, and into a large and bright room that appeared to be home office and family room rolled into one.

Pedro Avila stood by a massive dark wood desk and did not offer his hand as Cardenas introduced himself and Emilia. He was more handsome in person than in any of his interrogation videos. A starched blue Oxford cloth shirt, gray slacks, and tortoise shell glasses combined for a serious and casually professional look.

"This is my wife, Pilar," Avila said.

"Of course." Emilia nodded at the woman on the wide white sofa.

Pilar Garay de Avila did not offer a hand in greeting but simply stared angrily at the newcomers. It was clear that no courtesies would be extended.

Two attorneys were there. Introductions were made and a small argument ensued when notified they were not invited to participate. A letter from the Attorney General's office was produced and the two men parked themselves in the dining room.

Cardenas chose an overstuffed chair adjacent to the sofa while Emilia sat next to Pilar. Pedro Avila made a production of wheeling a large high-backed office chair from the desk to the sofa.

"I'm still mayor," he said and gestured to the lavishly appointed room. "Even under house arrest, I am always working for the people of Lindavista."

As planned, Cardenas set up the recording and began the interview, focusing on Avila. The questions weren't much different than what the mayor had been asked before, but Cardenas was much more skilled than their previous interrogator, Lieutenant Camacho, whom Avila admitted was still in prison.

Pilar did not acknowledge Emilia next to her on the sofa. The woman could have been a glass statue; perfectly composed, perfectly coiffed, perfectly aloof in a sleeveless white dress with a high neck and jazzy high-heeled sandals that called attention to the tracking device tethered to her ankle.

Emilia watched as Cardenas led first Pedro Avila, then Pilar, through the questions, trying to find a mistake or hidden link. Both were ready, having had a year, and their stories were watertight. Blame fell on the police and the ill-advised relationship with the El Choque "security club." Neither Avila knew what had happened to the bodies of the 43 students, but pointed out that Lindavista was making massive efforts to help the sorry little village of Amistad recover. A party with free beer, a clothing drive, a road paving project, and a grant of children's books for the primary school in the name of the people of Lindavista. All very well received, of course.

When Cardenas was done with his questions, Emilia turned to Pilar. "I understand your sister Adelita visited when you were detained."

"It was allowed," Pilar said quickly.

"That was very kind of her." Emilia smiled. Pilar was a block of ice; the woman wasn't going to give up any insights about the Santa Muerte worry beads unless Emilia established some sort of rapport. "I know visiting a detention center can be upsetting to some people."

"Adelita wasn't upset," Pilar said. "Family has to stick together in trying times. When falsely accused."

"Isn't her husband Erik Flores?" Emilia hoped she sounded sincere. "He owns the bus service that's the center of this whole controversy."

"Not through any fault of theirs," Pilar said with heat.

"Poor Erik has had a terrible time of it. He lost thousands of pesos because of what happened to his buses."

"And your sister didn't blame either of you for her family's financial troubles?" Emilia looked from Pilar to Pedro.

"Of course not." Pilar gave her head an indignant little shake that reminded Emilia of a parrot ruffling its feathers. "She's my sister. This is the fault of the police and only the police. I hope as soon as your report makes that point they'll take this ridiculous monitor off my leg and restore my husband's reputation."

"You and your sister must be very close," Emilia said, refusing to be diverted by the woman's little tantrum.

"Yes, we are."

"Is she older or younger?"

"Four years older."

"You're so lucky to have an older sister," Emilia said. She gave a little sigh and let the lie slip off her tongue. "I had to be the one to do everything first. Horrible peach lipstick. White pantyhose. Boyfriends with fast cars."

Pilar gave a little laugh and thawed a fraction.

Emilia flicked a look in Cardenas's direction. Pilar automatically glanced his way, too. On cue, Cardenas looked irritated.

The two women were suddenly united in resistance to the unfeeling police lieutenant. Emilia chose a uniquely feminine topic to nudge along the nascent goodwill. "Did your sister help plan your *quinceañera*? I have to come up with something for my niece and I've never done anything like that."

Pilar brightened and Emilia felt a thrill of triumph. "I can show you," the woman said.

As Pilar rose from the sofa and went to the bookcase, Emilia tried to catch Cardenas's eye. But he appeared for all intents and purposes to be wrestling with the audio program on a task force laptop, while oblivious to Pedro Avila's death stare.

Pilar returned to the sofa with a faded red scrapbook. "We had my *quinceañera* Mass at the cathedral," she said. "I was baptized there, too. The party was at the Princesa Maria Victoria hotel all night long, with a champagne breakfast in the morning."

Emilia made convincing impressed noises as Pilar reverently turned the pages of the scrap book. The snapshots were tucked into little black photo corners glued to the heavy scrapbook paper and mostly showed groups of people in overwrought ball gowns and pastel polyester tuxedos. Emilia's own coming out party had been non-existent; on her 15th birthday she was selling candy at the entrance to the Maxitunel to pay school fees. There was no money to squander on hotel ballrooms and lavish parties.

Pilar's finger slid down a page of six pictures and rested on her teenaged self in a pale blue tulle gown with a full skirt. Her hair was piled on top of her head and adorned with matching blue silk daisies. "I thought I was so elegant," she laughed.

"Did Adelita help pick out your dress?" Emilia asked, maneuvering for an opening.

"She helped with everything," Pilar replied. She tapped a picture of a big crowd of people. "Here she is."

"Which one is she?"

"There's a better one. Just the two of us." Pilar impatiently turned the page and a dozen pictures spewed to the floor by Emilia's feet along with a shower of brittle black crimped corners. "Oh, *por Dios*!"

"The glue must have dried," Emilia said. "I'll get them."

She scooped up the snapshots and quickly sifted through them as Pilar turned another page and fretted over the state of the album. The best photo was of Pilar in her puffy gown linking arms with a taller girl in a royal blue outfit with white silk rosebuds sprinkled across the bodice. The face was obscured by hideous blue eyeshadow and loops of brunette ringlets.

Emilia flipped over the picture to see if there was a label. Someone had written *Pilar Garay Villahermosa and Adelita Garay Luna: Preciosas!* The date of the *quinceañera* was penned below.

"Give those to me," Pilar said, as if Emilia had gotten fingerprints all over the photographs.

"Here you go," Emilia said and dropped the pictures on the table. Her own voice seemed to come from far away. "No harm done."

"Yes, that's the picture I was looking for." Pilar snatched up the picture of the two young women in blue. "We talked for hours about what color Adelita was going to wear. So when you start to make plans for your niece, decide on a theme color. Make sure no one wears the same shade as the birthday girl. Hers should be the lightest."

"The lightest," Emilia echoed. She watched Pilar put the picture back in the album while thinking furiously how to frame a question to obscure the intent. "You and your sister look very much alike," she began cautiously. "Do you . . . do you take after your father or your mother?"

"Our father," Adelita said. "We're actually half sisters."

Across the room, Pedro Avila cleared his throat. Pilar shut the album in a marked signal that the conversation was over.

"Thank you for your advice," Emilia said but the tiny bit of girl-to-girl rapport was gone.

The mayor stalked over to the sofa and put his hand on his wife's shoulder. Pilar remained sitting.

"How much longer are we going to have to endure this ridiculous house arrest?" Avila asked.

Cardenas stowed his laptop in its case and stood. "The Attorney General's office will be in touch with your attorneys at the proper time," he replied. He turned to Emilia. "Are you quite finished, Detective?"

"Yes." Emilia stood.

Cardenas gave the Avilas a curt nod. As when they arrived, no handshakes were offered or expected. Emilia resisted the urge to run as they followed the maid through the house and out the front door. The SUV with driver and bodyguard was still parked in front.

"We had to do it," Cardenas said as he buckled his seat belt. "But I didn't hear anything new out of Avila or his wife. He's a cunning bastard and this house arrest is a joke. What about you?"

Anticipation rippled through Emilia's veins. She fastened her own belt and tapped the driver on the shoulder. "Take us to the cathedral by the Plaza Bolivar."

CHAPTER 39

"To quote Captain Elizondo," Cardenas said. "This is not what I was expecting."

"Shut up," Emilia replied. "Keep looking for someone named Luna. It's not a common name, so it should stand out."

The leather ledgers stacked on shelves in the ancient stone-sided basement of the cathedral were more or less what she'd expected. The cathedral had adopted digital record-keeping ten years ago. For the four hundred years before that, the history of Catholic life in Lindavista had been written out by priests in ruled ledgers custom-made for that purpose.

To capture births, baptisms, marriages.

And deaths.

The secretary in charge of the cathedral's offices was loath to let the two police officers comb through the ancient books unsupervised, but Cardenas turned on the charm and won her over. Now they were crammed into the storage vault, surrounded on three sides by shelves of dusty ledgers. Every time they opened a new book, both Emilia and Cardenas sneezed repeatedly.

"They called it Black Lung in the Middle Ages," Cardenas grumbled after another bout, his eyes streaming.

Emilia answered with a fit of coughing.

From the task force files, they knew the year that Pilar

Garay de Avila was born. Cardenas pulled out the ledgers for the previous five years. Three hours later, Emilia found the simple entry recording the death of Monica Luna Fonseca and her burial outside the parish in the city of her birth."

Emilia copied down the name, date of death, and the inscription from the ledger. They kept going backwards in time, running fingers over the lines of fading ink. As the cathedral bells pealed to announce evening Mass, Cardenas found the entry for the baptism of Adelita Garay Luna, born to Ronaldo Garay Garcia and Monica Luna Fonseca.

"Adelita's mother died when she was almost three," Cardenas said. "Garay didn't waste much time. He must have married Pilar's mother right afterwards."

"We'd better go." Emilia closed the ledger in front of her, sending a grimy puff into the air. "The woman said they closed the cathedral after the evening Mass."

Cardenas sneezed so hard he almost fell off the rickety wooden chair.

They left the cathedral with the priest's final blessing in their ears. "I need food," Emilia said as Cardenas pulled open the heavy wooden door. "Time to think."

"I need a beer," Cardenas said. "Something to wash down the liter of dust I've swallowed."

He steered them across the Plaza Bolivar to the café and bought beer and thick *jamón Serrano* and tomato sandwiches. Emilia selected a table with a view of the bus station and took a long cold swallow of beer.

"This isn't a real meal," Cardenas said. "Just something to tide us over. Speaking of, did you notice that Judge Sarmiento never eats anything?"

"Too stressed." Emilia bit into the crusty roll and spiced ham, holding it with one hand while digging out her cell phone with the other.

"I thought maybe she'd fucked up the task force," Cardenas said. "On purpose. Took a bribe to fund her husband's campaign. But if that was true, he wouldn't have withdrawn from the race."

"Forget the judge," Emilia said. "She's in the dictionary under 'Incompetent.'" She opened the browser application and tapped in a name.

"What are you doing?" Cardenas polished off his first sandwich.

"She's his mother, you know," Emilia said.

"Who's mother?"

"Diego Barrielos Luna," Emilia said quietly. "The stories about him always mention the abusive father who raised him and the mother who abandoned him."

"Who abandoned him?" Cardenas paused, his beer bottle halfway to his lips.

"Monica Luna Fonseca," Emilia supplied. She slid the phone across the small table to Cardenas, so he could read the article in an online pop culture magazine. "The unknown mother is part of his narrative. The Barrel Bomber abandoned as a toddler, as if it explains his violence. This is her, I'd bet any money on it."

"Fuck me," Cardenas sputtered. "Do you think they're all related? Is that what this is all about?"

"Keep your voice down," Emilia said.

Monica had abandoned her son Diego, who grew up to become the Barrel Bomber, the same way Emilia's mother Sophia abandoned the son who grew up to become El Acólito.

Emilia put down her sandwich. The parallel between the two men turned it into ashes in her mouth.

"Okay, okay," Cardenas said. "*Rayos,* I can't believe this."

"I think if we found the church records for the village where Barrielos Luna was born," Emilia said. "We'd find that Monica Luna Fonseca first married a man named Barrielos."

Cardenas scrolled through the article. "Mateo Barrielos. The abusive father."

"Whatever." Emilia took the phone. Barrielos Senior was a minor character in the drama unfolding in her mind. "Monica has a son, Diego. But she can't stay. Maybe Mateo beats her. Whatever. She leaves the kid, runs away and comes to Lindavista."

"Where she meets Garay," Cardenas jumped in. "Marries him. Has Adelita and dies. For whatever reason, Garay sends her body to her hometown to be buried instead of burying her here."

Emilia stared at Cardenas. "*Madre de Dios,*" she said. "She was still married to Barrielos. They never divorced. I'll bet she was never really married to Garay. That's bigamy. He couldn't bury her with a sin like that in sacred ground. Everybody would know. Little Adelita would carry the burden of her mother's sin for the rest of her life."

"All right." Cardenas was keeping up. "So Garay solves the problem by burying Monica in her hometown. There's a funeral. Garay has little Adelita with him. Diego finds out he has a baby sister."

Emilia glanced at the dates she'd copied from the cathedral records and did some mental math. "He must have been 13 or 14 when his mother died."

"They both grow up." Cardenas swallowed the last of his sandwich. "Somewhere along the line, Diego reunites with his baby sister, Adelita."

"Who in turn connects him with her ambitious half sister, Pilar, and Pilar's up-and-coming husband Pedro." Emilia looked around at the ornate outdoor café, the well-maintained plaza. The pots of red geraniums. "That's why there's so much money floating around Lindavista," she whispered. "It's subsidized by Barrielos Luna."

"How does this tie into the missing students?" Cardenas asked. "Barrielos Luna was caught months before the showdown here. Don't you remember? Big army raid on his compound in the Sierra Madre mountains. Hermanos100 scattered to the wind and he's been in prison ever since."

Twilight deepened into early darkness. White lights strung across Plaza Bolivar switched on, giving the place a festive air. At the base of the statue, a busker began to play the violin, the instrument case open for donations at his feet. A man pushed an ice cream cart across the cobblestones, his bell tinkling merrily. People flowed from the cathedral into the square. Children made a beeline for the ice cream vendor while a balloon artist twisted tubes or air into skinny dogs and graceful swans for 20 pesos apiece.

"What if they're wrong?" Emilia asked.

"Who?" Cardenas asked. "The Avilas?"

"No." Emilia tipped the last of her beer into her mouth. The connection to the 43 missing students was there, but every time she reached for it, the answer slid away. Connecting the names had come quickly but now she felt slow and stupid. "The people who say Hermanos100 is broken. No longer a threat."

"*Rayos*." Cardenas rubbed a hand across his face. "You think Adelita's been running things for her brother while he's in jail?"

"I don't know," Emilia said helplessly. "But maybe that's why Pilar was so comforted by the Santa Muerte worry beads when she was in jail. They were like a message from Diego."

"Worry beads? You've lost me."

"In the video of her second interview." Emilia quickly related the discovery she and Anaya had made while watching Pilar's interview footage, which Cardenas had not seen.

"All right." Cardenas toyed with his empty beer bottle. "Pilar gets the message that everything is going to work out.

Adelita and Diego have everything under control. But he's still in jail. How does this help us find out what happened to the missing 43?"

"I don't know." There was no comfort in the words.

Cardenas got up and went to the café counter. When he returned with two more beers, Emilia narrowed her eyes at him. "Say what you said again."

"What did I say?" He drank a long swallow.

"Something about Adelita being in control."

"You're the one who said she could be running Hermanos100 now," he pointed out.

"What if she is?" The answer was there, if Emilia stretched hard enough she could touch it, grasp it, make a tight fist around it. "What if she primed seven *sicarios* to confess and take the heat off the real culprit?"

"Create a smokescreen with seven identical confessions?"

"She didn't know they'd be such morons to repeat the script word-for-word," Emilia theorized. "She just needed to distract attention."

"Okay, let's go with that." Cardenas cocked his head at her. "Which falls apart when we ask why they'd agree to confess if they weren't guilty."

"Like you've never run into a false confession before." Emilia rolled her eyes. "They agreed to do it to protect somebody else and knew they'd end up in Multifoco with the Bomber. Nothing too bad would happen to them besides getting beat up to confess. Once they got to Multifoco,

Barrielos Luna would take care of them."

"Is that why the warden got killed?" Cardenas asked thoughtfully. "Did he stand in the way?"

"Probably."

"Okay," Cardenas said. "Suppose we're on the right track. Pilar and Adelita and Diego are all half siblings. Adelita is running Hermanos100 while her brother is in jail. Reassures her sister when things get hot in Lindavista and gets seven idiots to lie in order to cover up for somebody else."

"Yes," Emilia agreed.

"So who are they all protecting?" Cardenas pressed. "Not the Lindavista police chief. They've thrown him to the wolves already. Mayor Avila? Adelita's husband Erik Flores? Who else is worth so much trouble?"

Across the street, the brightly lit bus station was doing a brisk evening trade. Six buses in their red, gold, and white Flores Transito livery waited under the awning. Inside the station, people swirled around the counter, purchasing tickets and waiting for their rides.

"Someone must have sat here," Emilia said. "Watching the front of the station that night. That's why they missed the bus coming out the other gate. It's not what was important about the maintenance area. It's what's so important about the buses leaving out the front."

"All the buses leave out the front," Cardenas countered. "Why should anybody watch?"

Emilia didn't answer. She pushed herself to reach farther,

to get the tip of her finger on the elusive answer.

A bus rumbled out of the station. The cleaning woman assiduously mopped the floor in its wake.

"I worked a smuggling case once," Emilia heard herself say. In her mind's eye, her fist curled around the answer and held on tight. "They'd built a tunnel alongside the Maxitunel into Acapulco. Used it to move drugs hidden inside water jugs."

"It's late, Detective." Cardenas tipped the last of his second beer into his mouth. "I'll pass on the trip down memory lane."

"Do you know what's the hardest part about digging a tunnel?" Emilia asked.

Cardenas sighed. "All right. I'll play along. Let's see. Not having it collapse?"

"No," Emilia said. "Getting rid of all the dirt."

CHAPTER 40

"An escape tunnel for Diego Barrielos Luna between the Multifoco prison and the bus station," Miranda repeated. "Using the Flores Transito buses to carry away the construction debris."

"That's why the police had to stop the buses," Cardenas said. "They were full of fucking dirt. The students commandeered the buses but no one knew where to or for how long. If the students did find the dirt, it would be easy to guess where it came from."

Miranda nodded, catching on quickly. "Which means that when Avila ordered the police to turn the kids over to the gang, he knew full well there would be no survivors. He was helping the sister-in-law dig a tunnel to get her famous big brother out of jail."

"Think of the network analysis with Barrielos Luna in the middle instead of the Avilas," Emilia said. "They all connect to him. He's the hub."

"You're right," Miranda said.

"Adelita's husband is in on it, of course," Emilia said. "Using the buses and the station was brilliant. With her sister Pilar and the mayor's office protecting them, even supplying a night watchman, it would have gone off without a hitch if it hadn't been for the students from Amistad."

"*Jesu Cristo*," Anaya muttered.

"Go back to the family," Elizondo said. "We've got to be

rock solid with these connections. Lindavista mayor Pedro Avila is married to Pilar, who is half sister to the wife of Erik Flores, who owns the transport concession for the city?"

"Adelita Garay de Flores," Cardenas supplied. "Whose half brother is the Barrel Bomber. Adelita and Barrielos Luna have the same mother. Pilar and Adelita have the same father."

All five of the task force members were crowded into Elizondo's hotel room in an effort to avoid Ramirez. Elizondo was in the desk chair, while Miranda and Anaya were propped against the desk and dresser. Cardenas lounged against the wall, his posture hiding his obvious excitement. Emilia perched on the edge of the bed, her heart beating like a jackhammer.

"This tunnel you say is being built." Elizondo looked at Emilia. "How long would it be?"

"Two miles," Emilia said. "A straight line from the Plaza Bolivar to the prison."

"A tunnel." Elizondo rubbed his neck as if it was stiff. "Under the highway and a ravine full of water."

"It's possible." Anaya nodded and shifted his weight restlessly. "I've seen longer and deeper going across the border with *El Norte*."

"How long would it take to build such a tunnel?" Elizondo asked.

Anaya shrugged. "Better part of two years, probably."

"About how long Barrielos Luna has been in Multifoco," Cardenas reminded the group.

"The bus station is the perfect cover," Emilia insisted. "People coming and going all the time. Buses to haul away the dirt. A cleaning crew to mop up behind."

"The weak link here," Elizondo said. "Is that the half sister would be running the Hermanos100 cartel. There's no evidence to suggest that's true."

"But what if it is?" Miranda mused.

Emilia jumped to her feet. *Por Dios*, why hadn't she seen it earlier? Barrielos could be on a bus right now, laughing all the way to freedom, that slick *pendejo* Lennox by his side. Thanks to her, they both knew that Adelita had come to the interest of the task force. The race was on to finish the tunnel and get Barrielos Luna and his seven disciples out of Multifoco.

"The tunnel is almost done," she blurted. "As soon as we leave Lindavista, they're going to get him out."

Elizondo's face tightened at her rudeness.

"If they started building as soon as he got to Multifoco," Anaya said. "She could be right."

"That doesn't mean they're ready to pull the trigger," Elizondo countered.

Emilia took a deep breath. "When we were in Mexico City, I was approached by a man claiming to be a diplomat from the United States embassy. He offered me a bribe to get the task force to finish early."

Elizondo rocketed out of his chair. Miranda's raised hand stopped the other man from speaking so that Emilia could continue.

"He made it sound like a reward, but I went to the embassy and made inquiries." She found the picture of Lennox framed in the doorway of the Saint Regis in her phone's photo gallery. "He isn't a diplomat. I don't know who he is besides a good actor. I assumed he worked for the Avilas. They had the most to gain from the task force accepting the Attorney General's previous findings and ending early."

Emilia handed her phone to Elizondo, aware of Cardenas staring at her in open shock.

After a moment, Miranda took the phone and gave a start when he looked at the picture on the screen. "I've seen this man," Miranda exclaimed. "He made conversation with me in the Starbucks in Mexico City. Has anyone else?"

He passed the phone to Anaya, who barely glanced at it and shook his head. Cardenas didn't take the phone when Anaya offered, instead muttering "No," while staring fixedly at Emilia.

Elizondo ended up with the device. "I presume you turned him down, Detective," he said coldly.

"I've never taken a bribe," Emilia said, torn between urgency and regret. "But he was quite convincing."

Adelita must have been desperate when she heard the task force was coming. The visit to Lindavista messed with the timetable to complete the tunnel. As long as the task force was in the city, there was too much attention on the bus station to whisk Barrielos Luna through it. At the same time, every day the tunnel was unused, the risk of discovery and failure went up. Hiring someone to pressure task force members as a representative of the powerful United States was quite ingenious.

"What excuse did he give for wanting the task force out of Lindavista early?" Miranda pressed.

Emilia nodded. "He told me it was because Judge Sarmiento was too distracted by the task force to negotiate Barrielos Luna's extradition."

The room was suddenly airless as all four men sucked in their breath in sudden stunned understanding. Cardenas slumped onto the bed.

"They need to get him through the tunnel before the extradition goes through," Elizondo said.

He tossed the phone to Emilia. She barely caught it.

"If we call the *federales* to raid the bus station and we're wrong," Elizondo said. "The task force is done. And the career of every person in this room as well."

Emilia's knees felt like rubber. She lowered herself to the end of the bed next to Cardenas. Her whole body vibrated from the tension bouncing off the four walls of the cramped bedroom.

"We've already put our careers on the line," Miranda pointed out. "By speaking to the families and hiding it from Ramirez."

"If we don't get in there," Cardenas argued, without acknowledging Emilia next to him. "They're going to get Barrielos Luna and the seven dwarves out of prison and we're going to look like fools."

Anaya unscrewed the top of his hip flask and took a drink.

"What about a vote?" Elizondo proposed. "Do we call in the *federales* or not?"

Emilia rubbed her eyes. They were all drained from the things they'd heard and seen that week; the disgusting dump, the anger and desperation of the families, the smug shit spoon-fed to them by the Avilas and men in prison.

"Maybe there's a middle way," Miranda said.

CHAPTER 41

"This guy Lennox," Cardenas said. "He's not the one you're taking a break from, is he?"

"Of course not," Emilia huffed. "He's some con artist who approached me in the Starbucks in Mexico City, just like Miranda. Why on earth would you think he was Kurt?"

"What kind of a name is Kurt?" Cardenas asked.

"Kurt Rucker," Emilia supplied, as she slid the task force laptop into its case. "He's a *gringo*. From New York. He manages the Palacio Réal hotel in Acapulco."

They were in the small dining room the hotel had provided for the task force's use, getting ready to implement the first part of Miranda's plan. Elizondo had left the hotel early that morning to make arrangements. Anaya would handle the last interviews with the men in Multifoco who'd given the duplicate confessions; his errand wrapped up the official schedule. Miranda remained in the hotel to draft a press report for Ramirez to pass to Judge Sarmiento that the task force was wrapping things up today in Lindavista and heading back to Mexico City tomorrow.

"No kidding." Cardenas gave a funny laugh. "I pictured you with another cop."

"Why are we talking about this now?"

"Because if your guy was this Lennox guy we'd be in trouble."

"I haven't betrayed the task force," Emilia said angrily.

Cardenas held up his hands in mock surrender. "Okay, I get it," he said. "But this habit of yours of leaking information in bits and pieces isn't exactly confidence building."

"That's not really the problem." Emilia stared at him. "The problem is that my private life is still private and I'm still not sleeping with you."

"What makes you think I'm so interested in your private life?" Cardenas began stacking files.

"You've been sulking since I told everybody about Lennox the other night," Emilia retorted. "I should have told you about Lennox first, right? Because you've staked your claim. In some weird way, because you want to sleep with me, I belong to you and that goes for everything I know about this case, too."

Cardenas slammed down a pile of folders as color rushed into his face. Papers spilled across the table and slithered to the floor. "You're way out of line, Detective."

Emilia clenched her fists by her sides. "But not wrong, eh, Lieutenant?"

Cardenas's jaw tightened in embarrassment. "I have not staked a claim. You're a cop, not a silver mine in Taxco."

"Thank you," Emilia said stiffly. She gathered up the papers.

Cardenas helped and in a minute they had reassembled the files. It didn't matter what order the papers ended up on; all the printouts, newspaper clippings, and handwritten notes were only for effect.

Flores Transito was housed in a five story building a few blocks west of the Plaza Bolivar and within walking distance of the city offices. The SUV swung into a visitor parking lot in the front of the building and the bodyguard hopped out to open the rear door. Emilia swung the laptop case strap onto her shoulder while Cardenas lugged the file box full of impressively thick folders.

The bodyguard came with them, making for a noticeable little parade as they entered the lobby. The task force had been successfully low key since arriving in Lindavista. But now, as Miranda insisted, they needed to go out in a blaze of attention.

Erik Flores's secretary came to the lobby to escort Emilia and Cardenas to an office on the top floor. They left the elevator, moved down a thickly carpeted hallway, and passed through a reception area. The style of the place was modern, with walnut wood furniture that looked like the overpriced stuff from Denmark in one of Kurt's hospitality magazines. The walls were pale blue and decorated with the same giant geranium logo plastered over the all-too familiar Flores Transito buses.

The secretary opened a set of double doors. Emilia walked ahead of Cardenas and his box of fake files and found herself nose-to-nose with the female version of the Barrel Bomber.

Like her half brother, Adelita Garay Luna de Flores had wavy hair, hooded eyes, straight brows, and a restless energy that filled the air like a static charge. Adelita made the most of her best feature with black eyeliner, shimmering pale shadow, and thick mascara. Taller than average, she wore a sleeveless belted red shirtdress that showed off tanned, muscular arms. She didn't have any tattoos.

Introductions were made and coffee was brought in as if this was a social call. Emilia made a production about setting up the task force laptop, while Cardenas fussed over the files he would be using as reference to guide the interview.

Adelita seemed perfectly at ease as she served coffee from the sideboard in her husband's office. If she knew Emilia had mentioned her name to her jailed brother, she certainly didn't show it.

Erik Flores was as buffed and toned as his wife in a yellow polo shirt and dark green cotton slacks. There were a few streaks of gray in his hair which the picture on the Flores Transito website hadn't revealed. Emilia wondered if the streaks were there for effect, a sign of his distress since the disappearance of the 43 students.

"Well of course, we want to be as helpful as possible," Flores said as he accepted a cup of rich-smelling coffee from his wife. "As I told Adelita just the other day, an impartial look at the whole mess was just what was needed. There's been too much bias on the part of the Attorney General's office."

"Shocking, so shocking," Adelita said. Her voice was low for a woman. She poured another cup and handed it to Emilia.

"To think of such things happening here in Lindavista,"

said Flores. "It's actually been quite hard to believe."

Emilia managed a brave smile to show she was on their side. "Lindavista is such a pretty city."

Adelita made sure Cardenas had cream and sugar for his coffee before seating them all in plush armchairs arranged around a small conference table. A large round silver tray held an assortment of framed pictures in lieu of a decorative centerpiece. Most of the pictures were variations on the family photo showcased on the Flores Transito website. Adelita, Erik, two children, horses and dogs. Others featured a lovely *hacienda* nestled amid pines by a gravel road.

Flores saw Emilia eyeing a panoramic view of pasture and lake at the foot of a craggy peak. "That's our ranch," he said. "We raise Sardo Negro cattle. Here."

He plucked one of the smaller frames out of the tray and handed it to her. A black and white cow with big drooping ears stared mournfully into the distance. "Very nice," Emilia said and showed the photo to Cardenas.

"We like to take the children out there," Flores said, replacing the picture after Cardenas murmured approval. "Make them understand the value of hard work."

"They both love to ride," Adelita added. "We have miles of trails."

"How lovely," Emilia said and woke the laptop screen.

Cardenas opened a folder stuffed with newspaper clippings. "Neither of you were arrested in connection with the events of 24 September, is that right?"

"Of course not," Flores said firmly. "I made a statement

to the authorities, of course. It was my company's buses that were hijacked, after all. But that is the extent of the Flores family's involvement."

"We lost hundreds of pesos," Adelita said. "But no one has been interested in hearing about that."

"I see, I see," Cardenas muttered. "Shall we start at the beginning? Tell us about that day. September 24. What did you do that morning, Señor Flores?"

Totally at ease, Flores recounted the sort of normal day that put him in the running for husband and father of the year. He brought his wife coffee in bed, supervised the children as they got dressed, and waved them off as the chauffeur took them to school. He and Adelita played tennis at the club that morning, which led to some friendly banter about who'd been the winner. Emilia felt an eye begin to twitch as Flores and Adelita slapped each other playfully.

"And after tennis?" Cardenas prompted, frowning at his supposed notes.

"I came to the office," Flores said. "Adelita had a luncheon with friends to plan a birthday party."

"Not just any party," Adelita smiled, showing perfectly straight white teeth. "Our son was turning 16."

"I recall her saying it had to be a man-sized party." Flores beamed proudly.

"Did you go to the Caritas Señoras rally in the zocalo?"

"No," Adelita said, a bit too fast.

Emilia gave into the urge to editorialize as she typed.

"Let's leap ahead a bit," Cardenas said. "At what time did

you hear that students from Amistad were at the bus station?"

"Quite late in the day," Flores said blandly. "The station manager called the police first, which of course as we now know, was probably a mistake."

"But you knew quite soon after?" Cardenas asked leadingly.

"Well, when everyone else knew."

The next three hours was more of the same. Cardenas asked non-threatening questions designed to imply that the task force was barely competent and Flores pretended to take them seriously. Emilia acted as note taker and sized up the woman across from her.

Adelita had the same raw energy as Barrielos Luna, the same shark-like smile. Barrielos Luna instinctively scrutinized everything and everyone around him like a predatory desert animal approaching a water hole. Adelita was the same, Emilia was sure, but had learned to hide her ruthlessness behind the carefully made up face and classy clothing. For the woman every interaction was a chess match, a game of strategy to win, an opportunity to destroy an opponent.

The one exception might be the husband. Flores and his wife appeared evenly matched on all levels.

In a way that Emilia couldn't quite define, they completely overshadowed Lindavista mayor Pedro Avila and his wife Pilar. Adelita and Erik were a thundering wind; Pilar and Pedro were the corn flattened before it.

"Your sister is Pilar Garay de Avila," Emilia said to Adelita when Cardenas finished his questions.

"Yes." Adelita clasped her hands. She wore a ring with a diamond roughly the size of Emilia's head.

"You visited her in prison."

"She was in an appalling situation," Adelita said.

"This must be so hard for you." Emilia worked her facial muscles into a sad frown. "To see her first in prison, and now under house arrest."

Adelita sighed. "We're placing great faith in your task force's ability to see reason. It's not for us to say who is guilty but we certainly know who is not and that includes my sister."

Cardenas kicked Emilia under the table. "I think we're done here, Detective."

Emilia straightened in her seat; the urge to press Adelita about Diego Barrielos Luna was almost overwhelming.

"Will you be needing to speak with my drivers?" Flores asked. "The station manager?"

How about your cleaning crew? Emilia bit her tongue.

"*Oye*, no," Cardenas said, playing the handsome idiot act almost too well. "We don't need to bother them."

"We don't have time," Emilia said. Her mental meter dinged; she couldn't keep up the sympathetic façade any longer. "The task force departs Lindavista tomorrow."

She watched as Adelita and Flores both froze. It was only for the fraction of a second, for the blink of an eye, but it happened. They thawed into exaggerated poses of relaxation. Flores settled his shoulders more comfortably in his chair while Adelita crossed her legs. A sandal-clad foot bopped to celebratory music only she heard.

"Yes," Cardenas said. "We head to Mexico City tomorrow morning. We're sure that we've collected all the critical information. If we can wrap this up early, we can all go home early, too."

"Maybe life can get back to normal around here," Flores said. "For you, too, of course. No doubt you'll be glad to get home."

Maybe it was Emilia's imagination, but relief—as subtle as a wafting scent— hung in the air.

The secretary came to escort them to the lobby and the waiting bodyguard. As Emilia walked out of the office, she wondered how long Adelita would wait before calling Lennox with the news.

He texted Emilia four hours later. The cell phone was set to Vibrate, making it rattle against the table next to Emilia's plate.

Elizondo nodded at her. "Just follow the script, Detective," he said.

The five members of the task force were gathered in the small dining room in the hotel eating a hasty meal. Ramirez was in his room with a stomach complaint, which led to a few morbid jokes from Cardenas, but it also meant they could speak freely.

Emilia clicked open the message application. Lennox was asking about the status of the task force, using the same language he'd done the other times. She took a deep breath and texted him that the task force was returning to Mexico City the next day.

Good news for me? Lennox replied.

99% certain will wrap soon.

Bounty is still available.

Glad to hear it.

Emilia read out the abbreviated dialogue.

"Reel him in, Detective," Miranda murmured.

Emilia suggested drinks at the Saint Regis tomorrow night.

Lenox texted quickly: *To celebrate?*

To talk $$$.

Both?

Maybe ☺.

Lennox answered with a thumb's up emoji.

Emilia felt shaky as she tapped the application to close it. "All set," she said. "We're meeting tomorrow night at the Saint Regis bar at 8:00 pm."

"Good," Elizondo said shortly.

Anaya wiped his mouth with the back of his hand. "I don't think this is fair to Cruz," he said to Emilia's surprise. "She was the one who figured out the whole tunnel scheme. She should be on the raid to find it."

"He'll expect to see me," Emilia said. She was the bait for

Lennox, whose unknown connections potentially made him very dangerous.

"Let me go instead," Anaya said to Elizondo. "This *pendejo* doesn't have to see Cruz. The cops in Mexico City just need someone who can finger this guy so they can pick him up."

"You haven't seen him," Elizondo pointed out. "You might not recognize him."

"I have." Miranda tossed down his napkin and joined the discussion. "And I agree with Detective Anaya. Detective Cruz should have the honor of participating in the raid. Without her, we'd never have gotten to this point."

Elizondo raised his eyebrows at the other captain.

"Detective Anaya and I will stay in Mexico City," Miranda said firmly. "We'll make the meeting at the Saint Regis and ensure that Lennox gets taken into custody tomorrow night."

"Does that work for you, Detective?" Elizondo asked Emilia.

"Yes." Emilia smiled gratefully at the two men across the table. "Thank you."

"That's settled then," Anaya said.

CHAPTER 42

The task force left Lindavista the next morning at 6:00, Ramirez unwittingly making a useful scene by complaining about the early start in the middle of the lobby. The same car arrangements prevailed as on the outward trip. Emilia was paired with Elizondo. They had with little to say that could be safely overheard by the driver and bodyguard, so silence prevailed. That was fine with Emilia.

With no reason to stop, they were in Mexico City by midday. After telling Ramirez they'd see him in the morning in the office, the five task force members checked into the Sheraton again. Emilia showered and topped jeans and cross trainers with a gray tee shirt and black denim jacket. She stuffed her toothbrush, two pairs of underwear, another tee, and all the tiny liquor bottles from the minibar into her shoulder bag before heading downstairs.

A taxi took her to the Centro Santa Fe on the western side of the city. The mall was huge and Emilia was glad she wasn't there to shop.

She saw Cardenas first, standing in front of the busy Crepes and Waffles restaurant, in jeans and a khaki bomber jacket, with a leather messenger bag slung across his chest. Elizondo arrived a minute later, with a knapsack.

Elizondo looked at his watch. "Barring unforeseen trouble," he said. "We'll make the rendezvous with an hour to spare."

He led them out of the mall and through a parking lot lit by the glow of a towering Palacio de Hierro department store sign. They piled into a rented Suburban, Emilia stretching out in the rear seat while Elizondo drove and Cardenas rode shotgun.

"Last chance for a no-go," Elizondo said loud enough for all to hear.

Neither Emilia nor Cardenas spoke.

The Michoacán *federales* met them at 7:00 pm in a small police station about 40 miles from Lindavista. They spoke for an hour around a battered conference table. Both Elizondo and the *federale* captain constantly checked their watches and the latter fielded a dozen calls on his cell phone. Emilia was so nervous she wanted to scream while Cardenas's knee pumped up and down furiously the whole time.

"You were right about that Lindavista cop," the *federale* captain said. "Lieutenant Camacho is loyal to the mayor and the chief of police in Lindavista, but there's bad blood between him and Erik Flores. Apparently, this Camacho was an admirer of Flores's wife back in the day and knew she was related to the Barrel Bomber."

"He chose to go to jail for collusion rather than admit the truth?" Elizondo asked.

"Nobody wants the Barrel Bomber or his sister after

them," the *federale* captain said.

"Did he admit that a tunnel is being built to Multifoco?"

"It took a couple of hours," the captain admitted. "But he finally broke. Just like you said. Excavated dirt gets loaded onto buses and dumped in a landfill south of the city. The students grabbed buses that had just been filled up. It was a case of bad timing. The chief of police panicked, thought the students had taken the buses on purpose."

"To expose the tunnel and the escape plan for Barrielos Luna."

"Yes."

"Flores paid the cops well," Elizondo said leadingly.

"Sure." The *federale* captain rubbed his forehead. It had obviously been a long day for him already. "Until now all of them kept their mouths shut. Let the morons who confessed take the heat and didn't rough them up too bad in gratitude." He checked his watch again. "We've had an undercover team in the Plaza Bolivar all day watching the bus station and so far, it's business as usual. Same at the Flores Transito offices—."

"What about the Flores ranch?" Emilia interrupted.

"It'll take us a couple of days to cover it," the *federale* captain said, clearly annoyed that she'd picked out the weak spot in his capabilities.

"Our priority right now is stopping Diego Barrielos Luna from escaping again," Elizondo reminded Emilia. "If we can do that, there will be time enough tomorrow for the rest."

Cardenas's knee was jiggling so fast Emilia wondered if

he was going to spiral up into the air, like a kid's toy helicopter. "I can't wait to surprise these motherfuckers," he said grimly.

"Keep it together, Lieutenant," she murmured.

Over the next few hours, the *federales* quietly put more assets in place around the Flores residence and offices, as well as the bus station. The captain received continual updates. As she waited, listened, and tried to eat the food supplied by the bewildered local cops whose station had been commandeered, Emilia pictured the scene at the Plaza Bolivar. Children's laughter at the balloon and ice cream vendor, frothy cups of cappuccino served up at the café, tourists pausing to take pictures in front of the museum after it closed for the day, the cathedral having another evening worship. A novena, perhaps.

Hopefully, no one realized that under the surface, Lindavista was preparing for war. Emilia closed her eyes and tried to pray.

Cardenas eventually bled off some of his nervous energy by pacing, but Elizondo wore the tension like a familiar coat. Emilia could tell he'd been through this sort of sting operation before.

She wondered if she'd ever be like that. So accustomed to hard things that neither her emotions nor self-identity could be touched.

At 11:00 pm, an hour before the bus station was scheduled to close for the day, the *federale* captain gave them the go-ahead to continue on to Lindavista. The southeast corner of the Plaza Bolivar, between the museum and the cathedral, was the rendezvous point. Elizondo's rental swung into line behind an unmarked sedan and headed south once more.

This time, the three task force members wore bulletproof vests with POLICIA stenciled across front and back. Everyone was armed.

CHAPTER 43

The Plaza Bolivar was quiet at 2: 00 am. From his seat on the rearing horse high above the ground, Simon Bolivar considered the starry sky. A streetlight by the museum glowed but the festive lights that crisscrossed the four corners of the plaza were dark. The cathedral loomed like a pale mountain.

Two teams of uniformed *federales* with long guns, followed by the three task force members, trotted to the cathedral and halted against the stone walls.

A row of mercury lamps buzzed with soft light near the roofline but otherwise the bus station looked curiously vacant. Big accordion metal doors closed off the archways that during the day were open to foot traffic. On one side of the building, the awning fluttered in the night breeze but no buses were lined up underneath as during the day. Emilia felt herself tense at the thought that they were being filled with dirt in the rear maintenance area right now.

"There'd better be evidence of digging, Detective Cruz," Elizondo said under his breath.

My thoughts exactly. Emilia focused on her breathing so she wouldn't hyperventilate. The air was cool but she was sweating under the bulletproof vest. In comparison to her chest, her head felt exposed and vulnerable in a POLICIA ball cap, but the automatic in her hand was big and reassuring.

The *federale* captain raised his fist in a form-on-me silent signal, then pointed ahead. His 5-person team sprinted to the bus station, leaving the task force members pressed against the cathedral wall. Five seconds later, metal cracked on metal and a steel accordion door slowly clicked up and out of sight. Emilia knew that the door to the rear maintenance area was being jimmied at the same time.

The uniformed *federales* disappeared inside the station. After ten long restless minutes, muffled gunfire whistled through the silence. Elizondo stiffened and all three task force members unconsciously raised hands to their weapons. As Elizondo's radio crackled with an "all clear" from the *federale* captain, a uniform stepped to the now open archway and waved them into the still dark building.

Once inside, the uniform rolled down the metal exterior door, and led them through the main passenger area, past the sales counter and the rows of plastic chairs bolted to the floor. Past the passenger loading zone and through an open door marked Employees Only. They passed through another door and ended up in the garage area. The lights were on, illuminating two huge maintenance bays, each occupied by a partially dismantled Flores Transito bus. The emergency exit doors in the rear and floor of both vehicles had been removed, revealing a long wire cage bolted to the undercarriage ready to be loaded with sacks of dirt.

Two men in grubby coveralls sat on the cement floor. One was bleeding from a shoulder wound. Both were cuffed with their hands behind their backs.

"They're just the night watchmen," the *federale* captain said sarcastically. He held up two push-to-talk radios, smaller and sleeker than the official ones his squad used. "Took these off them, along with handguns. But they both say they don't know a thing."

Emilia looked around. The huge garage bay doors were closed and she had to crane her neck to see the roller mechanism that raised and lowered them. Ceiling fans whipped the air below the double height corrugated metal ceiling. The dismantled buses were parked rear first, no doubt to facilitate loading.

A single shot and accompanying scream made her flinch and spin around. The *federale* captain lowered his handgun. Now both handcuffed men were bleeding profusely. The one with the new wound gasped for air as the other muttered a few words.

The *federale* captain jerked his head at two of his men. A moment later they'd found a door hidden behind a rolling tool chest. One of them shot off the lock and yanked open the door.

The small room had probably started life as a janitorial closet, but now was dominated by a trap door about a meter square set into the floor and hinged on one side. The *federale* captain grasped the rope handle. Two of his men trained rifles on the floor. Everyone else pressed against the walls.

The captain lifted the door. The hinges made no noise and Emilia heard everyone breathe again as it propped open of its own accord. An impressive hole about a meter in diameter gaped beneath.

No explosions or gunfire greeted them.

"*Rayos*," Cardenas said. "There really is a fucking tunnel."

The corner of Elizondo's mouth twitched.

Emilia was speechless.

The opening was ringed with cement; the hole went right through the slab foundation before it hit dirt. Looking down, Emilia saw a ladder bolted to the side that disappeared into the darkness. She estimated the bottom of the hole was at least 20 feet below the surface.

A switch was taped next to the first rung of the ladder. Cardenas bent and flicked it. Lights flickered on. No sounds of digging rose from the hole in the ground, only the soft electronic purr of an unseen power source. Cool air stirred as they all peered in.

"A generator, lights, and an air handling system," Elizondo said. "Serious operation."

"The two out there heard us coming in," the *federale* captain said. "Had enough time to dump their packs, close the trap, and lock the door to this room. Says there are two down there now. They take it in shifts. Two to stand guard, two to dig."

The other equipment in the small space included oxygen tanks, coils of thick yellow wiring, gasoline cans, light sockets and bulbs. The most remarkable thing, however, were two strange wire baskets with leather straps hanging off them, each filled with a bag of dirt that must have weighed at least 30 pounds.

The *federale* captain assigned men to guard the prisoners, the front entrance, and the maintenance area. Two were selected to enter the tunnel with him. Elizondo, Emilia, and Cardenas would follow in that order. Elizondo did a radio check with the *federale* teams. Emilia grabbed a flashlight as long as her forearm from the janitorial closet supplies, eliciting a smirk from Cardenas.

Emilia focused on not dropping it as she descended the narrow metal ladder. When she got to the bottom of the hole, she saw that the tunnel was tall enough for Elizondo to stand upright. It was wide enough for two to walk abreast, but half of the floor was taken up by a tiny track, almost like a miniature cog railway. The generator was located in a niche a dozen feet from the bottom of the hole, humming loudly but not enough to disguise the whirring of a fan. The light they'd seen turn on was the first of a rope of Christmas lights strung along the wall on the right side above the tracks. The glow was feeble. Emilia trained the flashlight on the ground ahead of Elizondo with her left hand and gripped her handgun with her right.

The tunnel sloped downhill. After 15 minutes of steady walking, the *federale* captain raised his fist to call a halt. The group stood without speaking and listened to the sound of burbling water.

"We're under the ravine," Emilia whispered.

They kept moving slowly and quietly, guided by the incongruous holiday lights. The faint gush of water gave way to the distant rumble of cars. They passed under the highway. Emilia found her breath coming in short, claustrophobic gaps as she imagined the tunnel collapsing and cars falling on them. Cardenas's breathing sounded uneven and hoarse behind her.

The *federale* captain turned and made a slashing motion across his throat. Emilia killed the flashlight.

Something ahead clattered, the sound magnified by depth and darkness. The floor vibrated. A quiet clicking noise filled the air as a small cart loaded with sacks of dirt rolled along the track toward them.

As it passed by and began to climb uphill toward the hole in the floor of the bus station, the lights strung along the wall sizzled and flickered. The generator apparently wasn't quite strong enough to power the tracks and the lights at the same time.

But more importantly, it meant that the excavators were ahead.

They kept walking single file in the wavering darkness. Emilia didn't turn on the flashlight again. The tunnel gradually eased upwards. The sound of traffic receded and she knew they had to be well within the perimeter of the prison now. Another cart stacked with bags of dirt clattered past.

They'd come more than a mile. The air was heavy and dry. It was getting hard to breathe.

The tunnel curved to the left, the first real change in direction they'd experienced.

Ahead of the three task force members, the three *federales* disappeared around the bend.

Elizondo slowed, Emilia and Cardenas still bunched behind him.

The lights winked again. They didn't come back on.

The darkness was absolute. Emilia wondered if she should turn on the flashlight or would it give them away; they were well under the prison building by now. Her ears strained to hear more than their footfalls. They could come upon the diggers any moment.

The tunnel exploded in gunfire.

Elizondo spilled backwards, cartwheeling onto the track and taking both Emilia and Cardenas with him as he fell. Emilia groped wildly, nearly blind in the darkness, as the three of them slid downhill in a tangled heap. They ended up in a pile on the tracks as rounds whistled past and pinged off the hard packed tunnel walls. As Emilia's vision adjusted to the blackness, another heavily laden cart rolled around the corner and zipped towards them on steel wheels.

Emilia managed to get past Elizondo's inert form. She jammed the end of the metal flashlight into a gap between the cogs of the track, snatching her hand away before the cart sheared off her arm. For a sickening moment, Emilia watched the cart slam into the metal rod of the flashlight and tip forward as if intent on jumping up and over this unexpected obstruction. At the apex of momentum, the cart wobbled and crashed down on its side, dirt bags thudding across the floor.

"They've got night vision!" The voice of the *federale* captain hissed from just a few feet away but Emilia couldn't see him. She squirmed forward, gun in her right hand, using the cart in the middle of the tunnel as cover. Cardenas wasn't moving. She didn't know if Elizondo was alive or not.

Gunfire filled the tunnel ahead of her. Emilia saw flashes of light. A red laser dot. Yelling. A scream cut through the sound and fury.

Then silence.

Emilia's head pounded in the thickening air.

A hand pressed hers and she nearly screamed.

Without making a sound, Cardenas eased toward her, crawling on his elbows to stay below the height of the overturned cart and contorting himself to get past Elizondo still sprawled on the track. He held both his gun and that of Elizondo. One side of his handsome face was streaked with blood. He smiled grimly at her, teeth shining white in the darkness.

They heard muttered voices. Low laughter that only three chickenshit *federales* had come. The rapid click of a radio button being pushed. Grumbling at the lack of response.

Cardenas laid down one gun, pretended to make a throw, and pinched his fingers together to mime a pincer movement. Emilia nodded and held her gun with both hands. She had been a street cop for years before becoming a detective but she'd never been in a pitched battle in the dark like this before. She willed herself to ignore the furious heartbeat pulsing through her veins.

As the disembodied voices tried their radio again, Cardenas swiftly worked open a bag and grabbed a fistful of dirt. He lifted himself up and hurled it over the cart. The shower of earth hit the tunnel wall and rained down in a gentle cascade.

When the figures in night vision goggles crept forward, Emilia threw herself against the wall to the left while Cardenas rolled to the right.

The two cops fired at the same time.

CHAPTER 44

"Any news?" Miranda asked as he and Anaya rushed into the hospital waiting room.

"Still in surgery," Emilia said.

"Hey," Cardenas said groggily, blinking at Miranda and Anaya from under a thick bandage across his temple. He unfolded himself from the chair where he'd been asleep for the last hour. "What time is it?"

"Noon," Anaya said. "You wearing that bandage to get out of work?"

Cardenas laughed and the two men clapped each other on the back.

Miranda knelt in front of Emilia's chair. "How are you?" he asked.

"Okay." Emilia felt her eyes well and to her surprise Miranda gathered her into a hug.

The *federale* captain and his men had died in the tunnel. Elizondo took two rounds: one in the neck and another in his left shoulder. Getting him out of the dark tunnel had been the stuff of nightmares.

The radios the *federales* used did not work so far underground so Emilia had stayed in the dark next to the barely breathing man, staunching the blood and talking and singing to ward off panic, while Cardenas retraced their steps through the tunnel to summon help. They carried Elizondo out on a makeshift litter and Emilia had never been so glad to see anything as she was to see the ambulance waiting for them next to the garage bay.

Miranda let her go with a smile of encouragement, and clasped Cardenas's hand. "You and Detective Cruz should be commended."

"That's what I told her," Cardenas said.

"I've called Efrain's wife," Miranda said, referring to Elizondo by his first name. "She's flying in tomorrow morning."

"How did she take it?" Emilia asked.

"She's strong," Miranda said. He sat down next to Cardenas. "Tell me exactly what happened. Every detail."

Cardenas touched the bandage on his head and winced. "Detective Cruz knows more than me," he said. "I took a nap halfway through the action."

They'd spoken to Miranda on the phone and given him a brief account of the tunnel raid, but now Emilia slowly recounted every step of the last day. Meeting the *federales* at the local police station. The easy entry into the shuttered bus station. The discovery of the tunnel, their long walk under the highway and the perimeter of the Multifoco prison, to the shootout with the tunnel excavators equipped with night vision equipment.

"The *federales* have arrested both Adelita and Erik Flores," Emilia wound up. "They're holding them at the army barracks. Lindavista is a little too hot right now."

"What about the mayor and his wife?" Anaya asked.

"They've been taken from their home and are at the

barracks, too."

Two doctors in surgical scrubs walked into the room. One held a clipboard. "Detective Cruz?"

Emilia shot out of the chair, her jeans creaking with sweat and dirt. "That's me."

Miranda rose to his feet, as did Cardenas and Anaya.

"For Efrain Elizondo?" the doctor said, looking at the anxious faces.

"We're all here for him," Emilia answered.

"He's out of surgery," the doctor said. "The bullet missed his carotid artery. As long as there's no infection, his chances of recovery are excellent."

"Can we see him?" Miranda asked.

"Just one visitor at a time in the Intensive Care Unit," the doctor said.

"You go," Emilia said to Miranda.

"I'll meet you at the hotel later," he replied and left the waiting room with the doctors.

Cardenas passed a hand over his face. "I need to sleep for about 12 hours," he said. "After that, I'd like a bottle of tequila and half a cow."

"*Por Dios*," Emilia said. "When was the last time we had anything besides coffee?"

"Yesterday," Cardenas informed her. "Maybe the day before. I've lost track of time."

"Do you think the driver is still around?" Emilia asked as Anaya followed her and Cardenas into the hall. A *federale* officer had driven them to the hospital behind the ambulance at 4:00 am as it screamed through the darkened streets of Lindavista.

"I'll drive," Anaya said. "We got a rental." He led them to the hospital parking structure and gave a ticket to the valet.

"I change my mind," Cardenas said. "First the cow, then tequila, then sleep."

Emilia hoped she didn't look as rough as she felt. "First a shower."

"He didn't show, you know," Anaya said as they waited for his rental car to be brought around.

"Lennox?" Cardenas asked.

Anaya nodded. "Just that. We had four undercover cops staged at the Saint Regis, plus me and Miranda. The guy never showed."

Emilia felt her blood run cold. Had someone tipped off Lennox? Did he know she'd set him up?

The valet brought the car. Emilia crawled into the back seat, too tired to be scared.

"Sit down, Detective." Even sitting in a hospital bed, with his upper body swathed in bandages, Elizondo projected authority. The police captain's voice was hoarse, but the doctors said the condition was temporary.

Emilia took one of the visitor chairs and perched nervously on the edge, clutching a collection of photos from Erik Flores's office. The television in Elizondo's room was on, the sound almost muted. News of the tunnel discovery was on every channel that morning, thanks to a *federale* press conference. The bus station was closed. Lindavista was humming with rumors and angry commuters.

The tunnel diggers had been inches away from breaking through the floor of Barrielos Luna's prison cell. If the drug lord hadn't been moved to a new cell by the late warden, he might have escaped already. Forced to accommodate his new location, the diggers had turned to the left, resulting in the trap-like bend.

The job of the task force members had been swallowed up by the *federales,* but to Emilia's chagrin, no one was talking about next steps.

Lennox was still at large and time was slipping away.

Judge Sarmiento was on her way to Lindavista. Miranda had spoken on the phone with her and the woman was livid at the actions the task force had taken without permission from the office of the Attorney General. Not only had they spoken to family members of the 43 missing, but they'd involved the *federales* in a hastily conceived and fatal operation.

Despite seven hours of sleep and a big breakfast, Emilia knew that fatigue was clouding her brain but she couldn't help feeling that the task force would be broken up as soon as the judge arrived and began the finger pointing that would end five careers.

Unless . . .

"Are you planning to go back to Acapulco when the task

force is done?" Elizondo asked.

"Yes," Emilia said, jolted out of her reverie. "That's where my job is."

"I'd like you to consider coming to Guadalajara and joining the police department there." The corner of Elizondo's mouth twitched at her reaction before he continued. "I can guarantee you a promotion to lieutenant and a slot in either Homicide or Vice."

Emilia hitched up her jaw. "You're offering me a job in Guadalajara?"

"We'd have to work on your tendency to withhold information, but I think you could have a very successful career there."

"*Oye*," Emilia blurted. "I've never been to Guadalajara." She wanted to smack herself for sounding like a schoolgirl, but his offer couldn't be more of a surprise than if she'd fallen out of an airplane.

"Less violent than Acapulco," Elizondo said. "But still challenging enough for an officer of your caliber."

"Can I think about it?" Emilia asked. "I mean, thank you. But—."

"Take a couple of days," Elizondo interrupted her. "I don't need an answer right away."

"Thank you."

"Now tell me what's on your mind." Elizondo pressed a button and the hospital bed whined into a more upright seating position.

"Judge Sarmiento is coming," Emilia said. "Unless we

find the bodies, she's going to call a press conference and say we've failed because we were distracted by Barrielos Luna and his family. Our impartiality was compromised by speaking to the parents. We got three *federale* officers killed."

"You have an idea, Detective," Elizondo said leadingly.

Emilia handed him the photos of the Flores family at play.

"I need a helicopter," she said.

Five hours later Emilia's stomach fell away as the *federale*-operated Black Hawk lifted, banked and headed east. Cardenas grinned like a kid and gave her a thumb's up sign. Emilia managed to respond in kind, even as she prayed not to get sick. Her flight helmet weighed a ton, but the conversation between the pilot and co-pilot crackling through the headphones was fascinating as they skimmed over the landscape.

She'd never been in a helicopter before, not to mention a *norteamericano* Black Hawk with two gunners in battle fatigues dangling their legs out the open doors, ready to fire on any threats. *Federale* helicopters had been shot out of the sky before by well-armed cartels. Mexico had learned to defend police operations the hard way.

"Coming up on the Colima dump," the co-pilot said and read off a set of coordinates.

They raced over the white ocean of trash, the smell rising

to greet them. A few tiny figures on the edges of the dump paused from their treasure hunting to look up at the helicopter and the guns trained down on them. No one waved.

And then the stench and the miles of refuse were behind them. The helicopter lifted over the jagged hills. Emilia's stomach settled down, lulled into submission by the craft's vibration, the strong and steady thump of the rotors, and the reassuring weight of her POLICIA bulletproof vest. She had no idea how fast they were flying.

"ETA is 15 minutes," the co-pilot's voice hummed through the headphones built into the helmet.

Once Elizondo gave the go-ahead, several photos were faxed to Anaya's contacts, who reached out to the geological survey people in *El Norte*. The photos were compared to satellite imagery and within hours they had the coordinates of the Flores ranch house.

The jumble of rocky and ribbed hills gradually smoothed into shallow undulations covered in scrub and streams. As the co-pilot announced that they were nearly to the target, Emilia and Cardenas both grabbed binoculars.

"We're looking for a burned-out zone," Cardenas reminded everyone, his voice canned and metallic in Emilia's headphones. "Away from the horse trails."

A dirt road led off a two-lane highway and wound around the rough terrain to the pretty *hacienda* with its clay tile roof and huge front porch. A gravel road looped invitingly in front of the house and led to several outbuildings. Big black and white cows roamed a fenced pasture.

In quick succession the Black Hawk passed over the house and two barns. There were no cars in the circular drive. No one came out to look at the unexpected sight of a military chopper. The cows appeared to have been abandoned.

"It's deserted," Emilia said.

"Bad news travels fast," Cardenas said.

Emilia kept her binoculars trained on the ground, her line of vision just over the gunner's shoulder. The gravel drive petered out in front of the last barn and the adjoining corral.

"I can see the horse trail," she announced, pointing so that Cardenas could also see the well-worn dirt path. "We won't find anything too close. Adelita wouldn't want the kids stumbling over anything."

Cardenas gave her another thumbs up as the helicopter banked and descended to keep the horse trail in sight.

"The house is our bulls-eye," the pilot said. "We'll fly widening circles in the standard search pattern."

Ten minutes later no one had seen anything like a scorch mark in the earth or any other evidence of fire. With the house now a hundred yards away, the helicopter began its second circular flight. Emilia wondered if this was a huge, stupid mistake. Adelita's gang had burned the bodies over a year ago; the landscape was stunted and parched but nature could hide a lot of evidence in a year.

On the third pass, Cardenas spotted the small black smudge on the landscape, nearly hidden by a copse of tall pines. He directed the aircraft and Emilia hung on grimly as the Black Hawk cartwheeled toward the spot.

The helicopter settled onto a patch of level ground about 500 yards away. The gunners hopped out. Emilia and Cardenas left their helmets in the craft and jumped onto *terra firma*. Cardenas grabbed Emilia's arm and they ran under the chop of the rotors together. She estimated they were about three miles from the house and barns.

"It's too small," Cardenas shouted to be heard above the continued rumble of the waiting helicopter as they looked at the patch of blackened dirt. "They couldn't have burned 43 bodies on a patch of ground this small unless they did it one at a time." He sounded close to tears.

"This has to be the place," Emilia hollered. Her ponytail swung wildly and her scalp prickled from the sudden easing of the helmet's pressure.

She was torn between elation and skepticism. Given the size of the charred circle, it was a miracle that Cardenas had spotted it. A fire was the only explanation. But he was right. Given Anaya's research into what it would take to burn 43 bodies, this spot was far too small. It might have been used for a sizeable campfire, but nothing more than that.

As she looked around, Emilia saw multiple tire tracks. A heavily laden vehicle had traversed the area, its tires sinking into damp earth that had hardened into telltale ridges in the dry season.

The tracks led into the pine trees. Beyond the foliage, she saw a flash of blue.

"*Madre de Dios*," Emilia said, her words lost in the

rhythmic chop of the helicopter. She grabbed Cardenas by the sleeve of his jacket with one hand and pointed with the other. "Look!"

"What?" Cardenas looked in the right direction. "What's that?"

They stumbled together over the uneven ground, through the broken brush, and into the pines.

Tucked under the trees, dozens of industrial steel drums were nearly hidden under a year's worth of dirt and spiders and fallen branches. Faded blue showed through the debris. Here and there, yellow brightened the cache.

Emilia caught a prickly pine branch to steady herself as she stared at the irregular rows of rounded metal. Each drum was shoulder height and nearly a meter in diameter. If she curled up, Emilia could easily fit inside one of them.

"*Rayos*," Cardenas swore and gestured at the ground.

Brown fluid leaked from the base of several barrels. Corrosion and rust stains revealed where the acid inside had eaten through metal and paint.

Emilia closed her eyes against a rush of tears. She listened to Cardenas count aloud.

He stopped at 43.

The wind sang a dirge through the trees. Or perhaps it was simply the churn of the waiting helicopter's rotors.

"Adelita did exactly what her older brother would do," Cardenas said, his voice breaking.

"She didn't have to," Emilia said. "She had choices."

CHAPTER 45

By the time Emilia and Cardenas returned to Lindavista, the initial shock had worn off. The day flew by with rounds of urgent phone calls to Mexico City and an emergency meeting with *federales*, Army officials, and people from the office of the governor of Michoacán. At 10:00 pm, Emilia, together with Cardenas, Miranda, and Anaya, left the hospital where they'd spoken briefly to Elizondo, and regrouped in the small dining room in the Hotel Independencia.

"Congratulations," Anaya said and poured them each a jigger of the best tequila the hotel could find.

"*Salud.*" Emilia raised her glass but the mood was somber.

"Kinda hard to look at this as a celebration," Cardenas said.

Miranda touched his glass to those of the others sitting around the table. "*Que vivas durante todos los días de tu vida,*" he said softly.

May you continue to live all the days of your life. Never had the classic toast carried more meaning. Emilia hugged each man and went upstairs.

The first person she called was Alejandro Baez. She apologized. The overdue conversation was quick and stiff.

Next, she called Silvio. His voice mail picked up and Emilia left a message telling him to watch the news tomorrow.

She changed her clothes and climbed into bed before making the third call. Not the office this time, but his cell phone.

"Hi, it's me."

"How are you?" Kurt asked.

"All by myself this time."

"Well, that's an improvement."

Emilia snuggled into the pillows. "I wanted you to know," she said. "We did it. We found out what happened to the 43 students from Amistad."

"Em, that's amazing," Kurt sounded thunderstruck. "Should I turn on the news?"

"Tomorrow," Emilia said.

"Are you all right?" Kurt asked.

"I'm fine," Emilia said. "A little shaky but it will pass."

She told him about the Avilas, and how Pilar led to Adelita and how Adelita led to Barrielos Luna. How the char woman continually mopping the bus station led to the tunnel. She told him, too, about the dark trek through the nearly finished tunnel and the helicopter ride over the Flores ranch to the cache of steel drums.

"So is it over?" Kurt asked. "Are you coming home?"

"I don't think so," Emilia said. This was the hard part of what she had to say. "We'll go back to Mexico City to write our report. After that, well, I've been offered a job in Guadalajara. Captain Elizondo from the task force is the head of Homicide there. He said I can choose between his unit or Vice. Either way, I'll get promoted to lieutenant."

"Promotion to lieutenant," Kurt said. "Hard to turn that down."

"It's a good opportunity," Emilia said.

"Sounds like it." Kurt's voice was hollow.

Emilia took a deep breath and closed her eyes. "I love you," she admitted for the first time. "But I can't stay in Acapulco."

"Because of me?"

"Because of a lot of things," Emilia said. "I'll always carry around what happened with Rafa Gamboa. You shouldn't have to carry it, too."

"Neither of us has to," Kurt said. "He's in the past. We accept it, deal with it, and move on. I love you, too, Em. We can still have a future together."

Emilia blinked rapidly to keep from crying. "I'd drag you down," she said. "Always twisting and turning, trying to figure things out. You don't deserve that."

"Listen—."

"No," Emilia said with finality. "Guadalajara needs to be a fresh start for both of us."

Across the miles, she heard Kurt let out his breath.

"I've kept the light on for you, Em," he finally said. "Now you're telling me to pay the electrical bill and move on."

"All the *gringas* at the tennis club in Acapulco will be thrilled." Emilia forced some levity into her voice as she wiped her eyes with the heel of her free hand.

Kurt gave a ragged laugh. "Maybe I'll write my phone

number on the bathroom wall."

"For a good time, call—." Emilia couldn't finish the sentence.

"Em." Kurt trailed off.

Emilia waited, wishing she could reach through the silence and hold him one more time.

On the balcony. Under the stars.

Finally Kurt cleared his voice. "Listen, Em," he said. "No matter how far we go in different directions, wherever life takes us, you'll always be important to me. Being with you was the best time of my life."

"I never wanted it to end," Emilia said, her eyes welling again.

"If you ever need me," Kurt said. "I'll be there. You remember that, okay?"

"Okay," Emilia whispered.

CHAPTER 46

Within a day, the national media narrative was cast in stone. The *federales* took credit for the find during a press conference hosted by the governor of Michoacán, as if to compensate for the loss of three of their finest. The task force was relegated to having played a mere advisory role, which was a gleeful black eye for the office of the Attorney General.

Even as the *federales* swooped onto the Flores ranch with crime scene investigators and equipment, Miranda called the representative of the families they'd met earlier. Two days after that, before the massive crime scene crew opened the first drum, the families held a candlelight vigil. It was both a celebration that the nightmare was over and a long-delayed funeral Mass. Thousands came from Michoacán and beyond.

The task force members all attended, even a heavily bandaged Elizondo and his wife. Emilia stood on the fringe of the huge crowd, shoulder to shoulder with Cardenas and Anaya. Candles were lit as the sun sank behind the pines and shadows played across the ribbons of fluttering crime scene tape. Firelight flickered across 43 giant posters, each the face of a young man whose life was cut short. Speeches and songs rang through the night, voices swelling with emotion.

Emilia held her candle and ignored the tears streaming down her face. It didn't matter that the task force would never be publicly recognized for what it had done. What mattered was that she had helped to create closure and had the respect of four good men. They'd all been strangers two months ago, now she knew they would be part of her life forever.

She'd never betray any of them.

Not even for Rafa Gamboa Escobar.

"When Diego Barrielos Luna was captured the last time," Judge Sarmiento said crisply. "The assumption was made that his organization was finally broken. That he would have turned it over to an unknown sister, was not considered, for obvious reasons."

"You didn't know she had a sister," Cardenas said, insolence in his voice.

The judge gave him a brittle smile. "Obviously this was a mistaken assumption. The Attorney General has you all to thank for the additional information."

Ramirez glowered as he wrote on his clipboard.

They were in a large conference room in the Lindavista city offices, which had been taken over by a squad of lawyers from the Attorney General's office. The oil drums had finally been opened and a complicated and painful sifting process to extract remains from the acid had begun. Teeth, bones, and belt buckles had so far been found. The families were already clamoring for DNA test results but the forensic investigation was going to take months.

"As we also now know," Judge Sarmiento went on. "Adelita Garay de Flores hired a *norteamericano* actor to impersonate the former Legal Attaché assigned to the United States embassy in Mexico City, in an attempt to pressure task force members to minimize time spent in Lindavista. The escape tunnel for Barrielos Luna tunnel was slated to be completed during the time the task force was there and they wanted to utilize it as soon as possible."

If anything, Judge Sarmiento was thinner than before. A severe but expensive black tweed pantsuit and copious amounts of eye makeup made her look even more anemic. Her wedding ring was conspicuous by its absence.

She'd come in with a phalanx of suits, including Ramirez, who'd pointedly not spoken to any of the task force members, as well as several men in black military uniforms without rank or insignia. Emilia assumed the hulking men were the beleaguered judge's new bodyguards.

No one had yet mentioned if the task force was going to have the opportunity to write a final report. Emilia hoped so, even if it was relegated to the Attorney General's trash can as the *federales* gave press conferences and bumbled their way around the Flores ranch.

"Given the rise of the Hermanos100 group under the leadership of Adelita Garay de Flores and her husband," the judge continued. "And the fact that this imposter is still at large and possibly making other arrangements for Señor Barrielos Luna's future as a free man, the Attorney General has decided to accede to Washington's extradition order and hand over Barrielos Luna immediately."

Emilia gave a little gasp and heard Miranda next to her do the same. Cardenas gave a snort. Elizondo nodded. Anaya was silent, eyes trained on the men in black uniforms.

"These gentlemen are from Special Forces." Judge Sarmiento indicated the men in black uniforms. "They'll be responsible for transporting Barrielos Luna to the border."

"Nice," Cardenas whispered.

Emilia had to agree. Mexico's secretive paramilitary Special Forces unit was regarded as the nation's elite. It had been formed to fight organized crime and cartel violence. No one knew how big it was, where the teams were based, or the names of the members. They fought with the same speed and weaponry as the violent drug cartels, never took prisoners, or made an arrest. Legend had it that they trained in Israel and had never lost a man.

One of the paramilitary uniforms rose to his feet. "We appreciate what you on the task force have done for the country." He spoke rapidly, but his eyes lingered on Emilia. "If any of you would like to accompany Señor Barrielos Luna," he continued. "To make sure he gets to the border and into the hands of the Drug Enforcement Agency, you're invited to come along. It'll be a quick trip that starts now."

Miranda and Elizondo exchanged looks, then Miranda smiled. "This is a young person's game," he said. "Captain Elizondo and I will sit this one out."

"*Rayos*," Cardenas swore joyously. "Count me in. I'd love to see that *pendejo* in *norteamericano* custody."

Anaya raised his hand. "Same here."

Elizondo leaned around Miranda to catch Emilia's eye. "Detective Cruz?" he said quietly. "We can talk when you get back."

Madre de Dios! Emilia clenched her fists in her lap. As much as she wanted to see Barrielos Luna rotting in a jail from which he'd never escape, there were no women in the Special Forces.

"If Detective Cruz would like to come along," the Special Forces man said. "We can make an exception."

"I'm in," Emilia heard herself say almost before he'd stopped talking.

As she walked out of the conference room behind the paramilitary team with Cardenas and Anaya, Emilia was so excited she could hardly breathe. She never would have imagined 60 days ago that she'd be riding with Special Forces to deliver the Barrel Bomber to jail in *El Norte*.

She'd thank him for the opportunity, but Emilia was also going to rub Silvio's nose in this for years to come.

CHAPTER 47

In the black paramilitary uniform and boots, her face and neck hidden by the Special Forces trademark balaclava mask, the only things that distinguished Emilia from the rest of the unit were curves and height. Anaya was the next tallest in the group of twelve. Cardenas was as tall as the Special Forces officers who'd apparently all been chosen for size.

And discipline.

"Radio rules are mission rules." The team leader, referred to only as Fox One, was clearly used to unquestioned obedience and loyalty from his men. As he seemed to know what he was doing, Emilia had no problem with that. "On a mission, operators have no identity besides this black uniform. No home. No family. Nothing besides a call sign. Nobody shares names, no personal information of any sort at any time. No exceptions. The package never gets any details about mission members that can be used to target us later."

His eyes raked over the entire group clustered in the locker room. The space, like the other parts of the unmarked base Emilia had passed through, was spartan and completely devoid of personal affects. There was only one bathroom, one place to change clothes, and one dormitory for sleeping. No accommodation was made to give her any privacy.

To their credit, the Special Forces guys treated her exactly the same as Cardenas and Anaya; guests who were expected to pull their weight and get the job done. No one leered or made jokes as she changed. Smart enough to take his cue from the paramilitary men, even Cardenas was all business.

Preparation for the mission was meticulous. After a physical, the twelve wrote their *cédula* national identification numbers on their upper arms, a grim reminder of the need to be identified in the event of a fatal encounter.

Each member was issued an untraceable burner cell phone and instructed in which pocket to store it. Personal cell phones were too easily traced and therefore not allowed. They were left, with the batteries removed, in the locker room.

Everyone carried a medical kit, again in a specific pocket, plus 1000 pesos cash, polarized sunglasses, and a mission-specific call sign card that would be meaningless to anyone else. Body armor with an integrated radio, a handgun with two extra magazines, and a high powered rifle completed each person's kit. Any personal items were limited to what fit in the last cargo pocket. Emilia took tissues, chap stick, and her Padre Pro rosary. Once upon a time it had saved her life.

They would travel in a convoy of three armored vehicles, with the respective call signs of Fox, Bear, and Lynx, up to the border city of Nuevo Laredo where they'd turn over the prisoner. Their leader's name was that of his call sign; he occupied the front seat passenger position in the first vehicle, a black SUV. The driver of that vehicle was Fox Two. Calls signs for the rear seat passengers were Fox Three and Fox

Four.

Emilia, Cardenas, and Anaya were invited to draw cards from a hat to determine their positions in the convoy. Anaya drew the Fox Four position, giving him a seat in the lead vehicle right behind the team leader.

Emilia found herself holding Bear Three, while Cardenas pulled out Bear Four.

"Best seats in the house," Fox One said. "You ride with the package. All you have to do is monitor physical status while the rest of us look out for the bad guys and potholes."

In this case, the package was Barrielos Luna. The prisoner would ride in the armored van with call sign Bear sandwiched between the two guardian SUVs. The trailing vehicle was Lynx, also with a team of four operators in it.

After a few hours of sleep in the dormitory, Emilia lulled by the snores of her new teammates, they headed into the vehicles before dawn.

"Good morning, Bear Three," Cardenas said to Emilia. The bottom of his stretchy balaclava was down around his chin.

"Bear Four." Emilia grinned as she helped swing open the van's the heavy bulletproof rear doors. A thick window separated the armored prisoner compartment from the cab where Bear One and Bear Two sat.

The Fox and Lynx teams loaded water bottles, ready to eat meals, and jerry cans of extra gasoline into the SUVs. The convoy was self sufficient for the entire 15-hour drive north; there would be no stops at commercial gas stations or rest areas.

Cardenas's excitement was palpable. "Excellent day for a little sightseeing."

"I couldn't have put it better myself, Bear Four," Emilia replied.

They buckled in, propped their rifles in the racks, and Bear One closed the doors.

Emilia had wondered if the rear of the transport van would feel claustrophobic, given that the windows were little more than long narrow slits covered by glass infused with metal webbing. But it was large and roomy and obviously designed to transport prisoners, suggesting that this was a routine job for the Special Operations crew.

On the left side of the van, a bench seat was fitted with a shoulder harness as well as riveted metal loops for shackles. It was long enough for someone to stretch out, suggesting the van was used for significant distances. Three conventional car seats faced the bench, with a customized console between each one to accommodate a rifle stock, handheld radio, and beverage cups. Each console had an emergency call button in case radios failed and the guards needed help. Every vehicle in the convoy would get the distress signal.

A reinforced metal plate slid across a bulletproof window looking into the van's cab. Bear One sat in the passenger seat. The driver was Bear Two. Both men were massive, humorless, and businesslike, much like the overall team leader Fox One.

Over the radio that delivered clear sound through her earpiece, Fox One gave the order to start engines and began the radio check. Emilia kept herself from giving an adrenaline-charged whoop and instead intoned "Bear Three, ready," when it was her turn after Bear Two. Cardenas grinned, the corners of his eyes crinkling in excitement, as he followed up with "Bear Four, ready." They listened as one after the other, the four members of the Lynx vehicle checked in.

"Radio check complete," Fox One said over the radio. "Let's roll."

Safe inside her paramilitary gear and the balaclava that hid every feature except her eyes, Emilia felt cocky as the three vehicles rumbled through the gates of the Multifoco prison half an hour later. She thought again that Silvio was going to be sick with envy when she told him about riding shotgun with Special Operations to deliver the Barrel Bomber to the *norteamericanos*.

Shackled with chains that ran from his handcuffs to his ankles, Barrielos Luna shuffled down the prison steps. The unformed prison guard held his elbows to keep him from tripping. They got him settled on the bench seat and chained to the purpose-made metal rings in the floor of the vehicle. The key to his restraints went to Bear One in the front seat.

Emilia admired how Special Operations protocol took every detail into account. By having a team member outside the compartment responsible for the key, the prisoner could not trick or bribe his guards into setting him free.

Barrielos Luna wore a dark gray sweatshirt and jeans with cheap cross trainers. He looked around alertly as he was guided into the van and the chains and seat belt fastened around him. Emilia saw the same restless energy and assessing eyes she'd seen before. The sinuous way he eased his head from side to side reminded her of a shark changing directions to look for smaller fish; first this way, then that as he sized up the people around him.

As the convoy left the prison behind, he fell asleep.

Emilia watched the sun come up through the narrow windows. The reinforced glass made the sky gray and overcast. The air conditioning kept the holding area of the van dry and stale. By the third hour she was thinking longingly of the fresh breeze, laden with salt and coconut oil, that perfumed the beach at the Palacio Réal hotel.

Guadalajara would smell differently.

Emilia gave herself a mental shake. Although she and Cardenas had nothing to do besides sit and stare at the sleeping and shackled prisoner, she couldn't let her thoughts wander. The radio murmured into her ear every few minutes as Fox One called for periodic radio checks or relayed route information from the central Special Operations unit monitoring their progress. The unit had a dedicated satellite link connected to sensors in each vehicle as well as their individual radios.

The convoy skirted Mexico City far to the east and stopped at a *federale* post before skirting the city of Queretaro. Barrielos Luna was marched to a toilet and

Cardenas had the honor of watching the infamous criminal pee. Cardenas would find some way to use the story to woo women, Emilia decided as she found the women's restroom. Bear Two stood outside the door while she used the facilities.

Food was eaten quickly. The three vehicles refueled and were on the highway again in ten minutes. Barrielos Luna shifted uncomfortably, his chains clanking against the floor of the van.

Fox One called a radio check.

Barrielos Luna closed his eyes again.

Highway traffic was steady, from what Emilia gathered from the radio conversations between the three drivers, who kept the convoy in the left lane. There were a few wry comments about cars that were slow to get out of the way as the convoy raced up behind them. Some took a bit longer, but eventually every car got out of their way.

They stopped to rest and refuel at another small *federale* post an hour north of San Luis Potosi. It was their halfway point; the convoy was making good time and slightly ahead of schedule. It was mid afternoon and the sky was a brilliant blue.

Emilia gathered that the local *federale* in charge was informed of the convoy's entrance only minutes before they arrived. The line of communication between Fox One and the post was complex; from Fox One to Special Operations central via satellite link, and from there to the regional *federale* command who was responsible for informing the local unit. The communications path meant that the *federale* post had no time to inform friends in organized crime, if so inclined. Of course, no one was told the identity of the prisoner. During each stop, Barrielos Luna was shielded from view.

Once again there was only enough time to use the facilities, refuel, and gulp a mouthful of protein bar before Barrielos Luna was chained in place and his seat belt fastened. Bear One clanged shut the double doors of the van, Emilia secured her rifle in its rack and buckled her seat belt, and Cardenas did the same. The van vibrated as the engine turned over.

In the vehicle ahead of them, Fox One called a radio check. Emilia and Cardenas each replied in turn. The process was routine now. The convoy hit the highway again, the van rocking gently as they gained speed and ate up the miles.

They were passing through a dry landscape marked by tumbleweed and broken billboards when Barrielos Luna smiled, showing his teeth like a shark about to bite.

"Hello, Detective Emilia Cruz," he said.

CHAPTER 48

Emilia's heart gave a lurch even as her body tensed. She didn't reply.

"Shut up, old man," Cardenas growled.

But Barrielos Luna had seen him blink. "She's very pretty under that mask," the prisoner went on. "Have you fucked her yet?"

"I told you to shut up," Cardenas said, this time with real menace in his voice.

Emilia stared past Barrielos Luna at the side window. The bulletproof glass turned the sky to dirty gray. The flat land beyond the edge of the highway was a murky sea.

"Just making conversation about our lovely companion," Barrielos Luna continued. "The first time I met her, she was nice to me. Wanted to know if we had a mutual friend."

"I said that's enough." Cardenas barked.

Don't let him get into your head, Emilia prayed silently.

Fox One's voice hummed through Emilia's earpiece. "Central, we have not seen traffic in either direction for the past seven minutes."

Emilia pressed a hand to her ear as she and Cardenas exchanged glances. Lack of traffic meant the possibility of a cartel blockade up ahead. Sometimes drug gangs set up checkpoints to extort money from travelers.

Other times it was to intercept specific vehicles.

Cardenas's forehead creased with worry beneath the

bottom edge of his balaclava.

"Requesting an immediate update from Highway Patrol. Over." Fox One sounded calm despite the unspoken question in his words.

"Bad news?" Barrielos Luna smiled. The shark smelled blood in the water.

"Nothing that concerns you, old man," Cardenas snapped. "Just sit back and enjoy the ride. It'll be over soon."

A new voice sounded in Emilia's ear, with the familiar buzz of a transmission from Central. "Fox One, Highway Patrol reports no traffic delays between your position and target destination."

Emilia found she'd been holding her breath and let it out slowly. The lack of traffic didn't mean anything in this sparsely populated part of central Mexico. The traffic would pick up when they were closer to Monterrey.

"I've travelled with Mexico's finest before," Barrielos Luna said. He lifted his chin at the rear double doors. "Always the same routine. Everything locked up tight."

"That's right," Cardenas said.

"Like travelling in a coffin." Barrielos Luna's voice pitched higher in a mocking tone. "Rolling coffins."

"Ignore him," Emilia said in a low voice to Cardenas.

"Detective Cruz and I have much to say to each other before our ride is over." Barrielos Luna thrust himself toward her as far as his chains would allow. "We must finish where we left off. Why so interested in Santa Muerte, my friend?"

"I'm not your friend," Emilia couldn't help saying.

"None of that," Barrielos Luna reproached her with a click of his tongue. "Santa Muerte can be a deadly foe or a beautiful ally. Which are you looking for?"

"What's he talking about?" Cardenas asked.

Fox One's voice filled Emilia's earpiece again. "Central, a helicopter is closing at high speed. Appears to be Highway Patrol."

Cardenas heard the news as well and relaxed. "Friends in high places," he joked.

Barrielos Luna smiled. Emilia's blood ran cold.

The look on the prisoner's face didn't escape Cardenas. "What's going on?" he asked.

"You shouldn't die thinking that Detective Cruz betrayed you," Barrielos Luna said to Cardenas. "No, it wasn't her."

Emilia unfastened her seat belt to creep forward and slide open the metal shutter covering the cab's rear window to look out of the windshield between the shoulders of Bear One and Bear Two. A helicopter hung in the sky as the convoy raced toward it. The highway was deserted but for the three vehicles.

"Your other friend," Barrielos Luna went on, the shark circling for a kill. "A homing device in his pocket in exchange for my promise to take care of his wife. Care for the insane is quite expensive, you know."

"What are you talking about, old man?" Cardenas barked, but there was fear in his voice.

"*Madre de Dios*," Emilia gurgled.

"You can die happy knowing la señora will have excellent care for the rest of her life."

Emilia keyed her microphone, forcing herself to stay calm instead of screaming Anaya's name. "Fox Four, Fox Four, the package—."

Fox One overrode her transmission. "Central, the helicopter has no tail number. Repeat no—."

A puff of smoke appeared next to the hovering helicopter. Something dark arced out of the sky toward the convoy.

The Fox SUV ahead of them reared up, like a stallion fighting for territory, before exploding in a hail of flames and metal.

Emilia heard herself yell.

The heavy van braked but was still moving forward when the concussion wave lifted it off the tarmac. Emilia crashed to the floor. The dull gray landscape in the narrow windows above the seat disappeared in flashes of red and yellow as the vehicle slammed into the burning Fox vehicle and kept going, Bear Two fighting for control. The helicopter was directly overhead; the roar and chop of the rotors vibrated through the armored compartment.

"Central." The radio filled with Bear One's shouting. "We are under attack. Repeat, under attack from airborne missiles. Fox is gone. I say again, Fox is gone."

"Drive, *drive*!" Lynx One broke in from the SUV behind the van. "We are taking fire from two bandits approaching from the rear."

Emilia got to one knee. The van bounced off the highway,

tilting dangerously as the tires sank into the gravel on the shoulder, and she spilled down again. Cardenas swept his rifle out of the rack and trained it on Barrielos Luna. "They won't get you alive," he said.

The van blasted onto the highway, rocking crazily, the landscape racing by faster than before. Emilia clawed her way into her seat. Barrielos Luna smiled.

"*Drive—.*" The transmission from Lynx ended in a screech of static as a second explosion rocked the van.

"Lynx One, Lynx One," Cardenas shouted into his mike. There was no answer.

Gunfire pounded the sides of the van like staccato bursts of death. Through the narrow windows, Emilia saw a truck speed beside them. A split second later it rammed the cab with a deafening crunch. A professional hit, just in front of the fenders. The van fishtailed across two lanes.

A second truck collided with the van. Emilia and Cardenas flailed helplessly against their seat belts and Barrielos Luna's chains rattled like castanets as the van spun across the empty highway.

Tires chewing into the dry dirt beyond the tarmac, the vehicle smashed headfirst into a lone pine tree. The engine died.

There was a moment of dizzy silence. Emilia and Cardenas automatically released their belts and grabbed their rifles. Emilia hit the emergency button on her console.

"Bear One, Bear Two," Cardenas croaked into the radio. "Do you copy?"

In lieu of a response, Emilia heard a grinding noise. The engine restarted and the van lurched backwards.

Before it had travelled ten feet, the doors to the van's cab disappeared in a coordinated explosion that rocked the van like a ship in a storm. Cardenas's lips moved but his words were lost in the din. Automatic gunfire cut down Bear One and Bear Two in seconds.

As the bulletproof glass separating the cab from the prisoner compartment groaned under the deafening spray of gunfire, Emilia keyed her microphone. "Central," she yelled. "Lynx is down, Fox is down. Bear One and Bear Two—."

Cardenas shoved Emilia out of her seat and onto the floor of the van just as the rear doors blew off. Choking smoke and molten metal rained into the compartment.

He dropped to one knee, partially shielding Emilia, and fired his assault rifle into the churning debris. Flat on the floor, Emilia fired until the rifle clip emptied, unable to see beyond the swirl. Return fire raked the seats where the two police officers had sat seconds before.

Cardenas jerked backwards, his body flopping against the base of the seats. He jerked spasmodically once, twice, and then lay still. Blood oozed over the floor of the van.

Crouched next to him, Emilia pointed her handgun at Barrielos Luna. The van swayed, buffeted by the wind kicked up by the helicopter.

Two swarthy men armed with rifles clambered over the twisted remnants of the door. Lennox, flushed with excitement in a khaki bulletproof vest, was right behind. He didn't recognize Emilia in the paramilitary uniform and mask but all three paused at the sight of her gun in Barrielos Luna's face.

"Leave her alone," Barrielos Luna ordered as they trained their weapons on Emilia. "Don't touch her."

"Tell them to go," Emilia rasped, her ears ringing. "Or I'll shoot you."

Lennox laughed at the sound of her voice.

"You're not going to shoot me." Barrielos Luna locked eyes with Emilia.

"I will kill you," Emilia said.

The helicopter landed on the flat brown land beyond the tree. Dust thickened and swirled through the compartment. The rotors throbbed impatiently.

Emilia inhaled the dense, dirty air through her balaclava. Her finger tightened on the trigger.

Kill him. She would do it.

"You're not going to kill me, Detective Cruz," Barrielos Luna held out his hands. One of the men cracked off the handcuffs with a huge wire cutter, while the other kept his rifle sighted on Emilia. "I have something you want and we both know it."

"You have nothing I want." Emilia's breath was loud and ragged. Yet she was locked in place, keeping the faith with Cardenas as his blood pooled under her knee. The gun was steady, her left hand wrapped around her right in the textbook grip. There were others outside the van compartment, shouting and firing guns. The crackle of flames was unmistakable.

Kill him. For Cardenas. For the team.

"El Acólito," Barrielos Luna said, massaging his wrists. "I know where he is and I'll find him before you do."

Emilia stopped breathing.

Barrielos Luna stepped out of the broken manacles that had kept his feet chained to the floor of the van. "I'll get El Acólito. You'll trade for him. Yes, *mi corazón*, you're going to be very useful to me."

Lennox helped him over the buckled and twisted metal where the rear doors had been.

For the 43. For all the others left to die in vats of acid.

Emilia pivoted on her knee, keeping her gun pointed at him. "I don't have anything you want," she shouted. "I'm not that important."

"You will be some day." Barrielos Luna looked back, his voice raised against the thunder of the helicopter. "You're famous as the lone survivor already. When it's time, I'll bring you El Acólito. In return, you'll do me a favor."

"He's nothing to me," Emilia screamed. "I'll never make a deal with you."

"Yes, you will," Barrielos Luna spat. "Whatever El Acólito is to you, you want him that much."

Flanked by Lennox and his men, he ran toward the waiting helicopter.

Emilia kept him in her sights but the gun wobbled in her hand.

If I kill in cold blood, who will I be?

The helicopter rose into the air, swung around, and beat its way into the sky. At the same time, tires spit rubber against tarmac and two dented trucks accelerated away.

Cardenas made a gurgling sound. His balaclava was off and his eyes were wide as Emilia tossed aside her handgun and frantically pulled out her medical kit. He'd been shot multiple times. Blood pooled under him and drained out of a fist-sized hole in his thigh.

"Nico," Cardenas whispered. His hand fluttered around the pocket reserved for personal items.

"We'll get you fixed up," Emilia gabbled as she wrapped the tourniquet strap around his upper thigh to staunch the flow. "You'll have cool stories to tell. Scars that will make you even more fascinating."

Even as she tightened the strap, she felt his life slip away. "No," Emilia yelled.

She snatched off her balaclava and started resuscitation, pressing on his chest and pulsing air into his mouth like an automaton. Cardenas's body was heavy and unresisting.

He was gone.

Emilia eventually slid her bloody fingers down his face, closing his eyes and soothing out the contortions of pain. A search of the cargo pocket yielded his small sketchpad. "I'll make sure Nico gets it," Emilia whispered and slid the pad into her own pocket. "I will tell him what a brave man his father was. And that he was my friend."

Emilia sat on her heels next to the body and the broken shackles, almost afraid to move and confront the silence outside.

"Central," she called into her microphone, her voice reedy and frightened. "Lynx One. Lynx Two. Anyone."

There was no reply. The radio was dead.

She climbed out of the van, catching her sleeve on the jagged metal where the doors had been ripped off.

The highway was empty, a dark ribbon punctuated by burning vehicles and nothing else. Except for the few scattered pines, the land on either side was flat and dry and brown.

The bodies of Bear One and Bear Two sprawled half in and half out of the cab of the van. Their eyes were open, their expressions neither afraid nor angry, only fixed and dead. Both had been shot multiple times. Blood spattered the interior of the cab. The bulletproof windshield was spiderwebbed with so many cracks it was opaque.

Emilia stumbled to the still burning hulk of the Lynx SUV. The passenger side doors were open. Lynx One and Lynx Four slumped sightless on the ground. They had used the doors as cover in an attempt to make a stand and fight. The interior of the vehicle was bathed in blood and the other two bodies were twisted and bloody. All four men had been shot multiple times and all bore the same hole in the forehead of a final execution. Barrielos Luna's men had been thorough.

A shadow slipped over the ground. Emilia raised her head to see a lone vulture circling above the still-smoking wreck of the Fox vehicle. She broke into a run.

The front end belched heat but the fire had burned itself out. The doors on both sides of the SUV were open. Three bodies lay on the ground; all still gripped rifles and handguns. Blood trailed from fatal wounds and spread across the tarmac, like water pumped from a broken well.

All had fought to survive.

Except one.

The rear passenger door was open. Anaya sat upright in the Fox Four position, a neat round hole in his forehead. His handgun was still holstered; his long gun still in the rack. He'd known death was coming and did not try to delay it.

Anaya's right hand was curled into a fist. The fingers were still pliable as Emilia peeled them away from the small object buried in his palm. A small metal object, no bigger than a matchbox.

So small, so deadly. When they were all excited about the possibility of a tunnel in Lindavista, this was why Anaya had volunteered to return to Multifoco. Said he'd interview the last of the seven who'd spouted identical confessions. No one had thought to check if he'd also visited Barrielos Luna.

He'd probably gotten to Lennox, too, before the planned meeting at the Saint Regis hotel. Warned him off in exchange for a deal.

Care for the insane is quite expensive, you know.

Emilia tried to raise Central on Anaya's radio, the only one besides hers not broken or covered in blood. Nothing.

Touching his body and the treachery it represented was loathsome. She reeled away, shaking uncontrollably. Emilia realized that she was going into shock.

Drawn by the instinct for carrion, more vultures circled in the clear afternoon sun. Emilia groped for the burner cell phone she'd been issued. Her fingers were clumsy. Her brain was shutting down. This was why there was a specific pocket for each item. In a crisis, rote memorization and muscle memory took over.

The laminated contact card fluttered to the ground as she pulled out the phone. She didn't pick it up. The icon for the satellite connection glowed on the cell phone's tiny screen.

Tears streamed down her face. Small buttons blurred. Her hands trembled. It took Emilia three tries before she managed to tap in the number.

The phone at the other end rang. And rang. Again and again.

Finally, a click. A live connection. A voice, a heartbeat, at the other end.

"Kurt," Emilia said. "It's me."

El Fin

Discover Emilia's next case in RUSSIAN MOJITO.

Let's Connect

Join the Crime Fiction Files newsletter for the encounters, experiences, and current events that shape author and CIA veteran Carmen Amato's crime fiction, including the Detective Emilia Cruz novels.

Get it here: carmenamato.substack.com.

There are extra goodies ahead, too.

A **favorite recipe** from a meal featured in the book,

A **Glossary** of Spanish words, and

An **excerpt** from the next Detective Emilia Cruz novel.

Carmen's Mod Mex Shrimp Cocktail

1 medium minced shallot

2 cloves minced garlic

1/3 cup Clamato juice

1/3 cup ketchup

2 tablespoons lime juice (preferably fresh-squeezed)

1 tablespoon lime vodka like Finlandia (optional)

½ teaspoon Mexican hot sauce like Cholula Original (more if desired)

Salt and black pepper to taste

1 pound cooked peeled shrimp (frozen is fine, but never use canned)

1/2 cup diced celery

1 cup diced cucumber

2 medium avocados, peeled, pitted and chopped

1/2 cup chopped fresh cilantro

INSTRUCTIONS

There is a lot of chopping and dicing for this recipe, all of which you can do ahead of time and refrigerate until needed, except for the avocado.

If using frozen shrimp, thaw in cold water. Drain and set aside on top of a bowl of ice.

For the dressing: whisk together Clamato, ketchup, lime juice, vodka, hot sauce, salt and pepper.

In large bowl, combine shallot, garlic, celery, and cucumber. Stir well. Add shrimp and mix. Finally add the chopped avocado. Pour dressing over the mixture and stir gently until everything is coated. Add more salt, pepper, and/or hot sauce as needed. You want a kick but not a burn.

This cocktail is traditionally served in wide-rimmed glasses, like a margarita glass, but in Mexico City I saw street vendors serve it in the local equivalent of Mason jars. Garnish with a lime wedge and a few sprigs of fresh cilantro.

Serve with ciabatta bread to sop up the yummy dressing and enjoy!

Glossary of Spanish Terms

Words and phrases commonly used in the Detective Emilia Cruz mystery series

Abarrotes: snacks

Agua de jamaica: cold tea made with dried hibiscus

Alcaldia: town hall and/or mayor's offices

Amigo: friend, buddy

Barrio: neighborhood

Cabrón: slang meaning dumbass

Campesino: subsistence farmers, country dwellers

Casita: little house

Cédula: identity card

Chica: girl

Comida: the main meal of the day, usually eaten in early afternoon

Conchas: sweet rolls topped with sugar and shaped like a conch shell

Dios mio: my god, an exclamation

El Norte: the United States

Federales: slang for the Policía Federal Preventiva, federal law enforcement agency

Guayabera: men's button-down shirt with a straight hem and multiple pockets

Halcone: word meaning falcon, used to mean a person acting as a lookout

Hombres: men

Jefe: chief, person in charge

Jitomate: tomato

Libraría: bookstore

Libro: book

Loco: crazy

Lotéria: lottery

Madre de Dios: Mother of God, used as exclamation

Maldita: damn, damned

Mercado: market

Mujeres: women

Muertos: papier maché skeleton figures used to decorate Day of the Dead altars

Narcomanta: banner bearing a message from a gang or cartel

Norteamericano: North American

Ofrenda: altar

Palapa: traditional Mexican shelter roofed with palm leaves or branches

Papel picado: streamers of tissue paper cut into silhouette designs

Parrilla: grill for food, usually assumed to be for meat

Pastelería: pastry shop

Pendejo: asshole, jerk

Permiso: excuse me

Placas: license plates

Prima: female cousin

Privada: enclosed subdivision and/or the gate to the

property

Prohibido el paso: "Keep out" warning

Queso fresco: soft cheese common in Mexican recipes

Rayos: exclamation, similar to "oh hell"

Reina: queen

Salsa verde: tart green salsa usually made with tomatillos

Sicario: cartel henchman or assassin

Talavera: hand painted pottery from Puebla

Taqueria: taco restaurant

Telenovela: television soap opera

Tiendita: little store

Tío/Tía: uncle/aunt

Zocalo: town square

An excerpt from RUSSIAN MOJITO, the next Detective Emilia Cruz novel

Emilia sat in the restaurant of the Palacio Réal hotel, inarguably Acapulco's most luxurious accommodation, and watched general manager Kurt Rucker fill two champagne flutes. The gentle ocean breeze ruffled his blonde hair.

"To second chances," he said and handed her a glass.

"Second chances," Emilia echoed.

Her heart constricted as their fingers touched. It was the day they met all over again, when she was mesmerized by the combination of sharp intellect, mental toughness, and compelling self confidence, all poured into an athlete's body.

They touched glasses in a toast to the future. Emilia took a sip of champagne and followed his gaze beyond their table to the setting sun as it spread ribbons of color over Puerto Marques, the bay-within-a-bay on Acapulco's southeastern side.

The curving shoreline was dominated by the Palacio Réal complex, including the flagship restaurant. Cantilevered over the ocean, the fine dining establishment was built to resemble a masted sailing ship. A cunning confection of canvas sails created a roof over the long teak hull as tables skirted in white linen and laid with antique sterling flatware evoked the dining room of a Spanish galleon.

"How does it feel to be home?" Kurt asked. His posture

was relaxed and comfortable but his ocean-colored eyes betrayed his concern for her.

"Awkward," Emilia admitted. Her smile failed and she drank some champagne to hide her shakiness.

Emilia ran away from Kurt and their life together in the Palacio Réal penthouse after the assault by Rafa Gamboa and the DNA proof that he was her brother. But even as police work took her to a task force in Mexico City and the abortive assignment with Special Operations, she'd been unable to break away from Kurt. Every long-distance conversation was both reassuring and agonizing; neither could say a final goodbye.

A waiter materialized with swirls of caramelized shrimp on gold-rimmed plates. The sweet scent of apple from Calvados liquor tickled Emilia's nose.

"Compliments of Chef Jacques, señora," the waiter murmured. He set down the appetizer and lit the candle on the table before melting away.

"It doesn't have to be awkward," Kurt said. "This is just the two of us."

"And all the ghosts of my past." Emilia heard the tremor in her voice and tried to pull herself together before she sabotaged Kurt's romantic homecoming dinner.

"We can leave the past where it is and move on." Kurt flipped his napkin into his lap. "Eat your shrimp before Jacques comes out of the kitchen and quits."

Emilia picked up her fork. In another life, the hotel's head chef had created his signature appetizer for her.

"I can't forget what happened," she blurted.

"No one expects you to forget, Em. But you still have a life."

"Rafa Gamboa is still out there," Emilia whispered, ignoring the beautiful food in front of her. "So is Barrielos Luna. He's like a snake. He's going to wrap himself around me and squeeze until none of us can breathe."

The man across the table from her was the only person who knew the truth about why Barrielos Luna let her live. Kurt had taken the news without flinching.

Now he put down his fork. "Em, you don't know how this thing with him is going to play out. Nobody does."

"He's out there," Emilia insisted. She was ruining the evening but she couldn't stop herself. "Him and his army of faceless *sicarios*. Waiting for me on some street corner. On the beach. *Madre de Dios*, at the next table eating Jacques's food."

"Or maybe he's dead in a ditch," Kurt said quietly.

"You once said," Emilia reminded him with a lift of one shoulder to indicate the hotel soaring up the cliff behind them like the architectural marvel it was. "If I'm in danger so is everyone in this hotel. I want to be with you and call this place my home again, but I can't put you in that position."

Kurt pushed aside his plate. "Tomorrow, Ronaldo Olivas and I are going to review the hotel's security program and make some upgrades," he said, naming the hotel's chief of security. "A beautiful woman who means a great deal to me once said she wouldn't live scared and I'm going to make sure when she's home, she's safe. And if she's safe, so is everybody else."

Emilia swallowed hard against a sudden lump in her throat. "That sounds like a lot of trouble for one crazy cop."

"She's worth it," Kurt said and stretched a hand across the table. "You're home, Em. We'll work it out, one day at a time."

Emilia wrapped her fingers around his. His hand was a lifeline pulsing with vitality and courage, pulling her out of a well of self-recrimination and fear.

"Okay," she breathed. "One day at a time."

"In a couple of years we'll step back, see how it's going."

The flippant remark made Emilia laugh, but Kurt's gaze was steady and unblinking.

He had a strength like steel, tempered long before he came to Mexico by years in his country's military. Kurt might manage a hotel now, but he'd been to war, confronted the enemy, seen pain and death.

That was why he understood her so well. They were both fighters.

Before she could say anything, a blur of white buttons and checked pants swept across the restaurant to their table. "Emilia!"

Jacques Anatole, a swarthy, lanky Frenchman in a chef's jacket, kissed her passionately on either cheek, half lifting Emilia out of her seat. "Your presence elevates us all. And this ogre is again tamed." He lifted his chin at Kurt. "You are a terrible boss."

"I can't be good at everything," Kurt said.

"He used to be modest," Jacques said to Emilia. "Now he is perfect."

Emilia laughed. The chef was the first member of the hotel staff who became a friend when she previously moved into the penthouse with Kurt.

"Now, to welcome back our prodigal daughter, I have for you a meal you will remember in song and verse and describe to your grandchildren with tears in your eyes." Jacques gestured dramatically to the plates in front of them. "First, you have my famous *camarones en Calvados*. Next a risotto with the essence of white truffle. Then, a morsel of fish that will melt in your mouth. A piece of skate like the wing of an angel, perfumed with herbs and posed with a mélange of vegetables. And for dessert, my fair lady's favorite cannoli with sweet *crema*."

"That sounds wonderful, Jacques," Emilia said. His fabled risotto was second cousin to *arroz rojo* but infinitely more exotic.

"I'll have the same," Kurt said.

Jacques glared at Kurt. "We're in training for the Ixtapa Half Ironman," he said. "I have beat you to the swimming dock four out of the last five mornings. No, my friend, you'll get a couple of chicken breasts, brown rice, and a spinach and beet salad. No dessert."

He pressed Emilia's knuckles to his lips and disappeared through the kitchen door.

"You didn't tell me you were in training for a race," Emilia said.

"It's not for six weeks," Kurt replied, gazing at the gently swinging kitchen door. "I should fire him."

"He's your best friend."

"Depends on what's for dinner," Kurt said.

Emilia laughed again. Familiarity was gently closing her wounds.

She felt . . . safe.

Almost.

She'd feel better once she attacked the long to-do list in her shoulder bag. Go back to work and wear a gun every day. Check the police database for any recent sightings of Rafa Gamboa and Barrielos Luna. Visit her mother and stepfather, and the rest of her extended family. Enlist the help of Padre Ricardo, the priest who'd been her mentor since grade school, to trace the original owners of the key.

Emilia's mushroom risotto was delicious and the fish was a work of art. She shared with Kurt, who was duly served with the high protein meal Jacques had promised. As they ate, Emilia thought of her suitcase, upstairs in the penthouse, waiting to be unpacked.

In the bedroom that used to be theirs . . .

She hadn't been with a man since the assault. She wondered if that part of her life with Kurt could be what it was before, or if Rafa Gamboa had stolen that from her, too.

"Where's your car?" Kurt asked.

"At the police station," Emilia replied. She put a piece of

asparagus on his plate, punctuating his beet salad with a stripe of green. "Silvio has the keys."

Kurt smiled his thanks and pronged the extra vegetable. "That's Lieutenant Silvio now, isn't it?"

"It'll be strange having Franco as my boss," Emilia admitted. "With him as the lieutenant, I'll be assigned a new partner. I hope it won't be a rookie like—."

She'd lost Kurt's attention. He was staring beyond her right shoulder.

"What's going on?" Before she knew it, Emilia was on high alert. Was Barrielos Luna behind her? Or a dozen armed *sicarios* as she sat in front of a half-eaten plate of fish and asparagus?

"Don't turn around," Kurt said.

"Tell me what's happening, Kurt." Was Rafa Gamboa and his sinister tattoo of Santa Muerte invading the Palacio Réal?

Emilia darted glances at the tables in her field of vision. Whatever was happening, the diners were unaware and focused only on themselves and their meals.

"Em, it's okay," Kurt said gently. "I just saw something odd."

Emilia couldn't shake her fear. "How odd?"

"Do you remember Sergei Porchenko?" Kurt asked. "Russian. Owns the Pacific Lotus hotel downtown. On the Acapulco Hotel Association board with me. He came to our World Cup party."

"His wife is named Magda," Emilia recalled, her heart

still thumping. "I spilled red wine on her."

"He's sitting in the corner in an Armani suit," Kurt said. "Opposite the bar. He gave his dinner companion a big wad of US dollars and thinks nobody saw."

"Oh." The tension that surged through her body ebbed. Emilia relaxed, but Kurt was right to be concerned. In Mexico, private cash transactions always meant trouble. Money laundering, bribes, cartel deals.

To make matters worse, Sergei Porchenko was Russian. Across Mexico, but especially in resort areas, the Russian mafia was making its presence felt, buying up condominiums, running prostitutes, and opening huge casinos. Money flowed through each operation, and in Mexico, money and drugs always swam in the same river.

Get RUSSIAN MOJITO on Amazon or at your favorite bookstore.

ABOUT THE AUTHOR

Carmen Amato is the author of the Detective Emilia Cruz mystery series pitting the first female police detective in Acapulco against cartels, corruption, and social inequality amid the hunt for Mexico's missing. Starting with *Cliff Diver*, the series is a back-to-back winner of the Poison Cup Award for Outstanding Series from CrimeMasters of America. Optioned for television, National Public Radio hailed it as "A thrilling series."

Carmen's historical fiction thrillers include *Murder at the Galliano Club*, which won the 2023 Silver Falchion Award for Best Historical.

Her standalone political thriller *The Hidden Light of Mexico City* was longlisted for the 2020 Millennium Book Award.

A 30-year veteran of the CIA where she focused on technical collection and counterdrug issues, Carmen is a recipient of both the National Intelligence Award and the Career Intelligence Medal. A judge for the BookLife Prize and Killer Nashville's Claymore Award, her essays have appeared in Criminal Element, Publishers Weekly, and other national publications. She writes the popular Crime Fiction Files newsletter on Substack.

After years of globe trotting, she and her husband enjoy life in Tennessee.

www.ingramcontent.com/pod-product-compliance
Lightning Source LLC
Chambersburg PA
CBHW030103310726
48970CB00004B/1124